IN HER OWN LEAGUE

Liz Tomforde is a *New York Times* bestselling author of sports romance novels that depict realistic and healthy relationships. Her books offer a mix of witty banter, undeniable chemistry, a healthy dash of spice and swoon-worthy men who look good in a uniform.

Born and raised in Northern California, Liz is the youngest of five children. She loves all things romance, travelling, dogs and hockey. When she's not travelling or writing, Liz can be found relaxing at home or listening to a good audiobook while on a walk with her golden retriever, Luke.

Visit Liz's website and subscribe to her newsletter at liztomforde.com. You can connect also with Liz on Instagram @liztomforde.author.

Also by Liz Tomforde

The Windy City series
Mile High
The Right Move
Caught Up
Play Along
Rewind It Back

A WINDY CITY SERIES SPIN-OFF

IN HER OWN LEAGUE

LIZ TOMFORDE

HODDER &
STOUGHTON

First published in Great Britain in 2026 by Hodder & Stoughton Limited
An Hachette UK company

The authorised representative in the EEA is Hachette Ireland, 8 Castlecourt Centre, Dublin 15, D15 XTP3, Ireland (email: info@hbgi.ie)

6

Copyright © Liz Tomforde 2026

The right of Liz Tomforde to be identified as the Author
of the Work has been asserted by her in accordance with
the Copyright, Designs and Patents Act 1988.

All rights reserved. No part of this publication may be reproduced, stored in a retrieval system, or transmitted, in any form or by any means without the prior written permission of the publisher, nor be otherwise circulated in any form of binding or cover other than that in which it is published and without a similar condition being imposed on the subsequent purchaser.

All characters in this publication are fictitious and any resemblance
to real persons, living or dead, is purely coincidental.

A CIP catalogue record for this title is available from the British Library

Paperback ISBN 978 1 399 74644 1
ebook ISBN 978 1 399 74645 8

Typeset in Fournier MT by Hewer Text UK Ltd, Edinburgh
Printed and bound in Great Britain by Clays Ltd, Elcograf S.p.A.

Hodder & Stoughton policy is to use papers that are natural, renewable and recyclable products and made from wood grown in sustainable forests. The logging and manufacturing processes are expected to conform to the environmental regulations of the country of origin.

Hodder & Stoughton Limited
Carmelite House
50 Victoria Embankment
London EC4Y 0DZ

www.hodder.co.uk

To my mom—
Who I lost three weeks after typing "The End" on this book.
This story showcases a strong woman, and my mom was the definition of strength and resilience.
I don't often write amazing mothers in my books, and I suppose that's because I knew that even a great fictional mother could never compare to how incredible mine was.
I'm so lucky to have had her for the years I did.
I love you and I miss you, Mom.

PLAYLIST

#	Title	Duration
1	She – BRNDN	2:28
2	Man I Need – Olivia Dean	3:04
3	Make Me Forget – Muni Long	3:58
4	F&MU – Kehlani	2:14
5	DAISIES – Justin Bieber	2:56
6	All Me – Kehlani feat. Keyshia Cole	2:58
7	God Went Crazy – Teddy Swims	3:03
8	I Do – Toosii feat. Muni Long	2:46
9	This Is – Ella Mai	3:26
10	Black & White – Teddy Swims feat. Muni Long	3:00
11	GO BABY – Justin Bieber	3:14
12	Different Too – Elmiene	2:45
13	Funeral – Teddy Swims	3:54
14	Keep Going (Aaaaahhhhh) – Mario	2:48
15	Photographer – BRNDN	2:12
16	Better – ZAYN	2:54
17	Useless (Without You) – Elmiene, Muni Long	3:07
18	Little Things – Ella Mai	2:52
19	Want You To Know – Bixst	2:48
20	Find Someone Like You – Snoh Aalegra	3:26

1
EMMETT

Is this the beginning of the end?

It feels like the beginning of the end.

At what point do I *know* this is my fate? That this is my last first day here. My last first staff meeting. My last first "hello" to the coworkers I haven't seen in months.

An offseason has never felt shorter.

Typically, I'm itching for baseball to return, counting down the days until winter is over, but not this year. This year, I've dreaded the idea of returning to my office at the field, knowing my every move is going to be analyzed.

Because this season, I have a brand-new boss—one that no longer sees me as the right fit to be the field manager for Chicago's MLB team, even though I've held the position for seven years now.

This morning, the film room is buzzing with noise. Every person who works for the Windy City Warriors, outside of the players, is packed in the stadium-style seats. This is the room we use to go over game film to prepare for an upcoming opponent, or when a one-on-one session is needed to make corrections.

Today though, we're sandwiched in here for our first meeting with the new team owner.

Reese Remington.

The thirty-five-year-old is the granddaughter of the previous owner, a guy who held the title almost as long as

I've been alive, an owner who allowed me to run my team the way I saw fit.

His granddaughter, however, judging by our interactions last season when she was simply training to take over, will be anything but hands-off.

Kai nudges my elbow with his from his seat next to mine. "What time do you want to meet tomorrow to go over the potential pitching lineup?"

"Let's say eleven thirty."

"I might have Max with me. I hope that's okay."

I give my future son-in-law a deadpanned glare. "Of course that's okay, Ace."

"I don't think you can keep calling me Ace. You're going to have a new ace pitcher this season. We just need to figure out who that is."

"You're always going to be Ace. Good luck to the next guy."

Kai, or Ace as we call him, was the Windy City Warriors' ace pitcher ever since he joined the team a few years ago. That is, until he retired at the end of last season, leaving me without my go-to guy on the mound.

But as much as I'm going to miss being able to count on him every few starts, I'm even more proud of him for making the decision that was best for his family. Especially because that family now includes my daughter.

A couple of years ago, the two of them met when Miller spent the summer nannying for Kai's son, and the rest is history. I couldn't imagine a better man for my girl. And now seeing Miller so calm and at peace here in Chicago with him and Max, it's hard to remember the wild child I raised who once never felt settled in one place.

As proud of Kai as I am for calling it quits when the timing felt right, he was missing the game before spring training even ended. So, though I may not have him on my roster anymore, I now have him on my coaching staff.

That's a perk of being the field manager of a Major League Baseball team. I get to hire my own staff, and there's no one more qualified to be my new pitching coach than Kai Rhodes.

The door to the packed and rowdy room opens and my body instantly tenses, expecting *her*, but when a short redhead with a bouncing ponytail and three coffees balanced in her hands ambles through the entry, I relax back into my chair.

"Did I miss anything?" Kennedy asks, taking the empty seat on my other side before passing Kai and me each one of the coffees.

"Not yet." I hold my cup up. "Thank you for this."

"Anytime, Monty."

"Happy official first day, Dr. Rhodes."

My words cause Kai to beam from the seat next to me, looking over at his sister-in-law.

A heat creeps up her cheeks. "Thank you."

Kennedy is not only the new team doctor, but she's also married to one of the players—Kai's little brother, Isaiah.

The Rhodes brothers have become a part of my family since we all landed in Chicago. There are times I take on a more fatherly role for them when they need it. There's not a huge age difference between us, just over a decade, so other times, I'm simply their friend.

Yes, they've both been my players and me their coach, but our bond is a whole lot tighter than that. It just so happens that Kai is marrying my daughter soon and Isaiah married the team doctor who I work with closely, so it's one big cluster of non-blood-related family.

"We'll see you guys for dinner tonight?" Kai asks.

She nods. "We'll be there."

"Same," I confirm.

Even though the film room is loud, I can hear the squeak of the door perfectly clear, and the sound has tension rippling through every one of my muscles.

Reese is the last to arrive and as soon as one high heel is past the threshold, my attention is immediately on her.

Short blonde hair cuts sharply below her jaw. A charcoal-gray pencil skirt paints her curves. Navy-blue eyes that are impossible to read coolly assess the room.

And when they slice to me, they silently scream how much she doesn't like me.

Well, I take it back. I guess she's pretty easy to read when it comes to me.

The unimpressed stare lasts only a second before she pulls her attention away and continues to the podium at the front of the room.

I don't know what it is about me that bothers her so much, that's caused such a bad taste in her mouth, but I feel the same way toward her.

However, I have my reasons.

First of all, the woman spent the entirety of last season informing me that her first year as the official team owner is the same year I'm up for a new contract. Like she needed to verbally remind me that the fate of my career lies in the palm of her hand this season.

Secondly, she's already been on my ass about schedules, budgets, and reallocating funds, as if *I'm* the reason certain departments of the organization are operating in the red, and not because her grandfather didn't have the energy to keep up. Truthfully, there's not an ounce of me that wants anything to do with the back end of how the club is run as long as my players are taken care of. I just want to coach baseball.

And lastly, her biggest fault of all . . . she looks like *that*.

My new boss is not only a pain in my ass, but she's also *stunning* and the first woman my body has decided to pay attention to in God knows how long.

Eventually the rest of me will get the memo that we don't like her. It just might not be until I'm packing up my desk at the end of the season because my new boss refuses to extend my coaching contract.

"You good?" Kai nudges my arm.

I clear my throat. "Yeah, of course."

"Okay." The word is laced with this annoyingly knowing tone that doesn't go unnoticed when he leans over to Kennedy and the two of them share a look.

"I saw that," I mutter.

Kennedy laughs. "We weren't trying to hide it."

Standing in the front of the room, Reese says something to the audience, but the crowd is so rowdy, everyone excited to see their coworkers after the offseason, that no one pays attention or tries to hear her.

I watch as her throat works its way through a swallow, like she's pushing down the nerves, hands tightly fisted to the podium. And I get it. Not only is she the first female team owner that the MLB has ever seen, but she's also the youngest.

But Reese is a boss. Not just *my* boss, but a gets-things-done, doesn't-take-shit-from-anyone *boss*. I saw it last year while she was training for this new role. She's the reason Kennedy is here and taking over the position she should've had years ago. Reese saw what her grandfather didn't—that the previous team doctor was a sexist piece of shit—and handled it. She fired him and gave Kennedy his job, making her the first female team doctor in the league.

As much as I don't love the idea of working for someone who doesn't want me here, Reese will be a breath of fresh air for this organization. But first, she needs to get through this staff meeting.

She opens her mouth to speak again, but no words come out, nerves holding her back, the room too preoccupied with their own chatter to realize she's here and asking for their attention. Her knuckles go white from her firm grip around the podium, her knees slightly shaking, which I can only see because I'm sitting in the front row.

The laughter and chat behind me is pissing me off for her.

Fuck. I internally berate myself for what I'm about to do. Blame it on my daughter. She's the reason I'm so damn soft.

"Hey!" I stand up, turning to face the room from my seat, and all eyes immediately fall to me. "Let's have a little respect, why don't we?"

The room goes silent at my tone.

"Fuck's sake," I mutter under my breath.

Sure, I come off like a grumpy bastard most of the time, a little intimidating with my build and tattoos, but anyone who knows me knows I'm a nice guy until you piss me off. And this is pissing me off.

I retake my seat, feeling Reese's attention on me, and it takes a moment for me to return the eye contact and look up at her.

She gives me a curt nod, her tone all professional when she says, "Thank you for that, Emmett."

And then there's that . . . *Emmett.*

She's the only person in all of Chicago who uses my first name when everyone else calls me by my nickname. And I know she does it on purpose, like she's refusing to allow any sort of comfortability between us. It's as if she's once again reminding me that she's my boss, I'm her employee, and regardless of how much time we're about to spend together this season, we aren't friends and we're never going to be.

It'll make it that much easier for her to fire me at the end of the year.

Fucking great.

"For those of you who don't know me, I'm Reese Remington." With the room silent, she confidently begins her first staff meeting. "The new owner of the Windy City Warriors."

"Emmett."

I'm mid-conversation with a few of the guys from my coaching staff. The meeting is over, so most everyone is simply catching up before calling it a day.

"Can I speak with you?" Reese continues.

I take a sharp inhale through my nose, gathering myself as I turn around to face her. "You're the boss."

"Surprised you remember that." Her eyes trail to the group of my video coaches. "In my office, please."

Reese shifts on her high heels, heading straight for the door, expecting me to follow.

Which I, of course, do.

Hands in my pockets, I trail her out of the film room down the hall and up two flights of stairs, headed for her office.

I keep my head down, partly to avoid watching the way her sinfully thick hips sway from side to side with each step she takes, but mostly because I feel like a kid in trouble, being called to the principal's office, and not like a long-tenured field manager with a winning track record and a World Series ring.

My jaw is tense for the entire walk to her office, but my chewing gum acts as a good distraction to anyone who might be watching this interaction. My players and staff have always known me as easygoing and confident.

But when it comes to Reese, I feel the complete opposite.

Who knows what she's going to throw at me on day one of this new season. All I know is that it's starting. Her mission to prove to herself that she doesn't need to renew my coaching contract next year starts today.

Once we reach the top floor, she turns the corner to her office and I follow, but stop short at the empty receptionist desk that lives just outside her door.

"Where's Denise?" When Reese doesn't answer, my eyes find hers. "You fired Denise? Are you serious?"

I get that the woman is wanting to make this place her own, but firing her grandfather's receptionist that worked here as long as Arthur did? What the hell?

Reese narrows her eyes at me. "Of course I didn't fire Denise. I've known her since I was born, but she wanted to retire, regardless of how many times I begged her to stay. I just haven't found her replacement yet. As much as you might not believe this, I'm not a monster, Emmett."

Reese doesn't give me a chance to respond, which is probably for the best, before she continues into her office and closes the door once I enter too.

The massive windows that look over the field are the first thing to draw my eye, the same way they have whenever I met with Arthur over the past seven years. The view from up here is probably one of the best in the city, and I can't imagine a better spot to watch a baseball game from.

Well, other than my prime spot against the railing in the dugout.

Even though the view is the same and this office is technically the one that I've been in countless times, it looks unrecognizable from the one Arthur used to occupy.

Reese has updated her desk to one that's sleek and modern, unlike the clunky one Arthur used to sit behind that was always covered in piles of papers and housed an outdated computer. Her chair is ivory and gold, unlike the cracked dark-brown leather one that used to reside there.

The piles of clutter that Arthur had accumulated over the past four decades are nowhere to be found, and Reese's office is now bright and light and clean. Sleek, modern, and neutral.

Exactly how I'd describe her fashion sense if I ever let myself admit that I noticed.

"Take a seat," she says, gesturing to one of the new chairs that sits opposite of hers.

For a split second, I let myself believe that maybe she's calling for a truce between us. That she knows as well as I do that this year is going to be a nightmare if we can't get along. But that idea is quickly dispelled when she says, "You need to fire one of the video coaches."

"Excuse me?"

"You have three on staff, when we've only ever had two. We don't have the salary space to pay three people."

What the hell?

"Arthur gave me permission at the end of last season to add a third. I just hired someone. I can't fire him."

"Can't or won't?"

I look her dead in the eye. "Won't."

"He should have never allowed that. The budget is a mess because my grandfather stopped paying attention to it. We don't have the funds to pay three people."

"Then take it from my salary."

Reese jolts back at my words, staying silent for a moment as she mulls over my quickly spoken statement. "No. It's not only the salary. It's the added expense of hotel rooms and food on the road. We don't need a third."

"Well, I'm not firing one of my guys. Two of them have been with me forever and the third I just upgraded from the triple-A team. His family just moved here, and his wife is expecting soon. He needs the salary raise."

Reese shows absolutely no emotion, those dark blue eyes unflinching. "I'm only paying two, so it's your choice who goes."

So much for "I'm not a monster, Emmett."

I can feel my grip tighten on the armrests of the chair, can feel my jaw tense so tightly I should probably be concerned for my teeth. "Not happening, Reese. Find money from somewhere else or take it from my salary. Your grandfather never would have asked me to fire someone who needed a job."

Exasperated, she pulls her attention from me, refocusing instead on something on her computer. "You may have had my grandfather wrapped around your finger, but I'm not him. Things are going to be different this year, Emmett, so you should probably get used to that idea."

Yeah, no shit things are going to be different.

And I hate that idea.

"Monty!" is the first thing I hear as I open the door to my daughter's house. "You color with me?"

"Absolutely I will." I lift my favorite three-year-old, slinging him on my hip and closing the front door behind me. "Missed you, Max."

He melts into my shoulder, already in his pajamas for bed as I carry him to the kitchen to find his parents.

"Hi, Dad," Miller says with a quick hug to my side.

I pop a kiss on the top of her head before she grabs the pasta dish she made for dinner and we slip into the dining room.

I knock fists with Kai and Isaiah when I find them at the table, setting Max on his feet. He pulls at my hand to take the chair where his coloring book and crayons are set up, climbing into my lap and picking a color for me, silently asking me to help him fill in the outlined image.

"Sorry, that was the new athletic trainer I hired." Kennedy hangs up her phone before taking the last empty seat next to her husband. "Her flight was canceled so she won't be here until tomorrow." She sighs, looking at the food on the table. "Thanks for making us dinner. We still haven't unpacked enough to find our dishes."

Max looks up from my lap. "Ken," he says, smiling up at his aunt.

"Hi, Bug."

Kai makes a plate of pasta and salad for his fiancée. "We'll come over tomorrow and get it finished."

"I can make it mandatory," I cut in. "Tell the team they need to get over to your place and help the new team doctor."

"Or they could just come help their teammate because they love me," Isaiah adds.

"Kennedy is in charge of their medical treatment," Kai reminds him. "I think they're going to be a bit more inclined to kiss her ass rather than yours."

"Monty. More." Max nudges my tattooed hand, the one with the crayon that's not working fast enough for him.

I quickly fill one of the outlined trees on the page. "House is good?" I ask Kennedy and Isaiah.

"It's perfect." She smiles.

Isaiah looks to his older brother and a content understanding passes between them. "I'm glad we're living closer."

Miller passes the breadbasket across the table, her eyes latched on me for too long as she does.

"Yes?" I ask suspiciously.

"Nothing."

"Since when do you have a filter, Miller? Spit it out."

"I just think it's nice that Kennedy and Isaiah are moving out of the downtown area and bought a house down the road from us."

"It is nice," I agree. "For them."

She focuses on the plate in front of her. "Nice enough that maybe you'd want to do the same."

I bark a laugh. "Nice try. I'm perfectly happy in my apartment in the city that's walking distance to work. I practically live at the field during the season anyway."

"I'm just saying, Dad, your whole family is out in the suburbs now."

"And I'm glad you four are all happily paired-off suburban couples."

"You could be happily paired off too, you know."

The disbelieving laughter keeps coming. My daughter has never been one to shy away from exactly what's on her mind. "Geez, Millie."

Kai shakes his head. "Let the man eat his dinner in peace."

"Oh, no, no, no." She holds a finger up. "You don't get to play Switzerland right now. You agreed with me when we talked about this last night."

I raise a brow. "You two talked about me last night? Nothing more exciting going on in your lives?"

"We just want you to be happy, Dad."

"And what makes you believe that I'm not happy? I've got my dream job and my daughter finally lives nearby. What more could I want?"

"A lady friend," Isaiah cuts in, talking over a full mouth.

"A *lady* friend?" Kennedy asks, unimpressed by her husband's choice of words.

"Yeah. A lady friend. A girlfriend. A wifey." He winks at her. "Or just a fuck buddy."

I palm both of Max's ears to cover them.

"Gross." Miller grimaces.

"Oh, come on, Miller. Look at the man. You think your dad looks like *that* and doesn't have fuck buddies? *Please*."

"Rhodes." I shake my head at him. "Shut up."

He smiles to himself before taking another forkful of pasta. "Sure thing, Coach."

"I'm happy, and I'm too busy to worry about anything other than work and you four." I uncover Max's ears. "Five," I correct.

"Just saying," Miller mutters under her breath. "Maybe it's your turn."

Until Miller met Kai, she had never mentioned the idea of me dating before, but now she won't let it go. Like she's so happy, she wants the same for me.

And I get it, I do, but I've already had my turn.

Sure, it's been twenty years since I was with Miller's mom, and I only had her for a year before we lost her, but I've experienced it. And then I was suddenly a twenty-five-year-old dad to a kindergartener who just lost her mom and wasn't biologically mine, and I was too busy to worry about anything else.

Now, I'm in my mid-forties and focused on my career. Happily, if I do say so myself, and too busy living at the field to meet someone.

With the stretched silence, Miller lets it go. "How was the meeting?" she asks us instead.

"Good," Kai exhales. "It sounds like there's going to be quite a few changes this year, but Reese was well-spoken. She's smart."

"Dad, it went okay?" Miller's tone is full of apprehensiveness.

"It was fine."

I don't mention the little conversation Reese had at me— yes, *at* and definitely not *with*—in her office afterward to inform me she was cutting a video coach position. I couldn't tell you if that's a good business move or not, and I don't necessarily care. All I know is the salary she wants me to cut belongs to a soon-to-be father who needs it.

A smile blooms on Kennedy's mouth. "It was really amazing to listen to Reese's vision for the team. I'm excited she's taking over as owner."

And even when the conversation shifts to subjects outside of work, the only thought that goes through my mind for the rest of dinner is . . . *that makes one of us.*

2
REESE

"Reese, are you with us?"

Hearing my name pulls my eyes up to find five too-intimidating stares mirrored back at me.

I have no idea what I missed from this meeting, focused instead on the printout sitting on the conference table in front of me. The column of red numbers has been stealing all my attention.

I clear my throat, finding Phil, one of the five members of the advisory board my grandfather had assembled when he was in charge. "I'm sorry," I say, holding up the red-riddled papers. "We need to go back to this. These are our yearly projections?"

"Correct."

"Most of the departments are operating in the red."

Phil laces his hands together, resting them on the table, a wholly unimpressed look on his face. As if he's about to have to repeat himself for the hundredth time to a child who can't seem to grasp a basic concept.

Except, I fully understand what's going on here. I simply don't understand how this has been going on for as long as it has been. Or why my grandfather's so-called "advisors" are so nonchalant about the club bleeding money.

And by the club bleeding money, what I actually mean is me. *I'm* bleeding money.

Because now that my grandfather has passed along our family legacy to me, I am the sole owner of the Windy City Warriors, and this money we're losing is coming straight from my own pocket.

I knew we were overspending. I just didn't realize how far it had gone.

The MLB doesn't implement a salary cap for teams, so this budget is more so an arbitrary number we try to work off to avoid certain league taxes and to make sure we're not spending money simply because we want to.

And clearly, judging by these numbers, my grandfather enjoyed spending money.

"Yes, Reese." Phil's words are said slowly, as if giving me the extra time to understand them. "As we discussed, with it being your first year as owner, we think it's best if you don't make any major changes, and instead build off the framework we built while Arthur was in charge."

"By operating in the red," I finish for him.

"If I'm remembering correctly, *you* were the one who decided to fire a long-tenured team physician mid-season last year, forcing your grandfather to pay out that contract while also paying Ms. Rhodes a new salary."

"Doctor," I correct. "Her title is *Dr.* Rhodes. And Dr. Fredrick is a sexist pig. I refuse to have someone like that associated with *my* club."

I catch the slight roll of his eyes and when I look around the room, I find that same annoyed expression mirrored back to me from the rest of the advisory board.

Well, everyone but Ed. Ed has always been my favorite. He's my dad's age and has worked under my grandfather for as long as I've been alive. He's also the only man on this advisory board who doesn't try to intimidate me.

Don't get me wrong, he still does. They all do to a certain extent, but Ed doesn't mean to. I simply want to do well in this new role, and they've all had a front-row seat to watch my grandfather's forty-year success.

"That salary bump was hardly a drop in the bucket," Ed

reminds the group. "Reese is right. Arthur was too loose with the budget his last few years here, but that's going to be a problem for her long-term if this continues. We're here to make sure she doesn't fail."

Again, there's this shared look among the other four, as if they were to silently say, "Actually, we're hoping that she does."

I'm well aware how polarizing my new position is. There's been a long-standing and very outdated position of "no women in baseball" and now, here I am, the first female team owner in MLB history.

There are far more people out there than the four sitting at this conference table hoping for my failure.

But I refuse to fail. I will do everything in my power to make my time here a success.

I've given up far too much to fail now.

And yes, I know that because I'm a woman, I will most likely have to work twice as hard and make our club's success twice as noticeable to have any hope of being viewed as the right person to operate this team.

"So where are we making cuts?" I ask the group.

Scott leans back in his chair, hands laced behind his head. "You tell us, *Stanford*."

He tacks on my alma mater with a patronizing edge.

"Why don't you say what you mean there, Scott."

"You spent all that money on a fancy MBA." He sits forward with confidence, hands folded together on the table. "Don't you think your time would be more valuable behind closed doors, focused on the business side of things? If you're so concerned about the club's financial state, why don't you leave the baseball operations to someone else."

"Someone else as in you."

This arrogant smile lifts on his lips. "Great idea, Reese. Look at you, making smart decisions for yourself."

Scott might be my least favorite of the bunch. While the rest are older, he's the youngest, closer to my age, and unbelievably entitled in his position.

It's not completely common for a team owner to be heavily involved with the everyday operations of their baseball club, but that's not how we run the Windy City Warriors. Yes, my grandfather was the team owner, but he was also the President of Baseball Operations—a position the other twenty-nine teams choose to hire out. Some clubs have both a general manager and a president. Some have only a GM to handle the day-to-day business of the team. Whereas in our club, the president takes on the role of a team's general manager. And now, that president is me.

In the past handful of years, before I was ready to take over, it all became too much for my grandfather to juggle on his own. He hired Scott to join the advisory board, but really, Scott was handling most of the baseball operations while my grandfather publicly held the title.

When he decided it was time to retire, though everyone knew I'd be taking over as owner of the team, most people expected me to name Scott as President of Baseball Operations.

I didn't.

Four of the five men in this room are still hoping I change my mind. And shoot, maybe everyone in the front office feels the same way. The players probably would want that too. And judging by the hate I've seen online, it feels like most of the fans in Chicago agree that I should hire out the position to someone who isn't me.

I mostly believe that I can do it. I know what I'm talking about when it comes to both business and baseball, but I can't lie and say it hasn't crossed my mind more than a few times that I might not be the right person for the job.

And it's hard not to let those thoughts creep in when the

only person who believes in me is me.

I gather a bit of courage, not allowing anyone in this room to realize it's forced. "As I've already stated, the President of Baseball Operations position is not up for discussion." Standing, I tap the stack of papers against the table to straighten them. "However, Scott, if you'd like to continue to be a part of this advisory board, I look forward to hearing your ideas on how to tackle this budget."

I catch a ghost of a smirk on Ed's lips as I bend down to retrieve my bag. "Have a good day, boys," I call out over my shoulder as I exit the conference room.

And as soon as the door closes behind me, I allow the façade to drop.

I'm screwed.

I already knew this new role was going to be a massive undertaking with very little support from those around me. But now I have to start the year off by making even more budget cuts than I originally planned, and people are going to hate me for it.

It shouldn't matter. This is a business after all, but I already feel like the outcast when it comes to the rest of the league owners, and I'd rather my own club not completely despise me too.

Bag slung over my shoulder, I bypass my office and head straight to the one place I know I'll get to be alone right now.

Things aren't so bad that we're at the point where I need to sell off shares or anything drastic like that. We have money. But people will be losing their jobs if their position is unnecessary. Players who aren't producing will be traded. When we hit the trade deadline this summer, I want to be buying players for the playoffs, not selling them, and I need room in the budget to do so.

I take the elevator down to the clubhouse level. Practice has been done for hours, so I don't expect to run into anyone down here, but as soon as the elevator doors open, I find one of the players standing on the other side of it.

And he's probably my least favorite of them.

Harrison Kaiser—one of the outfielders my grandfather picked up late last season, who gets paid way too much for what he does for the team. Not to mention I can tell that he doesn't mesh well with the other guys. Oh, and he's also kind of a patronizing prick and I find myself annoyed every time I have to sign one of his paychecks.

"Hey," Harrison draws out. "Where are you headed in such a hurry?"

"Just have a bit of business to attend to," I say with a forced smile as I slip past him. "Have a good night."

"Do you need me to help you find where you're going, sweetie?"

My back is to him so he can't see me roll my eyes, partly due to the pet name, but mostly because this guy has been here for only a handful of months, most of which were the offseason, while I've grown up in this clubhouse. I think I know where I'm going.

"It's Reese," I remind him, projecting my voice for him to hear as I continue down the hallway. "Or Ms. Remington, if you prefer."

I can hear his knowing chuckle from here. "Don't work too hard today. We don't need you messing up that pretty manicure of yours."

I wait until I hear the elevator doors close with him inside before holding out my hand in front of me.

My manicure does look good. The perfect neutral pink trimmed into a flawless almond shape.

I'll be sure it looks just as good on the day I sign his trade papers to a different team.

Thankfully, I don't run into anyone else. I don't need anyone to know where I'm going. This is *my* secret spot.

Well, I suppose the dugout isn't all that secret, but it's the last place anyone from the front office would look for me.

Once I'm out there, instead of taking a left to sit on the players' bench, I take a right. There's a small alcove on this side, just enough room for one or two people to sit. It's where the dugout phone lives on the half-wall. The same half-wall that gives this seat a bit of privacy and will block anyone's view of me if they happen to come out here.

This spot is meant for the field manager—though I've never seen a field manager who could sit through a game—but I've always viewed this little area as mine.

When I was a little girl and my grandfather was too busy working, I'd hide out here. It felt like my own little fort. I'd read or color in this spot. I'd hide from my parents if I wasn't ready to go home.

Last year, when I came back to start training to take over the team, I found myself out here once again. Not to hide from my parents this time, but to hide from everyone else.

All eyes have been on me since the moment I walked back into this organization last season, and every so often, I need a moment away from the scrutiny.

So, I get a bit of reprieve out here, and with the empty field and the silent stadium, it's a good reminder of why I'm doing this.

I take a seat and inhale what feels like the first deep breath I've had all day.

It's a beautiful evening in Chicago. The sun is starting to set, and the air is turning crisp from the lake.

It had been so long since I'd been back here, I almost forgot how much I love living in this city.

I almost forgot how much I love this team.

I always knew I'd come back, but I took enough time away to separate how I once felt about this team to how I need to view it now.

I grew up around this club, and this field holds most of my best childhood memories. I spent countless hours in my grandfather's office, listening to him talk about all things baseball. I spent endless summers staying up late to watch live games from his owner's box, all while cheering the players on by their first names because six-year-old me viewed them as my family. I mean, I practically lived at the field, and they did too, so I didn't quite grasp the concept that the reason I was spending every day with them was because this was their job, and they worked for my grandfather.

At the time, it just felt like one big extended family. From the front-office staff to the players to the ushers and concession stand workers. I had this naïve perspective of this place, and as much as I wish I could let myself view this team that way again, I can't.

Now that I'm in charge, I have to see it for what it is—business.

Baseball is a business.

Pulling my eyes away from the field, I refocus on the budget in my hands and flip to the coaches' salaries.

Where there are still *three* video coaches listed.

Because Emmett freaking Montgomery still hasn't let one of them go the way I told him to.

I still can't believe he offered up his own salary to cover someone else's.

I let my attention trail to his salary.

That number isn't listed in red.

It's printed in black ink but may as well be green because we're practically making money off his contract. My grandfather signed him at a steal years ago when he was coming into the majors as a field manager for the first time, but this is the final year on that contract. His value is too high that next year that number is going to skyrocket, and any team in the league who has the space in their budget will jump at the chance to pay him if we don't.

I truly don't know how we're going to afford him, and I've spent every day since joining this club trying to convince myself that he's not worth re-signing.

Talk about being disliked. If I were to get rid of him, the team would hate me. The city would despise me. The guy is beyond beloved here and had my grandfather equally wrapped around his finger.

That reason alone makes me want to hire someone new because there's not a world in which I'm going to bend to Emmett Montgomery's whims the way my grandfather did.

A couple of years ago, the Warriors' ace pitcher had a baby and needed a nanny. Emmett convinced my grandfather to have the club pay the nanny's salary.

Oh, and the new nanny? Yeah, she was Emmett's adult daughter. Convenient.

And of course, the pitcher's little boy and the new nanny needed to travel with the team, so my grandfather reconfigured a whole freaking airplane at Emmett's request.

It's no wonder we're so far in the red. My grandfather was throwing money at anything that would make his field manager happy.

That's not going to be the case this year, and if Emmett doesn't like it the way I suspect he won't, then maybe he should find himself a new team next season.

There's this buzz in my veins, this bubbling frustration just thinking about it.

I don't know what it is that gets so under my skin when it comes to him. It might just be this anxious gut feeling I have, knowing that he's not going to be able to view me as his boss. I'm a bit more than a decade younger than him. He's spent the last seven years working for someone else.

Then there's the fact that we couldn't view this club more differently. Emmett has the freedom to treat this team like his family—shit, half of them *are* his family—while I'm over here having to make the tough decisions that will cause people to hate me. Because this is a *business*.

I mean, he still hasn't let one of his video coaches go, and now I'm going to have to do it myself. He'll stay loved by everyone and I'll be the bad guy.

Lovely.

It doesn't matter. Who cares if I'm not liked, as long as I'm successful.

It's all business.

Standing, I grab my bag and shove the budget inside before turning the corner to head back to my office. Only to take one step before slamming face first into . . . a chest, I guess?

And I mean, I really slam into it. So embarrassingly hard that I practically bounce off it.

"Oh my fuck," I grunt out, taking a step back to balance myself, only to find that the arm wrapped around my waist is what's keeping me steady. I grab onto the forearm to give myself even more stability.

It's a nice forearm.

"Whoa, Reese. I've got you."

I'm really hoping this head injury has me hearing things because, unfortunately, without a shadow of a doubt, I know that voice.

Blinking a few times, I attempt to clear the image away of what I'm staring at right now. *Who* I'm staring at right now.

"Are you okay?" Emmett asks.

More blinking. All it does is completely clear my vision to find my *employee* towering over me, holding me steady on my feet.

Emmett Montgomery is a massive six-four former MLB

catcher who apparently still has all his athletic muscle. Probably more than he did when he was playing in his twenties.

And I'm not a small woman by any means. Five foot-seven and living somewhere between a size sixteen and eighteen depending on the day. But something tells me this guy could throw me around, no problem.

Okay. That was definitely the head injury talking.

"Reese," he repeats, chin dipped to make himself eye level with me. "Are you okay?"

He's got brown eyes. They're shaded by his baseball hat, but they're warm and concerned and that soft expression he's got right now is probably how he always gets exactly what he wants.

Not today, Satan.

Reaching behind me, I remove his hand from my waist and take a healthy step back, giving us distance. "My head is fine. Thank you."

"I'm not talking about your head. Are *you* okay? You seem off. Like something is bothering you."

Way too perceptive, this one. I'll have to remember that.

Straightening my spine, I tuck my short hair behind both ears and watch as his attention traces the stack of gold earrings up the ridges of them.

"The only thing *bothering me*," I say, bringing his attention back to my face, "is that *you* still haven't let one of your video coaches go."

He scoffs a laugh. "I see your feelings toward me didn't soften any with that hit."

"Why haven't you done it yet?"

"Because I already told you I'm not going to."

I shake my head in disbelief. "You have until the end of the week to make a decision, or I'll decide for you."

"Reese—"

"It's not up for discussion, Emmett."

We stand there, squaring off, neither of us backing down from our position. And just as I assumed, he seems to forget that he's working for *me*, not the other way around.

His jaw hardens, but then he begins chewing his gum to hide how tense he is, how angry he is with me for forcing him to do this.

"What are you doing in my dugout, anyway?" he eventually asks.

My defenses instantly shoot up. There's not a chance in hell I'm going to tell him I was having a sentimental moment in the place I used to hide out in as a kid.

"*Your* dugout?" I ask, brow raised. "Last I looked, my name was listed next to 'Team Owner.'"

Emmett's expression relaxes, this glint shining in his eye.

"What?" I ask, skeptically.

"I don't know. You're quick. You have a sharp tongue."

"Well, apologies that I'm not *softer* for you."

"I wouldn't want you to be. I raised a daughter who always had something to say. I don't mind the challenge."

I don't dare ask him why he's not with his daughter right now. I don't ask him why he's spending his Sunday night at the field when all the players and staff have gone home to their families. Instead, I take a step around him to head back to my office and get to work on this budget for the rest of the night.

"I'll see you on the plane tomorrow."

Emmett stops me with a hand around my bicep, causing me to turn back his way. "What are you talking about?"

"We have our first away series, Emmett."

"We do. And that's the only reason why you're coming with us, right? Because it's the first series of the season and not because you're planning to travel with us for every road trip?"

I can see why he's hopeful for me to confirm this. I didn't go to every road series last season while I was in training, and my grandfather gave up team travel years ago.

I fake confusion when I tell him, "Of course I'll be with you for every road trip," in my most innocent voice. "What kind of owner would I be if I didn't keep a close eye on how the team is performing? Or on how the field manager is doing?"

His eyes go wide with disbelief. "Your grandfather didn't travel to every game with us."

I shrug casually, turning on my high heels and enjoying the click they make against the floor with each step. Before I'm too far down the hall, I add, "Like I said before, Emmett, things are going to be different this year."

3
EMMETT

"Do you think if I went down a size in my uniform pants, it'd give me a better range of motion?" Cody, our first baseman, squats down into a deep stretch.

Isaiah laughs. "Range of motion? Really."

Cody's smile turns cheeky. "Might make my ass look better too. I don't know."

"Is that really the most important thing on your mind just before we start the final game of this series?" I ask, arms crossed over the dugout railing.

"Don't worry, Coach. My head is fully in the game. Been keeping a close eye on number seven over there."

Kai tries to hold back his laughter, but it slips out. "Yeah, I'm sure you have been."

Cody, our first baseman, and Travis, our catcher, are Isaiah's two best friends. And though I don't tend to choose favorites, Isaiah and Kai are basically family so Cody and Trav have become an extension of that.

Kai and Travis have always been my responsible, level-headed guys, while Cody and Isaiah are my two wild cards, always down for a good time.

I'd only admit it if they needed to hear it, but I really do love them. They make my job fun.

"What do you guys think of Natalie?" Travis asks of our new athletic trainer.

The three players are on the grass stretching, while Kai and

I rest our forearms on the railing that separates us in the dugout.

"Seriously, Trav?" I ask. "Not you too. Opening pitch is in ten minutes."

"Innocent question." He holds his hands up. "She seems like a nice girl."

"She seems like she's good at her job. Don't try to distract her from it."

"We don't need another Kennedy and Isaiah situation," Kai says.

"What Kennedy and Isaiah situation?" Kennedy asks, joining us in the dugout.

"There she is." Isaiah beams, bending over the railing to give his wife a kiss.

"The 'I'm obsessed with our athletic trainer' situation," Cody fills her in.

Kennedy's attention swings to Travis. "Leave her alone, Trav."

"Leave her alone?" Travis's tone is laced in disbelief. "We told Isaiah to leave you alone for three years then you went ahead and married him."

"Yeah, well. Blame that one on the tequila." She turns to her husband. "Great mistake, though, huh?"

"Best mistake," Isaiah adds in retort.

"I'm going to need everyone in the club to stop dating and marrying each other," I cut in. "It's starting to feel a bit incestual around here."

"Says the guy who is letting his daughter marry my brother."

"I don't let my daughter do shit. Have you met Miller? She's done exactly what she wants since the day I met her."

"Isn't that the truth," Kai tacks on.

"Where are you working today, Kenny?" Isaiah asks his wife.

"Bullpen. Will and Natalie are taking the dugout."

Everyone's attention swings to Travis, holding up his hands again. "Jesus. Okay, I get it. I'll leave her alone."

Then I hear it, the unmistakable click of a pair of high heels tapping against the cement walkway behind me. There's no need to turn around because I already know Reese is on her way out here from our visiting clubhouse.

"Hey, Reese," Kennedy says brightly, confirming my suspicion. "Where are you watching the game today?"

I keep my attention ahead, focused on my players warming up and Cleveland's stadium seats filling with fans. But I sense her, standing a solid ten feet away from us.

"I'll be in one of the visiting offices watching on a screen. I have some work to do but let me know if you need anything."

"Will do," Kennedy says. "I should get over to the bullpen."

"Same," Kai adds. "I'll walk with you."

They both take the steps up the dugout, headed for right-center field—where Cleveland's bullpen is. The other guys join them, leaving Reese and me alone in the dugout. Isaiah gives his wife a kiss and his brother a hug when they leave him behind in the infield.

"They're sweet together," Reese says, and for a moment I forget about my defenses and allow my attention to swing her way.

She's all business today. Light tan trousers that make her legs look about a mile long. Fitted cream-colored tank that seems like it was cut specifically for her body. Gold necklace that lands perfectly between her—

Fuck me, I feel like a creep.

She's your boss.

But regardless of her title, Reese Remington is one of the most beautiful women I've ever seen.

Ruthless but beautiful.

I refocus on the field ahead of me, shifting back to the conversation at hand. "They're a good match for one another."

The click of Reese's heels begins again, and out of my periphery, I can see her moving closer. My attention snags on the sharp angle of her hair just below her jaw, which could not have been a better choice of cut for her, before it trails to the elegant slope of her shoulder and down her arm. Which is when I remember to pull my eyes away again.

The soft notes of amber and vanilla from the perfume she wears invades my senses as soon as she gets close enough. And I know the scent is coming from her because it's all I could focus on during the flight here. Reese sits directly behind me on the team plane, and it was a nice reprieve from the guy-stench that typically fills our aircraft.

"We have a press conference scheduled after the game tonight."

"We?" I ask, skeptically. "As in, you and me? Why?"

Reese leans on the dugout railing next to me, mirroring my position, but she makes the move look a whole lot more graceful than the way my bulky frame is hunched over.

"Some of the bigger networks want to talk about our new relationship."

I turn in her direction, lifting my brow. "Our what?"

"Our relationship," she repeats. "Our *working* relationship. You know, the one where you're the long-standing field manager and I'm the new President of Baseball Ops."

"Well, I guess it's going to be an awfully short press conference seeing as we don't have much of a working relationship."

Other than the flight, I've hardly seen Reese on this road trip. I think it's obvious to both of us that we've been avoiding one another.

"We can fake one," she says simply.

"It'd be better if we actually had one." Standing, I turn to give her my full attention. "I want you to succeed here, Reese. You might not believe that, but it's true. And this season would run a whole lot smoother if we could communicate with one another. You run the back end of baseball ops. I run the games. We have to work together. I just . . . it'd be nice if we could try to get along. I get that we may never be friends, but I respect you."

"Do you?" Her question is almost testing in the way she asks it.

"Of course I do."

"Then why haven't you let one of your video coaches go the way I asked you to? It's the end of the week, Emmett."

Not this again.

I slightly roll my eyes. "Because I'm not fucking doing that."

"And so much for respecting me."

"I do respect you, Reese. But I wouldn't respect *myself* if I fired a soon-to-be father after I just gave him a promotion that he needed. That his *family* needed."

There's this heavy tension living in the silence between us, and if she's going to learn one thing about me, I hope it's this. That I'm not going to do something that goes against my beliefs, even if it risks my job or gets me shit from my boss.

Reese straightens her spine and lifts her chin as she looks up at me. "That's fine. I already took care of it for you."

The chill in my veins is instant. "What?"

"Nate. I let him go. He was the newest hire of the three. I gave you until the end of the week and you didn't do it, so I did it for you."

"What the hell, Reese?"

She doesn't say anything, doesn't have an ounce of remorse anywhere to be found in her expression.

It has me starting to rethink some things.

Yeah, sure, Reese is a boss. Arthur was too checked out, while she gets things done. But at what cost?

"Do you understand what this means for his family?" I ask, the desperation clear in my tone. "Exactly how heartless are you? Because I'm realizing it's more than I assumed."

If that hit landed, Reese doesn't let it show. She simply turns on her heels to leave. She doesn't throw a fit. She doesn't call me names. She just leaves.

But not before adding one more thing over her shoulder.

"Baseball is a business, Emmett. It'd be nice if you started viewing it that way."

You'd think that winning this series would help my mood.

It hasn't.

I'm still pissed. Even more pissed the longer I think about the fact that Reese fired one of my guys.

And now I have to sit in a press conference and pretend as if she and I have some cordial working relationship after she just did what she did.

Almost every major sports network is here, eager to cover this interview, which is a bit surprising. It's a Friday night in Cleveland, Ohio. We're being interviewed on the road. Both the NBA and the NHL are winding down their seasons, heading into playoffs. Shit, even the college basketball Final Four is this weekend, and yet *this* is what they want covered?

Sure, it's a big deal when one of the clubs gets a new baseball president, but I've never seen this much attention surrounding any previous transition.

"Should we get started?" Reese asks from the seat next to mine, countless microphones pointed in her direction.

Too many hands raise at once, but thankfully we have someone overseeing this conference who calls on the first reporter.

"Yeah, this one is for both of you. Have you two experienced any disagreements regarding the way you run the team, and if so, how has that been handled?"

I gesture for Reese to answer first because I can guarantee she's not going to like mine.

She's the picture of professionalism, sitting up straight, hands folded on the table in front of her. She's even got that sharp blonde hair of hers covering the stacks of gold earrings that sparkle up the length of her ears.

Don't get me wrong, those aren't unprofessional in the slightest. They just make her stand out a bit from the twenty-nine old guys who run the other teams in the league.

"Of course, there are a few small things we haven't entirely aligned on, but that's what communication is for. We both want what's best for the team, and any decisions we make are with that sole focus in mind."

Polished, professional bullshit.

I don't think I'd refer to firing someone from my staff as a "small thing."

With my turn to answer, I lean in closer to the mics. "This is Reese's team."

I can sense that most everyone is waiting for me to elaborate my answer, including her. But adding "our communication consists of her not listening to me" or "she does whatever what she wants" isn't exactly something I want to air out to the world, regardless of how pissed off and childish I feel.

But I'm also not going to lie by saying some shit about how we're a team and we're doing this together, so I sit back in my seat to signal that I'm finished with my answer.

Reese's face is etched in stone, unimpressed with my response.

"Okay then." The coordinator selects another raised hand.

"Yeah, this question is also for both of you. How do you feel the transition has been going so far? Reese, with you working so closely with an experienced and winning field manager. And Monty, for you working under someone other than Arthur Remington for the first time in your career."

Again, I look to Reese to answer first.

Reese gives a slight nod of her head. "It's still new. The season started only a week ago, but I look forward to working together this year. Emmett is well-loved so I'm eager to learn why that is."

Reese glances my way, a self-satisfied smirk on her lips.

All eyes turn my way and if Reese wants to play, we can fucking play. "Well, it may be new but I'm quickly learning that she's the boss, so whatever she says goes, right?"

There's a hum of laughter among the reporters and I allow my attention to drift over to Reese. The stoic princess cracks a bit, blinking quickly and swallowing hard, before resetting into her pristine posture.

Now I'm the one wearing a shit-eating grin.

"A bit different being bossed around by a woman, huh?" another reporter chimes in, the crowd continuing to chuckle along, and that instantly grabs my attention.

I dart my focus into the group of reporters, looking for who the hell just said that.

And that's when I realize what's going on. *That's* why they're all here.

This massive press conference is not because the Windy City Warriors have a new president. It's because that president is a *woman*.

That thought didn't even cross my mind, that her gender was the reason for this circus.

What a stupid fucking thing to focus on. If Reese were a man, I'd be equally pissed off about the shit they pulled today.

"Who said that?" I ask. "The 'being bossed around by a woman' comment."

A reporter raises his hand, and I instantly recognize him. I recognize all these reporters from various media coverages over the years.

It's one thing for me to give her shit because she can give it right back, but no one else here is allowed to make Reese uncomfortable in her position.

I focus on him, my tone sharp. "To make it clear, the original question was how I feel about working under someone other than Arthur Remington for the first time in my career. It was not 'how do I feel about working under a *woman*.' I think you all know I raised a daughter, so don't ever say some stupid shit like that to me again."

Reese offers me the smallest, almost undetectable but grateful smile aimed in my direction.

Fuck it. It may feel like we're on opposite teams most of the time, but when it comes down to it, we're on the same one.

The press conference continues.

"Reese, as you know, there's not many women in baseball, and there's never been one in your position of power. Do you feel like you're in over your head with this new role?"

I'm still fired up and about to speak into the microphone for her when Reese does so first.

"I'm not sure that your first statement has anything to do with your question," Reese says, completely composed. "Do I feel like I'm in over my head? No. Do I feel prepared with an extensive background and knowledge in both business and baseball? Yes. Next question."

Another reporter is called on.

"Yeah, this one is for Reese. What would you say to all the Warriors fans, and, well, most of the league, who don't believe you're the right man for the job?"

What the hell?

Again, she stays entirely undeterred. "I would tell them that they're right. I'm not the right man for the job. I'm the right *woman*. Next question."

I can't contain the laugh that charges out of me. Lifting my hat, I run a hand through my hair before replacing it. Then cross my arms over my chest and let the cameras pick up on the proud smile on my face.

"Reese, you don't have children or a spouse right now, but if that changes in the future, are you concerned about how you'd be able to balance your homelife and your career?"

Fucking hell.

I sit forward again, about to lay into this guy, when Reese puts a hand on my thigh to stop me. It's done so under the table so no one can see.

Light-pink painted nails, slender fingers, and a simple gold pinky ring. A complete contrast to my inked hand that's resting next to hers on my thigh.

Eyes finding hers, I settle back into my seat and allow her to answer for herself.

"It's Frank, right?" she asks the reporter. He nods in confirmation. "Frank, have you ever asked any of the other twenty-nine owners that question?"

He stays silent for a moment and not because he's trying to remember, but because he knows he's about to get called out.

"Have you ever asked any one of the players in the league who are fathers and husbands that question? Have you ever wondered how they're able to have kids and still go to work? I didn't think so. Next question."

"*Last* question," I cut in. "Because these ones have been awfully predictable."

Another reporter is called on. I believe her name is Kelly. She works for one of the major networks and has covered quite a few of our games over the years.

"Hi, Monty." She smiles at me. "I'll make this one less predictable for you. You've been in Chicago for quite some time now, and I'll be in town soon to cover a few Warriors' games. Do you have a favorite restaurant I should try?"

"Oh yeah, loads of them. I'm not much of a cook, so I'm a regular in the Chicago restaurant scene. I'll uh . . . get someone from our front office to email you a few recommendations."

"And these recommendations, would they be okay for someone to go alone, or is it best if I book for two? Because I'll be alone when I go."

"Jesus," Reese mutters under her breath.

"Um, well, most have nice bars you can sit at. I typically go eat by myself."

Kelly nods, still smiling my way. "Well, maybe you won't have to when I'm in town."

"Okay." Reese stands from her seat. "That's all for tonight. I hope everyone has a safe trip home. Thank you for your time."

I'm out of my seat too, chasing after her, but she's quick in those heels.

"Reese," I call out, jogging to catch up to her, but then slow to a speed walk to stay at her side. "Are you all right? Those questions were inappropriate."

"Yeah. They were. Especially the last one."

I grab her arm to stop her because I didn't expect to be getting my cardio in by sprinting through the visiting clubhouse.

She reluctantly turns my way and takes even more time to look up and meet my eye.

"Kelly?" I ask. "*That* was the question you felt was inappropriate?"

"Emmett, she was hitting on you."

Was she? I've been out of the game so long I didn't even notice.

My face must say exactly that.

"Seriously?" Reese asks, unimpressed. "You didn't pick up on that?"

"You seem awfully bothered about it."

She breathes a disbelieving laugh. "I could not care less. I would just prefer it if you didn't use our place of work as your own personal dating pool."

My smile only grows as I look down at her. The polished princess is flustered right now.

"Stop smiling at me like that," she huffs, walking away while I stay cemented in place, watching her go. "I'll see you on the airplane in the morning."

There's too much satisfaction in my tone, my cheeks a bit sore from grinning like a fucking idiot. "Have a good night, Reese."

"Don't tell me what to do," she calls back.

I burst a laugh. Maybe this sparring thing isn't so bad.

4
REESE

The elevator opens right into the living room of my condo on the penthouse floor.

The floor-to-ceiling windows that encompass my kitchen, living, and dining rooms are my only source of light, thanks to the glow of the surrounding buildings and the bustling city on a Saturday night.

I flip on the lamp on my entryway table and toss my keys into the small bowl next to it. I don't waste time before kicking off my heels, dropping my bag, and beelining for the kitchen.

Finding my favorite Pinot among the bottles of red, I uncork the bottle, pour a small taste into my favorite wineglass, and try it before deciding it's good enough for me to fill up the rest. As soon as it hits the back of my throat, I relax against the counter in the one place I feel like I can let my guard down.

I love this condo. It's luxurious and clean and mine. Furnished with the things I purchased or collected over the years. Decorated with the artwork I chose.

But most importantly, there's not an ounce of tension living between these walls. There are no feelings of resentment lingering in the air.

I never understood how much I would value my own space until I shared one with the wrong person. And having a place that I can unwind at the end of the day, now that I spend my days doing a job that is under a constant microscope, has become priceless to me.

Sure, this penthouse is massive and meant for more than one person, but I'm not going to attempt to justify it. I understand I'm privileged to be born into the family I was born into, but I've also worked hard to get to where I am. I work hard so I can buy myself nice things. I shouldn't have to sacrifice what I want just because I'm alone. If that were the case, I'd be sacrificing for the rest of my life.

And I'm okay with being alone forever. I've already had to choose between my career and a life that would look a whole lot different than the one I'm living now. I chose my career and would make the same choice again. I've learned and accepted that most men don't find my job impressive. They find it intimidating. They don't want a woman who works twelve-hour days. They don't want someone who travels half of the year.

No, not all men. Just all the men I've met.

Sure, there are times I feel lonely, but that's a rarity. I grew up as an only child and learned how to entertain myself. I enjoy my own company. I'm happy with who I am. And at this point, I've switched off the part of my brain that actively looked for a partner.

When I was given the choice between two different life paths, I chose this one, and if this is everything life has in store for me, I'm still happy I made that decision.

I take a long sip of my wine and take in the view I paid for. The sun has almost fully set, leaving a slight glow through the endless skyscrapers, and the combination of the sunset and the city lights is breathtaking.

There was a time in my life that a Saturday night was a bit livelier than how I tend to spend them now, but then I turned thirty and learned that a hangover could last multiple days. Or if I'm missing out on sleep, it could take me an entire week to catch up on it. So, if I'm not at the field watching a game or lingering in my office, I've come to stick to my single glass of wine and a hot bath on a Saturday night.

With my glass in hand, I head to my primary suite to do just that.

This week was exhausting from travel and games, but when we landed at O'Hare this morning, instead of heading home, I went straight to my office at the field. I spent the day watching film of the other teams, working on ways to reallocate funds, and checking in on our minor league system. Those kinds of things.

The work doesn't stop, and that's what I like. It keeps me busy. I like to be busy, but every once in a while, I also like to wind down.

Keeping the bathroom lights dim, I light a few candles and turn on some music as the bath fills. I do all the extra stuff too, adding Epsom salts and grabbing my latest book. Why the hell not, you know? If I'm going to do something nice for myself, I'm going to indulge in every second of it.

After tossing my clothes into the hamper, I slip into the bath and let the water soothe my tired body.

I didn't give myself a moment all week to realize how tense I've been. It feels like I've been in a constant state of fight or flight. Fighting to prove I can do this job when most people want me to run away and hand the team over to someone else.

Take last night's press conference, for example. It took everything in me not to let them see how those questions affected me. Sure, I'm confident enough in myself that I can handle some scrutiny, but it's human nature to want to be liked. To be accepted.

To have just one person tell you they think you're doing a good job instead of being told the opposite while also being recorded for your response.

Then there was Emmett, sitting right next to me at the time.

Sure, we started off going at each other, but then he was kind of . . . protective.

I could sense how badly he wanted to step in during those questions. I could see how offended he was on my behalf. I would imagine a lot of that comes from him being a girl dad, but I couldn't let him defend me.

I'm a woman working in a man's world and the last thing I need is for a man to speak on my behalf. I have to do it myself.

But I don't have to defend myself tonight. Tonight, I'm off the clock.

I take another sip of my wine before closing my eyes and resting my head back on the bath pillow, ready to fully relax.

Until my phone dings.

The audible whine that involuntarily comes out of my throat is a bit pathetic for a thirty-five-year-old, but come on now.

For a split second, I consider not looking at it. But then there's a bigger part of me that's convinced this could be another team and with an amazing trade opportunity. And if I don't answer, I'll always be known for my first act in office being that I missed a historic trade deal.

Dramatic, yes. But that's the kind of pressure I'm under to get this right.

Water dripping from my hand, I grab my phone. But it's not one of the other clubs in the league messaging me.

It's my field manager.

Emmett: It's a Saturday night, so I'm sure you're busy, but when you get a moment, can we chat?

My thumbs hover over the keyboard, unsure of what to reply. Should I reply? Or should I let him believe I have a more exciting life than the one where I'm home alone, sitting in the bath on a Saturday night off work?

Me: Why are you working on a Saturday night?

Emmett: I'm always working. It doesn't stop.

Me: Yeah, I get that.

Emmett: Can I call you?

Can he call me?

My eyes immediately dart downward . . . to my bare tits. To my stomach and thighs just below the surface of the extremely clear water.

Really not the most flattering angle on anybody, I swear.

It feels . . . *inappropriate* to take a phone call from my employee while bare-ass naked in my bathtub. But before I can tell Emmett it's a bad time, my phone starts buzzing with a call from him.

Shit.

I quickly turn my music off before answering the call, attempting to make my voice sound as professional as possible. Because a professional tone would indicate that I'm definitely *not* naked right now.

"Hello?"

"Bad time?" Emmett asks.

The worst time, actually.

"Of course not. What's up?"

"I just got a strange email from Scott asking me to join your advisory board meeting on Monday. Arthur never had me join those, so I wasn't sure if that was your idea or . . ."

It's impossible to mask the frustrated huff of air I blow out. "Nope. Sure wasn't."

Scott is really trying to go around me to add another person that doesn't agree with me into our meetings. I'm already outnumbered. What more does he want?

I guess that's an easy answer. He wants the city's beloved manager to see *him* as the better fit for president.

"I'll tell him no, then," Emmett says easily. "It's your meeting. I'm not sure why he's asking me to get involved."

"I'd appreciate that. And thank you for checking with me first."

Look at me, being cordial.

"Of course. You're the boss, Reese."

"I do love when you remember that."

He laughs under his breath and, shockingly, I find a smile on my mouth from hearing it.

"Have a good night," he says.

"Don't tell me what to do."

His chuckle is this warm rumble that fades into a still silence on the line. It stays that way for a while, allowing this shift that feels a bit more personal than professional. Not quite friendship, but maybe allies.

"Emmett?"

"Yeah?"

"I just . . . thanks for trying to have my back during the press conference last night. I didn't get a chance to thank you. So . . . thank you."

"That was all you, Reese. You held yourself together far better than I would've if I were in your position." He pauses for a moment. "Don't let them push you around, okay?"

"Only you?"

"Yes," he says, his tone attempting to remain serious. "Only I can push you around."

That shift feels even stronger. Like maybe, just maybe we could call a truce and work together amicably.

It's what has me asking the next thing without fully thinking it through.

"Actually, Emmett. Maybe you *should* come to the advisory board meeting. If you want to. I might need an ally."

"Is that what we are now? Allies?"

"We could be. We have a long season ahead of us. It would be nice to get on the same page with how we're running this team."

He hums into the line. "You know allies are sometimes referred to as friends."

"Don't push your luck."

There's a beat of silence before he says, "I'm still upset about what you did to Nate."

"I know."

"But if you want me to go, I'll be there. Whatever you need."

It's strange. Every now and then, I'll see this gentle side of him. It's probably the side that raised a daughter. It's probably the side that the players get when they need it, which has them all so attached to him. You wouldn't know it from the way he looks, all big and broody, covered in tattoos, but I'll admit, I could see the appeal of Emmett Montgomery if I looked for it.

As I hold the phone to one ear, a strand of my hair falls into my face on the other side. I lift my hand out of the water to push it back and, without thinking, create a splash loud enough he can hear through the line.

That's confirmed when he asks, "Are you swimming right now?"

Yes. "Yes" would be the right answer. Or taking a dip in the hot tub. Or doing the dishes. Literally anything other than, "I'm taking a bath, actually."

There's far too long of a silence on the other end, until finally his deep voice says, "Oh."

Why the hell did I just admit to that? Now he's probably picturing me naked.

"But don't picture me naked or anything."

What is wrong with me? Who says that to their employee? *Don't picture me naked, you know, just in case you were thinking about doing that.*

I'm expecting him to tell me he's hanging up so he can call HR, but instead I'm met with my very own retort. "Don't tell me what to do."

Now I'm the one left speechless on the line.

After I can't seem to come back with any sort of response, Emmett fills the lingering silence. "I'll let you get back to your naked bath, Reese."

"Yep. Thanks."

"Enjoy it."

Before I can find some words that somehow might push this conversation back onto the professional side of things, Emmett ends the call.

5
REESE

The conference room is silent as I sit at the head of the table and wait.

Four of the five members of the advisory board take up each side of the rectangular table with Emmett sitting opposite me.

Scott is late and something about that feels personal. Like he's taking control by making me wait for him. Similarly to how him inviting the team's field manager to the meeting *I* called felt like a power move.

The tick of the clock on the wall is the only sound in the otherwise silent space. I've tried my best not to look up and across from me. I've tried my best to avoid Emmett at all costs.

Don't think about me being naked.

Don't tell me what to do.

Tentatively, I let my eyes drift to him.

Thankfully, he's not looking in my direction, instead focused on the clock on the wall, telling us all that the meeting was supposed to start seven minutes ago.

I never let myself realize it before, but Emmett Montgomery is hot.

Like sinfully hot.

I thought I'd turned that part of my brain off, the part that could even be attracted to another person again. But then something about that reporter practically asking him on a date during our press conference and our conversation while I was in the bath reminded me that I'm still a woman and that man is fine as hell.

Apparently the "older guy thing" is doing it for me these days.

My eyes trail over his jawline. To the way it moves as he chews a piece of gum, and even that part of him is attractive. It's hard and sharp, covered in a perfectly trimmed beard that's peppered with just a bit of salt. His ball cap is pulled low and his Warriors' long-sleeve is tight against his wide shoulders and chest, bunched up at the sleeves where I'm then graced with those cut forearms covered in black ink that extends down the back of his hands.

My attention follows up the center of his chest where our team's logo lives, to the pair of sunglasses resting on the collar, then up to his face again.

Only to find him watching me.

Those brown eyes are hard to see under his hat, yet I can still see the glint that shines in them. His lips lift on one side, this all-too-knowing look plastered on his handsome face before he leans back in chair, folds his hands over his stomach, and doesn't break eye contact with me as he continues to chew his gum.

I simply scowl at him, and Emmett's low chuckle is covered by the sound of the door opening.

"You're late," Ed reminds Scott as he strolls into the conference room, one hand tucked into a pant pocket, the other holding a coffee from my favorite coffee shop a few blocks over from the stadium.

"Am I?" He slaps a hand on Emmett's shoulder before taking the last empty seat at the table. "Good to see you, Monty. Glad you could make it."

I can sense Emmett hesitating. "Reese asked me to join."

Scott takes a sip of his coffee, turning his chair to face me. "Reese, you called this meeting. Go ahead."

Most of the advisory board seem completely uninterested that they're back here so soon after our last meeting. And as the owner of the franchise, I don't technically have to run a single decision by anyone else first.

But even though I feel knowledgeable and qualified, I'm still new in this position. And this group of people has decades of experience in advising my grandfather. It seems like a waste not to use them. It's what I pay them for, after all.

"I want to look into trading Harrison Kaiser," I say simply.

The room goes eerily silent.

Until finally, each and every man on the advisory board bursts into laughter.

Well, everyone but Ed. He offers me an apologetic smile, but nothing about that expression tells me he agrees with me either.

"That's a good one, Reese," Phil chuckles. "What are we really doing here?"

I don't let their reactions deter me. "I want to look into trading Harrison Kaiser."

The laughter slowly dies down as the room begins to realize that I'm completely serious. I watch as they look around at one another, watch as they silently ask each other if I've lost it.

Scott is the first to speak up. "No."

"He's here on a two-year contract and getting paid way too much for it," I explain. "We could use those funds elsewhere."

"Absolutely not. I'm the one who got him here last season. We aren't trading him."

"And you offered him more money than he's worth."

"He was the biggest pickup of the season!" Scott raises his voice at me. "Every playoff-bound team wanted him and *I* got him."

"Reese," Phil cuts in. "Your first act as president cannot be to trade one of the most sought-after players just months after we worked so hard to get him here. You'll be the laughingstock of the league."

Ed puts his hand over mine in a move that reminds me so much of my grandfather. "Don't you think you'll need him for a long playoff run if we make it that far?"

"Yes," Scott answers for me.

"No," I quickly argue. "I have someone else in mind to fill his role. Someone in our minor league system."

Scott scoffs. "Who?"

I pause, unsure if I want to tell him about my long-term plans or about the player I haven't been able to stop watching film of. Really not the best sign that I'm not sure if I can trust someone from the advisory board.

"That's what I thought," Scott says when I stay silent. "There's no one in our minor league system that could even be considered a possible replacement for Harrison Kaiser. Are you out of your goddamn mind?"

"Hey," Emmett cuts in sharply. "Do not speak to her like that."

I let my eyes drift to him to find him already staring back my way.

And he's pissed.

At Scott, I'd like to think. But you never know with Emmett and his players. He's too attached to them.

My hope with inviting him to this meeting was to have another voice on my side. I know I'll get Ed to understand my point of view and having three of us against four are better odds than only having two.

"Let's have a vote," Scott says.

"What?" We don't vote here. I'm in charge. These meetings are simply to advise me, not to force my hand in a certain direction. "No, that's not how this wor—"

"Everyone against trading Harrison Kaiser, raise your hand."

Four hands shoot up instantly. Every member of the advisory board.

All but Ed.

Four against three as I knew it would be, but again, this vote doesn't mean anything. I have the field manager on my side. I have my grandfather's longest trusted advisor.

Those four hands are still lifted in the air when, cautiously, my attention drifts back to Emmett. He's watching me from across the table, jaw hard, hands gripping the armrests of his chair, white knuckles and all.

Until he slowly raises his hand too.

And that single hand in the air is the only one that bothers me.

I don't know how to explain it, but everything in me deflates. I really let myself believe we could be on the same side.

So much for a truce.

We hold eye contact from across the table and I feel my own expression morph to mirror his. Hard. Angry. Disappointed.

No, we aren't allies, and we sure as hell aren't friends.

"There we have it." Scott is far too chipper for my mood right now. "We're not trading Kaiser."

"Great." Standing abruptly, I grab the handles from my bag, slinging them over my shoulder. "Thanks for the meeting."

I'm pushing open the conference room when I hear someone at the table mutter behind me, "She's not cut out for this position."

Just make it to your office. Just hold it together until you can get to your office.

I'm used to being undermined and brushed off, so that's not what has me upset.

I thought, I really thought that after that press conference, Emmett and I could get on the same page. Maybe not privately—I know we're going to disagree on things along the way—but publicly, I hoped he'd have my back.

I pride myself on rarely getting rattled when it comes to work, but I feel it right now.

I move with quick strides, thankful as ever that I'm a pro in heels, when I hear someone jogging behind me.

"Reese!" Emmett calls out, anger clear in his tone.

No. Hell no, I'm not talking to him. And he doesn't get to be the angry one right now.

I turn into the open doorway, pass the empty receptionist desk and dart into my office, slamming the door behind me.

Only for that door to fly open a second later.

"What the hell was that about?"

I turn on him. "You can't just barge in here!"

"What would you have me do? Make an appointment with your receptionist?"

He gestures that way, showcasing the empty desk.

I really need to find a replacement for Denise.

Emmett closes my office door, harder than necessary, leaving us alone inside.

I slip behind my desk, standing while he takes the other side, looming over me.

Ready for battle.

"What are you thinking? Harrison Kaiser. Really, Reese?"

"You already voted against my decision. You didn't have a word to say while we were in the meeting, but *now* you want to argue with me about it?"

"Yes, I want to argue with you!" He lifts his hat, running an aggravated hand through his hair before replacing it. "And no, I'm not going to argue with you in front of *them*. But privately, if I think you're making a huge fucking mistake, then yes, I'm going to tell you."

"Have you ever chased after my grandfather to tell him he's making a mistake?"

Emmett pauses for a moment, his voice a bit more even. "I don't have to tell you that you have way more eyes on you than your grandfather ever did. Every decision you make is going to be plastered across headlines, Reese. Every mistake you make is going to be put under a microscope."

"Well, I don't think it's a mistake. I think it's the right decision."

He laughs in disbelief. "Of course you do. And let me guess, you're going to do it, regardless that no one agrees with that decision. History already tells me that you don't give a shit about what I want anyway. Why even have me in that meeting?"

It feels a touch too vulnerable to admit that I thought maybe, just maybe, he'd see my vision. That he'd have my back. That we could make a good team together.

So instead, I go with, "Harrison doesn't even mesh well with the other players."

"And how would you know?"

"I just . . . I can tell."

He scoffs. "I spend all day every day with those guys. You're grasping at straws here."

I can sense him hoping that I'll back down now, that I'll maybe take a seat so we could have a civil discussion about this. But I don't. I stay standing, facing off with him.

"Goddammit, Reese." Emmett begins pacing my office. "Did something else happen with Kaiser that you're not telling me about?"

"No. No, nothing else happened. But he's expensive and I have a plan."

Sure, Harrison tends to talk to me like I'm a silly girl who has no idea what they're doing around a baseball field, but I can handle that. I'm not so sensitive that I'd make a business decision of this magnitude just because the guy calls me "sweetie."

Emmett stops in the middle of my office, brows cinched and trying to read me. "Why?"

"Why what?"

"Why are you coming in here and trying to change *everything*?"

Is *that* what he thinks I'm doing? Because I'm not. There's so much history of this franchise that I want to protect.

"I have a vision for this club and some decisions that my grandfather made need to be undone in order for that to happen."

Emmett stays silent, watching me. And he looks utterly heartbroken as he does.

"Like me," he finally says.

"What?"

"I don't know why I'm always so surprised by your decisions. It's so easy for you to drop people, like they mean nothing. And we all know I'm next." Emmett shakes his head, headed for my door. "Thanks for the reminder, Reese. I won't be surprised when it's my turn."

6

EMMETT

"Big hit!" Max says, pointing at my desktop computer while sitting on my lap.

"That was a big hit," I agree. "That's Isaiah."

"Yeah. Zaya."

His little finger smears across my screen, attempting to follow his uncle as he runs the bases while we watch game film together.

My daughter is sitting on Kai's lap on the other side of my desk, both watching their son help me prepare for tonight's home game. All while wearing a jersey with his dad's old number on it.

"What do you think, Bug. Do you think I should play Isaiah tonight, or should I bench him?"

Max giggles in my lap, as if that was the funniest thing he's ever heard, and Kai and Miller join in.

We all know I'm not benching my star shortstop.

"No way!"

"No?" I ask. "What if Auntie Ken asked me to bench him for annoying her with that song he always walks out to?"

Max thinks it over. "Hmm. Then yeah."

This time *I* laugh. "Yeah, that's what I thought."

"Bug," Kai begins. "Are you going to come see me and Monty in the dugout before the first pitch?"

"Yeah. And me and Mama watch Dada coaching."

Max's attention focuses back on the computer screen,

watching highlights from last night's game, while I look across at my daughter.

She grew up just like this, coming to the field to watch me coach.

I've spent the last twenty-plus years raising that girl and wanting only this—for her to find her happiness, no matter what that may look like. At the time, I didn't know it was going to be my star pitcher and his son to bring that into her life, but meeting Kai and Max grounded her in a way I could've only hoped for.

More than any job I've had, more than my time in the league as a player, more than the World Series win as a field manager, what I am most proud of in my life is her. Anything I've ever done is for her.

"Max, what do you say?" Miller asks. "Do you want to go find Isaiah and Auntie Ken before the game starts?"

Max's big blue eyes widen in excitement, his silent way of saying yes.

"Well, let's do it." Miller stands from Kai's lap.

"And the boys?" Max asks as I help him down.

"We'll go see all the boys. I bet Cody and Trav are looking for you right now."

Reaching up, Max puts his hand into his mom's.

Miller wraps her arm around me in a side hug. "Good luck tonight, Dad."

"Thanks, Millie. Love you."

"Love you too." She bends over to quickly kiss Kai. "Good luck, baby."

"Thanks, Mills. Love you."

As soon as my daughter and Max are out of my office, I scowl at my future son-in-law.

"What?" he asks, confused.

"Don't copy me."

Kai chuckles. "Get over it, old man."

"You're only like a decade younger than me."

"All I heard was 'younger.'"

"Shut up and let's talk about the pitching strategy for tonight."

Laughing, Kai pulls out his iPad and starts spouting out facts about the other team's batting lineup. Through the window behind him, a flash of blonde steals my attention. I keep my eyes locked there, willing for it to return, when finally, Reese walks by my window with someone I vaguely recognize from the ticket sales department.

They stop right in front of my office, right in front of my window, as they continue their conversation, giving me a perfect view.

She's all business tonight, as always. Sharp line to her short hair, sky-high heels, and a pencil skirt that's practically painted to her curves.

And she's *smiling*, which is only worth noting because I haven't seen it in over a week.

We have yet to speak since that advisory meeting last Monday. Well, I guess what I mean is that we have yet to speak since we got into it in her office right afterward.

And yeah, I've fucking noticed.

I've noticed that she hasn't once come to the dugout before a game this week. I noticed that she hasn't accommodated a single request for joint interviews with me. I noticed she hasn't been around the clubhouse much, instead staying upstairs in her office during this home-stint.

I also noticed that she hasn't made a move to trade Harrison Kaiser.

Reese is clearly pissed at me for not having her back last week, but I'm just as pissed that she continues to prove me right. I'm pissed that she doesn't hold an attachment to any part of this baseball club that I love so much. Not the staff and, clearly, not the players.

"Monty," Kai says, earning my attention. "Did you hear me? Do you know who you might want for middle relief tonight?"

I keep my eyes locked on her, watching her smile and enjoy whatever conversation she's having with someone who isn't me.

"No." Even *I* can hear the distraction in my voice. "Game-time decision, I guess."

Out of my periphery, I watch as Kai follows my line of sight. "Do you need to go speak with her?"

"Nope." I clear my throat, attempting to refocus on this meeting with my pitching coach.

But I'm having a hard time keeping my eyes off my window, wondering if the reason Reese is down here, near my office, is because she's finally going to talk to me.

She ends her conversation with a kind smile to her employee before her attention drifts to my office window.

First to Kai, who earns a polite grin and a small nod of her head in greeting.

Then to me, which is when her expression completely shifts.

To nothing.

It's neutral. Blank. I don't get a smile, but I also don't get that scowl I kind of miss.

Reese doesn't seem angry.

No, she seems entirely disinterested with me, and I hate *that* even more than if she were fuming at me.

Reese's eyes meet mine for only a fraction of a second, not letting them linger in the way I've caught her before. Almost instantly, she pulls her attention away and leaves the perfectly framed spot outside my office window. And I'd bet money she'll be up in her office for the rest of the night, watching the game from her million-dollar view.

"So, by 'you don't need to talk to her' what you meant is 'she won't give you the time of day.'" Kai laughs. "What the hell did you do?"

"Nothing. We had a disagreement last week and neither of us has gone out of our way to smooth things over yet."

"Kennedy raves about her, and from what she told me, Reese seems level-headed. Especially for all the shit she's getting online for her new position. Your disagreement must have been pretty heated for her to react to you like that."

"It was nothing. We'll both get over it eventually."

"Don't you two have the commissioner's conference coming up?"

I audibly groan, head falling back. "Fuck me. I almost forgot about that."

Toward the beginning of every season, the commissioner of the MLB hosts a gathering for all the teams' owners, baseball presidents, and field managers. And since Arthur has always held two of those positions, I've gone to the last seven conferences with only him.

And this year, I'll be going with Reese.

The location never changes and neither does the schedule. The commissioner hosts a few lectures throughout the day then a mixer at night, giving all the teams a chance to get together just once without a competition attached to it. There's no getting out of it for either of us, and I already know that Reese and I are going to have to at least pretend to be a united front while we're around all the other teams.

Kai laughs. "I'd apologize before you go if I were you."

"Except I don't have anything to apologize for."

"If you say so."

My pitching coach refocuses on the strategy for tonight's game, but there's something nagging me again, the way it has all week. Something that Reese said in our heated argument.

I lean back in my chair, folding my hands behind my head. "Ace, can I ask you something?"

"Of course."

"What do you think of Harrison Kaiser?"

Behind his glasses, he lifts his brow in surprise. "As a player, or as a person?"

"I already know what kind of player he is."

Kai sighs, leaning back in his chair. "He's not my favorite."

"Why?"

"We were on the same team for only a few months, so I might not be the best judge of character."

But he is. Kai is steady and perceptive. I wouldn't care if he only knew Harrison Kaiser for a day, I'd still trust his opinion on the guy.

When I don't interrupt him, Kai continues. "He's arrogant. And not in a goofy, Isaiah kind of way, but in an elitist way. With how much he's getting paid, I know his attitude rubs some of the guys wrong. He likes to talk shit about other players, and you know how close our team is, so no one really fucks with that. He doesn't join any of the team outings. He's never come to our house when Miller does her baking nights for the guys, even though he's always invited."

He pauses his own rant, slowing himself down. "To put it simply, Cody can befriend a brick wall if asked to and even he's not a fan. But . . ." Kai tosses his head from side to side. "I also know he's fast as hell and can outrun anyone around the bases and in the outfield, so it's not like he's going anywhere either."

I'm shocked silent, frozen in my chair.

"Should I continue?" Kai asks. "Because I can."

"Why did I not know about this? I'm around you all every single day."

"We're adults, here to do a job. No one is going to come running to your office to bitch about someone's personality not meshing."

Well, I feel like an idiot.

Reese told me this and I didn't listen. I was so adamant she was wrong, that there was no way she could know about our team dynamics better than me.

Fuck. Apparently, I do need to apologize.

My future son-in-law studies me. "Why do you ask?"

I exhale a resigned breath. "If I tell you something, it needs to stay here."

"Of course."

"That disagreement me and Reese had, it was over Kaiser. I sat in on an advisory board meeting where Reese proposed trading him and no one agreed with her, including me."

Kai's eyes widen with surprise. "Who would she replace him with?"

"I'm not sure. She didn't give details, only that she had someone in mind. But she said something about him not meshing with the team, and I didn't believe her. I thought she was just pulling something out of thin air to back up her idea."

"Wow." Kai pauses for a long moment. "That's impressive, that she was able to pick up on that. Most owners wouldn't give a shit about team personalities, let alone notice on their own."

"Yeah," I sigh, running a hand down my face. "I underestimated her."

Just like everyone else.

7

EMMETT

Leaning a shoulder against the lobby wall, I wait.

Reese already texted me that she was running a bit behind and would just meet me in the hotel's main ballroom where they've set up a bar and some high-top tables, but I didn't have it in me to make her walk into tonight's cocktail mixer alone.

I was surprised when her name popped up on my phone screen thirty minutes ago, because that one text is about all the communication we've had.

We didn't speak on this morning's flight to Las Vegas. We sat next to each other on the plane, but Reese had her headphones in and worked the entire time.

When we arrived at the hotel, we didn't say a word, simply gave the receptionist our IDs to check us in. Once we received our room keys, we went our separate ways, and the conference schedule kept us apart for the rest of the day.

Reese attended a few events for the owners while I went to the get-togethers for the field managers. The commissioner spoke. We listened. Then we all hung out, shooting the shit during our downtime.

I've got quite a few friends who manage other teams, which is the only part of this yearly conference I enjoy. We get to catch up without the pressure of a game looming over us. Sure, there are a few coaches who don't exactly get along, but they're all fairly good at faking it in these group settings.

It doesn't make a whole lot of sense that this conference is held in Vegas every year. There are no major league teams here currently and the commissioner's office is located in New York. Yet, every year, for twenty-four hours, we all gather here. And judging by the debauchery that I've seen some of these guys get up to over the years, I think I might be the only attendee who despises having to trek all the way out to Nevada for one night.

Personally, I can't stand this part of the job. The ass-kissing. The showing off to other teams. By the time the cocktail mixer rolls around every year, I've got about an hour left in my social battery before I head back to my room for the night. I can't remember a conference I've attended that I wasn't counting down the minutes until our flight out or when I could get back to my team.

So, knowing there's only one hour that I might get to speak to Reese after more than a week of silence, I wait in the lobby for her so we can walk in together.

This level of the Vegas hotel is reserved for the conference, which is a whole lot quieter than the casino. So, when the elevator finally dings, landing on this floor, it earns all my attention.

But even if I were surrounded by hundreds of people, even if I couldn't hear myself think, my eyes still would've found her as soon as the doors opened.

Reese is standing in the elevator by herself, riffling through her tiny purse for something and not realizing that I'm standing on the other side, utterly speechless.

I've mostly seen my boss in business attire. But tonight, she's wearing a dress. It's dusty blue and cut perfectly to highlight every inch of her. A dress that I can't decide if I'd like better on her distracting body, as it is now, or seeing it sprawled across my bedroom floor.

Okay. What the hell is wrong with me?

It doesn't matter that she and I don't get along most of the time. It's becoming increasingly difficult to view my boss as *only* my boss when I haven't felt this level of attraction to someone in years.

Not that I'd ever act on it. I respect her too much to risk her reputation or my own job for something as minor as physical attraction.

There's also the fact that I'm older than her and also her employee. I'm self-aware enough to admit that I already know Reese would never see me in that way.

She walks out of the elevator, still looking through her purse until she finally finds the lip gloss she was searching for. She's got the top off and the applicator partway to her lips when she looks up and finds me waiting for her.

Leaning a shoulder against the wall, hand tucked into a pocket.

A little bit hypnotized.

"Oh," she says. "I uh . . . you didn't have to wait for me."

It's about the most she's said to me all week, but I'm not paying much attention to her words. I'm fixated on the way her eyes trail down my body, on the way her cheeks earn a slight flush as she takes her time looking.

I typically live in my athletic clothes and baseball pants when I'm at work, but tonight, just like the other ninety or so men in there, I'm wearing a suit.

Miller was over at my apartment this morning, and I asked her to grab me a suit from my closet so I could pack. I wasn't at all surprised when she picked my dark green one, seeing as it's her favorite color. And judging by the way my boss is looking at me right now, I need to thank my daughter for choosing this one.

"I uh . . ." I rub my palm over my beard. "I didn't want you to walk in alone."

That blank expression she's worn around me all week softens in a way she rarely lets it. "That was thoughtful of you."

There's a moment of silence as I replay her words.

"I'm sorry," I tease. "Was that a compliment you just accidentally let slip out?"

I watch as the smallest tic lifts the corners of her lips, but she tries to cover it by sliding the gloss over her lips, leaving a soft-pink shine in its wake.

"My bad. I won't let it happen again."

As she speaks, a bit of gloss smears just on the outside ridge of her lip and I can't seem to help myself. Something about her not only speaking to me but bantering with me again has me pushing off the wall, closing the distance between us.

Reese's eyes stay on mine the entire time, and when I reach her, I carefully swipe the bit of stray gloss off her skin with the pad of my thumb. "You look . . ." *Stunning. Breathtaking. Absolutely unreal.* "Beautiful."

Reese's eyes widen only a fraction and it's enough to tell me that was the wrong thing to say.

"Nice, I mean. You look nice. Fine. Average at best. And honestly, I wouldn't notice otherwise."

Reese tilts her head to the side, trying to suppress her grin. "Is that what you used to tell my grandfather when you two went to these things together? That he looked beautiful."

"Absolutely. So don't assume that's something I reserve only for you. That's just a typical thing I like to say to my bosses."

"Hmm," she hums. "Glad to see you're keeping things so consistently professional."

That's my new rule. If I wouldn't say it to Arthur, I shouldn't say it to Reese.

I clear my throat. "Shall we?"

Reese gives a polite nod of her head and, like instinct, I reach out to place my hand on her lower back, wanting to usher her to walk ahead of me. But, thankfully, I stop myself before I make contact.

Even though we're dressed like this, this is not a fucking date. This is a work event and the last thing she needs is to walk into a room of her peers and the commissioner of the league with her employee's palm sprawled across the small of her back.

Instead, I shove my hand back into my pocket and just pray I find a way to get my shit together at some point tonight.

I can feel this uneasy, nervous energy radiating off her the closer we get to the ballroom door, and that's only amplified by the way she constantly turns her head and checks her surroundings.

I'm not used to seeing Reese flustered and uncomfortable, but I did just wipe her lip and tell her she looks beautiful, so I assume what she's desperately checking for is the nearest exit and the quickest path to get away from me.

I give her a bit more distance, staying another step behind. But when I reach out to open the ballroom's door for her, she quickly covers my hand with hers to keep the door closed.

"Emmett," she sighs, turning to face me. "I know we're having some differences right now, but just for tonight . . . can we be on the same team?"

"We're always on the same team. That's literally why we're here. Because we are on the same team."

"You know what I mean. It's been a hard day, and I have a feeling tonight isn't going to be any easier."

There's a lot more that needs to be said, mostly an apology from me for not hearing her out about trading one of my players. But that's a conversation for a different time.

"What happened today?" I ask.

"Nothing I didn't expect."

I'm not positive I know what she means but my instincts are screaming that I'm not going to like the answer when I find out.

"So maybe, just for tonight, we can call a truce?" There's a bit of vulnerability in her voice that I'm not used to hearing from her.

I nod to agree. "Of course, Reese. Whatever you need."

She exhales, and the weight on her shoulders seems to lighten a bit. "Thank you."

"Do you want to talk about it?"

"No. I'm a big girl. I can handle it." She takes her hand away from mine, allowing me to open the door. "Let's just get this over with."

I pull the handle inward. "That's the spirit."

That one and only hour I was planning to stay has come and gone.

So have an additional two.

Don't get me wrong, I don't want to be here. I'd rather be just about anywhere else *other* than here, but I'm sure as hell not going to leave Reese on her own.

I've only ever worked for one Major League Baseball club so I don't personally know many of the other team owners, but I can say for certain that they're all a bunch of pricks.

Hidden in the back corner of the bar with a bourbon in hand, because I really am done with the socializing part of today, I watch it all unfold the same as it has for the past three hours.

Technically, Reese is with all the other owners on the other side of the room, trying her best to network and include herself in the conversations happening around her. But since we've been here, I've witnessed every single one of them brush her off.

She might be standing nearby, but they're doing their best to make sure she knows she is not *with* them.

It's a sea of white-haired men in ill-fitting suits. The blonde bombshell stands out no matter where she goes but even more so being the only woman among her peers who are all at least thirty years her senior.

I'm sure they don't think they're being absolute dicks by excluding her, and I can guarantee at least half of them don't even know the meaning of the word *sexist*, though they're the walking definition. But I know the way some of these guys think. Fundamentally, they believe that women should stay out of sports.

They'll do their one female hire to dodge the scrutiny from the public, but it's never in a higher-up position.

Then in comes Reese, equal on their level and done so without their permission.

She's got a glass of red wine in her hand and is doing her best to listen and contribute to the conversations around her, and my heart kind of breaks watching her have to try so hard.

Eventually, Reese says something to a group of men, but then, once again, one of them shifts his shoulder slightly to edge her out of the discussion. She keeps her head held high, not letting anyone notice that being ostracized by her colleagues is bothering her. But I can tell. I've watched it bother her all night.

This must be what happened earlier today and that just fucking sucks.

Once again, Reese checks her surroundings, the same as she's been doing for the last few hours. There's this nervous energy about her tonight that's unnatural to the Reese I've been getting to know.

She's the embodiment of confidence, or at least does a good job of putting on that front. But tonight, even though she's trying her best to seem self-assured, everything in her body language screams that she's on edge.

As her eyes track the room, they eventually land on me. Her

shoulders drop a hair, but her smile is weak, like she's a bit embarrassed that I witnessed her being outcasted by the fellow club owners.

I nod my head toward the door, silently asking her if she wants me to help her get out of here, but she simply gives me a small, indiscreet shake of her head before focusing on her phone in her hands.

My own phone dings and I pull it out of my pocket to read the text.

Reese: You don't have to wait for me.

Looking up, I shoot her a glare for thinking I could leave her like this.

> **Me:** We're on the same team tonight. Also, fuck these guys.

She chuckles, holding up the last of her wineglass in a cheers from across the room. I do the same with my bourbon before bringing it to my lips, keeping eye contact the entire time to watch her finish the last of her glass.

> **Me:** What are you drinking?

But Reese's phone must be on silent because she doesn't see my text come through when she turns back to the group of twenty-nine other owners, doing her best to get involved.

"Hey," I say to the bartender as he makes his way to the far end of the bar. "What kind of red do you have?"

He looks behind him at the uncorked lineup of wine. "We have a Cab, a Zin, and a Pinot. But if you're wondering what she's drinking . . ." He points in Reese's direction. "She's drinking the Pinot."

"How'd you know it was for her?"

He grabs the bottle of Pinot and pours it into a fresh glass. "You've had your eye on her all night."

"Yeah, it's not like that. She's my boss and she's having a rough day, is all."

He slides the wineglass over to me. "I'm not here to judge. And I signed an NDA to work this event tonight, so I'm not saying a word. Another bourbon?"

"Please." Over my shoulder, I look back in Reese's direction, only she's nowhere to be found. She's pretty impossible to miss in that blue dress tonight, so I'm assuming she ran to the restroom or something and I'll get her this glass of wine when she comes back.

"So, is she his boss too?" the bartender asks. "Because he hasn't been able to keep his eyes off her all night either."

He points in a different direction than I was looking, and I follow his outstretched finger to the far corner of the room. Reese's back is to me, but her posture is tense, her shoulders lifted nearly to her ears as she speaks to someone.

I vaguely recognize the guy. If I'm remembering correctly, he was introduced earlier today as the newest assistant to the commissioner. I couldn't tell you his name if my life depended on it, but he's younger than me. In his thirties, if I had to guess.

To be frank, I don't care to know *anything* about him other than why Reese is so nervous speaking to him.

"Thank you," I say to the bartender, throwing a twenty in his tip jar before taking the wineglass in one hand and my bourbon in the other.

Pushing off the bar, I'm quick to cross the room.

"Monty! My guy!" Seattle's field manager swings an arm over my shoulder, stopping me in place. "You are . . ." He stumbles over his words. "Coming out with us."

"No, Bill. I'm not."

"You never come out with us. We're in Vegas!"

I slip out from under his arm, continuing to cross the room. "That's because I'm too old for that shit."

"I'm older than you!"

"Exactly!" I call over my shoulder.

Another one of the coaches steps in front of me, blocking my path. "Montgomery. Monty," he says, drawing out my nickname.

"Yeah?" My tone is exasperated as I look past him to check on Reese. They're still standing in the same spot. She seems just as uncomfortable as she did before. He's got a smile I'd like to knock off his face.

"I gotta ask you something."

I close my eyes in frustration. I've been hiding in the corner of the bar for the past few hours. He couldn't have asked me then?

"Yep?"

He leans in closer, his voice low. "Arthur's granddaughter." As soon as those two words are out of his mouth, I feel every muscle in my body tense, wary to hear what else he's going to add on to them. "What's her name again?"

My jaw is tight as I speak through my teeth. "Reese."

"Reese! That's right. What's her story?"

"What do you mean, what's her story? She's the new owner of the team and acting president. She took over for Arthur after last season."

He laughs. "No, I don't care about any of that. Is she single?"

"Seriously?" I blow past him, maybe hitting his shoulder with mine as I do. "Stay away from her," is my only answer.

"Geez, Monty. Sensitive topic, I guess."

Finally, I reach her, and I can feel the tension radiating off her body as I approach from behind. I put both our glasses in one of my hands, using my other to palm her mid-back. It's an appropriate spot that no one here, especially someone who works in the commissioner's office, would think twice about.

From behind, I bend down close to her ear. "You okay?"

Her nod is a bit stiff, but the rest of her seems to relax a bit.

Reaching around her, I steal her empty glass, setting it on a nearby table before slipping the new one into her hand.

"Thank you," she whispers.

I'm typically one to introduce myself when someone is standing nearby, but for whatever reason, fuck this guy.

"Aren't you going to introduce me, Reese?" he asks.

I feel her deep inhale against my palm.

"Emmett, this is Jeremy." Over her shoulder she looks up and meets my eye, trying to silently tell me something before she adds, "My ex-husband."

8
REESE

"Well, I hope you're taking care of our girl out there in Chicago," Jeremy says.

It takes everything in me not to roll my eyes. *Our girl?* Please. He's only laying it on thick now that another man is around.

"She takes care of herself just fine," is Emmett's answer.

And there's something about the conviction in his tone that reminds me that I do.

Being ignored by every other team owner in the league did a number on my self-confidence today, so I don't mind having a bit of it restored by the one person in my organization whose approval I'm finding myself eager to earn.

"I bet she does." Jeremy's attention swings back to me. "It's been a long time, Reese. You look good."

I want to tell him he looks exhausted from kissing up to the commissioner all night. But I don't. Because I'm so fucking professional.

The sentence is barely out of Jeremy's mouth when Emmett's fingertips curl against my back. "Excuse us, but I need a word with my boss in private for a moment."

"No problem." Jeremy keeps his eyes on me. "I hope we can catch up soon."

Not that I was going to agree, quite the opposite in fact, but before I can say anything, Emmett's palm presses against my back, ushering me away from my ex.

"Why are you acting like a jealous boyfriend?" I ask over my shoulder, though my words are a bit slurred.

There's an annoyed rumble in his tone as we continue toward the exit door. "Do not ask me that right now, Reese."

I do my best, pressing my lips together and holding back my laugh. But I'm tipsy, so one slips out anyway.

We continue through the crowd when Emmett leans down, speaking quietly for no one else to hear us. "Are you okay?"

"Yep."

"Are you sure?" I don't miss the concern in his question.

"Super totally sure."

I am fine, but like Jeremy said, it's been a long time since we've seen one another. And I spent most of the day on edge, knowing I was most likely going to run into him here and just praying I wouldn't have to hear him say, "I told you so."

Thankfully, my field manager got me away before he could.

Emmett opens the main door for me, allowing me to exit first before he closes it behind him, blocking out the buzzing noise of everyone partying inside.

I'm still buzzing though, that's for damn sure. Having no one to talk to all night gave me plenty of time to drink this wine. And I am feeling it.

The lobby's silence is a stark difference to the noisy ballroom-turned-bar, so Emmett's voice is perfectly clear when he says, "Let's get the hell out of here."

"Where are we going?"

"Anywhere other than here. You don't need to be around these people any longer than you already have been."

As much as I hate to admit it, Emmett is a calming presence when he wants to be. Sure, he's excellent at going toe-to-toe with me, but I'm learning he's equally talented at composure when the moment calls for it.

He also does a good job at differentiating between those two instances, a trait I'd imagine he developed by raising a daughter.

As we make our way to the elevator, he takes two plastic cups by the water station and pours our drinks into them, handing me my wine once again. We go two floors up to the casino level and as soon as the elevator doors open, cigarette smoke chokes the air.

It's even louder than the ballroom was downstairs, so when Emmett puts his hand on my lower back to usher me through the swarm of people, he has to lean in even closer to say, "Outside."

He keeps his fingertips pressed into me, guiding me through the drunken crowd. It's an eclectic group. Bachelorette parties. Twenty-first birthday parties. Some random guy who looks like he just lost his life savings at a blackjack table.

Vegas is weird.

I'm buzzed, but definitely not drunk enough for this. But then Emmett slips his arm around my waist because there're way too many people we're attempting to move through. And it's then I realize that, nope, I am drunk enough for this. Because I'm not trying to pull away from him.

The outside air is by no means fresh, but it's so much better than the stale recycled air in the casino. Our hotel is right on the main strip, so though it's late already, the sky is still illuminated from all the Vegas lights.

"Are your feet okay to walk?"

I look down at my heels. "I could run a marathon in these babies."

I couldn't even finish a marathon in running shoes, but he doesn't need to know that.

"I'm sure you could, Reese. Walk with me, then."

"Are you going to ask me about my ex-husband while we're on this walk?"

"There're a lot of things I want to ask you while we're on this walk. I didn't know you were married before."

"That's not a question." I take another long sip of my wine from my plastic cup like the fancy bitch I am. "And of course you didn't know that. There're a lot of things we don't know about each other."

Looking down, he arches his brow at me. "Maybe we should change that."

Fuck me, he looks good in that suit. Perfectly fitted to his wide body, tatted hands spilling out past the cuffs at his wrist. And thick thighs that want to test the durability of the fabric in the way it pulls across his muscular legs as he takes each step.

And no baseball hat tonight, letting me witness his handsome face without the shadow of a brim to conceal it.

"Did you know he was going to be here?" Emmett asks.

"I assumed he might be. I heard he had a new position in the commissioner's office. Hey, look! Isaiah and Kennedy got married there." I point at a small white chapel, recognizing it from a particular newspaper article.

Without paying attention, I step off the curb to cross the street and almost eat shit as I do.

"Okay." Emmett loops an arm around my waist to steady me. "So much for that marathon."

"It's not my fault that I'm buzzed. No one would talk to me. I got bored. I was nervous. And why am I telling you anything?"

"You don't have to tell me shit, Reese. But I like the idea of you starting to talk to me again."

Arm still around me, he leads me into a different hotel. The air isn't as stale here. The crowd isn't as rowdy. Near the entrance, there's a small cocktail bar that's hidden and quiet. Emmett gets us a spot in the back where two plush chairs face one another. He orders us another round before he sits and gives me every ounce of his attention.

His position is widespread and sprawled out, his legs open around mine. The outsides of my knees kiss the insides of his in a way that feels far too intimate because he's my employee, so I cross one leg over the other to buy myself some space.

But then Emmett leans his elbows on his knees, crowding me again, and I don't have it in me to lie to myself a second time by pretending I don't like it.

I've truly never felt small in my life, but the way this man's body covers mine in this protective manner has me thinking that if I ever gave myself permission to feel fragile, it'd be safe to do so here.

"So talk to me," he urges.

My lips are loose tonight. "Jeremy is kind of a prick. He doesn't come off that way, but—"

"Oh, no. Trust me. He comes off that way," Emmett interrupts. "Did you get him a job?"

"You mean in baseball? No. We met years ago when he was doing data and analytics for the MLB and living in San Francisco. I was finishing my MBA at the time. But maybe you already know that. I don't know what you know."

"I don't know much, Reese. I think that may be part of the issue with us. I don't know much about you at all." The server drops our drinks off. Emmett pushes my wine toward me. "But I'd like to."

A warmth rushes my cheeks at the soft and sincere way he says that. Or maybe it's the wine that's making me hot. Who knows at this point. But I'm starting to understand how my grandfather had a hard time saying no to this man.

"I know what you're doing."

"Keeping your buzz going, so you keep talking to me. Oh, no. You caught me."

"You're doing a great job. Keep it up."

I try to hide my smile behind my glass and watch one mirror on Emmett's mouth as he brings his bourbon to his lips.

"We were married for three years," I tell him.

"Amicable separation?"

I toss my head from side to side. "Once I came to terms with what our marriage was to him, then yes. He tried to take the team from me. It was easy to walk away after that."

I take another sip of my wine. "I grew up around the clubhouse. I knew I was going to take it over one day. But my grandfather wasn't going to just hand over the team without any experience. I had to get my MBA. Did that. I had to intern with the MLB, learning the baseball side of things. Did that. Started working for the San Francisco office, educating myself on the game from the numbers point of view. Did that. Met Jeremy there. Got married. He tried to take the team from me. That's super fucked up, right?"

"Yeah, Reese. That's super fucked up."

"I mean, people can change their mind. It happens all the time. But the things he suddenly wanted came out of nowhere. He had never mentioned wanting any involvement in running the team, then all of a sudden, he wanted in on all of it. He assumed marrying into my family gave him that right. My grandfather was pissed. I was pissed. You'd be pissed too, right?"

He crosses his arms over his chest. "I'm currently pissed."

I hesitate when I realize I've probably already said too much. "I don't want to just sit here and shit on Jeremy."

"Well, that's too bad. Because I do."

I huff a laugh. Okay. Maybe I do too. "He legally wanted fifty percent of the team ownership to be under his name."

"Wow. He can go fuck himself for expecting that."

"I know! Right? Fuck him!"

"Fuck him!" he echoes.

I sit back in my chair with a heavy sigh. "Emmett, I know you think I'm being careless with some of the decisions I've made, but I promise you, I'm just trying to do my best. You have no idea how desperate I am to do well."

My field manager's face softens with understanding.

"Is he who made you so nervous today? You seemed on edge all night, looking around."

"Oh God." I exhale a self-deprecating laugh. "You noticed that?"

He brings his bourbon to his lips, watching me from over the rim. "I had my eye on you most of the night."

That heat rushes up my face again. And though I like the way those words sound coming from him, we both know that's not what he means. He was simply trying to have my back tonight, the way I asked him to.

"One of Jeremy's selling points for him taking over instead of me was the concern that if I were the face of the team, no one would give me the time of day. And today only proved that he was right. His theory was on full display for him to witness."

"He wasn't right."

"Emmett—"

"He wasn't right, Reese." His words are laced with so much conviction even *I* almost believe them. "And I'm really fucking tired of people telling you that you can't do this job."

"No one thinks I know what I'm doing, including you."

He pauses for a long moment and when he speaks again, there's this regretful tone to his voice. "I need to apologize—"

"You don't need to do that."

"Yes, I do. I need to explain myself because the last thing I want is for you to view me with any sort of comparison to them." He nods in the direction of the hotel we're staying at. "I don't like how you were being treated tonight."

"I can handle it."

"Yeah, I know you can. But that doesn't mean you should have to."

Those kind brown eyes are filled with an apology he doesn't owe me. Because in this moment, for the first time today, it feels like I'm not entirely alone. And that means more than he probably realizes.

I shrug nonchalantly. "I'll feel better when we finish the season with a better record than each and every one of them."

A warm laugh bursts from Emmett's chest, instantly bringing a smile to my lips. "You read my mind. This conference is supposed to put the competition on pause, but watching those other owners around you tonight, all it did was make me want to beat every one of their teams on the field for you."

"For me, huh? You're the one up for a new contract this season. Don't you think a winning record would benefit *your* case?"

"Yeah, well, why can't it do both? You said it yourself, Reese. We're on the same team. Don't you remember?"

I find him with a teasing yet testing smile on his lips and I mirror it with my own.

"Yeah, I remember."

9
EMMETT

As soon as I'm back in my room from my morning run, I slip off my sweat-soaked shirt, tossing it on the floor to remind myself to separate it from my clean clothes when I finish packing.

While we were only in Vegas for one night, Reese and I are headed straight from here to San Diego to meet the team for a series of road games. I had to pack more than I would for a simple overnight stay and don't want my workout clothes stinking up everything else I'll be wearing the rest of the week.

Typically, I find this little conference a waste of time, taking an entire day away while in season, but I learned more last night than I ever thought I would.

Not about baseball or the inner workings of the league, but about Reese.

It was the first time she's shown me any real vulnerability, and instead of resenting this time away, I was grateful for a chance to be alone with her. Where she couldn't hide in her office, and I couldn't hide behind my team.

It was . . . *nice*.

I'm still catching my breath from my run when my phone rings. I dig it out of my running belt to find a picture of my daughter covering the entire screen and her name scrolling across the top.

"Hey, Millie," I say through hard-earned breaths as I answer the phone.

"Hey, Dad. Just calling to check in on you. How was the conference?"

"It was . . ." I hesitate. "Not as terrible as it usually is."

"Glad to hear it. Is that because your hot boss was there? Reese is a little nicer to look at than Arthur, huh? *Oh my God.*" I can hear the grimace in her voice. "Is that why you sound like that? Like you're completely out of breath. Is she there with you right now? What the hell did I just interrupt? Jesus, Dad. Are you sure you're healthy enough for those kinds of activities?"

I shake my head, though she can't see me. "Hey, Miller?"

"Yeah?" She laughs.

"Shut up."

Her laughter only grows.

I love my daughter but goddamn, the girl can talk shit. She can take it too, which is what I get for raising her around a baseball team her entire life.

"I did an early lift and just got back from my morning run. So, while yes, I'm definitely healthy enough for *those kinds of activities*, that's not what's happening right now. Get your mind out of the gutter, you freak."

She chuckles on the line.

I go into the connected bathroom, turning my hat backward and grabbing a clean hand towel to run over my face, trying to clean up the dripping sweat.

"What are you up to?" I ask.

"Me and Maxie boy just got on the plane and it's making me miss the season we got to fly with the team through the private airport. TSA was a nightmare today."

"Yeah, I bet Max is missing it too. Do you remember how hard he used to sleep on the team plane in that bed that was set up for him in the back?"

"Well, I can promise you, he's having no issues with that. We've been in our seats for all of five minutes and he's already passed out in my lap."

"When he wakes up, tell my boy I say hi and that I can't wait to see him."

"I will."

"I can't wait to see you too, Millie. I'm glad you two are joining us for a couple of road games."

I saw my daughter just yesterday morning, but now that I'm spoiled enough to have her living in my same city, I'll take every chance I can get to spend time with her.

It's been just the two of us for the past twenty or so years, and while Miller is building her own family now, she's the entirety of mine. Maybe it's why I'm so close to my players and staff I work with. When Miller left home at eighteen and I moved into coaching in the majors, I was all of a sudden alone, and the team became my new extended family.

"I'm looking forward to seeing you too. Kai is having so much fun, Dad. He's loving coaching the guys."

"Well, he's damn good at it too." As I sling the hand towel over my shoulder, a knock sounds on my hotel room door. "One second, Millie. I think housekeeping is here already. They must not know we have a late checkout."

Crossing the room, I keep the phone pressed to my ear and open the door.

But it's not housekeeping I find on the other side.

It's Reese.

"Morning," she says with a smile, but her mouth quickly drops into parted lips when her eyes drift down my sweat-soaked face, over my bare chest that's still pounding as I continue to catch my breath.

"Hi." I sound just as surprised as she looks right now.

As she stands on the other side of the door, I let my eyes roam. If she weren't right in front of me, I'm not sure I'd recognize her. She's in a pair of well-fitted blue jeans, and I've never seen her wear denim before but *goddamn* it looks good stretched over her thick thighs. Her high heels have been swapped for a pair of sneakers, and her typically sleek blonde hair is covered in a Warriors' team hat, the ends curled in a loose, casual wave.

It's a stark contrast from the business Barbie I usually see around the office. Today Reese looks more like the baseball-loving girl next door and it fucking works for her.

It works for me too.

"Dad?" My daughter's voice in my ear acts as the coldest kind of shower. "That's your hot boss at your door right now, isn't it?"

I close my eyes for a moment. "I gotta go, Miller."

"I'm sure you do. Tell my new stepmom I said hi!"

"Something is seriously wrong with you, you know that? Who the hell raised you?"

Both Reese and my daughter laugh, but thankfully, my boss can't hear Miller through the phone.

"Love you, Dad."

"Love you too. Fly safe and I'll see you tonight."

I hang up the phone, giving Reese my attention again. "Sorry about that," I say, using the towel to wipe my face again.

When I sling it back over my shoulder, I don't miss the way her cheeks have turned a shade of pink or the way those blue eyes work their hardest to focus on my face.

She clears her throat. "Miller is coming to San Diego?"

"She is. Max too."

"You know, I've never formally met her before."

"You haven't?" My head rears back. "How is that even possible?"

"I've seen her around the field with you, Kai, or Kennedy, but yeah. I haven't met her myself."

"I'll introduce you this weekend. But fair warning, she's absolutely insane and will most likely say something highly inappropriate, so just ignore that."

A smile lingers on her lips. "I'll keep that in mind."

I lean a shoulder into the doorway and catch Reese quickly checking me out again.

I like working out to clear my head and to strengthen my body, but my boss's attention will be good motivation too.

"What's up?"

She hesitates. "I just wanted to apologize for being a little word-vomity last night. It was a long day, and that wine was disturbingly easy to drink."

"You don't need to apologize for anything. It was nice . . . talking with you. Buzzed or not."

"It was." She takes a deep breath, rocking back on her heels. "And I was thinking that maybe we could call a truce that lasts longer than just last night."

I feel my smile fighting its way through. "I think I'd be up for that."

"Perfect. Because I want to take you somewhere before our flight."

"Right now?" I glance down at my bare chest, reminding Reese I'm half naked.

"You can put a shirt on first."

"Are you sure you want me to do that?"

Her mouth opens to say something in retort, but nothing comes out. "Just meet me in the lobby in five, Montgomery."

"Montgomery, huh?"

Reese starts toward the elevators, not taking the bait.

"Montgomery is awfully close to 'Monty'! You know, the name that all my friends call me!"

She's got this playful smile on her lips as she looks back at me over her shoulder. "Never going to happen!"

I pull the foldable seat out next to Reese before sitting in it. We're up high, sitting out in right field. I wouldn't exactly call these seats nosebleeds, seeing as most triple-A stadiums aren't big enough to have nosebleeds, but they're the closest thing you can get to them here.

While Las Vegas doesn't have any major league teams, they do have minor league ones, and it just so happens that our triple-A team is in town to play theirs.

I still can't get over seeing Reese pull out her phone at the front gate to scan the tickets she purchased online. It was so . . . normal of her.

"You know you could've called ahead and told them we were coming. You didn't have to buy tickets and I'm sure they would've found you a closer seat."

She shrugs, a smile on her face and eyes on the field. "I know, but I didn't want to make the players nervous knowing we were here. And besides, when was the last time you got to just sit and watch a game? Don't you miss watching baseball as a fan?"

Yeah. I do. I really do. Other than highlights, the only full games I watch these days are our own.

We won't get a full game in today, maybe only three or four innings before we need to head to the airport for our flight, but I sit back in my seat and let myself enjoy it.

"Have you always been a baseball fan?" I ask Reese.

"Yes. I would beg my parents to bring me to the field and let me spend time with my grandfather. I loved everything about it. The people who worked there. The fans that were so diehard and *so* superstitious. I practically lived at the stadium during the summer, staying up late and watching every home game, and I truly can't think of a better childhood than the one I had."

I know there's a game starting right in front of us, but I keep my eyes on her. I didn't know that extending our truce would also extend Reese's honesty with me but I'm glad it does.

She laughs at herself. "I used to invite the players to my birthday parties because I genuinely thought they were my friends. I didn't pick up on the fact that it was their job to spend every day at the field. That they weren't just there because they wanted to be, like I was."

"And did they go?"

"Of course. Probably because my grandfather was the team owner, and they felt as if they had to."

I think about my team and the way they are toward Max, loving him as if he were one of the guys. Or the way my college players were with Miller while I was raising her, always hyping her up when she brought homemade cookies to share with them.

"I doubt that. Baseball is one big family. I know you don't see it that way, but it is. I bet they went to your birthday parties because you were one of them."

She stays silent for a long moment, eyes on the field.

"I know it is," she finally says. "I know how much community and comradery there is. I grew up in that environment, Emmett. I'm not just some random owner, fresh out of business school with no connection to this team. This team is my family's legacy. This is my childhood and all my best memories.

"I know you think I'm coming in here and trying to blow everything up," she continues. "But I promise you, I'm not. I want to better this team because I love it. I want to be able to give other people their best memories too. Whether that be the days they spend at the field as a fan or the years they spend in a Warriors jersey as a player. I know you think I'm heartless, but every decision I've made is to preserve the thing I love most in hopes that other people will continue to be able to love it too. In order to do that, I don't have the luxury to view this as anything but a business right now."

Words stick in my throat because this is just about the most open I've ever heard her.

And I like it.

This version of Reese . . . this version is dangerous for me.

She swallows hard. "Look, this needs to stay between us, but my grandfather wasn't paying a whole lot of attention the last few years. He was spending far too much money and now our budget is a mess, and I feel partly at fault for that."

My brows cinch together. "How is any of that your fault? You weren't there."

"Exactly. But I was supposed to be. He wanted to retire years ago and I was ready to take over, but there was one problem."

Everything we discussed last night comes flooding back.

"You were still married," I realize.

"My grandfather wouldn't sign the team over, for good reason, until he was sure that Jeremy would have no legal claim to it."

"Wow." I sit back in my chair. "I had no idea. I knew Arthur was ready for retirement, but I assumed he was holding out because he still loved it."

"He did, but he wasn't invested the way he used to be. He wanted to be home with my grandmother more, so he made decisions like hiring Scott to run the baseball side of things and spending money just to make others happy."

There's something in the way she tacks on that last part that feels directed at me, but that wouldn't make sense. Arthur never spent extra money on me, unless she's referring to that extra video coaching position that I'm still not entirely over.

But hearing her speak about the love and responsibility she feels to this team brings a whole new wave of understanding that I didn't have before. Maybe she really did have to cut that position, and that realization makes me feel like an absolute dick for not being the one to do it.

Reese refocuses on the field, clapping as our first batter makes his way to the plate. "Let's go, Braden!" she yells, hands cupped around her lips.

I glance in her direction, a little confused. "You sound like you know him."

She seems just as puzzled when she looks my way. "I do."

"You've met him?"

"Of course I have. I've met his whole family. His mom made one of the best lasagnas I've ever had."

"You've had dinner with him? And with his family?"

"Yes, Emmett," she says with a slight chuckle. "I've met all of them. During the offseason, I traveled the country, introducing myself."

I'm shocked silent but somehow am still able to exhale a question. "Why?"

"Wouldn't you be a little freaked out if the franchise you're signed with got a brand-new president and owner all in one go? I wanted to be able to put faces to names and ease any concerns they might have. These guys are our future players."

I should probably focus on reiterating how impressive that is, that she went out of her way to do that. But instead, I'm still having a hard time finding words, so again, I give her only one.

"*Our?*"

She shoots me a deadpan look. "We'll see."

"What about the guys on the Warriors?"

"I met most of them last year while I was shadowing and they're kind of stuck with me all season. Plus, they don't need as much assurance. They've already made it."

"You seriously made sure to meet every single one of these guys and their families?"

She nods as if it were no big deal, eyes on the game.

I've never known an owner or president to take that kind of initiative. But when I think about my own time, coming up through the developmental system and hoping to one day play in the majors, I would've felt so valued as not only a player but also a person if the team owner went out of their way to meet me.

"Well, Reese. For someone who views baseball as just a business, you sure met a lot of families."

She slightly shakes her head, still unable to take her eyes off the game.

And when Braden hits a double, it feels like I'm watching the baseball fan version of Reese next to me as she cheers for him.

She tells me all about the second and third batters in the lineup as they each make their way to home plate. She tells me where they went to school, how long they've been playing, and where they're from. She even spews out some of their stats from memory. And I'm not talking about the simple stats like their batting percentage that's displayed on the jumbotron.

She recites their weighted on-base average and their OPS all from the top of her head.

Then she follows it up with things like, "His sister is a senior in high school this year," and "He's also very talented at the guitar."

I swear I'm living in an alternate universe where everything I thought I knew about this woman has flown right out the window. Yes, she's business savvy and will be great for the franchise in that regard, but she also knows the game. Far more than anyone realizes.

She also cares for these players' well-being far more than *she* realizes, but that's a conversation for a different day.

That apology I already owed her becomes even more imperative.

"Reese." My tone is serious as I turn slightly in my chair to face her. She hears it too, evident in the way her smile drops soberly. "I need to apologize."

"It's fine, Emmett. I promise."

"It's not, though. I shouldn't have undermined you the way I did during and after that advisory board meeting. I'm sorry."

She offers me an understanding smile. "Well, thank you for saying that. And I'm sorry for not giving a heads-up about wanting to trade one of your players."

A concessions worker slowly scales the steps, a hot dog sign plastered to the heated bag he's wearing.

"Want one?" Reese asks, and though I know she's trying to change the subject, I'm starving, and a hot dog sounds delicious.

Reese starts to reach into her purse.

"Yes, but put your wallet away. I can buy you a goddamn hot dog." I hold up two fingers to the concessions worker, exchanging cash for two hot dogs. "But I'm capped at that."

Chuckling, she pulls out the relish and mustard packets, assuming the prior conversation is over, but I need to explain myself.

"Reese," I say again, placing my hand over hers to stop her from unwrapping her lunch. "The reason I was so upset after that meeting is not just because you wanted to trade one of my players."

Slowly, she turns in her seat, giving me her full attention.

"You're making history this year," I remind her. "And I'm not sure if the weight of that has fully set in for you yet. And no, I don't think you should base your decisions on the scrutiny you're under, or the fear of what others may say, but in that moment, it felt like you were about to make this career-defining decision, and I wouldn't be able to protect you from the aftermath of it."

I expect her to interrupt me, to say something along the lines of "I can handle it," but she doesn't. She simply hears me out.

"And it's not just protecting you for this one season," I continue. "It's about protecting the legacy you're going to leave for all the women who will come after you. There are girls who love this game the same way you do, who are going to be looking up to you. I think about the little girl *I* raised and the world that's not set up for her success. I think about how much I would've loved for there to be women in positions of power for her to look up to the way you are now. And it scared me to think about what they were going to say about you in the press. Trading Kaiser would put so much heat on you, Reese, and I was afraid that you didn't fully grasp the weight of that, and I was scared *for* you. I took it out on you, and I'm sorry for doing that."

She swallows hard, eyes bouncing between mine. Her lips open then close, no words coming out, so I press her for them.

"What?" I ask.

"I think . . ." She shakes her head. "I think I'm starting to get the hype surrounding you."

I exhale a laugh, and the tension breaks in such an easy way.

I pull my hand away so she can eat, but before I can, she grabs it, stopping me.

"Thank you," she says softly. "For looking out for me. I try not to focus on the bigger-picture-type things because they feel heavy and overwhelming when I think about them. I already feel so much pressure every single day just doing my job, that if I think about the history books and the girls I want to inspire, I'm afraid I'll be paralyzed with expectations."

"Yeah," I breathe out. "I can see that."

"So how about I focus on the task at hand, making this team the best it can be, and if I make a decision that you think could harm the legacy I want to leave behind, you raise that concern to me and we talk it through. Deal?"

"Deal."

She lets go of my hand, but I don't want it back.

I like listening to her speak. I like the way she handles herself. I like her sharp mind and her quick wit.

I think I might just like *her*, which is a real problem when I think about protecting her legacy. The last thing she needs is her employee crushing on her.

"*This* is why I wanted to bring you here," she says, nodding toward home plate. "That's Milo Jones."

The name sounds vaguely familiar, but not enough for it to scrounge up any memories.

"He's twenty-two years old. From a small town in New Mexico. Played center field for his local community college and is the player I wanted to call up as Kaiser's replacement."

"Why have I barely heard of him?"

"He was undrafted. I found him a few years ago because my car broke down and the auto shop where I was towed was next to a community college and there just happened to be a game going on. He's wildly talented but didn't grow up playing competitive ball or anything like that, so he's needed some polishing. He started all the way at the bottom in the rookie league but has quickly moved his way up, just starting triple-A this season."

My eyes flit to the jumbotron displaying his batting average, but that's not a clear enough number to let myself get excited.

"OPS?" I ask, referring to the combination of on-base percentage and his slugging percentage.

"It's .920."

"Jesus."

On the third pitch, I watch as Milo swings the bat in the most natural and athletic way, connecting with the pitch. He hits what looks to be a double, the ball landing near us in right field, but with how fast he is, he stretches it to a triple, sliding into third base.

If he's that fast in the infield, I can't wait to see him let loose in the outfield.

"Damn." I exhale a laugh and when I look at Reese out of the corner of my eye, I find her watching me knowingly. "You think he's ready?"

"Only one way to find out."

I like the confidence. I like that she's willing to bet on herself and the player *she* found.

"In case no one has told you today, you are very good at your job."

She smiles proudly. "Thank you."

We get back to the hot dogs in our hands, dressing them with a couple of condiment packets. But there's no onions on it and hardly any relish in the packet so my hopes aren't too high for it.

We take a bite at the same time.

"Oh, that's so bad." She spits it right back into the foil wrapping.

"That's terrible." I find the will to swallow down that single bite but wrap the rest for the trash can. "Ours are so much better."

"So much better. We need to get back to Chicago."

There's this ease and playfulness between us today, including a whole lot of honesty, which has me asking the question I've had lingering on my mind all week.

I take her hot dog and re-cover it, getting them both ready for the trash while trying to keep my question as casual as possible. "You were pretty adamant about trading Kaiser, and that vote didn't mean anything. You don't need the advisory board's approval."

"I know I don't."

My eyes meet hers. "So, why haven't you done it yet? Just because they didn't want you to?"

"No." Reese's voice is soft and earnest when she admits, "I haven't done it yet because *you* didn't want me to."

10

REESE

It's a perfect Sunday afternoon in San Diego. The sun is shining over the field, and the stadium is already filling up with fans, ready for the first game in this series.

So, because of the weather, and maybe a few other reasons too, I make my way out through the visiting tunnel instead of hiding out in an office the way I have the past handful of games.

The dugout is practically silent as I step into it, with every player on the team currently out on the field warming up or back in the training room getting pregame treatment. The only chatter is from our field manager, who is leaning up against the barrier that separates the dugout from the field, speaking quietly to Kai Rhodes' son. Max is sitting on the railing and Emmett is hunched over behind him with a single arm wrapped around the little boy to keep him steady. His other is pointing out toward his players and explaining things in Max's ear.

His grandson's ear?

I don't exactly know if he refers to himself as that, but his daughter is marrying Kai soon. And though she's not Max's biological mother, everything I know about their situation tells me she is his mom.

But the idea of Emmett being someone's grandfather seems entirely unfathomable. He's only in his mid-forties and not to mention, he looks like *that*. He's at an age that he could be a father to a toddler himself, and the fact that his daughter is old enough to be Max's mom means he must have become a dad when he was extremely young.

I wonder where her mom is. Was Emmett married before too?

"Mama!" Max points to Miller, who is crossing the field to them after visiting the bullpen.

Oh, I should go. A sense of urgency takes over, pushing me to leave. I already felt as if I were intruding on a moment with Emmett and Max, but with his daughter here too, it seems even more invasive.

But before I can turn down the tunnel and go back the way I came, Miller's eyes move from her son up to me. And when she lifts her hand in a polite wave as she approaches the dugout, it catches Emmett's attention.

"Reese," Emmett says, standing straighter, arm still secured around Max and eyes wide like he just got caught doing something he shouldn't. "Sorry. My family was just stopping by. They're headed up to their seats now."

He really does have it ingrained in him that I don't care about the sentimental part of this whole thing. Maybe he forgot about our conversation at the game yesterday, or maybe he's just waiting to see if my actions back up my words.

"That's okay. They can stay for however long they'd like."

His worried expression melts, giving me a look that's equal parts impressed and appreciative.

I take a step forward. "I was just . . ." *Stalking you. Being an absolute creep. Checking out how good you look in those baseball pants.* "Coming to say hi before the game."

His voice and smile go soft. "Well, hi."

"Hi."

"Hi!" Max yells, waving his hand in my direction.

"That's right, Bug. You call them out just like your mama taught you."

"Really, Millie?"

Miller just shrugs, entirely proud of herself for saying it like it is. Because she knows as well as I do that I'm not here because of a simple hello. I'm here because I'm starting to have a hard time staying away.

"Hi." I smile at Max before shifting my attention up to his mom. "And hi. I'm Reese."

Crossing the dugout to join them, I hold my hand out to shake hers. It's formal and a bit stiff but also seems like the correct way to introduce myself to my employee's daughter.

Because that's who Emmett is to me.

"Miller." She shakes my hand. "I can't believe we haven't been introduced before. You're all I ever hear about anymore. Reese this and Reese that. Isn't that right, Dad?"

He stares at her dumbfounded. "I truly don't know where I went wrong with you."

Miller just laughs and I watch as this loving smile blooms on Emmett's lips from hearing the sound. You can tell they equally adore each other. It's obvious by the way they feel safe enough to playfully talk a bit of shit.

"We really are headed up to our seats now, though." Miller lifts Max into her arms. "We'll see you after, Dad. And, Reese, it was nice to finally meet you."

"It was. Enjoy the game."

After Max and Miller say their goodbyes to Emmett, he turns my way. "Remember when I said she was going to say something inappropriate, and that you'd have to ignore it?"

I lean a hip on the railing next to him. "So, you talk about me, huh?"

"Talk is a loose term." A grin hitches on one side of his lips. "I was more so complaining about you."

I do my best to hold back my laughter. "I really am living rent-free in that head of yours to be complaining about me in your free time."

"You have no idea. And are you trying to tell me that you don't complain about me outside of work?"

I tilt my head in faux confusion. "Why would I ever think about you when I'm not at work?"

He huffs a laugh. "You're terrible for a man's ego, Reese."

"Thank you. I was worried I might be losing my touch."

Leaning closer, Emmett props his elbow on the railing, resting his cheek against his closed fist. And I find myself leaning into his space too.

"Where are you watching the game today?" he asks.

"I was thinking I'd take a seat in the stands for once. Watch it with the fans."

"That sounds nice. Which section can I look for—"

"Monty!" a woman calls out from the field, interrupting his question. "Hey!"

It takes me a moment to register who she is before realizing it's the reporter from that press conference who was hitting on Emmett in front of me . . . and everyone else.

"Oh. Hey . . ." He hesitates before saying her name as almost a question. "Kelly. You're covering the game today?"

"I am. Do me a favor and save me a postgame interview? It'll give me some brownie points with my boss to get a one-on-one with everyone's favorite field manager."

"I doubt I'm everyone's favorite."

She puts her hand on his upper arm, and I feel my eyes widen as I watch the contact. "Maybe not everyone's. But you're mine."

I want to like her. I want to root for her. I want to see more women succeed in male-dominated fields the way she is, but *good God*. It takes everything in me not to roll my eyes.

Is everyone just completely obsessed with this guy?

"I'll be covering the whole series actually," she continues. "And I believe I'm staying at the same hotel as your team. What do you think about extending that interview over dinner?"

Well, damn. I admire the courage, but it doesn't change the fact that I find myself hoping he turns her down.

And he does . . . kind of.

"As tempting as that sounds, my daughter is in town for this series, so we have dinner plans. But thank you for the invite."

I can't quite tell if he's turning her down because he wants to, or if his plans with Miller truly are the reason he can't get together with her later.

Apparently, Kelly can't quite decipher Emmett's motives either. "Totally understandable. Family comes first. But I'll be at the hotel bar tonight if you feel like a nightcap afterward."

"Sorry," I cut in before I can think better of it. "But the game is about to start, and we need to finish prepping."

Kelly's expression gains an annoyed edge when she looks at me, but she's all smiles again when turning to Emmett and saying, "Good luck out there."

"Yep. Thanks."

Emmett slowly turns back to face me, single brow raised and the most knowing grin on his lips.

"What?" I ask, entirely innocent.

"We need to finish prepping for the game?"

"Yes. You need to focus."

"*I* need to focus?"

"I think we *all* just need to focus. And you know, getting friendly with a reporter wouldn't look good for the club."

Now he can't hold back his laughter. "You make it sound as if I'm sleeping with her."

It takes everything in me not to ask if he has.

"Which I'm not, by the way," he supplies

"Didn't ask."

"But you wanted to."

I open my mouth to tell him he's wrong, but judging by that stupid smirk on his face, he'd know I was lying.

"And we're not *friendly*," he continues. "I hardly know her."

"She called you Monty. You said it yourself. Your friends call you Monty."

"*You* don't."

"Well, we aren't friends, Emmett. I'm your boss."

He leans in closer, looming over me and keeping his voice low for only me to hear. "It's always good to remind yourself of that when a female reporter, who I barely know, starts making you jealous, huh? And just so we're clear here, there's no part of me that wants to be *friends* with you, Reese."

Just a few weeks ago, that statement would've meant something entirely different. But I catch the insinuation in his tone.

It's dangerous. Whatever game is going on here.

And I can't seem to stop myself from playing.

I look up at him through my lashes. "I don't want to be friends with you either."

"Good." His voice is a deep timbre that I can physically feel crawl under every inch of my skin. "Glad we're on the same page."

11

EMMETT

Sitting up, I grab the water bottle off the nightstand, unscrewing the cap and bringing it to my lips to chug. But I quickly find out that there are only about three drops of water left and they do absolutely nothing to quench my thirst.

Fuck this night.

The sushi we had for dinner has me parched as hell. I can't seem to find the right temperature to regulate the room to a comfortable spot. And all of it conspires to keep me from finding a moment of sleep.

I sound like a goddamn diva but fuck it. Maybe I am.

The neon green numbers displayed on the bedside clock remind me that it's just after two in the morning and I'm far too old to still be awake. And right now, the only thing I can focus on is the lack of water in my hotel room and how dehydrated I am, so I decide to start there.

I find a pair of gym shorts in my suitcase and throw on the shirt I was wearing earlier today to head down to the lobby. I shove my feet in a pair of shoes by the door, grab a room key, then try to fix the thermostat one last time. I press the down arrow, but the screen is displaying the lowest setting at sixty-five, though it has to be at least another ten degrees warmer than that. I toggle with the fan switch, but still nothing in the room changes.

The hall is silent when I step out of my room, the elevator is empty as I ride it to the main level, and the small market next to the lobby is fully stocked, *thank God*.

I grab the largest bottle of water out of the refrigerator, unscrew the top before I've paid for it, and chug it back.

It's fucking glorious.

Cold and refreshing and makes me believe I may actually be able to get to sleep now. But that hope is quickly paused while my head is tipped back, mid-swallow, and I hear a familiar voice in the lobby next to me.

"Any room would do," Reese says.

"I'm so sorry." That must be the man working behind the front desk. "But we're completely sold out for the night."

Turning the corner, I find Reese at the front desk, pleading eyes locked on the hotel employee. Her nose is a bright pink. Her cheeks too. Even her lips seem to have shifted to a different color than they typically are as they tremble with each word out of her mouth.

I can't quite tell if she was crying, if she's sick, or if she's just really cold.

But then her clothes answer that question for me.

Her blonde hair is tucked beneath the hood of a sweatshirt. But that sweatshirt has one of her work blazers over it. And not in a fashionable way. But more like a "I'm cold as hell and didn't pack any warm layers because I'm in San Diego so why would I" kind of way. I can also tell she's wearing at least two pairs of yoga pants right now with tall socks pulled up over them as high as they can go.

But the most shocking part may just be the slippers Reese has on her feet. I never thought I'd live to see the day when polished Reese Remington was caught out of her hotel room in a pair of slippers instead of her high heels.

It all contributes to the way I'm cautiously walking toward her as if I were approaching a feral animal who's hurt and just needs a bit of help.

"Please," she begs. "You must have a hotel partner close by who you could call and see if they have an extra room available? I just need to get a few hours of sleep."

"I'm sorry, ma'am. There's a popular convention going on this weekend. All the hotels have been booked out for months."

Her face is equal parts desperate and defeated.

"But I'll send the mechanic up as soon as he gets here."

"Okay, great." There's a flash of hopefulness in her tone. "And when is that?"

The employee looks down, probably checking the day's schedule. "He'll be in at nine."

Reese exhales this whiney groan sort of sound before dropping her head onto her folded arms and resting on the check-in desk.

I take another cautious step closer. "Everything okay?"

She perks up but then rolls her eyes and drops her head back down when she spots me. "You're too late. Your reporter girlfriend just left the bar with someone else, but you might be able to catch her if you hurry."

I bite back my laughter. "Well, aren't you just a ray of fucking sunshine at this time of the day."

"Not tonight, Emmett. I haven't slept and I'm too exhausted to spar with you."

"Good. I may actually win one for once, but then again, probably not." I lean an elbow on the desk next to her. "I haven't slept either."

She's got this optimistic look of comradery when she lifts her head again. "Is your room also so cold that you can no longer feel your fingers?"

"I'm having the opposite problem. It's a little too warm."

"God, that sounds like heaven."

"The thermostat seems to be broken."

"Sorry about that, sir," the front desk employee cuts in. "As I was telling Ms. Remington, our maintenance staff will be here at nine and can take a look for you. We seem to be having an issue regulating the temperature on your floor right now. Not sure what's going on with the system."

"And you have no other rooms she can get some sleep in until then?"

"I'm so sorry, but we don't. We're at full capacity." He directs his attention to Reese. "But we'll make sure that you're not charged for your stay tonight and I can send some extra blankets up to your room."

She offers him the best smile she can muster, which is a pretty sad and pathetic one if we're being honest. "Sure. Thank you."

"Or if you'd like, I can see if I can find you a room outside of the downtown area. You may have to take a rideshare about twenty minutes—"

"That's not happening," I cut in. "She can stay in my room."

The words are out before I can think better of them.

"No." She huffs a startled laugh before redirecting her attention to the hotel employee. "Yes, please. I'm fine jumping in a rideshare."

"You're not getting in a rideshare in the middle of the night to find a random hotel twenty minutes away, Reese. You're staying in my room."

"Don't tell me what to do."

"Don't be ridiculous and I won't have to. I'll call Kai and Miller to see if I can crash in their room."

"Absolutely not. They have a sleeping toddler with them. The last thing I need is for you to wake them up because your boss is too much of a princess to sleep in a slightly chilly room."

I place the back of my hand against her pink cheek, and I'm stung with how sharp the cold is. She's more than slightly chilly. She's absolutely frozen right now.

"Jesus. How fucking cold is your room, Reese?"

I can tell she wants to lie to me, to tell me it's just a few degrees below comfortable, but thankfully she's too tired to attempt to bullshit me. Sure, she doesn't give me any response, but that's enough to let me know it's unbearably cold in her room.

"You're going to get sick if you go back in there. You'll be lucky if you haven't already. You're sleeping in my room."

"Emmett, I can't do that."

There's enough conviction in her tone that it makes me pause. I don't want her to do something that will make her uncomfortable, but I'm also not going to let her drive across town with a stranger to some random hotel, because that's something that will make *me* uncomfortable.

I keep my voice low for only her to hear. "You can't do that because you're uncomfortable with it, or you can't do it because you're worried someone might find out?"

She doesn't respond, but she looks up at me, making eye contact and silently telling me her answer.

"No one will find out, Reese. Everyone is in their room asleep, and you can have the bed. Besides, if I were you, more than anything, I'd be more concerned that someone might catch you in this outfit."

She exhales a laugh, and I watch as her walls retreat just a hair.

I turn to the staff member. "Can you have a rollaway bed sent up for me, please?"

He offers me a sheepish smile. "They're all being used tonight, unfortunately."

"Of course they are."

I look to Reese, letting her be the one to make the final call on this.

"We'll figure it out," she says, completely defeated. "Let's just go. I'm exhausted."

I hold up the two water bottles, one unopened and one nearly empty for the clerk to add them to my room charge.

"Those are on the house," he says.

"Should be. Making me share a room with this one and all."

Reese just shakes her head at me, but I see the smile playing on her lips as she turns toward the elevator. "I'm going to be real freaking pissed if you end up being a snorer."

12

REESE

I made a quick detour to my room, deciding I'd rather not sleep in my blazer tonight, swapping into a matching pajama set instead.

And no, the matching set has nothing to do with the fact that I'm going to be sleeping in Emmett's bed tonight. I wear a pajama set every night, whether someone is going to see me in it or not.

The chill in my room hasn't let up and the silk fabric on my sleepwear has only made it worse, so I grab the spare blanket off the bed and wrap it around me like a cape for the short walk down to Emmett's room. But the blanket is also freezing just from being folded on the bed directly under the AC unit, so it does absolutely nothing to help the bone-chilling cold that I can't seem to shake from my body.

"Cute slippers," Emmett says from down the hallway, leaning a shoulder into his door to keep it slightly cracked.

"Get fucked."

He bursts a laugh and it's just about the only sound I don't seem to hate at three in the morning.

I don't do well without sleep. In fact, I'm kind of a terror without it. And yeah, maybe that makes me high maintenance, but I don't see anything wrong with being high maintenance when I'm the one taking care of the maintaining.

I pay to get my nails done every two weeks. I pay to get my hair cut and colored every six. And yes, I require eight hours of sleep every night. If those things make me high maintenance, then fuck it. I love being high maintenance.

Emmett steps into his room as I approach, holding the door open for me to enter too.

Once I'm inside, the first thing I notice is the change in temperature from my own. It's distinctively warmer, thank God.

Then I note the lack of light. His room is dim, with only the glow from a single lamp on the nightstand to illuminate a path toward the bed.

It gives off an . . . *intimate* vibe, but I really wish it wouldn't.

His bed is unmade. His reading glasses are on the nightstand. His suitcase is propped up on a stand, unzipped and open, giving me a sneak peek of the clothes I might see him in this week.

But as his boss, I should never know what he packed in his suitcase. I should never see his unmade bed or know which side he prefers to sleep on.

I would catch so much heat from my grandfather, the advisory board, and the press if anyone found out that I slept in my employee's hotel room.

In my employee's *bed*.

"Do you want me to take the floor?" Emmett asks, startling me out of my daze.

Yes. "Yes" is the only correct answer.

"No," is what comes out instead. "Don't you think you're a little old to be sleeping on the floor?"

"Damn right, I am." He ambles right over to his side of the bed.

Okay. We're doing this. We're really doing this.

I'm not sure what other response I was hoping for. Maybe I was looking for more of a fight. Maybe I assumed he'd insist he sleep anywhere else but next to me. Maybe I was hoping one of us would have just a bit of willpower.

I stay stuck in the entryway, still shivering from my cold pajamas, my cold blanket and being back in my cold room for only a few minutes. But then I feel the first warm flush to my skin I've experienced all night.

Because standing next to the bed, Emmett reaches over his head and pulls off his shirt in a single, fluid motion.

And fuck me, he's delicious to look at. Tall and wide with bulky shoulders and inked arms. His chest is splattered with dark hair. His body narrows at the waist, but he's not so cut that you can see the complete outline of each and every one of his ab muscles. Instead, he's thick and muscular, including those thighs that are practically eating the athletic shorts stretched around them.

I've already seen him with his shirt off, already have the image ingrained in my memory, so this is nothing new. But I've never seen Emmett take his shirt off just before I'm about to crawl into bed with him.

"You could . . . keep that on," I croak out.

He lifts an unimpressed brow in my direction. "I'm good, but thanks for the offer."

Emmett makes a move to tug at the waistband of his shorts as if it were instinct for him to remove them before bed. Which means he probably sleeps naked or, at the very least, in only his underwear.

Which, again, I shouldn't know.

It takes him less than a second to realize his mistake, before adjusting his waistband back low on his hips to keep his shorts on. Then he climbs into bed, pushing the sheets and comforter off his heated body, and with his long legs spread out and one arm folded behind his head, he finds me still stuck near the entryway.

"C'mon, princess." He pats the mattress next to him. "I want to get some sleep."

I don't tend to get nervous, but this is making me nervous. *He's* making me nervous. He shouldn't look so good when he's so tired, and I shouldn't be crawling into bed next to him.

Removing my slippers and keeping my blanket-cape on, I climb onto the mattress and very quickly realize that this is a queen bed and not a king by the way I can feel his body heat as soon as I lie down.

It's lovely, but he's already too close.

Once my head hits the pillow, Emmett turns off the light, coating the room in darkness.

I can't see anything. I can't hear anything either, other than the slight chatter of my own teeth. Every muscle in my body is firing, doing its best to warm itself up. Lying on my side, facing away from him, I pull my knees to my chest, trying to find as much warmth as possible.

"You're still cold?" he asks quietly from behind me.

"Freezing."

"Take that blanket off. It's only making you colder."

"I just need some time to warm up and I'll be fine."

There's a moment of silence. A moment where I think he's let it go, but then he whispers something highly inappropriate into the otherwise silent room.

"I can warm you up."

Looking over my shoulder, my eyes shoot to his, and I've adjusted enough to the lack of light to find him lying on his side, facing me.

Emmett tentatively reaches out, tucking my hair behind my ear before brushing his knuckles across my cheek so I can feel exactly how warm he is.

I practically purr as I lean into his touch.

"Lose the blanket, Reese, and come here."

"Emmett."

"Don't be weird about it. Just come here. I'm not going to get any sleep if you're over there squirming all night, trying to warm yourself up."

I can't. I shouldn't.

There's too much on the line.

This baseball club.

His career.

My career.

My reputation.

The fact that I'm the first ever female team owner and now I'm lying in a bed with my field manager.

But he is right about this blanket being too cold, so I decide to shed it to the floor by the mattress, and instead of moving closer to him, I reach down to the end of the bed where his sheet and comforter are shoved and pull them over me, all the way up to my chin.

He doesn't say anything about it and neither do I.

This will do just fine . . . eventually.

Minutes pass and I do my best to warm myself up. In fact, I'm practically praying that my body will stop involuntarily shivering. That my teeth will stop chattering. That I'll stop squirming on the mattress next to him.

When I can't seem to do it myself, Emmett slips his arm under the sheet, draping it over my waist and sliding his hand between me and the mattress. Then he easily scoops me up, pulling me back to meet his chest.

And that swift and effortless movement just causes a whole lot of other inappropriate ideas to play in my imagination. Because just as I suspected, this man has no problem tossing me around when I've never had the privilege to be tossed around before.

The legs of my pants and the back of my top have ridden up, putting that small part of us skin to skin. The warmth of his body on mine is almost painful thanks to the quick and sharp shift from cold to hot. But that sting subsides when Emmett removes his arm and scoots back just an inch so that we're no longer touching, but still close enough that I can steal his warmth.

Slowly, my muscles begin to uncoil themselves. My skin begins to calm.

"This okay?" he asks quietly, but his lips are so close to my ear that the rumble of his voice sends a shiver down my spine.

Which is not too helpful on the whole "getting warm" thing.

I swallow. "Probably not."

"Why not? We're basically . . . hugging. Hugging is totally fine."

"Yeah, we're just hugging. In your bed. With my ass against your crotch."

"Semantics."

"Just . . . keep your dick away from me."

I can hear the smile in his reply when he says, "Don't tell me what to do."

Emmett's arm is awkwardly resting above the pillow where my head is before he adjusts it lower. And as if on instinct, I lift my cheek for him to put it under my head before resting it back on the inside of his bicep.

He sucks a sharp inhale at the contact.

"I know I'm cold but suck it up. You asked for this."

His silent laugh rumbles the bed. "I'm burning up, so trust me. You feel good."

You feel good.

All I can think about is how those words would sound coming from his lips in an entirely different setting. Does Emmett Montgomery praise women when he's in bed, or does the grumbly bossy thing seep into that part of his life too?

Why am I hoping it's a combination of both?

And what the actual fuck is wrong with me?

I haven't been interested in anyone in years. In fact, I've practically sworn off men since my divorce, and suddenly the one man to snag my attention is one that's currently on my payroll.

Real professional, Reese.

"Did you have a nice time with Miller?" I ask, because that's a normal train of thought. Who goes from wondering how someone likes to fuck to asking whether that same someone enjoyed his time with his daughter?

I won't be holding my breath for one of those World's Greatest Boss mugs anytime soon.

"Yeah, it was nice," he says softly. "I'm always stoked when I get the chance to see her while we're on the road."

"You two are close."

Emmett hums this sleepy sound. "Of course we are. We practically grew up together."

"Yeah, there's not a big age gap, huh? You must have been young when you became a dad."

He hesitates for a moment. "I was maybe nineteen or twenty when she was born."

"And where's her mom?"

Though we're not touching other than my cheek on his arm, I sense his entire body go rigid behind me.

What the hell is wrong with me?

"What?" he asks, but it's not confusion in his tone. It's shock.

Shock that I felt as if I had any right to know the answer to that question, I'm sure. I guess I just assumed that since I drunkenly told him all about my divorce, he'd want to soberly tell me about his.

"I'm sorry," I quickly blurt out. "That was inappropriate of me to ask."

"We're sharing a bed, Reese. I don't know that either one of us is the best judge of what's appropriate and what's not these days."

His honesty acts as a reality check for me. Because if he's saying it like it is, I can no longer lie to myself by going with his original "we're just hugging" theory.

I go to move away, to create some distance between us, when Emmett grabs my hip to stop me. He flexes his fingertips, curling them into the softness of my belly and keeping me exactly where I am.

"Stay."

"Don't tell me what to do."

His head drops to mine, his beard tickling the skin at the back of my neck when he breathes a laugh.

"Emmett, we shouldn't be doing this."

"Stay anyway."

I don't have a retort for him, but I also don't have the willpower to move away.

Instead, Emmett scoots closer, curling his body around my own. His knee grazes the back of mine. His foot brushing against my ankle. And his hand . . . his hand is still firmly planted on my hip, calloused and warm and real fucking distracting.

Silence lingers for a long while and it acts as a test to see if one of us will move away, to see if one of us stops this and reestablishes some professional boundaries.

Neither of us does.

"Do you really not know about Miller's mom?" he finally asks.

I shake my head against his bicep, and I feel it flex under my cheek, which would account for the way his fingers are curling into a fist before eventually relaxing.

"Miller's mom died."

Oh, shit.

"And I have a feeling that if you didn't already know that, then you probably don't know that Miller isn't biologically mine."

What?

There's so much important information coming at me at once, and I can't seem to organize it quickly enough to give him a thoughtful response.

"Miller's mom's name was Claire," he continues. "Claire and I started dating shortly after I was called up to the majors. Miller was four years old when I first met her, and just after she turned five, her mom died from cancer."

Any words that might possibly convey how sorry I am stick in my throat. "I . . . I don't know what to say."

"That's okay. It was a long time ago."

"You adopted Miller," I realize.

"I did."

"Did her mom ask you to do that?"

Emmett exhales behind me. "She did. She was a single mom without any extended family, and she knew that when she passed, Miller wouldn't have anyone."

"But she had you."

"Yeah, she did. And she ended up becoming my entire world. I quit playing that year and settled down in a small town in Colorado to raise her. She was so young at the time and had just lost the only parent she'd ever known, so she needed some stability, you know? I couldn't travel the way I was."

I could not be more thankful I'm turned away from him right now as I screw my eyes shut and let my heart ache for this man who I've always believed cares just a little too much.

But thank God he does.

"Were you scared?"

"Terrified." He breathes out a laugh. "I was suddenly raising this kid, but I was still a kid myself. I was twenty-four or twenty-five at the time and just winging the whole fatherhood thing because I had no idea what the hell I was doing. So that's what I mean when I say Miller and I grew up together. We both were just trying to figure it out."

It's no wonder Emmett is all about family. He fought hard for his.

"And Miller," I begin. "Is she okay? I can't imagine losing my only parent."

"She is now. She was so young when Claire passed that she doesn't remember a whole lot about her, but she carried a lot of guilt for a lot of years. Mostly about me quitting baseball when I did. And that I stayed to coach at our local college instead of taking one of the MLB coaching positions I was offered over the years because I didn't want to uproot her. But I think meeting Max gave her a whole new perspective on how I felt when I met her."

"Oh my God," I exhale in realization.

Miller is Max's parent in the same way Emmett is hers.

Emmett smiles and I feel the curve of it against the back of my neck. "Kind of a fun little parallel."

"So, you really are a grandpa. Maybe not biologically, but still."

He laughs, his entire body rumbling against mine. "You really know how to humble a man, Reese. And yes, I guess technically I am. There's no blood relation between me, Miller, and Max, but yeah. They're my family. So whatever title that puts on me, I'm good with it."

The smile on my lips feels good. The sound of his laughter feels warm. It's nice to be able to bounce from serious to unserious with him without either of us missing a beat.

"Well, just so you know, you don't look like a grandfather."

"Hmm," he hums, pulling me closer. "No?"

"Not even a little bit."

"What about the bit of gray I got in my beard?"

"It works for you."

"Does it now?"

"Unfortunately."

His head dips lower, falling into the crook of my shoulder as he gets comfortable, and I can sense he's getting close to finding sleep.

But I'm not ready yet.

"Emmett," I whisper.

"Mm-hmm."

"Is that why you're so close with the guys on the team?"

He inhales a breath as he thinks it over. "Yeah, I suppose so. Sometimes you're just needed. Whether that's as a coach, a mentor, or a friend. And I like being able to be whatever is needed for them. I like taking care of people too, I guess. Or maybe it's just that I really love my job."

A smile pulls at my lips. "I remember when my grandfather got you to come on board. I wasn't involved with the team yet, but I knew he'd been trying for years to get you to join the coaching staff."

Emmett hums this sleepy sound, and it's confirmation that this conversation is going to be over sooner than I'd like. "I didn't let myself take a job in the majors until Miller was old enough and off doing her own thing. It was the right decision to stop playing when I did, but I won't lie and say it hasn't been my dream to come back. Coaching feels like my second chance in a way."

Well . . . shit.

He's making it awfully hard to keep my emotions out of the business side of things. Yeah, Emmett Montgomery is going to be expensive next season, but I'm starting to believe he might also be worth the investment.

His breathing grows slow and steady against my back, but I'm desperate to know more. I may never get this chance again, just him and me in a quiet room being honest and vulnerable.

Knowing I'll most likely only be able to get one more answer out of him, I pick the question I'm most eager to know.

"Did you ever meet someone else after you lost Claire?"

He's quiet for a long moment and it's then I realize I've lost him to sleep.

Probably for the best, I suppose. I doubt there's an answer to that question I'd love to hear.

With the room silent and his body behind mine, keeping me warm, I close my eyes and look for sleep too. I've just about found it when Emmett finally speaks up and gives me his answer.

"No," he says, and it's hardly a whisper. "I didn't have it in me to move on."

13

REESE

"Hey there, Reese's Pieces."

Looking up from my desk, I find my grandfather wearing a proud smile on his lips, watching me from the entryway of his office.

My office, I mean.

After spending my entire life coming to this office to visit him, it's strange to think the situation is reversed now.

"Hi, Grandad." I scoot my chair back away from my desk. "What are you doing here?"

"Just coming to see my favorite granddaughter. You're working away, I see."

Rounding my desk, I meet him at the door, pressing my cheek against his and leaving a kiss there. Then I pull the chair out that lives opposite mine for him to take a seat.

For a man in his late seventies, he's still active and mobile, but he's definitely begun to slow down over the years. It's evident in the way he takes his time walking to the chair, and even more so in the way he cautiously lowers into the seat.

And it all just makes me feel even more guilty that my poor choice in a life partner is the reason he had to keep working longer than he wanted to.

I retake my seat behind my desk. "What are you really doing here? Because I know you didn't just come all the way down to the field to say hi to me."

He chuckles a hearty laugh. "Ed and I are grabbing lunch and meeting with Denise so we can go over the last of the details for my retirement party. But getting to say hi to you is definitely a bonus."

"Denise is planning your retirement party?"

"Of course she is. That woman practically planned my life for the last forty years. I wouldn't trust the job to anyone else."

"Any chance she wants to come out of her own retirement and start planning *my* life? I'm in desperate need of a receptionist."

"Yes, you are. I should not have been able to get into your office so easily. But no, Denise worked for me for too long. She earned her own retirement."

"Well, it doesn't mean I won't give it a solid effort when I see her at your party. Are you excited for it?"

"I am. It's not necessarily that I'm looking forward to celebrating myself, but it's not often you get to have everyone who has played a part in your life all together in the same place. Well, other than your own funeral, and unfortunately, I won't be there to enjoy that party."

"Geez," I laugh. "Well, *I'm* looking forward to celebrating you."

My grandfather's kind and loving smile begins to fade, and I note the moment his entire demeanor switches into business mode. It's even evident in his tone when he says, "There is one other reason I wanted to come see you today."

The energy in my office switches up immediately.

I sit up straighter, folding my hands and resting them on my desk. I'm no longer a granddaughter speaking to her grandfather. I'm the new team owner speaking to her predecessor.

"What's going on?" I ask.

He exhales a long sigh, pulling out his phone. "Scott found this online. It's not an official news report or anything like that, and it's clearly just a rumor, but there's an anonymous post on this website. Read . . . Red-something."

"Reddit," I finish for him.

"That's the one. Someone is claiming they saw you leaving Monty's hotel room early one morning last week when you all were playing in San Diego."

The blood instantly drains from my face.

"Now, obviously that's not true," he continues. "Anyone who knows you two personally knows that you don't exactly get along, but these are the kinds of rumors that people are going to want to spread about you, and I just want you to be aware of it."

It's shocking that I can hear him through the buzzing in my ears, or that I'm still sitting straight regardless of the pit in my stomach.

How could I be so reckless? What the hell was I thinking?

I attempt to calm the tremble in my voice when I ask, "What do the comments say?"

"I don't know about all that. Scott just sent me a . . . what is it called when you take a picture of something?"

"A screenshot."

"He sent me a screenshot of the post. Not sure how much traction it's gotten, but he was able to find it."

Yeah, I bet he was. I'd imagine that Scott has a Google alert set up for my name, looking for any information he can use as ammo against me.

And I gave him some. On a silver platter.

I chose to go to Emmett's room that night. *I* chose to sleep in his bed. *I* brought this on myself.

I can ignore all the bullshit online regarding my abilities or questioning if I'm cut out for this job. But this? This is something *I* did. This isn't some made-up story. Someone *did* see me leave his room.

"Reese," my grandfather says, and when I finally meet his eyes, I find him studying me. "This is simply a made-up rumor, right?"

I swallow hard, doing my best to compose myself. "Of course it is. You may adore Emmett Montgomery, but you know I can hardly stand the guy."

"Give him a chance, Reese. I think he can change your mind."

He already has.

"I just wanted to make you aware of this post, that's all," he continues. "Not to accuse you of anything, but to remind you that you're under far more scrutiny than I ever was. All I want is for you to succeed. This is everything you spent your whole life working toward. Shoot, you gave up your marriage for this."

"I didn't give up my marriage for this. Jeremy gave up our marriage when he decided to try to take this all from me."

"But that was also your decision to not let him. You chose this baseball club because this was your dream, and I just need you to remember what you've given up to be here. I didn't choose you as my successor simply because you're my granddaughter. I chose you because I believe you're the best person for the job. But just because you're the right fit for this position doesn't mean you're not going to have to work twice as hard to be taken half as seriously. You know that. You've known that for years leading up to this. You can't ever give them a reason to talk about you, Reese. Okay?"

I nod in agreement. "I won't."

I won't make that mistake again.

"All right," he says, slowly standing from his seat. "You're leaving for a few games in Detroit?"

"I am. Our flight is at nine tomorrow morning."

"Okay. I love you."

"Love you too, Grandad. Tell Ed and Denise I said hello."

As soon as he's out of the door, I count to twenty, giving him enough of a head start before I freak the fuck out.

What am I doing? How could I ever think that staying in his room was acceptable? When did I become so reckless?

I grab my phone off the desk, but I don't dare look for that post while here in my office. As my grandfather reminded me, I don't have a receptionist to go through first, and the last thing I need is for someone to walk in on me having a mental breakdown while reading a supposed rumor about me and my field manager that is very much true.

Leaving everything else behind, I take only my phone and head straight for the one place I'll be able to hide at this time of the day.

The team is off today after a series of home games and before we leave on another road stretch tomorrow. The only guys that were at the field this afternoon were those coming in to get treatment by the medical staff, but even those players have left by now.

So, with the clubhouse level left empty, I make my way through the tunnel that leads to the dugout, then take a seat on the right-hand side where the field manager's spot is, hiding behind the small partition that blocks it from anyone else's view.

Grabbing my phone, I pull up Reddit and it doesn't take long until I find the post my grandfather was referring to.

This is the only post this anonymous account has ever made, and it quickly details what they saw as I left Emmett's room. The exact pajamas I was wearing. The slippers on my feet. My blonde hair that was completely disheveled, which they say is due to an activity we definitely did *not* participate in.

The walk of shame they claim to have witnessed was simply a walk back to my room around nine thirty a.m. after the front desk confirmed the HVAC system on our floor had been fixed. And yeah, I looked disheveled because I was running on only a few hours of sleep.

As exhausted as I was, the final words Emmett said to me that night are what kept me up.

I didn't have it in me to move on.

What the hell am I doing? I'm putting my reputation on the line by playing with fire with a man who admitted to me he didn't have it in him to move on.

I don't blame him. Who can blame someone for being unable to move on from the person they loved and lost? But I should really get my shit together and listen to what he's trying to tell me.

I scroll down to read the comments on the post. Some of them are predictable, calling me names and claiming I'm trying to sleep my way to the top.

To the top of what, though? I'm already the sole owner of this entire baseball club.

A few comments call out the original poster for making it all up. A couple of comments reiterate how excited they are for a woman to oversee her own team. But there's one comment that steals all my attention.

I heard she was married before and the guy only wifed her up so he could take part ownership of the team. Maybe Monty is doing the same kind of thing. He's up for a new contract next year, so who can blame him for playing his cards right and having a bit of fun while doing it?

It takes everything in me to ignore that comment, but I won't lie and say it doesn't eat away at me. I can't say I'm fully confident in my ability to read others' intentions after what happened with Jeremy.

Do I believe Emmett is pretending to get close to me so that I won't be able to let him leave for another team after the season ends? Do I think he's lying about wanting to protect me just so I'll keep him on my payroll? I don't want to. I can't imagine that's the case, but again, I've been blinded before.

There's a reason I swore off personal relationships when I took this job, and this right here is a prime example. I'm letting what I've learned about him cloud my business judgment.

I'm second-guessing myself.

I don't have time to second-guess myself. The rest of the league is doing that enough for me already.

I need to refocus. No more getting distracted by good-looking men with sweet stories about why they love their players and family so much. I have too much on the line to lose sight of what my end goal is here, and that's to make this baseball club the most successful it can be.

The last thing I need is headlines swirling with rumors about the team owner and field manager.

"Reese?"

Emmett's voice pulls my attention up from my phone screen to find him standing in the dugout, directly in front of my secret spot. And while yes, this is technically the field manager's spot, he's off duty at the moment.

"What are you doing down here?" he asks.

"Nothing." I quickly stand, locking my phone screen and slipping the device into the back pocket of my trousers. "Just leaving."

"This is the second time I've found you in my spot. Are you waiting for me or something?"

There's a playful smile on his lips and I can sense him gearing up for whatever quick retort I might come up with.

But I'm not doing that anymore.

"Have a good night, Emmett," I say, turning to leave.

He gently grabs my arm to stop me, spinning me back in his direction. "Hey, everything okay?"

"I'm fine." I steal my arm back, stepping a healthy distance away.

"Okay." It comes out as more of a question. "I'll see you on the plane in the morning, I guess."

Because of course we're heading on the road again tomorrow. Where we'll be staying in the same hotel. Where more rumors can circulate.

I can't avoid traveling for the entire season, but I can give it a pause to give whatever might be spreading online about us time to calm down.

"Actually, I'm going to stay back this time."

"What?" His brow furrows. "Why?"

"Because I can watch the games from here and I need to be in my office this week."

He's quiet for a long moment, clearly taken aback by my sudden coldness toward him. "Okay. I'll call you and bring you up to speed with anything you missed each night after the games."

"I'd prefer it in an email."

"An email." He huffs a small disbelieving laugh. "I don't think I've ever emailed you."

No, he's just called me while I was naked in the bathtub.

"Well, we should start using that form of communication going forward. There's no reason for you to call or text my personal line unless it's an emergency."

He searches my face, his brown eyes etched with hurt, and I feel like an absolute piece of shit for making him feel that way.

But it's for his own good. It's for both of our own good. He wants to coach here next year? He wants to work in the same city where his daughter lives? Well, that's not going to happen if rumors start flying about an inappropriate relationship between him and his boss.

"Did something happen?" he asks softly, taking a step forward.

I take a step back. "Of course not. I'm just resetting some boundaries we seemed to have forgotten about. For our working relationship."

I watch as his expression shifts when he realizes what's happening here. "Right. Our working relationship."

"Yes. So, good luck to you and the team this week. I'll see you when you're home."

"Are you sure you're allowed to say that to me? That's not too inappropriate for you?"

"Emmett—"

"No, you're right, Reese. The conversation was needed and I got it. Loud and clear. Thanks for the reminder, *boss*."

14

EMMETT

When the team plane landed back in Chicago, I didn't go from there to my apartment.

I probably should have. There's no reason for me to be at the clubhouse on a Friday night when everyone else has gone home to their families.

But I guess that's also exactly why I'm here, and already forty minutes into a grueling leg workout.

My job and my daughter are the two biggest pillars in my life, and with one of those occupied tonight, I'm left with my work. And even if there's technically no work to be done with the night off from practice and games, I'd still rather be alone here than alone in my apartment.

Miller invited me over for dinner, but Kai was on the road all week too, and as sweet as her offer was, I know she'd rather spend time with just the three of them.

I'll grab some takeout for dinner on my way home, but until then, I plan to waste as much time here as possible. The gym connected to the training room has enough equipment to keep me busy for hours, and with how frustrated I've been this week, I could use the outlet.

With my music blasting over the gym's speaker system, I add another plate on either side of the squat bar before ducking under it to position myself for another set. I haven't lifted the bar off the rack just yet. I allow myself to stand and fume a little first.

A couple of months ago, I would've appreciated a little time away from my boss. I probably wouldn't have even noticed if a stretch of time had passed without seeing or speaking to her.

But this week, I fucking noticed.

I noticed the stench on the team plane without Reese sitting behind me. I've grown accustomed to her perfume distracting me on those flights. I noticed her absence from the dugout pregame. I noticed the extra room key that was left behind at the front desk when we checked into our hotel.

And the worst part about it is I have no idea what her sudden distance is all about. Last time Reese gave me the cold shoulder, I earned it. But I thought things were good between us now.

Something new I learned this week? How Reese signs off on her emails.

Best Regards, Reese Remington.

Initially, I didn't listen to her request that I only contact her via email. After our first game on the road, I texted her about an injury that was bothering one of our players and letting her know I was going to sit him for game two.

She didn't respond.

I called her after our second game to keep her in the loop of why I needed to pull our pitcher in the middle of the fourth inning.

She didn't answer.

And after the third and final game, I relented to emailing her the way she asked me to.

I didn't have anything new to say that day. I just wanted to see if I'd ever hear back from her. And via email, I finally did.

Thank you for the update. Best Regards, Reese Remington.

Best fucking regards.

I'm tempted to add yet another plate onto the squat rack because there's a part of me that believes the frustration thrumming through me could help me set a new personal best tonight.

But there's no one here to spot me and though I may be irritated and want to take it out in the gym, I'm not an idiot.

With the bar balanced across my shoulders and my hands firmly wrapped in place, I lift the bar off the rack and power through my set of squats while watching my form in the mirror.

The music helps. The dark gym helps. But mostly, it's the maddening question of what I did wrong that fuels me.

Maybe I shouldn't have told Reese about Miller's mom. Maybe it freaked her out that I haven't dated anyone seriously in over twenty years. Or maybe I read it all wrong, and misunderstood what I thought was flirting all this time. Maybe she truly does just see me as her employee and I crossed a line with her.

I re-rack the bar before standing to my full height, taking deep breaths to try to calm my pounding heart.

That felt good, though. I could go all night. Pushing my body is a welcome distraction.

Pulling off my shirt, I use it to wipe down my face before giving my muscles a couple of minutes to recover before my next round. I stand behind the squat rack, leaning my arms over the bar to rest and catch my breath.

It shouldn't bother me so much. I have too many other things to focus on. My kid. My kid's kid. My team. Whether I'm going to have a job at the end of this season.

I should be concentrating on the future of my career, but instead, I'm too busy pondering if my boss knows I'm crushing on her and wondering if she ever felt the same. I thought you grew out of this phase after your early twenties, but here I am, smack-dab in my forties and wishing I could read that woman's mind.

Get your shit together, Emmett.

I don't hear the door open, my music is far too loud for that, but the light that reflects off the mirror in front of me, coming from the crack in the doorway, draws my attention.

Through the reflection, I watch as Reese walks into the gym.

She probably didn't know I was in here with how dim I keep the lights, but as soon as she steps inside and hears the music, even though she's wearing her own earbuds, she looks around the room until she meets my own waiting gaze through the mirror.

Reese stays frozen by the door, and I don't move from my spot at the squat rack.

We simply watch each other through the reflection, not saying a word, once again in the same room after nearly a week.

I haven't seen her since I ran into her in the dugout, and I assumed I wouldn't until some point tomorrow during our afternoon game. I purposely avoided the top floor tonight just in case, and I didn't check for her car in the parking lot because why would I? Why would she be here on a Friday night anyway?

Reese opens her mouth and says something, but when I can't hear her, I realize my music is still blaring over the speaker system.

I push off the bar to grab my phone, lowering my music almost all the way down before turning to face her.

"I was just saying sorry," she says, and for a moment I allow myself to believe she's referring to the distance she's kept this week. But then she throws her thumb over her shoulder toward the door. "I didn't know you were here. I'll go."

That'd be for the best. My only hope of concentrating on the rest of this workout would be if she left.

I shrug casually. "You own the place. Do what you want."

I find myself hopeful to hear one of her little quips. "You're right. I do," or "It's always nice when you remember that."

But instead, Reese stays silent, and I hate that more than any jab she's ever thrown my way.

"Do your thing," I continue. "I'm almost done anyway."

She offers me this small, almost pitying smile and I decide I absolutely hate that too.

Reese grabs a yoga mat and lays it out on the floor in the corner of the gym. Unfortunately, that corner just so happens to be the one directly behind the squat rack, and I'm given a prime view of her through the mirror on the wall when I return to the bar for another set.

She puts her earbud back in and starts with a stretch, reaching up toward the sky before folding in half to touch her toes.

And I'm fucking staring.

I don't know how long it's been since my last set, and I can't seem to pull my attention away from her long enough to start my next one.

She looks good.

Her blonde hair is halfway clipped up, keeping it out of her pretty face. She's in a matching workout set because of course she is. The woman is always polished and perfectly coordinated, and clearly that extends to her time in the gym.

The berry-colored leggings paint her thick legs, and the matching sports bra just barely holds her in. She's soft everywhere and I fucking love that. I love that she doesn't hide it either. She's confident in her body and my type to a T.

It's the bit of motivation I need to start my next set because, yeah, she's my type. I lift heavy for a reason.

Watching my form in the mirror, I'm only three reps in when my eyes drift to her corner. She's got one arm reaching over her body in another stretch, but it's done so a bit mindlessly. Instead, her focus is locked on my reflection, snagging on my thighs as I sit deep in a squat.

As I push through the movement, her attention follows, until finally, her eyes catch mine.

I want to tease her. I want to give her a bit of shit for checking me out. But I also don't want her to stop, and with her new professional boundaries, drawing attention to the fact she's close to crossing them would only cause her to put up more.

But neither of us looks away from the other. There's a beat of silence and I'm tempted to fill it with the question I've been wondering all week.

What the hell happened?

It's on the tip of my tongue when Reese pulls her eyes away from mine and moves into another stretch. I get back to my workout and sink into another squat, doing my best to focus on my form, and only my form, when I look into the mirror.

That's only successful for about two more reps because out of the corner of my eye, I watch as Reese spreads her legs into a wide stance, then folds in half at the hips to put her palms flat on the mat.

The dim light sets a moody glow over her body and *good God*, she's about to spill out of that fucking bra with the way she's bending forward. If she does, there's no doubt my knees will give way under this amount of weight.

Without finishing my set, I slam the bar back onto the rack, partly out of frustration, but mostly because I'm going to drop it if I don't get it secured as quickly as possible.

The bang startles Reese, her eyes shooting up to me. "Are you okay?"

"Yep." I pace the small area around me, hands on my hips and keeping my eyes down. "Fine."

I take a few deep breaths before returning to the bar. I lift it off the rack again and sit myself into a deep squat at the exact moment Reese decides she needs to stretch her calves. Hands and feet on the mat, ass in the air and done so facing the opposite wall from me.

Is she fucking with me?

She has to be fucking with me, right?

I barely get through the one single rep, too distracted and too mesmerized by the way her body moves, by the way her ass jiggles. By the way she won't fucking talk to me.

Giving in, I re-rack the bar for the last time. And I'm still as frustrated as I was when I started my workout, aggressively removing the weighted plates and putting them back where they belong.

"I'm done," I exhale in defeat. "The place is all yours."

I don't know why I announce it. I supposed it's in the hope she'll say something to me in return.

She doesn't.

Reese has moved over to the free weights, but I don't look in her direction again as I grab my T-shirt, phone, and water bottle and head toward the small locker-room-type bathroom attached to the gym. I keep my eyes down, locked on my phone screen, disconnecting my music from the surround-sound speaker.

"Emmett," she says, stopping me before I've slipped out of the room.

I can feel how hopeful my expression is when I turn back to face her, eager that she'll talk to me for longer than one clipped sentence.

There's an apology in the way she looks at me from across the room. It's enough to tamp down a bit of the frustration I'm feeling toward her. Because whatever is going on, that look on her face lets me believe there might be a part of her that dislikes her new rules too.

Reese opens her mouth, then closes it again, and when she finally does speak, all I get is a simple, "I hope you have a good night."

I hate this.

"Yeah," I force out. "You too."

With that, I round the corner behind the half-wall that separates the bathroom from the gym.

Hands on the sink, I dip my head.

I need to let this go. Who cares if I can't remember the last time I was this attracted to someone? Who cares that I can't remember the last time I was this interested in every word that came out of someone's mouth?

She's my boss. It was never going to happen anyway.

Turning on the sink, I splash a bit of water on my face. I was planning to shower here before heading to my apartment, but knowing Reese is right on the other side of this wall, working out in that tight little outfit, it seems like a terrible idea. I'll let my imagination run wild in the privacy of my own shower at home.

I wash my hands and slip my sweat-soaked shirt back on when the creak of the gym door opening grabs my attention.

Did she leave already?

I'm about to go check when I hear one of my players speak.

"Hey, sweetheart," Harrison says. "I didn't think anyone else was going to be here. What are you doing here on a Friday night?"

Every one of my senses goes on high alert as I listen in.

"Reese. Ms. Remington. Boss," she says, no humor to be found in her tone. "Any of those would work."

It's hard to hear everything that's said between them, but what I do catch, I don't fucking like. He's patronizing in both his tone and his words.

Everything Kai said about him has already given me a new view of the guy, and I've had a hard time with him since. I've tried to keep it as professional as I can, but I'm learning I'm not great at that.

Not with Reese and, in a different sense, not with Harrison.

He makes a few snide remarks about how she may want to use smaller weights. He tells her he missed her on the road trip to Detroit. And he once again asks her what she's doing here on a Friday night.

It takes everything in me not to go out there and rip into him for the way he's speaking to her, but I also know that Reese would hate it if I jumped in to rescue her when she can handle it herself. So instead, I continue to listen.

"I own the place," she says simply. "So what exactly are you doing here?"

Harrison chuckles in this demeaning way, and this whole interaction is showing a side to him I've never witnessed myself before. "I left my car here during the road series, so my buddy here dropped me off." And apparently, there's two people in there with her. "I was just showing him around the beautiful facility that *you*, as you pointed out, own."

That checks out. I remember parking my truck in the private lot next to his car earlier tonight. Didn't think much of it until now.

"Is there a bathroom around?" Harrison's buddy asks.

"Through there," Harrison says. "I gotta use it too."

It's not that I care if he knows I'm here, but I'm real curious to hear what else he might have to say when he thinks no one is listening. So, for that reason, I slip into a shower stall before Harrison sees me.

"*That's* your boss?" his friend asks.

He scoffs. "Yeah, exactly."

"She's hot."

Okay. Get fucked.

"Dude, it's embarrassing," Harrison whispers. "I play for the one fucking team that's run by a woman. She's out of her league."

All I see is red.

That anger that had begun to tamp down from that last interaction with Reese quickly amps back up. My blood goes hot, and any energy I may have expended on that leg workout comes flooding right back, giving me the overwhelming urge to punch this guy straight in the face.

They finish their business and exit the bathroom, but before they leave the gym, Harrison says one more thing to Reese. "If you need Friday night plans, I know of some ways to keep you busy."

As soon as I hear the door to the gym close, I leave the shower stall, exit the bathroom, and immediately find Reese already looking in my direction. As if she knew I overheard everything and would have something to say.

"Has he spoken to you that way before?"

She sighs. "Emmett—"

"Reese." There's even more anger and urgency in my voice the second time. "Has he spoken to you that way before?"

She doesn't say anything, but her silence is enough of an answer for me to know that that little interaction was nothing new.

I already know why she doesn't want to confirm it. She doesn't want me to think her idea of trading him has anything to do with the way he addresses her. And I know by now that Reese would put all of that to the side for the good of the baseball club. If she felt he was the right player for her team, she wouldn't dare think of getting rid of him simply because he's a patronizing little prick.

But I fucking would.

I shake my head, utterly pissed off that I didn't know about it sooner. Then I look her dead in the eye, arms crossed over my chest when I say, "Trade him."

15

REESE

"What's up with Monty today?" my grandfather asks from the seat next to me. "I've never seen him like this before."

From up in the owner's box, I watch as Emmett returns to the dugout after spending a few minutes on the field, getting in the umpire's face. To be fair, the ump has blown too many obvious calls, but Emmett typically handles that kind of thing with a bit more of a level head.

I attempt to keep my tone uninterested when I say, "Not sure."

But the problem is that I'm very much interested in just about everything regarding that man.

It's an abnormally hot day in the city, and we just so happen to have a game smack-dab in the middle of the warmest afternoon hours. And because of it, I fear the heat is getting to everyone.

Emmett.

The umpire.

Me.

Regardless that I'm sitting in my air-conditioned suite, every inch of me is on fire from just watching the game.

Well, if we want to get specific, it's from watching the field manager.

Thankfully, my grandfather is too oblivious to notice that I haven't been able to pull my attention away from the dugout. And I'm lucky this suite is situated above the stands off the third baseline, where I'm granted a bit of privacy unless someone knows to look for me up here.

Anyone who saw that rumor online, the one about me leaving Emmett's hotel room, would quickly learn it wasn't just a rumor by the way I can't tear my eyes off him.

I kind of... missed him this week.

A sentiment I swore I'd never feel when it comes to Emmett Montgomery.

I missed the shit-talking. I missed knowing he had my back. I missed being able to talk to the one person in the entire franchise who truly sees how hard it is for me to be a woman in this industry.

I just missed him, and yes, I know I brought this on myself. It took everything in me not to respond to his text or answer his call, but I know I'm doing the right thing by keeping our communication professional and putting a safe distance between us for now.

To him, maybe our flirty banter was no big deal. Maybe to him, me cutting off any personal communication was a drastic move because he never felt the danger of coming too close to crossing a line.

Maybe that's why he's so upset with me.

But for me, I felt myself getting too close. I felt myself realizing I liked things about him I swore I never would.

Sure, of course, I find Emmett physically attractive. Just take a second to look at the man and you'd understand. But it's what's inside I thought I was safe from. His personality was what I believed I couldn't stand. Unluckily for me, his heart is now the thing I find most attractive about him.

Or is it? Because my view during this game has been unreal.

Emmett's got his baseball pants on today as per usual, but instead of the uniform top, he's wearing a white team-issued shirt made from a thin athletic material. It's practically see-through in the way it clings to his wide back and rounded traps. He's held the same position the majority of the afternoon, standing at the edge of the dugout and leaning his forearms over the railing, pants stretched over his thighs and ass.

"You know who's been asking about you?" my grandfather asks, and holy shit, I forgot he was here.

Am I drooling? My freaking grandfather is next to me and I'm drooling over my employee.

The picture of professionalism, I swear.

"Reese's Pieces," he says, almost singing my name to gain my attention.

"Sorry." Shaking my head, I focus on him and not on the man in the dugout. "Who?"

"Ed's son. Michael."

"Asking about me how?"

My grandfather's bushy brows lift, as does that knowing smile on his lips.

"Okay, matchmaker." I chuckle. "You know I'm not looking to date anyone."

"Yeah, yeah. And I don't believe you."

This sweet old man has a hard time fathoming that his granddaughter could be happy and content all on her own.

"I enjoy being single," I remind him. "It's nice not having to think about anyone other than myself."

"But wouldn't it be nice to have someone thinking about *you*? And trust me, honey, you wouldn't mind the right person occupying all your thoughts. It's quite nice, actually. You just need to meet someone new."

My grandfather, bless him, has been on about me finding someone since I became single. And granted, he knows a bit about that. My dad's mom passed when I was a baby, and a handful of years later, my grandfather met the woman I now refer to as my grandmother. He spent some time alone but now has been happily married for almost thirty years. But not everyone is so lucky to get a second chance at love.

Some people only get one. Like me.

I've been on my own so long now that I couldn't tell you what it feels like to have someone think about me. There's no one around to witness my every day—my mundane moments or my biggest accomplishments. I only have me, and though others might find that discouraging, to someone who's been with the wrong person, it's rather hopeful. Sure, I may be alone, but at least I'm not questioning anyone's motives for being in my life anymore.

As if he could read my mind, my grandfather adds, "They're not all Jeremy, you know."

Maybe. But why risk finding out?

My focus drifts back to Emmett in the dugout.

This week, I had a hard time ignoring that comment I saw online. The one about him getting close to me so I'd renew his coaching contract at the end of the year. It's hard to fathom it being true, but I've been wrong before, and keeping a distance between us not only keeps rumors from circulating, but it also takes that concern off the table.

It's the bottom of the seventh and we've got Harrison Kaiser on second with two outs, when Isaiah Rhodes strikes out at bat. Down 4-1, with two innings to go, we're not playing our best today.

Blame it on the heat. Blame it on the travel. Blame it on any one of the million possibilities there could be to having an off game. It'd be impossible to play a perfect 162.

What I don't expect to blame it on is player dynamics, but two of them are practically getting into a fight on their way back to the dugout.

Harrison is in Isaiah's face, saying something to him, which I assume is about Isaiah's not so pretty at-bat or the fact that he couldn't bring Harrison home. Isaiah shakes his head, continuing to the dugout and trying to shrug him off, but Harrison doesn't let up. He keeps talking shit, pushing his chest against Isaiah's shoulder.

I can tell you right now, he picked the wrong fucking guy. And not because I think Isaiah Rhodes is going to do anything about it. He's laid-back and just wants everyone to have a good time. But his field manager views him as part of his family, and I know how Emmett gets when someone he cares about is disrespected.

And just as I suspected, Emmett's protective side comes roaring to life when the two players near the dugout. He reaches over the railing, stopping Harrison at the top of his stairs by grabbing the front of his uniform and pulling his attention to Emmett instead of Isaiah.

Then he lays into him.

I mean, he fucking lets him have it.

I, obviously, have no idea what he says, but I can tell it's working by the fear on Harrison's face. It doesn't hurt that Emmett's practically towering over the guy.

This little interaction is going to be all over the sports networks tonight, and I have a feeling Emmett could not care less.

I also have a feeling that the verbal lashing he's giving his player is not only about protecting Isaiah, but it also has a little something to do with what he overheard in the gym last night.

Emmett says one final thing and gets a tense head nod from Harrison. The force with which he was holding on to his jersey has the opposite effect when he releases him, and Harrison practically falls down the dugout stairs.

"Kaiser might be a problem," my grandfather says.

I love my grandfather, but yeah. No shit. It's exactly what I've been saying since I took over.

"And wow," he exhales. "I have no idea what's gotten into Monty. I've never seen him this riled up before. Plan to get questions about that interaction in any interviews you have coming up this week. Go in prepared with a way you can spin that so it doesn't look like our field manager has a personal vendetta against one of his players."

But he does.

With the conviction in which he told me to trade said player last night, I can promise you it's personal.

I hate to admit it, but the protective thing is kind of doing it for me.

And by kind of, I mean completely. It's completely doing it for me.

"I hope everything is okay with him," my grandfather adds.

I huff a laugh, shaking my head in disbelief. "Of course you're not upset that he just created a PR nightmare for me. Emmett has always been your golden boy."

"I don't know that I'd put it like that."

"Oh, come on. You threw money at any and everything he ever asked you for. I think the title is almost an understatement."

My grandfather's gray brows knit in confusion. "What are you talking about?"

"Emmett." I gesture toward the dugout just as the players begin dispersing to their positions in the infield and outfield. "You let the club pay for anything he wanted. Things we didn't exactly have the budget to cover. Whatever his star player needed, he got for him. From you."

"Hey now." He holds a hand up. "You're as big a Kai Rhodes fan as any of us."

True. But not the point I'm trying to make here.

"When Emmett asked that Kai have a nanny to travel with the team, you paid that salary. When Emmett asked that two of the plane seats get removed and, instead, have a crib installed for Max, you also paid for that."

His confusion only deepens. "No, I didn't."

"Well, then who did?"

"Monty."

I open my mouth to say something, but no words come out.

"Those expenses came out of Monty's salary," my grandfather admits, and the revelation nearly knocks the wind out of me. "He didn't want anyone to know, so we agreed to tell people that the club was paying for everything. A couple of years back, Kai almost retired. Not because he wanted to, but because he felt he had to when his son was born. Monty wasn't going to let him, so he covered the nanny salary. Before Miller came around, there were a lot of them. But he especially didn't want his daughter to know her paycheck was coming out of his."

No. That can't be true. Not because I don't believe my grandfather, but because this information contradicts every belief that formed my opinion about Emmett.

"And the plane thing," he continues. "It wasn't as expensive as you'd think. But the guys who run the hangar where we park the aircraft, Monty gave them his two season tickets that year in exchange for getting it done. So technically, that was free."

All this time, I truly thought that Emmett had taken advantage of my grandfather's kindness to get what he wanted. All to find out, it was his own kindness that made sure Kai had the resources he needed for his son so that he wouldn't retire before he was ready to.

I truly can't find words, so my grandfather fills the silence.

"Haven't you deep-dived into that year's budget? The numbers might look a bit confusing due to where they're allocated, but if you look hard enough, you'll see where that money was coming from."

Of course, I haven't investigated that year's budget yet. I haven't been able to get further than last season. Instead, I formed an opinion off what I was told instead of looking into it myself.

"One day, you'll see what I see, Reese. That guy right there is not only a fantastic manager, but he's a gem of a human."

Little does he know, I already see it. And that's the problem.

I find him in the dugout once again, jaw ticking with frustration from that interaction with Harrison. But then when Isaiah bounds up the stairs with his hat and glove in hand, headed for his place in the infield, Emmett stops him and pulls him into a hug to speak quietly in his ear.

I can sense by the way Emmett's shoulders relax that he's no longer acting as the protective hothead. He's in full-on father figure mode, and the quick switch-up is, unfortunately, very attractive.

Isaiah nods and when they pull away from each other, he's got that goofy grin back on his face. Emmett cups the back of his head, playfully shaking him before sending him onto the field for the top of the eighth.

He's good down to his core, isn't he?

The players adore him. My grandfather adores him. And I think I might kind of adore him.

Which is just fucking great.

This is the man that changes my mind? The one I can't have. The one I shouldn't want. My goddamn employee.

And as if he knew I was having an existential crisis over him, Emmett has the audacity to grab the nearest water bottle and take a long drink before pouring the remainder down the back of his neck to cool himself down.

Fuck. Me.

Fuck this heat. Fuck my hormones too.

He may be cooling himself down, but I don't think I've ever been so warm. Or so annoyingly turned on. It's like I'm watching the start of one of those male revue shows and I've got a front-row seat.

It feels criminal that I don't have a bit of cash on me.

Will they need to change the age rating of this game on the television networks?

The water rains down his back, causing that already thin shirt to practically disappear against his skin. It clings to every hill and valley, showing off every detailed line of that black ink.

"Well, that's one way to sell tickets," my grandfather says, laughing next to me.

Good God.

I need to go hide in my office for these final two innings. Alone.

Emmett turns, tossing the empty bottle onto the bench behind him. And then, as if by instinct, he looks up.

To my box. Right at me.

He does it in a way that tells me he already knew exactly where I've been for this entire game.

There's a hardness in his jaw and an intensity in his stare, but neither of us breaks eye contact.

It reminds me of the way we watched each other through the mirror when I found him in the gym last night.

It reminds me of the way he might watch a woman as he's making her come.

My grandfather, bless his sweet innocent soul, lifts a hand to wave at the man I'm currently having all sorts of inappropriate thoughts about.

Emmett's gaze ticks over to my grandfather and he raises two fingers in the air in a casual wave. Then his eyes track back to me one more time before he turns away and refocuses on the game.

Apparently, everything about today is hot, and right now I'm playing with fire.

Maybe it's not Emmett that's awakened the side of me I thought I shut off years ago. Maybe I'm lonelier than I believed. Maybe I do want to be with someone, and *that's* the issue I'm having here. It's not Emmett.

It *can't* be Emmett.

I need it to be anyone *but* Emmett.

"Ed's son . . ." I begin.

My grandfather perks up next to me at the mention. "Michael?"

"Go ahead and give him my number. I think you're right. I think it'd be good for me to meet someone new."

16
EMMETT

"That's my new favorite one," Travis declares, spoon pointed in the direction of the lemon mousse Miller prepared.

Although, I know that dessert is not as simple as a mousse. I know it has some fancy name I won't be able to pronounce.

"I think the chocolate still wins." Isaiah takes another bite of each dessert just to be sure.

"Well, good news for both of you." My daughter throws her dish towel over her shoulder. "They're both getting added to the menu."

"This is the best side gig anyone could ask for," Cody says, mouth full as he speaks. He then proceeds to steal the lemon mousse from Travis, finishing the rest before anyone could have a chance to sample it again.

"Dad, which is your favorite?"

I can't tear my eyes away from my first baseman as he inhales the dessert, not giving himself time to even take a breath.

"I don't know." I grimace, watching him. "Kind of lost my appetite."

"Sorry, Coach." Cody finishes the last bite before taking a deep inhale, sitting back in the stool at my daughter's kitchen island to stretch his stomach. "She's too good at this."

That she is.

Miller has always been an excellent baker, something she took up when she was just a kid because I was, admittedly, pretty terrible in the kitchen. Thankfully, my shortcomings caused her to experiment and find her passion, and after years of traveling the country to create Michelin-star dessert programs, she's now got her own patisserie right here in Chicago.

Every so often, when she's looking to create new menu items, she has us over for a taste test. Sometimes it's just me and the Rhodes brothers. Other times Cody and Trav join in. And when she's experimenting for a full menu revamp, the entire team piles into their home to sample each item.

Baking for her loved ones is what helped her find her passion again after a bit of burnout, and years later, it's still a part of her process.

"But, Dad, if you had to choose one," Miller begins again, "which one was your favorite?"

"Millie, you know I can't choose. I think they're both excellent. People will be lining up for them."

She offers me a grateful smile, and I watch the moment she catches herself.

At times, I still find her looking for my approval. Whether it be in small things like a dessert preference, or bigger things, like which wedding dress she should choose.

She's better about it now, but there were a lot of years that Miller lived her life as if she were in debt to me. As if me leaving my career and becoming her dad required her to prove that she would be successful in return.

Miller just being Miller is all I could've asked of her, and up until she met Max, I don't think she ever really believed that was enough. But she's a mom now. It's good to see her understand how I feel about her because she loves Max in the same way.

Speaking of my favorite three-year-old, little Max comes waddling into the kitchen, pajamas on and hair still damp from his bath. He holds his hands up for me to pick him up off the ground.

"Hi, Bug," I say, sitting him on my lap at the kitchen island. "Cool PJs."

"They're doggies." He points at a golden retriever then to a black lab.

"I see that."

"Five minutes, Maxie," Kai says, strolling back into the kitchen. He eyes the empty glass jars and dirty spoons before shifting his attention to Cody. "Seriously, man?"

"What?" His voice is as innocent as he can muster. "I'm sorry. But you weren't here."

"I was giving my kid a bath. You're in *my* house and you couldn't have saved me a bite of the dessert *my* fiancée made?"

Cody pauses, thinking it over. "No."

Miller chuckles. "I made an extra of each for you. They're in the fridge when you're ready. The other two are for Kennedy. She's on her way."

"I mean . . ." Isaiah lifts a brow, cheeky smile on his lips as he speaks to his future sister-in-law. "Ken and I are married, so technically, what's hers is mine, right? Because I could for sure go for another round if you want to pull those out of the fridge."

"Why are you like this?" Kai asks his brother before turning to Miller and bending to kiss her. "Thanks, Mills."

I cover Max's eyes, but he just giggles as he attempts to pull my hand away. "Save it for the wedding."

Miller gets that look on her face, the one where her lack of a filter won out and she's about to say something I don't want to hear.

"Sorry to break it to you, Dad, but we didn't really save anything for the wedding."

"C'mon," I groan. "There are some things a father doesn't need to hear about."

She shrugs. "Now you know how I feel when I have to listen to all my friends refer to you as my 'hot dad.' Or when all the guys on the team talk about you and Reese needing to . . . *release some tension*."

My attention shoots to my three players, and not a single one of them tries to deny it. In fact, Cody is too busy licking the glass jar clean like a goddamn dog.

"You guys can't say that kind of stuff."

"Well, sorry that it's true." Travis shrugs, no apology in his tone.

"That's how rumors start, and Reese has too many eyes on her right now for that kind of talk."

"No one is saying that you guys have," Isaiah explains. "Just that you should."

"You of all people should know how hard it is for a woman to succeed in this business," I tell him, reminding him of his wife. "The last thing Reese needs is her players talking about her having some sort of inappropriate relationship with the field manager. You guys have to understand that she, more than any other team owner in the league, has to keep things professional."

"No, we get it," Cody says. "It just seems like you're trying awfully hard to remind yourself of that too."

The boys all laugh.

"All right, well you can all go fu—" Looking down at my lap, I find Max's big blue eyes staring up at me. "*Find* something else to talk about."

"Nice save, Grandpa," Kai taunts, nodding toward his brother. "What I want to know is what the hell was up with Harrison going after you today?"

"I don't know," Isaiah exhales. "That guy is a cancer. Just look at how many teams he's played for over the course of his career. I doubt it's a coincidence that he's always moving around. Not that it matters. With how hard Arthur and Scott worked to get him last year, it's not like Reese is going to get rid of him now."

"I wouldn't be so sure about that," I mutter under my breath. All eyes shoot to me.

"What do you know?" Isaiah asks.

Even though Isaiah is practically family, he's still a player and I can't have the team knowing about the inner workings of trades and pickups before they happen. We don't need rumors circulating the locker room, and I don't need Reese getting heat for a decision before she's even officially made it.

So, I look for a different answer that's equally as true. "Well, the optics aren't great when a field manager and a player get into it mid-game, now are they? But I'm only guaranteed to be here until the end of the season. So, who knows, maybe I'll be the one to go."

"Yeah, Dad." Miller leans her elbows on the kitchen island opposite me. "I've never seen you get in a player's face like that."

"He deserved it."

"I can't imagine the boss was too stoked about that," Travis cuts in.

"I wouldn't know how she feels about it. I didn't see her post-game."

"By the way, I really like Reese," Cody states, his typical happy-go-lucky demeanor switching up the mood. "I think she's doing a good job."

That earns my attention. "Yeah?"

"Yeah. And I mean more than just running the team. Did you know that next week is my thousandth game with the Warriors? I didn't even know that was a thing, but she's flying my parents out here for the game. I thought that was so cool of her."

You'd think after everything Reese told me at that minor league game about her love for her family's team that this wouldn't shock me, but still, it does. She loves to preach that baseball is only a business, so it's always a little surprising when she proves herself wrong.

I nod in agreement. "That is really cool of her. I'm glad your parents will be there."

He smiles. "Me too. My mom is excited."

"Reese hooked up my family too," Travis cuts in. "You know when we were in Detroit last week and my mom and aunt came to game two of that series? Well, Reese found out they were going and bought them seats directly behind home plate." He chuckles to himself. "I could hear those two yelling behind me the whole freaking game."

"Reese wasn't even on that road trip," I remind him, a bit of disbelief laced in my tone.

"Exactly."

Before I can wrap my head around this new information, Kennedy comes in through the front door.

"Sorry I'm late," she says, immediately finding Isaiah. "I got stuck at work longer than I planned. It felt like everyone came in for treatment today. Well, except for you three."

"It was a dessert day," Cody explains as if that explains anything at all.

Isaiah wraps an arm around his wife, pressing a kiss to the top of her hair. "I made sure we saved one of each of the desserts for you. Other people wanted to eat them, but I said no way. Those are for my wife, and if she wants to share when she gets here, that'll be her decision."

Max giggles in my lap, already picking up in his three short years that his uncle is the comedian of the family.

Kennedy cocks her head to the side. "Why do I have a feeling that none of that happened?"

Miller rolls her eyes. "Nice try, Rhodes."

I don't hear what else is said, instead distracted with my phone that's buzzing and the name that's scrolling along the top.

Hesitating, I stare at the incoming call before I stand with Max tucked under one arm. "Sorry, Bug. I have to take this."

Setting him on his feet, he instantly climbs onto his uncle's back instead.

"Everything okay?" Kai asks.

I hold up my phone to show him the screen as I start down the hall. "Nate's calling."

His expression matches my own surprise from seeing my former video coach's name. I've called him multiple times since Reese let him go, and he's yet to answer a single one.

"Nate?" I ask, answering the phone as I slip into Max's bedroom. I close the door behind me so no one else can hear this conversation. I have a strong suspicion I'm about to get cussed out or called a well-deserved name for promising him a job I couldn't deliver.

What I'm not expecting is the unmistakenly cheery tone in his voice when he says, "Hey, Monty!"

I'm clearly confused, and don't do a great job of hiding it. "Everything okay?"

"Yeah, man. Things are great. Look, I'm sorry I haven't answered. Life has been a bit hectic lately."

I exhale a sigh. "Nate, I'm so sor—"

"But I just wanted to call and say thank you."

There's a long pause on the line, my confusion evident once again. "For what?"

"For calling Seattle's coaching staff and recommending me. They reached out to me a couple of hours after the Warriors let me go. Offered me a full-time video coach position."

Words stick in my throat, but the first thought that runs through my mind is the realization that Seattle is Nate's home team. Both he and his wife are originally from Washington.

Then there's the reminder that I didn't call anyone.

I should've. I was just too busy being pissed at Reese.

"So, between the cross-country move," he says, "and becoming a dad. Oh yeah! Big news. I'm a dad now. Hailey gave birth last week to our daughter. I'll send you a picture. She's beautiful."

I exhale a small laugh. "Congrats, man. Being a girl dad is the best. Everyone is healthy?"

"Yeah, everyone is great. And it really is such a blessing that we have both our parents here to help while I'm traveling for work. And none of that would've happened if I was still in Chicago. So, I just wanted to call and say thank you so much for whatever strings you had to pull to get me a job back home."

It doesn't take me long to figure out who exactly made that call.

It's the same woman who seemed so nonchalant when she told me she let Nate go.

The same woman who I called heartless because of it.

The same woman who already had a job lined up for him with a different team.

"Nate, I'm so happy for you guys, but I've got to be honest. I wasn't the one who made that call."

There's a lingering pause on the line.

"Then who did?"

"I can't say for sure, but I believe that was Reese."

"Wow," he exhales. "I . . . I don't know what to say. She barely knew me, but was apologizing profusely when she let me go, so I guess I'm not all that surprised. I need to give her a call this week and thank her."

I nod, though he can't see me. "I think that would mean a lot to her if you did."

"Thanks for everything, Monty. I loved being a part of your staff, but I really am glad that we ended up back here and things worked out the way they did."

"Happy to hear it, Nate. Tell the family I said hello and I'm looking forward to catching up when we play each other this year."

We say our goodbyes and I hang up the phone, but before I rejoin everyone in the kitchen, I find my text thread with Reese.

There are a few blue bubbles of previous messages I've sent her that never got a response, thanks to our new *professional boundaries*. But I refuse to send her an email when this conversation—this *apology*—requires a face-to-face.

I don't have it in me to receive another "Best Regards" in response.

After how this last week has gone, I have zero expectations that she'll respond, but still, I give it my best shot.

> **Me:** Hey, are you at the field? I need to talk to you.

I give it a few minutes and when the message not-so-surprisingly goes unanswered, I leave Max's room to grab my truck keys.

I've run into Reese a couple of times at the field so I'm starting to learn she likes to spend her time off there the same way I do. It may not be for the same reasons, but it's a Saturday night and if I weren't at my daughter's house, I'd find something to keep me busy at work. I have a feeling that's exactly where she is.

I grab my truck keys off the entryway table and head back into the kitchen to say a few quick goodbyes when I remember our team doctor just came from the field.

"Kennedy, was Reese still at the stadium when you left?"

She thinks it over. "I don't think so. There were only a couple of cars left in the lot, and I didn't see a light on in any of the offices upstairs."

Shit.

Well, there goes that idea.

Something about this feels too pressing to leave until tomorrow. Yeah, I'm frustrated that she's upholding these professional boundaries out of nowhere, but I don't care about that right now. I care about the fact that I was way too hard on her about Nate, when all along she was making sure he was taken care of because she didn't have room in the budget to take care of him herself.

The more that realization settles in, the more of an asshole I feel.

I desperately need to apologize.

I lift my phone to call her when a text pops onto my screen, and it's been so long since I've seen a message accompanied by her name that I have to do a double take just to convince myself she actually responded to me.

Reese: No, I'm not at the field.

Me: Where are you?

I say my goodbyes, hugging my daughter and loving on Max for a moment before heading toward the front door to go find Reese.

Reese: Across town. I won't be going back to the field tonight.

Me: Where across town?

Reese: At a new restaurant called the Brass Fork. About to eat dinner.

I've heard of it. Never eaten there myself, but I know it's nice. There's a good chance my henley, jeans, and baseball hat won't get me through the door, but it's worth a shot.

Me: I'll come meet you.

Reese: You can't.

Me: This is work-related. I promise I'm not crossing any of your boundaries.

I'm out the door and reversing my truck when she responds with a message that has me putting it right back in park.

Reese: I'm on a date.

I reread that message a few times, and I like it less and less with each pass.

She's on a date?

Am I jealous? Fuck yeah, I'm jealous. I'm jealous that she'll hardly talk to me and now someone else gets the privilege of having her attention all night. I'm jealous she's out with someone else in public because that person, unlike me, is not her employee.

But I don't know why she'd think her being on a date would deter me. All it does is add fuel to the fire. Has she met me?

I throw my truck in reverse, but before I start driving, I send her one more text.

> **Me:** Great. When is that over? I'll be the one taking you home.

17

REESE

"Thank you so much for dinner," I say, walking next to Michael as we head for the front door.

"Of course. I had a nice time."

"I did too."

"The food was great."

"So good."

I don't miss the way we're both trying to get to the exit without either of us bringing up the idea of a second date. I think it was fairly obvious early on into dinner that we each got the friend vibe from the other.

"So, uh . . ." Michael holds the front door of the restaurant open for me. "I'll probably see you around the field at some point. My dad has been wanting us to go to a game together."

"That sounds great. I'm sure I'll see you around."

He's got this polite smile as he looks down at me, neither of us knowing how to end this as we awkwardly stand on the sidewalk outside of the restaurant. But then his attention flicks to the street.

"Is that . . ."

I follow his line of sight.

No fucking way.

I didn't entirely believe Emmett when he texted to tell me he'd be the one taking me home. I kind of thought it was simply said to stake his claim without doing anything to back it up.

But here he is, leaning against the hood of his truck, arms crossed over his chest, exuding all the confidence in the world. Waiting to pick me up from the date I was on with someone else.

I can say with certainty that there's nothing between me and Michael. Because after two hours of conversation, I didn't once feel an ounce of the need I have just from making eye contact across the sidewalk with Emmett.

Something is seriously wrong with me because at this point, even him finding street parking on a Saturday night is attractive to me. Then you add the black jeans, gray henley rolled to his elbows, and a ball cap, and I'm just kind of done for.

Which is fucking fabulous, you know. The whole point of going out with someone after years of actively being single was to prove to myself that I could replicate my attraction to Emmett.

Spoiler alert: I can't.

Emmett pushes off his truck, meeting us on the sidewalk. "Sorry to interrupt."

No, he's not.

He watches only me but speaks to Michael as he does. "A work emergency came up and I need to speak to my boss." For a brief moment, his eyes pan to my date. "In private."

"Totally get it." Michael holds his hands up before looking my way. "You're good, then?"

"I'm good." I offer him a polite smile. "Have a nice night."

"You too." Smiling, he nods to Emmett before he takes off in the opposite direction that I'll be headed.

I watch his retreating back, waiting until he's a far enough distance away before I spin back on my field manager. "What are you doing here?"

He doesn't react to my tone. "I told you. I'm taking you home. Also, what was that? A little fight from the guy would've been nice. Another man just stole his date."

"You didn't steal anyone." I roll my eyes because that seems a whole lot safer than jumping him in public. Which is exactly what I want to do. "And I'm good on the ride," I say, taking a couple of steps in the direction of my condo. "I live within walking distance."

"Reese." Emmett takes a couple of quick steps with those long legs to meet up with me, standing in my path. "You've avoided me for too long, and I need to talk to you. Let me take you home."

I look back at his truck. "I'd rather walk."

His set jaw tics, before he runs a palm over his beard in frustration. "Okay," he relents on a long exhale, moving out of my path. "Fine."

I take a couple of steps, the stilettos of my heels clicking against the cement. But he's not walking with me, so I turn back to find him stuck a few paces back.

"Well, are you going to walk me home or not?"

"Oh." He perks up, nodding quickly. "Yeah. Yeah, I can do that."

I try to bite back my grin as he jogs to catch up to me, slowing to a walk when he meets my side.

"Hi, by the way," he says softly. "You look absolutely stunning."

Well, fuck me.

"Thank you."

"Are you cold?"

I should be cold. I'm wearing only a silk cocktail dress that lands at my knees and has a slit up my thigh, but I'm not. It's a warmer night in Chicago, not to mention the blush taking over my entire body just from being around this man again.

Part of me is tempted to tell him that I am cold just to see if he'd offer me his henley and walk the rest of the way to my apartment shirtless.

Professional boundaries, Reese.

"I'm good. I'm actually kind of warm. So warm. I don't need more clothes. I could take this dress off because that's how warm I am right now."

Stop. Talking.

My wide eyes shoot to his, finding him watching me with that stupid freaking smirk on his lips.

"Are you thinking of me naked right now?"

He offers me a single, slow nod. "Yes, I am."

"Don't do that."

"Don't tell me what to do."

Swallowing hard, I quicken my pace, needing to get home before I do something rash. But Emmett's long legs hardly have to make an effort to keep up with my new pace.

It's as if abstaining from his presence over the last week has only made me want him more. But this is not one of those romantic cases of distance making the heart grow fonder. This distance has only made me weaker.

"What's the work emergency?" I ask, taking a sharp left onto my street.

And it's then I realize I've never taken a man to my condo. I've never taken *anyone* to my condo. Not that he's coming *into* my condo, but it's become such a sanctuary for me after my divorce and taking over this new position that I've never taken anyone into my space, let alone allowed someone to know where I live.

This is fine. We'll separate at the front door. Or maybe the lobby. Or maybe my elevator.

"I hope this emergency you're referring to is an emergency apology," I say, chin held high, quick tempo to my feet. "My inbox has been flooded with press requests, wanting the inside scoop about what happened with you and Harrison today."

Emmett chuckles. "Yeah, I'm not apologizing for that."

Never thought he actually would.

"And why is that?" I ask.

"Because I'm not sorry."

Looking up, there's not an ounce of apology on his features.

And fuck me, I like that too. I like that he's owning it. I like that part of what happened during the game today happened because he was protecting me.

"The way I see it," he says. "Now you can blame it on me. When you trade Harrison, and the media wants to give you shit for it, you can say it's my fault. It's right there on camera for everyone to see that he and the field manager weren't getting along."

I stop in my tracks and eventually Emmett realizes I've stopped walking when he stops too, turning back to face me.

"Are you saying you did that for me?"

He shrugs. "I'd be lying if I said I didn't enjoy it. But . . ."

I cock my head to the side. "Emmett."

He takes slow steps to meet me on the sidewalk before he lifts a hand and gently pushes a strand of blonde hair behind my ear. He leaves it there, cradling my cheek.

"It's not going to be pretty, Reese. The press is going to put you through the wringer. The fans too. But if I can take some of the heat off you, I will."

He's really got to stop. The professional walls between us are becoming far too fragile.

"Thank you," I exhale and watch the way his eyes fall to my lips as I do.

"Why have you been avoiding me?"

His soft brown eyes search mine, looking for the answer, and the desperation in his inquiry breaks my heart a bit.

But I've been avoiding him for his own good. An excellent reminder I need right about now.

I gently circle his forearm with my hand, pulling his palm away from my face. "I'm almost home. What is it you needed to speak to me about tonight?"

He exhales a sigh, understanding my wish to change the tone of things when the two of us fall into step again.

"Nate called me."

Oh.

"And I needed to say thank you."

I quickly nod, wanting this conversation to be over as soon as possible. "Of course."

"Why didn't you tell me you had a job lined up for him?"

Maybe because I shouldn't have cared that much. I didn't know the guy, yet I felt terrible for having to let him go. I didn't have it in me to make a cutthroat business decision without giving him a backup option, though a stronger businesswoman probably would've been able to stomach it.

My voice is small. "I don't know."

"You let me call you heartless, Reese. You hardly batted an eye all while knowing you had him taken care of."

"It's fine, Emmett."

"No, it's not." He stops again, grabbing my arm to stop me as well. "I never should have spoken to you that way."

"You were upset."

"Yeah, and that's not an excuse. I'm sorry for what I said. Clearly, I didn't know you yet. I didn't understand how you operated. I had no idea you'd make sure he got a job close to family. I had no idea you'd make sure my players' families were at their important games or that you'd be so invested in our developmental teams. I didn't know you then and I'm sorry for making the wrong assumption."

As much as I liked that he didn't apologize for his interaction with Harrison, this apology feels good. It's unnecessary because I was making assumptions about him then too. But it's nice to know he sees me even when that's not the side of me I'm trying to put on display for the rest of the league to witness.

"Thank you for saying that," I whisper. "I recently learned I may have made some wrong assumptions about you too, so I guess we're even."

"Yeah?" His eyes tick to my lips. "Like what?"

"Like the fact that you covered the salary for Max's nanny, even before that nanny was your daughter."

"Oh." Realization dawns on him. "Please don't say anything to anyone. I don't want Kai or Miller to feel—"

"I would never say anything. But you do know that you're already underpaid for your position, right? Let alone secretly giving part of that salary to someone else."

He shakes me off. "I make plenty."

A throat clears near us, and I turn to find my doorman standing outside of my building. Because that's where we've been stopped this whole time we've been whispering, apologizing, and staring at each other's mouths. Right in front of my building.

"Hey there, Keith." I hold up a single hand in a wave. "Didn't know you were out here."

"Evening, Ms. Remington."

I throw a thumb in that direction. "So, this is me," I tell Emmett.

"I see that." A ghost of a smile lifts on his lips. "Thanks for letting me walk you home."

I should leave it at that. He's giving me an out. But after a week of avoiding him, I find myself desperate for just a few more moments.

"I'm not home yet." I slowly start toward the entrance, nodding for him to join. "I've got to make it to the top floor."

He shakes his head, following me. "Of course you're on the top floor."

There's no hint of judgment in the way he says it. It's stated in a way that he already knew I bought the condo on the penthouse level because he knows I like nice things. He's not giving me a hard time for having preferences. He's simply making it known that he's aware of them.

We say our thank-yous to Keith as he opens the main entry door for both of us and when we hit the lobby, Emmett veers for the primary elevator bank.

I slip my hand into his to stop him. "This way," I say, nodding toward my private elevator on the opposite side of the main room.

"You have your own elevator."

"I do."

"As you should."

Letting go of his hand, I swipe my keycard over the sensor, opening the elevator doors. Once inside, I tap it again, this time adding my thumbprint before pushing the button for my floor.

I'm able to get to any floor from this elevator, but seeing as this opens right into my condo, no one else can get onto mine.

The doors close, and out of the corner of my eye I watch as Emmett takes in his surroundings, his attention snagging on the emerald marble encasing us. On the intricate design pieced together on the floor. On the gold handrails and crystal buttons for each floor.

He doesn't make some judgmental statement about excess, nor does any part of him seem intimidated. Two reasons I've never wanted anyone to see where I live now. Because I bought the place that *I* wanted post-divorce, and the last thing I want is to hear anything negative said about my sacred space.

"This place suits you, Reese."

Standing shoulder to shoulder, eyes locked ahead on the door, Emmett brushes his pinky against mine.

It's intentional. It's the simplest of touches yet feels far too intimate for what it is.

The tension feels far too thick in this little box. The small amount of newfound privacy allows for the electric charge between us to simmer and heat to an unhealthy level.

As we go up through the floors, I can sense my pulse quicken, can feel the beat in my chest grow to a thundering pound when Emmett not only brushes his pinky against mine again, but wraps it fully around, holding on to that small part of me.

"Emmett—"

"How was your date?"

Looking up, I meet his eye. "You sound jealous."

"I am."

I take a step back for my own sanity, but it doesn't last long before he follows me with a step of his own.

"I'm jealous that this little red dress you're wearing tonight was for him and not for me."

He takes another step toward me, and I take another step back. Like some sort of practice dance that gets rudely interrupted when my shoulders hit the cold marble wall.

A breath hitches in my throat. "I didn't go on a date to make you jealous."

"Well, you made me jealous anyway."

Emmett's big body crowds me in the corner of the elevator, tattooed hands meeting the wall on either side of my head. And *God*, he looks downright feral as he looms over me like this. Like a predator who has finally cornered their prey.

"So why did you go?" His voice is pure gravel.

"I don't know."

He shakes his head in disapproval, bending his neck so his lips are just a whisper above my own. "Why'd you go, Reese?"

His attention dips to my mouth. Maybe waiting for my answer. Maybe waiting for me to lean up and fill the space between us. Maybe waiting for me to give him permission. I'm not entirely sure.

"Tell me."

I swallow hard, not breaking eye contact. "Because I was trying to forget about you."

There's the quickest flash of relief on his face, and I can practically feel the race of his heart pick up from here, even with the couple of inches of space still between us.

His brows furrow, pleading eyes locked on mine. "Did it work?"

"Not even a little bit."

He closes his eyes, standing to his full height and gathering himself. He takes a moment, before he turns his hat around, brim to the back.

"Good," he exhales, craning over me again, the skin of his lips brushing my own when his mouth moves to whisper, "Tell me I can kiss you."

It's part dare, part command.

And yet still a fully frantic plea because we both know if one of us is going to give permission to cross the line, it's going to have to be me.

I slightly shake my head against his. "Don't tell me what to do."

"Reese."

"Emmett, you work for me."

He hesitates for a moment, but there's no mistaking the conviction or desperation in his next words.

"Fire me."

18
EMMETT

She seems to have no retort, words sticking in her throat.

There's a heavy, heady silence in the air, only the rhythmic beep of the floors we're passing echoing through the elevator. A countdown of sorts, reminding me that this moment is almost over.

Reminding me that we're potentially crossing a line and I couldn't care less about the consequences right now.

God, I just want her to kiss me. I'm desperate for her to make the first move because there's a complicated power dynamic between us, and I need Reese to give me the green light here.

Unfortunately, she doesn't.

She doesn't kiss me. She doesn't say a word. She simply holds her ground, pressed against the wall.

Dammit.

I just told her to fire me. And yeah, I'm pretty sure that's exactly what's going to happen. I won't be surprised when the head of HR calls me into their office on Monday for making a pass at my boss.

Maybe at some point during our working relationship, I'll figure out how the hell to be professional around her, but today is clearly not that day.

I pull back, giving her space to breathe, but can't help the utter defeat etched on my face. My ego isn't so fragile that I'm upset at her for rejecting me, but that doesn't mean I'm not disappointed.

More beeps echo off the walls as we pass more floors, climbing to the top of her building.

Reese holds eye contact with me, and for turning me down, it's a boldly confident move. Which is just another thing I like about the woman. She can reject me and not pretend to be shy or apologetic about it.

But as we watch each other, Reese's right hand reaches out to the panel next to her, finding the emergency stop button on the wall.

Holy shit. *Press it. Press that button.*

She does.

The elevator jolts to a stop just a few floors below the penthouse level.

There's a moment that we stand off and I can hardly get my breathing under control. It's erratic. Frenzied. A physical manifestation of how I feel right now.

Her cherry-red lips open, and all I can think about is how fucking badly I want to smear that color all over her mouth.

"Well, what are you waiting for, Em?"

Is she trying to kill me, letting that little nickname slip off her tongue?

It used to bother me that she wouldn't call me Monty, but this new name has me hoping I'll never have to hear her call me Monty when "Em" is an option.

I don't have it in me to rush this. Instead, I step into her space again, running the back of my hand softly against her cheek. Dragging the pad of my thumb over the red stain on her lips. Cradling her jaw before my palm drops down the column of her throat.

"What are you thinking about right now?" she asks softly.

I breathe a laugh, unsure I could form a coherent thought even if I tried.

But the one that comes to the top of mind is, "Finally."

All that frustration, all that pent-up sexual tension, all the weeks of bickering come to head and the metaphorical dam breaks.

With both hands, I take her face and finally press my lips against hers.

She melts against me instantly, this sweet sigh of relief slipping past her mouth.

She's soft everywhere. Soft lips. Soft body.

There's a moment that I linger there, mouth fused to hers but doing nothing more. A silent reminder that this is her last chance to keep things from going any further between us.

She doesn't stop me.

Instead, she wraps her hands around my forearms, pulling me in even closer.

That's when the energy truly changes.

The kiss turns feverish. Frantic. Fucking perfect.

My body covers hers, pressing her against the wall behind her and taking what I want from her mouth. She pushes against me, working to steal back some control, that constant back-and-forth between us evident even in the way we kiss.

She'll figure it out eventually—that's not how it's going to work between us here.

Lips parting, her tongue dusts against my lower lip in a way that sets my entire body ablaze. It's this soft slide, this tempting lick, and the groan that rumbles up my throat is possibly the most desperate sound that's ever escaped me.

Fuck it. Maybe she should be in charge.

But Reese only plays with me. She only tests and nips.

I need more.

So, I tilt her chin up and slip my tongue past her lips, letting it slide against her own. I tease her. I savor her. I torture her.

Reese leans in, but I slightly pull back, taking control of the tempo between us.

She squeaks out this mixed sound of both torment and pleasure that goes straight to my cock. My already half-hard cock that's currently pressed against her lower stomach.

"You might be my boss out there," I remind her. "But here, when we're like this, I'll be the one in charge."

She practically purrs under the instruction.

"You like the idea of that?"

"Yes," she hisses, pushing her hips out. "And apparently you do too."

I don't have a shy bone in my body right now, so with my mouth on hers, I press into her, letting her feel exactly what she's doing to me.

"God, you feel good, Em." Her lips dust against mine as she rocks her body in rhythm with my own.

"Call me that again."

She smiles this mischievous grin against me. "No."

Well, so much for being in charge.

"You're not very nice to me."

Her smile only grows, so proud of herself.

"Fine." I let my hands drift down her body, touching every dip and curve that I normally don't have the pleasure of getting my hands on. "I can think of a few ways to make you scream it instead."

When I meet her thighs, I curve my palms around the back of them, cupping her ass and lifting her in the air. She gasps in surprise as if she's never been picked up before, but it doesn't take long for her to figure it out. She crosses her arms behind my neck. She wraps her legs around my waist, exactly where I've needed them to be.

With her at eye level, I really take her in. She's so incredibly beautiful that it kind of hurts to look at her. Like this overwhelming awareness that I'm batting so far out of my league here and trying my best not to point it out.

Soft blonde hair, gold lineup of earrings, red lips that are already smeared outside the edge.

She drops her forehead to mine, running her hand through my beard, her fingertips scratching the skin there. "Why are you looking at me like that?" she asks.

"I don't know how to look at you in any other way. I've tried."

"I can't get you out of my head," she admits, and goddamn, it feels good to hear her voice exactly how I've been feeling.

"That makes two of us." I lift a hand, pushing a strand of hair behind her ear that can't seem to stay out of her stunning face. "Where were you this week?"

The question doesn't cause her to pull away, but she doesn't answer me either. Instead, she shakes her head before stealing any protest I might have right off my lips with another kiss.

Her mouth moves over mine as I push her back against the wall, her legs open wide and her dress bunched around her hips as I rub the rigid seam of my jeans against her. Holding on to her ass, I do it again and again. Over and over as she whimpers against me.

I'm so hard and she feels so good. It's been so goddamn long that I, a fully-grown man, might just come in my pants tonight.

I don't remember ever feeling this desperate for someone. Ever wanting someone like this. Ever needing someone in this way. Yeah, sure, maybe you could chalk it up to the whole forbidden boss thing, but in my gut, I know it's more than that.

I couldn't tell you the last time this part of me came to life. I've been focused on being a dad. Focused on being a coach and a mentor. Spent so many years trying to be everything else for every*one* else, but right now . . . right now I like being a bit selfish. I like taking something that I want only for me.

I focus on the way Reese's fingers tighten in my shirt as she fists the fabric. On the way her body trembles. On the way my hands are full in the best way possible.

Reese's legs tighten around my hips. "Right there."

I roll into her again, moving my lips across her jaw, biting and licking and soothing my way down the column of her pretty throat. Her perfume invades my nostrils as I work my mouth over the delicate skin of her neck and I'm fucking feral for it.

For her.

She has no idea how long I've wanted her, even if it was just a physical need at first. She has no idea how positive I was that she couldn't want me back. I'm a fairly confident guy, but having this stunning and successful woman wrapped around me has me *soaring*.

I drag my mouth over her collarbone, my fingers curling over the little red strap to pull it off the slope of her shoulder. The pounding of her heart thunders against my lips as I dip lower, needing to take her in my mouth.

With her dress hanging partway off, I run the pads of my fingers over the neckline, finding the ridge of her strapless bra. I'm half a second away from yanking it down, so close to having my lips wrapped around her, when the fucking intercom blares into the tiny box, stopping us in our tracks.

"Ms. Remington," someone says over the emergency speaker. "Are you okay in there?"

Hands cradling either side of my neck, she closes her eyes before dropping her forehead to mine.

Puffy lips, pink cheeks, hair mussed from the wall behind her, and a pretty dress halfway slipped down her arm.

A little disheveled for the polished princess I'm accustomed to seeing, but not as wrecked as I'd like to make her.

"Yes," she says on a desperate exhale, doing a terrible job of hiding what the hell we were doing in here. "Sorry about that. I must have accidentally pressed the stop button."

"Of course." There's this knowing edge to his voice. "I'm going to restart it on my end, and it may take a minute or two before it gets going again. Just expect a bit of a jolt when it restarts."

"Yeah," she huffs, still doing her best to catch her breath. "Thank you."

The line beeps, telling us it's disconnected.

I can't help but chuckle. "He's going to think we fucked in here."

"We probably would've if he didn't stop us."

She gently uses the pad of her thumb to clean up the red off my lips.

My eyes search hers. "Are you okay?"

She nods, offering me a small smile.

I carefully pull her strap back over her shoulder, covering her up again before I get her back on her feet. I let her fix her dress, pulling it down her hips before I take a step back to where I can see her properly.

I run my fingers through her short hair, my calloused thumb rough against her soft skin as I swipe against her cheek. "I want to do that again."

She closes her eyes for a moment, and I can almost see the regret take over. "Emmett."

I shake my head, refusing to believe this is about to go the way I think it is. "Please don't."

"Emmett," she says again, stepping into me and looking up, making sure my attention is locked on her. "You should know that someone saw me leave your hotel room when we were in San Diego."

The blood instantly drains from my face. "What?"

"It got posted online somewhere. Nothing official, just a rumor, but—"

"Fuck," I exhale. "*Fuck*, Reese."

All her new rules, all her new boundaries. They all make perfect sense now. How terrifying that must have been for her to know we got caught. I mean, what happened that night wasn't necessarily inappropriate, but I'm sure whoever saw her the next morning thought it sure as hell looked that way.

And here I am, showing up like a fucking caveman to pick her up from a date because I can't handle the thought of her being with someone else.

"That's my fault," I tell her. "I'm so sorry."

"I chose to be there too."

The elevator jolts, restarting, and like an instinct, I reach out to steady her.

And even that feels like it's crossing a line now, let alone what just happened between us.

Her blue eyes look up at me with this begging, pleading expression. "Emmett, we have to stay away from each other."

I hate the words though I know she's right.

It's too dangerous for her. There are too many eyes on her. There are too many naysayers thinking she can't do her job.

If anyone found out she was making out with her employee in an elevator...

"I know," I agree, hating the way the words taste coming off my tongue. "I know. You're right. We do."

She offers me a thankful yet pitying smile.

"But not like this last week. Please don't avoid me again like you did last week."

The elevator stops on the top floor, opening right into Reese's condo, but I can't bring myself to pay attention to her place. I'm too busy watching this woman, trying to read her.

"Promise me, Reese."

"I won't, but we have to keep things professional. This—" She circles the area around us. "This can't happen again."

"Yeah," I breathe out. "I know." The agreement sounds fucking depressing as it slips off my lips.

And I'm not just saying that to agree with her in this moment. I fully understand nothing can happen between us again. It's too risky now that even one rumor is circulating out there about her.

What the hell was I thinking? I'm putting her career and reputation at risk. Something I promised her I'd protect.

Reese steps off the elevator and into her condo, turning back to look at me. "Thank you for walking me home."

I nod, trying to find a smile for her. "Thanks for letting me steal you away from your date."

She huffs a laugh, offering me a small smile in return, but it's a sad one.

Then we watch each other as the elevator doors close, knowing it's the last time we'll get to look at each other in this way.

19
REESE

"Is there anything else that you or your department needs?" I ask Kennedy.

Sitting in the chair on the other side of my desk, she scans the notebook in her hand, bulleted with all the points we discussed over the last hour of this meeting. "Not that I can think of at the moment."

"Your staff is being respectful of your position? Has everything been okay with the transition?"

"They are and yes, it's been smooth. I think taking over as lead doctor in the final few months of last season helped with taking over the role officially this year."

"And the players. Are they being good to you and your team?"

She hesitates for a long moment. "Most of them, yes."

Kennedy doesn't have to explain. I'm Harrison's direct superior and he can't even find it in him to respect me. I'm sure she's been on the receiving end of his patronizing comments a time or two.

"I'm taking care of that," I attempt to reassure her without being too descriptive of my plan.

She nods in agreement.

"And Natalie, is she doing okay in her new role?" I ask, referring to the new athletic trainer Kennedy hired to replace her former position. "Is there anything I can do for her?"

Kennedy gains this proud smile on her lips. "She's doing well. She's a hard worker. Smart. Driven. And the boys are officially giving her shit in the training room when they come in for treatment, which means they like her."

"She sounds a lot like you."

"Well, I think we both know it takes a certain personality and . . . *backbone* to be a woman in this industry."

"That it does." There's a hint of exhaustion in my tone.

She cocks her head to the side, studying me. "And how are you doing?"

"I thought I was heading up this meeting, Dr. Rhodes? I'm supposed to be the one checking in on you."

"Yes, but if you're in charge of everyone else, then who are you supposed to vent to? Just because you're the boss, doesn't mean you can't bitch every once in a while. So let's hear it."

Sitting back in the chair, she wears this cheeky, knowing smile that reminds me far too much of the one I always see on her husband.

She has a point. They don't say "it's lonely at the top" for nothing, but that's what I signed up for with this career. You get a lot of criticism simply from being a team owner, but then you add in my being the first woman in the role. Even more so, you add in that I'm running the baseball operations of this franchise too, and it's just been a lot of hate. Or at least, that's what it feels like.

The hateful ones are always the loudest.

But Kennedy is still my employee, and as much as I believe she'll understand having to deal with some of these same sentiments herself, it's still my responsibility to shoulder. I don't want the criticism I receive to affect anyone working under me.

"It's been . . ." I search for my words carefully. "Loud."

Loud headlines. Loud naysayers. Loud doubts that come creeping into my own mind sometimes.

"I get that. I see the headlines online. Try your best not to listen to them. The only people who truly know how this club is operating and how well you're doing are the ones who work for you."

She hasn't been in the advisory board meetings to know that not everyone who works for me thinks I'm doing all that great.

"Thanks, Kennedy. I appreciate that."

"Well, thank you for the meeting." She stands from her seat. "It's nice to have these monthly catch-ups."

"Of course. But if anything comes up before the next one, you know where to find me."

"Thanks, Reese. Will I see you at the team potluck next weekend?"

"No," I quickly answer. "I'll let the players have their fun."

"I'm not a player and I'm going. My entire staff is going. You should come. It's always a good time and a nice way to get to know people outside of the office."

I offer her a thankful smile. "It's a little different for me."

As in, no one wants their boss, the person who signs your paycheck, the person who determines the fate of your career, around when you're just trying to have a good time with your friends.

"Well, if you change your mind, you know where we'll be," she says on the way out of my office, passing the still-empty receptionist desk. "Have a good day, Reese."

I haven't made too many public moves yet, mostly just been working on cleaning up things on the back end. But promoting Kennedy Rhodes to lead doctor last season was my first big decision, and I'm happy to say I haven't second-guessed that choice once.

I can only hope to make future decisions with as much confidence as I did that one.

Speaking of decisions I need to make, I have a couple of receptionist interviews lined up for this afternoon. Grabbing my bag, I loop it over my shoulder and leave my office for a conference room on the second floor that will feel less intimidating than interviewing in my office.

It's a quiet day around the offices, so I don't see too many people on the way to the elevator, and it opens on my floor immediately after I press the button for it.

As soon as I step inside, I'm instantly hit with a flashback of last Saturday night.

My back against the wall.

Legs wrapped around Emmett's waist.

His lips on mine, trailing down my neck, over my collarbone. How close he was to pulling down my bra and wrapping his mouth around—

"Can you hold that for me?"

Oh God. I'd know that voice anywhere.

I hold a hand out to keep the doors from closing, giving my grandfather time to come around the corner.

I love the man, but unfortunately, he's the very last person on Earth I'd like to see right now, while I'm busy replaying every second of what I did with my employee last weekend.

"Oh, there's my girl," he says brightly, taking his time getting into the elevator next to me.

Gathering myself, I pop a kiss on his cheek as the doors close with only us inside. He pushes the button for the floor directly below us while I choose the second level, right above the clubhouse.

"Are you feeling okay?" he asks, the back of his hand meeting my forehead. "You're awfully flushed right now, honey. A bit warm."

If he only knew.

"I'm fine," I lie. "Just a warm day out."

"Don't worry. I'm not here to check up on you. I was just saying hi to some old friends in the ticketing office. Thought I'd make my rounds and see who else was here today."

My grandfather, like me, loves this place. This was his life for more than four decades. He spent as much time here as I do now. I can't imagine how strange the transition has been for him, regardless that he was ready to call it quits.

So, I'm never surprised when I find him lingering in the halls every other week or so.

"You know you're welcome here any time," I tell him. "If you ever want to come sit in my office while I'm working or if you need me to make up an excuse for why I need you at the field, so Grandma doesn't give you a hard time, you just let me know."

He chuckles. "That's why you're my favorite."

The doors open on the floor he needs and the one person I both long to see and also need to avoid is standing on the other side, waiting for the elevator.

Emmett's eyes are downcast on his phone as the doors slowly open, but he finally looks up once they're fully ajar.

There's the smallest hint of surprise on his face when he meets my eye, but that look slowly morphs into this sweet smile that sets every inch of me on fire.

I find myself giving him a mirror grin in return.

We've barely seen each other since that kiss. Not entirely intentional, just being busy with our work. And the times we have seen each other have been across a crowded room or in a congested dugout. Which is purposeful. We're both doing our part to stay away as best we can. To keep a healthy distance.

"Hi," he breathes out, eyes locked on me.

That warm fever my grandfather was so worried about? Yeah, it's back.

I open my mouth to say something, but my grandfather beats me to it.

"Monty!" he bursts, taking a step to get off the elevator. "So good to see you. How have you been?"

Emmett tries to bite back his laughter as he looks at me, both of us clearly having something else on our minds.

"Hey, Arthur. I'm good. How are you?"

"I'm great. Enjoying retirement."

"So that's why you're at the field today?" he teases. "Enjoying your retirement?"

"What can I say? This place is like a drug."

Emmett uses his arm out to keep the elevator doors open, allowing for my grandfather to take his time getting off. "That it is, Arthur. Have fun today."

My grandfather's smile is boyish and excited because he gets to make the rounds and see some of the people he misses from his daily life.

"Love you, Reese's Pieces!" he calls out over his shoulder.

Emmett steps into the elevator next to me, but doesn't select a floor, clearly going to the same level as me. The doors close and an instant wave of déjà vu crashes over me again, even stronger this time now that the man at the center of those memories is standing next to me.

Alone.

For the first time since we kissed.

Through the reflection in the metal doors, I see the way my body involuntarily leans in his direction. Like a flower finding the sun. But it's not one-sided. Emmett is doing the same, his arm brushing mine, his fingers skating the backs of my own.

The silence is suffocating. The knowledge of where we are now and where we were the last time we were alone sits heavy in the air between us.

"Well, so much for staying away from one another," I say, trying my best to break the tension.

It doesn't work, so Emmett gives it a shot.

"This uh . . ." He looks around. "This looks awfully familiar."

I huff a laugh and through the reflection, I see the smile he's wearing as he looks down at me. His fingers find the spaces between mine, dangling there but nothing more, and something about that small point of contact takes the edge off.

"So, Reese's Pieces, huh?" His tone is all tease.

"No. Don't even think about it."

"Ironic nickname, if you ask me. Named after a candy when there's nothing really all that sweet about you."

I try to bite back my grin. "Thank you. That's the way I like me."

Looking up, I find him watching me, his voice all soft. "That's the way I like you too."

I'd really like to kiss him again right now.

The string keeping us apart is pulled too tight, tempting to snap at any moment, but thankfully, that tension is relieved when the doors open on the second floor.

Taking a deep breath, I inhale some of the new air that wasn't stuck with us in this elevator, that hasn't been laced with not-so-innocent touches and soft-spoken words.

Emmett's fingers leave mine, his palm finding the small of my back, and even that touch, which is seemingly normal and appropriate, feels anything but. It pricks my skin with acute awareness, sensing the pad of every one of those five fingers pressing into me.

His other hand gestures for me to exit first. "After you."

Swallowing, I gather myself and take a step forward, needing to get to these interviews and just hoping like hell I don't come off as flustered as I feel right now.

"Where are you headed?" he asks, stepping off the elevator with me.

We both stop just on the other side of the doors before we'll separate for our destinations.

"I have interviews. I'm finally going to hire a receptionist."

He hums this disappointed sound.

"What?"

"I'm going to miss being able to barge in there any time I want, is all."

"Even more of a reason to hire someone as soon as possible."

He smiles.

I smile at his smile.

We're both just really fucking smiley today, aren't we?

We linger there, him rocking back on his heels, me shifting my weight from foot to foot. Having absolutely no reason to continue this conversation but also not wanting it to end.

I throw a thumb in the direction of the conference room. "So, I should—"

"Are you coming to the team potluck next weekend?"

"I'm not," I quickly answer for the second time today. "That's a team thing."

"Exactly."

"I'm not sure the guys would want the person who holds their careers in her hands to attend their team-bonding event. Can't imagine that'd be very relaxing for them."

"They would want you there. They do. You're a part of this team, Reese, and it would be good for you to start seeing that."

I notice the way he says it would be good for *me*, not them. Because I'm the one who needs convincing.

I'm tempted to give him a quick and sure no. The way I did when speaking to Kennedy about this same subject. But something about Emmett asking me to join is tempting me to do so.

It'd be much simpler for me to keep some boundaries in place when it comes to the guys on the team. To try my best to view these players as pieces of a puzzle and not people. Because that's what I should do. Remain detached. Keep things strictly on a business level.

And naturally, I'm not good at that at all. Instinctually, I probably care too much.

But then I think about all the teams I grew up around as a little girl and how much fun I had with them. How so many of my best childhood memories are from simple events just like this one.

"I . . ." I hesitate. "I don't know what I would bring."

Not a no. Not a yes.

Emmett's lips tick up in a small smile. "Anything. I'm a terrible cook so I'm making Miller bring a second dish for me. Buy something premade at the store. Show up empty-handed. It doesn't matter. Just show up."

Just show up. I could maybe do that.

"I'll think about it."

"That's all I'm asking for." He nods in the direction of the conference room. "Good luck with those interviews. Make sure you hire someone that won't make me wait forever when I want to meet with you."

Emmett turns back to the elevator, pressing the button for it to come pick him up.

My brows furrow in confusion. "You didn't need to get off on this floor?"

"No. I'm headed down to the clubhouse."

The elevator doors open and he steps inside.

"Then why did you get off here?" I laugh.

"I haven't seen you in a few days. I figured it was a good way to steal a couple extra minutes of your time." The doors begin to close on him, but I watch the way his eyes trail down my body. "You look good today, boss."

20

EMMETT

Isaiah and Kennedy's backyard is packed with all the players from the team, everyone from the Health and Wellness Department, the team photographers, equipment managers, and social media staff.

Essentially, it's every person from the franchise who is involved in each game we play, both home and away.

All but one.

The Rhodes' new house is stunning, and their sprawling backyard is just as impressive. There are plenty of tables and extra chairs for sitting, and lawn games are scattered across the grass. The weather is perfect, as is their view of the nearby lake.

I've been over a few times since they moved in early spring, but it's fun to see them host their first gathering. They may have been an unlikely pair in the beginning, but they're good for each other and I'm proud of the life they've built for themselves here.

"Can I get you another?" Kai asks, holding up his empty beer bottle.

I check the one I'm currently nursing. "I'm good. I'll wait until we eat."

"What did you bring?"

Shrugging, I bring the bottle to my lips. "I don't know. Whatever Miller made for me."

Kai chuckles. "Well then apparently you contributed a watermelon and feta salad, and I brought a corn and tomato dish I can't pronounce."

"How innovative of us."

Kai looks around the busy backyard. "Reese isn't coming?"

I down the rest of my beer. "Apparently not. I invited her last week, but that was also the last time I was alone with her to ask."

I've seen Reese every day at the field, in that polished pencil skirt with her sleek blonde hair, fully in boss mode and focused solely on her job. We've hardly been alone since that kiss. It's this torturous game of being in the same room with her but not being *with* her in the slightest.

Then there's the reminder that this isn't a game at all. This is her reputation at stake, and that's enough to reinforce my resolve of keeping my distance.

At least that's what I tell myself until the side gate to the backyard opens, and all that willpower I've been trying to muster since leaving Reese's condo threatens to crumble at my feet.

Reese steps into the yard, serving dishes in her hands with that perfect pink manicure wrapped around them in a white-knuckled grip.

I've seen Reese outside of work enough times now that I shouldn't be shocked when she's not wearing her business attire, yet still, she somehow takes me by surprise.

She's traded her usual pencil skirt for a pair of well-fitted jeans and light-yellow cardigan, unbuttoned at the top. Casual but still completely put together. She swapped her stilettos for a pair of Chucks and added a bend to her sharply cut hair, which is tucked behind one ear, showcasing those earrings my attention tends to snag on.

She looks fucking adorable, and I think she might cut my dick off if she ever heard me call her that.

The buzzing chatter of the backyard around me silences, and at first, I think it's one of those cliché movie moments where the guy locks eyes with the woman he's gone for and everything else around disappears to nothing.

And while, yeah, I've got my attention locked on Reese, the sounds around me didn't falsely fade out. The backyard conversations and laughter truly did die down because everyone is looking in her direction too.

Reese glances up to find just about everyone staring at her and the panicked expression on her face cracks my heart in two. Her hands are full, her blue eyes are wide, and I've never seen her less confident than she seems right now.

I want to rush over to her, wrap her in a hug, thank her for coming, and tell everyone to be fucking normal about the team owner showing up to join us.

But I can't because every person watching works for her. And that kills me.

I take Kai's empty beer. "Go help her."

The words are barely out of my mouth before he's already taken off in her direction.

God, she looks so freaked out right now and I feel terrible. And helpless. I feel really fucking helpless. As someone who prides themselves on taking care of my people, just standing here doing nothing is torture.

I know people are staring in her direction simply because they're surprised to see her outside of work, but if they can just go back to whatever the hell they were doing before she walked in, that'd be great.

Isaiah is the one to break the awkward silence, *thank God*.

"Welcome!" he says, loud enough for everyone to hear. Which isn't all that loud because, again, everyone is just silently watching her.

He meets her at the back gate the same time his brother does.

Kai takes the dishes from her—three, to be exact—and Isaiah points her in the direction of the drinks, the bathroom, and where the food will be served.

The backyard is still way too quiet and I'm about two seconds away from grumpily growling something that will definitely out the fact that I'm more than a little smitten by this woman. But thankfully, Isaiah beats me to it.

"Okay, everyone. You all see her literally every day. Stop being weird and go back to whatever you were doing."

There's a nearby speaker system that hasn't been used yet today because it's been so loud back here, but Isaiah turns it up and the music is enough to ease the uncomfortable void.

I know I didn't raise those boys or anything, but there's still a swell of pride for them handling the situation how I hoped to handle it myself.

The people around me slowly get back to their previous conversations, and I give myself to the count of ten until I'll allow myself to go see her. By then, enough people will have found something else to focus on rather than the team owner.

One.

Two.

By the time I get to three, Miller steps out of the backdoor slider and spots Reese slowly and unsurely migrating to join the party. And my daughter, my beautiful, sarcastic, doesn't-give-a-shit-about-making-anyone-uncomfortable daughter beelines right for my boss and wraps her in a hug.

Reese is stiff as a board, and I can't help but laugh from my spot across the yard.

But that's Miller for you. She has no boundaries in the same way she has no filter. You feel uncomfortable and unwelcome? Well, she's going to hug the shit out of you until you realize you're wanted here. Either that or she'll make some inappropriate joke at your expense that'll break the ice real freaking quick.

Finally, I watch as Reese's stiff shoulders loosen, and she hugs my daughter in return.

I'm always proud of my girl, but I could not be more thankful she is who she is, that she doesn't have a shy bone in her body or give a shit that she just caught my boss off guard. Because I can already sense that Reese is a bit less guarded.

I don't know what number I'm supposed to be counting, but it's got to be past ten by now, so I toss the two empty bottles in a nearby recycling bin and take a step in her direction right as Isaiah places the last platter on the food table.

"Food is ready!" he announces loudly enough for everyone to hear.

An instant swarm of people head in that direction, but I'm just trying to get to Reese.

I veer through bodies, pushing my way through the crowd, trying to find her. Every once in a while, I catch a glimpse of blonde hair or a peek of that yellow sweater. But there's so many people here it feels as if I'm swimming upstream and unable to make any progress.

Until I do, and realize I've passed her, finding her in the middle of the line to get food along with everyone else.

Cutting into the line, I slip in right behind her.

"Um, Coach." Cody taps my shoulder. "You cut in front of me."

Reese's back is to me, not acknowledging that I'm standing directly behind her, but I see her body move in a silent laugh and know that she's aware I'm here.

I look over my shoulder at my first baseman. "I've got to be honest, Cody. I truly could not care less."

"Yeah, totally. Me neither. It's not like I've been waiting all day for this or anything."

Reese has this stunning smile on her face, trying to hold back her laughter when she turns back to Cody. "Do you want to go ahead of me?" she asks him. "I don't mind."

"Oh, no. That is so nice of you, Reese, but to be honest, I just really want to hold this over his head for a while. Thank you, though."

She turns back to walk forward with the line, and Cody looks at me, pumping his brows a couple of times like a fucking idiot.

Shut up, I silently mouth.

"I just love that you can read my mind, Coach. We're so connected."

I step forward in line, keeping myself only a few inches behind Reese, my chest real close to her back. But we're simply in line for food, so this is an innocent enough position if anyone were watching.

"So, what did you bring?" I ask quietly.

The corners of Reese's mouth turn up, keeping her focus ahead of her.

"I brought a loaded focaccia with prosciutto and arugula. But then I got worried that people might be vegetarian, so I also made a caprese salad. But then that has dairy, and some people are dairy-free, so I also made this cucumber and avocado dish, just in case."

"You brought three separate dishes?"

"I was nervous no one would like the one I brought. At least now I have better odds."

I do my best not to tease her, but my cheeks hurt from the splitting grin I'm trying to bite back. Business Barbie is fucking endearing, and she has no idea.

My fingers are itching to touch her, to place my hand on her hip and give her a squeeze. To wrap my arm around the front of her shoulders and reassure her that she's doing great.

But I can't. Because I work for this woman along with everyone else at this potluck.

Instead, I keep my voice low and my mouth close to her ear when I say, "I'm glad you're here."

She looks up at me over her shoulder, brows pinched. "Are you sure it's okay?"

"Without a question. You're a part of this team too."

The crease between her eyes softens, and *God*, she looks so fucking kissable glancing up at me like this. It'd only take me craning my neck to meet her lips with my own.

And I'm hit with the harsh reminder that I don't get to do that again.

We're nearing the start of the food tables, but the coolers of drinks are lined up right before, so that's the task I choose to distract myself with.

"What can I get you to drink?" I ask.

"What are you having?"

"I'll probably stick with a beer."

"Is there a seltzer?"

"Any specific flavor?"

"Whatever looks good."

I grab one that looks to be the most popular flavor since it's the last one left, then grab a Corona for myself. And that only makes me think of Miller, so I grab her one too. It's the least I could do for her being welcoming to my boss.

I hand Reese the cold can, lacing the necks of the two beer bottles between my fingers, and by the time I've got the cooler closed, we've made it to the front of the table.

Reese grabs a paper plate from the stack, but when she also tries to snag all the different disposable utensils, she fumbles a bit with her seltzer.

"I got you." I grab all the needed utensils for both of us, including a stack of napkins. Then I take her plate, exchanging it for the beers in my hand. "You just tell me what looks good when we pass it."

She gives me this look, as if silently telling me that my making her a plate for dinner looks a bit odd. A bit questionable. Possibly inappropriate. But I ignore it.

I situate a second plate in one hand, including the forks, knives, and napkins, using my free hand to serve us both food. Anytime we pass a dish that looks remotely like one that Reese described bringing, I ask for confirmation if it is. When she points out the three that are hers, I make sure to add a healthy serving of each on my plate.

Our plates are full by the time we reach the last table where the desserts are displayed.

"Oh shoot," she says.

"We can come back for this."

Reese lifts a brow in my direction.

"I mean *you* can come back for this. Alone. By yourself."

She laughs under her breath, slowly walking away from the table of sweets. And that pure look of disappointment that she doesn't have enough room on her plate for dessert is just another thing I like about the woman. "Okay."

Using one of the plastic forks, I push all the food on my plate together, mixing the flavors in a way they probably shouldn't be. But it buys me a bit of real estate along the edge. "Which one looks the best to you?"

Reese hums, stepping back to the table as she eyes each and every one carefully. "Maybe that one?"

"Good choice." I add a scoop of my daughter's blackberry cobbler to my plate for her. "Miller made this one. Well, I'm pretty sure she made most of these."

"Did she? I haven't gotten a chance to try one of her desserts before. I've heard the guys on the team raving whenever Kai brings her cookies to the field."

"She's incredible. You have to check out her patisserie."

"I'd love that."

"I'll take you sometime."

Reese opens her mouth to say something but doesn't. A heavy pause lingers, and it's then I realize my mistake.

"Or you could take yourself," I amend.

We get through the food tables and move out of the way for everyone waiting behind us.

"I want to go sit with Miller." I nod toward the direction of that picnic table. "I haven't caught up with her yet today."

"Sounds good." Reese holds out the two beer bottles in exchange for her plate of food. "You're a good dad, you know that?"

I should give her the plate. I should let her go sit wherever she wants. I should put a bit of distance between us to keep any rumors from starting up.

But she can't say things like that and expect me to leave her alone.

"Come sit with me."

Reese hesitates, her eyes discreetly bouncing to the people around us. "I don't know if that's such a good idea."

I start in that direction with her food, not giving her much of a choice other than to follow me.

"It'll be fine, Reese. You're going to sit on the bench next to me, not on my lap. I don't think anyone is going to have something to say about us sitting at the same table."

"Just keep it professional," she mutters under her breath, walking at my side.

"What do you think I'm going to do while we're eating dinner with my daughter and my pitching coach? Stick my tongue down your throat?"

She smacks me in the bicep with the back of her hand, and I catch the sly little grin on her lips.

"You're thinking about me sticking my tongue down your throat right now, aren't you?"

She gives me a single nod of her head. "Yep."

"Keep it professional, Reese."

"Don't tell me what to do."

We join Kai and Miller at a picnic table. I set Reese's plate in front of her, then her utensils, and she places the two beers next to me.

We take the bench opposite them, and thankfully Reese is too busy tucking her legs under the table that she doesn't catch my daughter grabbing my attention.

Miller lifts a single yet knowing brow. *Should I call her Mommy?* she silently mouths.

Fucking hell.

"Behave yourself," I quietly remind her.

"What?" Reese asks.

"Nothing," Miller and I quickly say at the same time.

Kai just laughs without a care in the world because for once he's not on the receiving end of Miller's asinine comments.

"I brought you a beer, but I'm starting to regret that decision." I push the Corona across the wooden table to her.

Miller hesitates, looking at the bottle, then to Kai.

"What?" I ask.

Kai gives the smallest nod of his head, a weirdly eager look on his face.

Miller wraps her hand around the beer, but instead of bringing it to her lips to take a sip, she pushes it back in my direction.

From next to me, Reese lets out this excited little gasp. The sound is fucking adorable and so unexpected coming from her, but I have no idea what she's figured out that I haven't.

"Can't drink that," Miller states.

My eyes bounce from her to Kai then back to her, both of them watching me expectantly.

"No way."

Miller huffs a laugh, her smile blooming, waiting for me to confirm I've figured this out on my own.

"Are you pregnant?"

She nods frantically.

My voice goes all soft. "Are you really?"

"Yeah."

"Oh my God." I stand from my seat as she does the same and I meet her, wrapping my arms over her shoulders and pulling her into a hug. "Holy hell. Congratulations, Millie."

My mind is all over the place. Is she feeling okay? Is she excited? Does she need anything from me?

Then it moves on to the same thought process that occurs anytime something big happens in Miller's life.

I wish Claire were here to see this.

I'm so thankful I get to be a part of Miller's important life moments, even though her mom can't.

And finally, I wish I had someone to share this with.

"I'm going to give you guys some privacy," Reese says from her seat at the table.

"Stay," Miller and I say at the same time, pulling back from our hug just long enough to watch Reese freeze halfway to standing.

I wait until she swings her legs back under the table, retaking her seat before I go back to hugging my daughter.

"I'm so happy for you."

"Thanks, Dad."

"You're feeling okay?"

She nods against me.

"Are you happy?"

"So happy."

"Good." I swallow hard. "That's all I want for you."

Her grip around my waist loosens so I pull back, hands on either side of her face. How this is still the same girl I used to play dress-up with or who hung out in the dugout during my practices, I have no idea.

Kai smacks me on the shoulder, so I move on to him, giving him a hug as well.

"Love you, Monty."

"Love you too. I'm so excited for you guys."

The girl I spent the last twenty years focused on raising is now raising her own family. That's both incredible and terrifying. Miller doesn't need me in the same way she once did, but that's the whole fucking point, right? I raised her to be her own person.

"Does Max know yet?" I ask, retaking my seat at the table.

Miller shakes her head. "We're going to tell him tonight."

"He's going to be stoked. I'm so happy for you three."

Miller leans her head on Kai's shoulder before he wraps an arm around her and places a kiss on the top of her head. And in that brief moment, I feel like an interloper intruding on a private moment. It's kind of a big deal the first time you tell your parent that you're also going to be a parent. And though Miller already is, becoming Max's mom didn't come with an announcement.

So yeah, I feel like an intruder, sitting across the table and watching my daughter share this important moment with her person.

But my attention is quickly stolen when, under the table, a hand smooths over my thigh, squeezing just above my knee.

Reese smiles brightly up at me, her blue eyes shining under the summer sun. Clearly, so excited for me and the news I just received.

And that's when I realize, for the first time in an awfully long time, I got to share an important moment with someone too.

21
REESE

"I had a really nice time today," I tell Kennedy, standing toward the edge of the open backyard. "Thank you for inviting me and for hosting."

The sun is beginning to set. The crowd has started to dissipate.

"I'm glad you came. I hope you felt welcomed by everyone."

"I did. You were right. It was a good opportunity to get to know people outside of work."

After I ate dinner with Emmett and his family, we separated from one another for the rest of the potluck. But I caught him watching me at one point while I was deep in conversation with some of the medical staff. I caught him looking again when I was laughing at some ridiculous story one of the players was telling me.

It was nice. It took a minute, but eventually it seemed as if they all forgot I was the boss, and instead treated me as if I were one of their own.

"I'll take the credit for you coming," Kennedy says with an edge of humor. "But I have a feeling I wasn't the one who got you here."

She discreetly tips her head to the side, and I follow to find Emmett making his way out to us. Hat pulled low over his eyes. Hands casually tucked in his denim pockets.

"Hey," he says, attention locked on me. "You doing okay?"

"Yeah. I'm great."

"I'm going to go help Isaiah clean up," Kennedy says, starting in the direction of the house.

"Can I do anything?" I offer.

"Nope. No. You two just enjoy . . . the party."

She departs, leaving Emmet and me alone at the edge of the yard. The setting sun casts this warm glow against his face, and I'm thankful no one is too close by to watch me admire him. I truly don't think he understands just how handsome he is.

"Walk with me?" he asks, nodding toward the walkway around the edge of the lake.

Hesitating, I scan the yard. A sunset stroll with him sounds equal parts lovely and like a terrible idea. But a substantial amount of the rest of the staff has gone home and, well . . . I want to spend time with him.

"Okay," I answer quietly.

We walk for a minute or two in silence, putting space between us and our coworkers, while also keeping distance between us. There must be at least four feet of walkway to separate us. Which is for the best. Whenever we're shoulder to shoulder these days, Emmett's fingers find their way to mine.

To ensure that doesn't happen, I cross my arms over my chest as well, really adding to the distance thing.

"It's beautiful out here," Emmett says, breaking the silence. "You don't get this in the city. Of course, we have the lake, but not this kind of quiet."

It really is stunning. The sun sparkles off the water and the trees line the walking path. Then you add this hot older guy at my side, and yeah. The view is a bit breathtaking.

"Would you ever want to get out of the city and move to the suburbs?" I ask.

He breathes a small laugh. "Not anytime soon. Maybe I'm doing it all backward, but I spent most of my twenties and all of my thirties in the suburbs. Well, it was more like the country, I suppose. In fact, there's a lake with a similar feel to this behind the house where I raised Miller in Colorado. But I guess now I'm making up for the parts I skipped by trying to be a bit selfish. Having the job I want. Living in the city I love."

Those last two sentences might not intentionally be directed at me, but we both know the future of where he works and lives rests solely on *my* shoulders.

"Would you ever . . ." I hesitate. "Live in a *different* city? Maybe work for a different team?"

I know it's a silly question as soon as it's out of my mouth. Of course, the answer is no, but the man kissed me stupid *one* time and now I'm over here imagining any plausible scenario where I wouldn't be his boss.

Which is also ridiculous for more than one reason. He already told me he didn't have it in him to move on from the woman he loved twenty years ago. I should really believe him.

Emmett eyes me, probably wondering what kind of ludicrous daydream I'm creating in my head, so I pull my focus away and instead watch the sun lower a little more.

"Never mi—"

"No," Emmett answers simply. "If you would've asked me that a few years ago, I probably would've had another answer for you, but things are different now. My daughter is here, settled down for the first time in her adult life. Max is here. The Rhodes boys are here. I wouldn't leave now."

Of course. Why did I even ask that?

"But I'll be just fine with whatever happens at the end of the season," he continues, and it's then I realize he thinks I'm asking because I've dangled his contract renewal over his head and not because I have a big, irresponsible crush on the guy. "If I couldn't work for the Warriors, I'd maybe move back down to the college level, but I'd stay local."

What?

Does he not realize what he just said?

My heart breaks a bit at his answer because I don't think he even sees it. It's so ingrained in him to just take care of everyone else.

"Isn't that exactly what you did when Miller was young? Gave up your career and started coaching college?"

He thinks it over for a moment before exhaling a small laugh. "Well, maybe I'm not so great at being selfish after all."

He's so good. So kind. So grumpy when he needs to be, and I just want to protect him and make sure he gets everything he wants out of life. Coaching for *this* team. Living in *this* city.

He and I will never be more than that one kiss, but at least I have the power to make sure the two things he wants out of life continue to happen for him. And in that sense, holding his future in my hands doesn't feel like a burden. It feels like a privilege.

"Especially now," Emmett says. "After that little announcement today, I'm not going anywhere."

I can't help but smile thinking about his reaction. How sweet he was with her, how excited he was for both of them.

I playfully nudge his shoulder with mine and that's when I realize the distance we were trying to keep between us has practically all been eaten up. But we're far enough down the walkway that I don't know if anyone back at the house could see us anyway.

"Did you know they were wanting a second?" I ask.

"Yeah, I knew they wanted Max to have a sibling close in age. They're getting married later this summer, but Miller isn't exactly the traditional type. Her being pregnant at her wedding is pretty on-brand for her."

The more I hear about her, the more I like her.

"Good for her. She knows what she wants and doesn't care what other people think."

"She is excellent at not giving a shit about what other people think." Emmett chuckles. "Not sure if that's an only child thing or just a Miller thing."

We continue to walk, but he closes even more distance between us, his arm rubbing my shoulder every few strides.

"Did you ever want more kids?" I ask.

Looking up, I find him smiling to himself.

"What?"

He shakes his head. "I like that you said, 'more kids' instead of 'your own.' You have no idea how many times people have asked me if I wanted to have kids of my own."

"What a strange perception of your relationship with your daughter. Have they not seen you two together?"

"That's always bugged me. Especially when it was said in front of her. But to answer your question, no. I never wanted to have more kids."

I nod in understanding, assuming that part of the conversation is done.

"Aren't you going to ask me why not?"

"You don't have to explain yourself to me," I say simply. "Whenever I tell people I don't see myself having kids they love to back that up with endless questions. So, unless you want to talk about it, you don't have to."

The smile on his face is soft as he watches me, walking at my side. "I've never talked to anyone about this, so maybe I do."

"Then please, explain yourself."

He breathes a small laugh. "I first want to say that I love being Miller's dad. Best thing I've done with my life."

"Emmett, that's obvious. You don't have to preface anything."

"But I kind of got thrown into the deep end then spent a solid thirteen years drowning, trying to figure out how the hell to be a parent. And on top of it, how to do it alone. It was exhausting and scary but also really fucking rewarding. And I am so beyond grateful that Claire chose me. But there's another side of me that's also looking forward to figuring out who I am outside of just being a parent. Miller has her own family now, and doesn't need me in the same way, and that's terrifying. But that's also really exciting. And I know I'm not making any sense right now."

"You are. You made a lot of sacrifices at a very young age that you were happy to make, but you're also allowed to be excited to live your life for yourself, Em."

"Yeah." He nods. "Yeah, I think that's exactly what it is."

"And just so you know, you did an excellent job on your first try. Thrown into the deep end or not."

His lips tilt on one side. "Thanks for saying that. She's absolutely unhinged half the time, but you can't win them all."

"That's what I like about her. Also . . ." I use my palms to cover my eyes. "Oh my God, I am so sorry for being there when she told you today. I was so out of place and that was such a special moment for you two, and—"

"No." Emmett stops walking and grabs my arm for me to do the same, pulling my hands away from my face. "No, I'm glad you were there. It was . . . *nice* getting to share it with someone. There were so many times when she was growing up I wished I had someone to celebrate with. It's been lonely in that regard, so today was really nice. It's really nice having someone to talk to about it all."

Good God. My heart physically aches at the sweet words. At the soft way he says them.

He's so deserving of literally anything he wants, and it's difficult to stop myself from basking in his warm attention.

How lucky am I to be the one he looks at? For *me* to be that person he wants to talk to.

His smile is a bit shy and, regardless of the distance we're supposed to keep, or the professional wall that should be rebuilt, I just want to hug the man.

So, I do.

Not paying attention to how far we are from the house or who may be watching, I kind of throw myself at him, reaching up and wrapping my arms around Emmett's neck to hug him.

For the first time ever, I realize.

He's frozen for a moment, clearly caught off guard, but eventually he pulls his hands from his pockets, wrapping one around my lower back, the other sliding into my hair.

"Thanks for choosing me to talk to," I say quietly.

He buries his face against the curve of my shoulder and holds me tighter. "I'm so glad you came today."

"I am too."

22

EMMETT

"And I'm sitting Travis tonight," I tell Reese as we go through tonight's lineup together, sitting on opposite sides of her desk.

"Is he okay?"

"Yeah, just the usual wear and tear. He took a hard bounce to the mask in yesterday's game and needs a night off to rest."

"But you're sure he's okay? Does he need anything?"

"He's a catcher. He's tough."

"Okay. But please let me know if he needs anything more than just a night off."

I lift a brow. "How business-minded of you."

"Yeah. Well, he's a piece of the business."

I hum. "Sure."

"Leave me alone," she says playfully, refocusing on her computer sitting on the left side of the desk.

She looks good there, the field and stadium working as a backdrop for her.

I've spent a lot of time in this office, meeting with her grandfather over the years. But Arthur never looked that good sitting there. The energy in this office was vastly different. Before this season, I never dreamed of sweeping an arm over this desk to clear it off because I think the team owner would look fucking lovely spread across it.

I also never looked forward to my pregame meetings with Arthur the way I look forward to those same meetings this year. In fact, they've become one of my two favorite parts of game days. The other being the dugout visit from Reese that happens before the first pitch.

Pale pink nails type away at the keyboard as she chews on that bottom lip, slipping it between her teeth in concentration as she works.

I've come to find out I thoroughly enjoy watching this woman work.

I like how focused she is. I like how smart she is. I like that she loves this team and these players as much as I do, even if she has a hard time admitting that she sees this franchise as more than just a business.

With all her attention locked on the screen, all my attention is locked on her.

Then I remember I'm not allowed to look at her the way I am now. I'm not even allowed to close her office door during these meetings in fear someone might get the wrong impression of us being alone.

Reese reads something on the screen and exhales—the sound part relief, part centering breath. "Well, it looks like this trade will be official by morning."

Whoa. I've been waiting to hear her tell me that for weeks now.

I sit up straighter in my chair. "Yeah?"

She scans the email again. "Obviously nothing is official until the paperwork is signed, but it looks solid."

I study her for a moment. "Are you nervous?"

Reese allows herself to be honest with me when she nods to tell me yes.

I bask in her vulnerability. Though Reese is always sincere and straightforward when it comes to business, she's not always open regarding how those business decisions make her feel. She has to put on a professional and unbothered mask in front of the press, and there's no way she'd ever tell reporters she's scared about the backlash from her first major move as president of the team.

But she's telling me.

"You'll be okay," I reassure her. "I'll back you up with the media. The boys aren't going to be upset in the slightest, so you don't have to worry about them. And you're doing what's best for your team, so just remember that."

"Yeah." She offers me a small smile. "You're right. Thank you for that."

"When will you tell him?"

"As soon as the paperwork comes through. It's going to be my first time telling someone they're no longer on the team." She drops her head into her hands, rubbing circles along her temples.

"You have no reason to be nervous about that conversation. However you decide to tell him, he deserves it."

"He's still one of your players, Emmett. Wouldn't you prefer I be gentle?"

I sit back in my chair, arms folded over my middle. "There's rarely a time I prefer you gentle, Reese. In fact, I prefer most things a little rough."

She quickly picks up on the innuendo in my tone. "Don't flirt with me, Montgomery. We're at work and I'm your boss."

I huff a laugh. "How could I ever forget?"

Refocusing on Reese's desk in front of me, I add our backup catcher's name and number onto the lineup card where I typically place Travis.

I continue to fill the lineup with the guys who are playing tonight when, on my very last name, a set of well-manicured pink nails lands on the back of my hand, contrasting the black ink they're tracing.

I freeze with the pencil in my grip, watching the way Reese's fingers languidly follow the outline of my tattoos.

"Your daughter's sleeve matches these flowers."

It feels like all the oxygen has left my lungs by her not only touching me but doing so while at work. But I somehow find enough air to say, "I had them first. Miller copied me."

Reese chuckles, fingers still drawing soft lines over my tattooed hand. "I don't blame her. They're awfully pretty."

"Thank you."

She eyes them, head cocking to the side. "They'd make a beautiful necklace, don't you think?"

My eyes shoot to hers, finding a mischievous little grin on her lips after delivering an inappropriate line of her own.

My boss just told me she thinks my hand would look pretty around her throat, and I couldn't agree more.

"Don't put ideas in my head," I warn. "And don't flirt with me, Remington. We're at work and I'm your employee."

"Just reminding you that two can play that game," she says, a self-satisfied smile on her face as she pulls her hand away.

But I catch it before she can place it back on the keyboard, letting a couple of my fingers fall into the spaces between hers, my thick knuckles alternating with her narrow ones.

"Are you sure you're going to be okay tomorrow?"

Her expression goes soft, and I love seeing her soft with me. "I'll be all right."

"Call me if you need me."

"You know I can't do that, Emmett."

"Call me anyway."

She takes a deep inhale, slowly releasing the exhale. "The press is going to ask you all sorts of questions about Harrison's trade. You'll probably have your hands full tomorrow."

"I don't mind. After that little elevator ride, I think we both know by now I like having my hands full."

Her mouth pops open, eyes shining with mischief. "Okay. We really have to stop."

"But I *really* don't want to."

Before she can try to tell me to keep things professional or throw out a line of her own, a knock raps on the doorway behind me.

Her playful expression swiftly morphs to panic, and I feel it mirrored on my own face when I realize our hands are still slightly intertwined on the desk between us. Whoever it is, they're standing directly behind me, and I'm just praying that my back is fully covering anything they might see.

"So, yeah. The lineup looks good to me," Reese says, tapping the paper under our hands.

"Great." I lift the lineup card, making a too obvious show of it in hopes of proving that we were focusing on it and not each other.

Reese's eyes slowly move to the doorway over my shoulder. "Scott," she says. "What can I do for you?"

Fucking hell. Of all people.

"So much for that new receptionist," I mutter under my breath.

She ignores me.

"Can I have a word with you?" Scott asks. "In private."

"Of course." Reese shifts her attention to me, a professional, stoic expression back on her face. "Thank you for meeting. Best of luck tonight, Emmett."

Message received.

I need to go, but the last thing I want is to leave her alone with Scott. Not that I have a choice. Whatever that conversation entails, it's most likely far above my pay grade.

Standing, I slip the lineup card back into the folder I brought with me and push the chair in. "Scott," I say, passing him on my way out the door.

"Monty."

Just past the threshold, I turn back to check on her, but before I can make eye contact, Scott closes the door on me.

Because he can.

Because he can be alone with her.

Because no one is talking about Reese sneaking out of *Scott's* hotel room.

What the hell am I doing?

That was far too close a call.

I swear that woman turns me reckless every time she's in my vicinity. And to have Scott, out of everyone, almost catch . . . whatever that was. The guy is gunning for her job and I'm risking everything simply because I want to flirt with her for a few minutes and hold her hand across her desk.

I have to stop. We both know that nothing can come from this, and I told her I'd stay away. As much as I hate the idea, I need to be better about keeping that promise.

I'm disappointed in my own lack of restraint as I head down the hall for the elevators, needing to get to the clubhouse. The offices are empty today with it being a Sunday, so I'm surprised to find that when the elevator doors open, someone is inside and gets off on this floor.

But it's not just anyone. It's the same guy Reese went on a date with a couple of weeks ago.

"Hey, it's Monty, right?" he asks, a smile on his face when he spots me, like he's absolutely thrilled to see me here.

I'll tell you right now, the feeling is not reciprocated.

I want to remind him that we're not friends, so he doesn't need to call me by a comfortable nickname. But then again, I've also grown attached to only one specific person calling me by my first name.

"Yeah," I say, studying him. "Remind me of your name again?"

"Michael." He holds his hand out to introduce himself.

I shake it, but it's done so hesitantly, trying to figure out what he's doing here at the stadium, and even more so, why he got off the elevator on Reese's floor.

She didn't seem all that interested after their date, right? Or did I read that entirely wrong?

"Nice to meet you," I lie. "Are you lost?"

"Nope. I'm here for the game tonight."

I nod slowly. "Well, the box office is out front. You can get your tickets there."

He laughs, assuming I'm just giving him a hard time.

I'm not. He can go now.

"I'm here as Reese's guest. She invited me to watch the game from the owner's box tonight."

What the hell?

"Did she now?" I ask, the tension in my jaw obvious as I speak. "How . . . generous of her."

"Totally. It should be a good time." He smacks my shoulder like I'm his fucking pal. "Well, I'll see ya. She told me to meet her in her office, so I'm just gonna . . ."

He steps around me, and that's when I realize my stance. I'm taking up the majority of the hallway, legs spread and shoulders wide, as if I could stop him from getting to her simply by standing in the way.

But the reality is, I can't do anything.

I can't stop him.

I can't be more than her employee.

I can't stake some sort of claim over a woman who I can never be with.

I can't even be seen with her in public the way he can.

"Good luck, Monty," he calls out, and I'd like to respond by telling him to get fucked. But the dude seems like a genuinely nice guy.

Unfortunately.

How lucky is he that he gets to be here with her.

How lucky is he that he gets to be *seen* with her.

I don't know if I've ever been more envious of another person in my entire life.

23

REESE

"Drinks are in here," I tell Michael, showing him the mini fridge in my suite. "But if there's anything you want that you're not seeing, we can get it for you."

"This is amazing. The view is . . ." He shakes his head in disbelief. "Thank you for hosting us."

"I'm happy to." I gesture to Ed. "Your dad has watched quite a few games from up here with my grandfather, so he can show you anything I may have missed."

Michael slowly migrates through the suite, checking out the television screens and the spread of food as Ed stays by my side.

Since Michael moved back to Chicago last month, Ed has practically been floating on cloud nine, having his son home again. And after Michael mentioned that his dad had been wanting to get him to a game, I figured why not let them enjoy their day together from my suite.

I'll probably watch the game from my office or see if I can get away with doing a couple of incognito laps around the stadium, but I'll leave the suite to just the two of them.

"Thanks so much, Reese," Ed says to me quietly. "I can't think of a better way to spend the day with my son."

"Of course. You're both welcome anytime. After all the years you've worked with my grandfather and now me, it's the least I can do."

He nudges his shoulder into mine. "Michael mentioned that you two went to dinner a couple of weeks ago."

I offer him a placating smile. "We did. It was nice, but I think we'll be better off as friends."

Ed chuckles. "Yeah, that's what he said too, but a father can dream."

"Well, I hope you two have fun together today."

"We will." Ed takes off to join his son. "Thank you again."

Before I go, I check the view, watching the seats slowly fill with fans. The sun has begun its descent, the stadium lights have just kicked on, and I couldn't ask for a more perfect Sunday night for baseball.

I adore these kinds of early summer nights. The weather is starting to warm up, but the humidity is still low. Though there are still plenty of rainy days, they just make these dry ones all the more special.

I want to get out there. To feel the buzz of the fans, to experience that pregame energy in the dugout. To get a quick moment alone with the field manager before the first pitch is thrown out.

Letting my eyes drift down to the dugout, I find Emmett in his usual spot, leaning his elbows on the railing that acts as a barrier from the field. He's alone, and it just makes me that much more eager to get down there for my new favorite pregame ritual.

I say a quick goodbye to Ed and Michael as I rush out of the suite and down the hallway. I press the button for the elevator a few too many times, and when it drops me on the clubhouse level, I should be embarrassed with how quickly my heels tap against the cement, hurrying my way outside.

"Hi, Reese!" Isaiah calls out, jogging past me in the tunnel to the field. "Bye, Reese!"

"Good luck!" I shout at his back, where the number nineteen is stitched on his jersey.

In the distance, I watch Isaiah smack Emmett on the back as he passes him, jogging up the steps to the field. But once he's out of the way, I realize Emmett is no longer alone in the dugout the way he was when I was spying on him from my suite.

The reporter who has made it clear on multiple occasions that she's interested in him is out there too. Kelly, I believe is her name.

I'm not usually the type to stand back instead of going after what I want. But in this case, I'll never get to have who I want, so I stay hidden in the empty tunnel.

Emmett's back is to me, but I can see Kelly's face clearly from here. It's beautiful. *She's* beautiful, as is that beaming smile she's wearing while talking to my field manager. I can't hear what they're speaking about, but the body language is far too casual to be an interview. Not to mention, she doesn't have a recorder or a notebook in her hands right now.

Whatever they're talking about is personal. And all I can focus on is how lucky she is that she gets to speak to him in a personal manner while in public.

She's got this twinkling glint in her eye as she looks up at him, and I know that sparkle all too well.

And I hate knowing he has the same effect on others. I feel a bit possessive over his attention, though I have no right to it. With what he told me at the potluck, now that he's starting to focus on himself more, what if that includes dating? What if he meets someone he's allowed to be with publicly? And what if it happens while he's working for me?

At some point, I'm going to have to figure out how to be okay with seeing him with someone else. But today is not that day. Today, I have no intention of being okay with it. Today, I'm going to be irrationally jealous over the idea.

I don't ever remember being upset at the thought of Jeremy moving on after me. Jeremy and I were married, so I suppose that idea should've stung, while Emmett is simply someone I've kissed once. He's someone I thought I couldn't stand only a few months ago. He's my employee.

And yet, the idea of Emmett being with someone else ties an uncomfortable knot low in my stomach that makes me feel a bit sick. And that alone is terrifying to admit.

Emmett says something and it must be the most hilarious thing to ever come out of that man's mouth because Kelly falls forward in laughter, long hair brushing over his chest, a hand circling his forearm for balance.

When she stands up straight again, she waves him off, trying to catch her breath because she simply can't find it in her to stop laughing at him.

Okay. Well, he's not *that* funny.

From here I can see his back shake in a laugh as well and decide that's about all the torture I can take for tonight. Without making it out to the dugout to visit pregame, I turn around and head for my office.

Yeah, I'm jealous.

But I'm not jealous of just *her*.

I'm just jealous of anyone who is not me.

I'm jealous of anyone who doesn't have to keep up professional boundaries, because the last thing I want is to be *professional* with Emmett Montgomery.

The gym is mostly dark, but of course it is.

Everyone is long gone from the stadium by now, leaving me here alone. It's the first time I've left my office since the game started, and I waited around in hopes of getting the place to myself.

I'm amped up. A little bit pissed off, though that's not necessarily aimed at anyone in particular.

I'm just mad.

I'm mad at the headlines that haven't been written yet, but will inevitably circulate regarding tomorrow's trade.

I'm mad at our 6-4 loss tonight. I guess.

And I'm mad at Emmett, for making me like him so much. Truthfully . . . screw him for doing that.

I connect my music to the surround-sound speakers, turn the incline up on the treadmill, and start my evening workout with an uphill walk.

I don't even make it a mile before the gym door opens, and through the mirror, I watch as Emmett barges in, breathing heavy and dripping sweat. It cascades down his bare torso, down his abdomen, following that same trail of dark hair that leads right to his . . .

Nope. Not thinking about that.

Definitely not looking in that direction either. Because again, screw him. For what? I don't know exactly, but whatever I'm so upset about, he seems like a solid choice to direct my anger toward.

His chest rises and falls in quick succession as he attempts to steady his breathing, and it doesn't take a rocket scientist to piece together he just came from a run.

As soon as he hears the music playing, he pulls out his earbud and finds me in the reflection of the mirror.

He doesn't say hi, he just grinds his molars, allowing his jaw to tic, as if my mere presence is offensive to him tonight.

Well, right back at you, buddy.

What the hell is that about? *I* didn't do anything to deserve a cold shoulder. He's the one who . . . who . . . well, he didn't do anything wrong either, I suppose, but two seconds of being in the same room and he's already annoying me.

The way he doesn't say anything annoys me.

The way he gave someone else his attention tonight annoys me.

The way I can't have him annoys me.

The way he looks so fucking good after a run especially annoys me.

The fact that he even *likes* to run.

Honestly. Who the hell likes to run? He's a monster, I swear.

Emmett opens the small cabinet near the door, pulling out a hand towel to wipe over his face, and I notice he doesn't put his earbud back in. As if he's waiting for me to be the one to break the silence. Expecting me to.

Well, joke's on him because I'm suddenly petty as hell tonight. I refuse to be the first one to say something. I'd rather work out in silence anyway.

He tosses the towel over his shoulder and heads to the free-weight section, taking a bench—a bench I now realize has his shirt sprawled over it and a set of heavy dumbbells on either side. He must have been in here long before me, and though this is technically *my* gym, I suddenly feel as if I'm intruding on his alone time the way I assumed he was interrupting mine.

That annoys me too. I thought I was here first.

Ten minutes in, we're focused on our own workouts, neither of us saying a word. The silence wouldn't bother me so much if I could stop catching his eye in the reflection or if I could find a hint of willpower and stop watching the way he's moving those dumbbells with ease.

My brain is a little traitor and quickly does the math on how much he's lifting in continuous reps. It's half my body weight and he's making it look easy. Seems like he could easily lift a hell of a lot more if he wanted to.

If he had the right motivation.

Good to know or whatever.

The weights land on the ground in a heavy thump after he's done with each set, and it doesn't take long for me to realize he's not dropping them because he's worn out and no longer has the energy to set them down carefully. He's dropping them loudly because he's throwing a fit.

And why? What did I do?

Is this because we lost? We lose plenty. Losing every so often is a part of the endlessly long season.

I stop the treadmill and before it's slowed to a complete stop, I hop off and head for the exit, deciding I'll come back when he's done, and I can work out in peace. Without all the noise. Without all the tension. Without all the daggers he's sending me through the mirror.

My hand is on the doorknob when he finally breaks the silence.

"What are *you* so pissed off about?"

Finding him in the reflection, he's leaning forward, elbows on his knees and attention on his phone.

"Me?" I exhale in disbelief. "I'm not the one throwing dumbbells around like a fucking drama queen."

He doesn't look up from his phone. Doesn't answer me.

"Is this because we lost?" I ask.

"I'm just having a night, Reese."

"Yeah. Well, I'll let you have it alone." I push the door open to leave.

"You never answered my question." His words work, stopping me in the doorway. "I know why I'm upset, but I can't piece together why you would be."

"Funny." I spin back to face him. "I was just thinking the same thing."

Finally, he glances up from his phone, and this time he doesn't use the reflection to find me. He looks me straight in the eye.

His attention draws me back into the room, closing the door again, but keeping my back flush to it.

"I saw your favorite reporter," I let slip.

His dark brows raise. "You're joking, right?"

I keep my shoulders straight, owning the statement, though I didn't necessarily intend to be the first of us to be honest.

"You don't get to be upset about that," he decides.

"I can be upset about whatever I want."

"Bullshit." He stands from the bench seat, shirtless and angry and so goddamn delicious to look at. "I have no idea what would make you upset about that anyway, but whatever the reason, it doesn't matter. Not when you brought a fucking date to the game."

A date?

"What are you talking about?"

He stalks toward me. "Matt or Mike or whatever the hell his name is. The guy you spent the whole game with, in your suite. Did you forget about him already? Kind of how you forgot about him real quick after your last date, huh?"

I have the boiling urge to tell him to fuck off, but I'm also so confused and need him to keep explaining himself.

Then I realize what and who he's referring to. The date that I used as a way to try to forget about *him*.

"Michael?" I ask for clarification.

"Sure."

He's pissed because Michael was here?

I scoff a disbelieving laugh. "Okay, now you're the one who's kidding, right? You don't get to be mad about Michael."

The muscles under Emmett's beard clench as he takes another step in my direction. "I know I don't. Just like you don't get to be mad about that reporter. Because we're just coworkers, right, Reese?"

"You do know that Michael is Ed's son, right? Ed, who is on the advisory board. Ed, who knows that I am not interested in his son. Ed, who watched the entire game from my suite. With his son. Just the two of them."

I watch as a bit of realization dawns on Emmett's face.

"I take it you didn't look up there once today, did you?"

He doesn't respond, but I already know the answer.

"So no, you don't get to be pissed off that Michael was here," I continue. "And especially not when you were busy giving one-on-one interviews in *my* dugout."

He takes a few more calculated steps toward me, and I can sense the frustration thrumming though him as he watches me. "On game days, it's *my* dugout," he says coolly. "Is that why you didn't come see me before the first pitch? Because that reporter was there?"

"Is that why you were flirting with her? To get back at me because you thought I brought a date today?"

"Answer my question."

"Don't tell me what to do."

He takes one final step, looming over me, big and pissed off. Sweat drips down his temples and continues to run over the dark splattering of chest hair. It takes everything in me not to reach out and run my fingers through it because fighting with him is kind of turning me on.

"Fine," I answer. "Is that what you want to hear? That you made me into a jealous and petty woman for the first time in my life? Does that make you happy, Emmett?"

"Yes."

I startle, head rearing back, but I have nowhere to go with the door behind me.

He bends, making himself eye level, and the attention is intoxicating. The way he smells. The palpable energy radiating off him. That possessive spark in his eye.

"I want you as irrational as you make me." His tone is laced with frustration. "And I wasn't flirting with her."

"You were laughing with her."

"Well, Reese, what would you have me do? Yell at the woman and tell her I'm only allowed to laugh around my boss?"

"Yes."

He lifts a brow in surprise.

I shrug, entirely unapologetic. "You said you wanted me irrational."

There's the smallest, almost undetectable twitch of his lips. "I can't be a dick to a random reporter. Besides, you tend to steal all my fight these days. I don't have much left to share when I use it all on you." Emmett cages me in with his arms on either side of me, palms flush against the door and eyes locked on mine. "You should know better than anyone that I wasn't flirting with her."

I roll my eyes. "Sure looked like it."

He shakes his head, his breath fanning over my lips as he speaks. Then he kicks my feet wider, slipping his big thigh between my legs as he presses me against the door. "Have you somehow forgotten already? Do you need a reminder of what it looks like when I want a woman? You should know that better than anyone."

The evidence is right there, resting on my hip.

He's so close, his lips are so close. All I'd have to do is tilt my chin up and my mouth would find his. All I'd have to do is slip my hand into the space between us and wrap it around him.

I tilt my hips, rubbing against the muscles in his thigh, and *God*, I don't think I've ever wanted anything more than I want him right now.

His calloused hand circles my throat. Light pressure. Warm skin. "You were right."

I attempt to hide my moan. "About what?"

"My hand." His eyes appraisingly assess my neck. "It does make an awfully pretty necklace."

He uses his hold on me to tilt my jaw toward him before he bends down and kisses me.

And holy hell does he kiss me. There's this deep ache in the pressure with which his mouth presses to mine. A desperation in the way his tongue slides over my lower lip, begging for me to open for him.

I do.

Willingly. Compliantly. Like putty in his hands.

He groans this primal sound when I slip my tongue into his mouth and it acts as a sounding alarm. Reminding me where we are. Reminding me of *who* we are.

We can't do this. Not again. And especially not here.

"Emmett." I find the will to turn my face away, breaking the moment. "You know we can't do this."

It's exhausting, trying to constantly do the right thing, but the consequences of doing the wrong thing in this scenario feel too big to ignore.

Heavy breaths are shared between us as a beat passes. His brown eyes search my face, as if he were looking for the moment I'll change my mind. But when I don't, he drops his forehead against mine for only a second before he pushes himself off the door, leaving an aching emptiness between my legs.

"And that's why I'm having a night." Turning, he walks away, creating some much-needed distance. "Because it can't be me."

"How do you think I feel?" I ask in a raised voice directed at this back. "I was perfectly happy running this team alone. *Being* alone. I hadn't even looked in a man's direction until your stupid hot face started showing up everywhere. With your stupid big body and your stupid big heart."

He watches me over his shoulder, a bit of surprise etched on his face by my sudden honesty.

"You're so worried about some other man? I *wish* I could want someone other than you. That would solve a lot of problems for me, Emmett. So, you're not the only one who gets to be mad about it. I'm pissed off too!"

"Well, that's just fucking great, Reese!" He throws his hands up, turning to face me. "Do you know how frustrating it is that the only person I want to talk to, I can't, unless I make up some ridiculous work-related excuse? Do you realize how maddening it is to want someone for the first time in twenty years only for that woman to be my boss? Just being around you is the biggest fucking tease of my life, and most days I can hardly stand it. Your presence is infuriating to me, and still, I can't stay away. I *hate* that you made me want you."

Alone, some of those statements should sting, but they don't. Not even a little bit.

I scoff. "You did the same damn thing! You made me want you, so why the hell are you fighting with me about it?"

"Because! If I'm not fighting with you—" He stops his shouting, scrubbing a palm over his mouth, as if he were tearing off the filter. "If I'm not fighting with you, then I'm too busy wanting to fuck you."

And there they are. The words are out in the open for both of us to hear.

We stand off with one another, heaving chests and unsteady breaths. Just waiting for the other to break the rules. To cut the tension. To just give in already.

Neither of us do.

Emmett exhales a resigned sigh. "And we both know that can't happen."

His shoulders slump and I feel mine deflate the same way, both of us giving up the fight. There's not much more to fight about. We both want something we can't have, and there's not a whole lot either of us can do about it.

Emmett shakes his head and slowly makes his way to the bench he was using earlier, sitting and leaning against the back support. He runs his fingers through his hair before linking them behind his head and staring off into nothing. Too exhausted. Too defeated.

I should leave. We both need space to let that heated moment cool. But when I reach for the door, I don't have the will to push it open and go.

My head is screaming to create some distance, but my head is the last thing I want to listen to right now.

I take the door handle and pull inward, making sure it's closed. Then I turn the lock.

To keep others out? To keep us in? I'm not sure. I'm not thinking all that clearly at the moment.

Crossing the room to meet him, I don't let myself second-guess what I want. This is his fault, I decide. Looking like that. Fighting with me like that. *Wanting* me like that.

Emmett's corded thighs are spread with the bench between them, so facing him, I swing one of my legs over to straddle his lap. There was a time I might be too self-conscious to drop my full weight, but then I turned thirty years old and stopped giving a shit. So I sit, resting my entire body on his.

He doesn't even have to adjust to hold me, his muscular legs having absolutely no issue balancing me.

"Reese—"

"Just . . ." I take his face in both hands, fingers smoothing over the short hair behind his ears. "Shut up for a second."

Then I do the most reckless thing possible, and while at our place of work, I press my mouth to his.

24
EMMETT

Reese is kissing me.

Again.

I could've sworn it was a one-time thing, but here we are, her soft lips nestled against mine. I've been dreaming of this, and I'd tell her that if my mouth wasn't currently occupied.

She's pure confidence in the way she holds my face in her hands, kissing me exactly how she wants. Confident in the way she just came over and sat on my lap like a goddamn queen taking her rightful throne.

Reese goes after what she wants. It's one of the sexiest traits about her, and right now, she wants *me*.

I wish I could want someone other than you.

Those words feel like they're etched into my chest, creating this desperate determination to ensure she never will.

I'm angry and turned all the way on.

Irrationally angry because some random guy was here in her vicinity. Rationally angry that I can't have her.

But right now, she's sitting on *my* lap. Kissing *me*, so I should really tell my brain to shut up so I can focus.

This kiss is smooth, entirely in sync, as if the one and only kiss we shared before tonight made us experts in one another.

She pulls her mouth away, hands still cradling my skull, navy-blue eyes searching my face. Waiting for me to stop her. Waiting for me to be the responsible one here.

Fuck it.

I'm tired of being responsible. I want to be selfish. And I'm certain, this is what I want. *She's* who I want. Fighting with her already has me ready to combust, and for just once, I want to do the wrong thing.

"Did you lock the door?" I ask.

"Yes."

"Are there any cameras in here?"

I've never wondered until now. Never cared either.

This mischievous smile tilts on her lips.

"What's that look for?"

"Wouldn't that be fun to watch? A little gym porno."

"Jesus," I exhale. "Fancy Reese Remington sounds real good saying things like 'porno.'"

"I'm not always fancy, you know. I can get dirty too."

I hum at the thought, running my fingertips languidly down the column of her spine. "I can't fuck you in the gym, Reese."

Partly because she deserves better than that, and partly because I'm scared she'd regret it tomorrow. I couldn't handle it if this woman looked at me with regret. I like her too much. Respect her too much.

Her shoulders instantly sag, this bratty little pout pulling on her lip.

"Cameras?" I ask again.

"No."

"Good." Leaning in, I run my tongue over her puffy lower lip jutting out. "Don't pout. You're too much of a boss to pout about not getting your way. I'm not going to fuck you here, but I'll make sure to release some of that anger of yours."

Her eyes trail down to the space between us, snagging on the bulge in my shorts, and my cock instantly jumps at her attention.

"You're hard already."

"Yeah. Well, this is what I look like when I want someone. Here's your reminder, Reese. I walk around this clubhouse with a constant hard-on from my boss, not from some random reporter."

She hums this satisfied sound, perfectly manicured hands landing on my shoulders. Those light-pink nails drift down my chest, over my abdomen, trailing south in a way that has my body fucking aching for her touch.

She draws a torturous circle through the line of hair just above my shorts before trailing south to toy with the elastic waistband.

"So, this is for me?" she asks.

"It's *because* of you."

"But is it *for* me?" Her eyes bounce up to mine, innocent and testing all at the same time. "You're not going to fuck me, but do I get to touch it?"

Does she get to touch it?

Fucking please. She can touch it. Twist it. Lick it. Stroke it. Treat it like a fucking bop-it, for all I care.

Without waiting for my answer, Reese runs her palm over the front of my shorts and I'm officially dying. Because this has got to be what heaven feels like, right?

"Shit." Head dropping back, I watch her. "Yeah, baby, you can touch it."

Over my shorts, she wraps her hand around my cock and squeezes. And when she strokes me from root to tip, I watch those blue eyes widen as if she were mentally measuring my size.

I don't ask her if she's sure about this or give her a chance to second-guess. Because I know if I give either of us the space to think clearly about what we're doing and where we're doing it, this will abruptly end.

I'm amped all the way up, not thinking clearly, and I could not care less that, for tonight, I've given up the fight.

With my hips chasing her palm, pushing into her touch, I slip my hand into her hair, gripping the strands and pulling her mouth back to mine. I breathe against her parted lips, and it feels like my first deep inhale of fresh air after weeks since the last time I got to do this.

She's everything, kissing me like I'm hers, stroking me like she owns me. And for this moment, I let myself believe that I could be. That she does.

Reese wiggles against me, circling with need. She's on my lap, but not flush to me, the empty space between our hips acting like the worst kind of tease. Though, I'm the lucky one who's got her hand wrapped around me while she's out there chasing nothing with her hips.

I'm so focused on her mouth, on the way her lips are soft yet sure, that I can't concentrate on what I want to touch for the first time. I feel like a kid on Christmas morning who wants to play with every toy at once.

"Em," she pants, pulling away to rest her forehead against mine. She must notice my tense fists, opening and closing, trying to figure out where to lay my hands first. "Touch me."

"I can't decide where," I exhale on a laugh.

She smiles against me, a soft palm running through my beard. "Everywhere would be a good start."

I focus on her thighs, thick and balanced on my own, those light blue leggings of hers acting as a second skin. Then there's her tits, heaving with labored breaths behind a matching sports bra that can barely hold her in. And I can't help but dream about feeling them pressed against me, maybe getting my mouth wrapped around one. Her stomach curls over the waistband of her leggings, and *fuck*, I want to touch that too.

She's squirming against me, a shuddering little mess, and it reminds me of exactly where I want to touch first. Where I *need* to touch first.

Smoothing my palms over her thighs, I languidly run them upward, and when they meet her hips, I curve them over, grabbing her ass and pulling her forward to rock against me.

She moves her hand out of the way, running it up my bare torso. And the small brush of friction, when her body finally rubs over mine, almost makes me come undone with that one single stroke.

"*Oh*," she cries, cheek falling against my own, a single hand cradling the back of my head while the other grips the bench behind me. She curls her hips forward the slightest amount and her entire body shivers when her clit coasts over the head of my cock.

"That's it," I encourage. "Use me, Reese. Or let me use you."

She agrees eagerly, letting me move her body exactly how I want, pushing and pulling her by her hips and *good God*, I'm going to come in my fucking shorts.

The fabric of her leggings creates this delicious slide against my cock, though I wouldn't be mad if what's left of our clothing could disappear. But then I'd just be tempted to slip into her, and like I said, I'm not going to fuck her here.

Her lips work a path over my throat as I allow my hands to explore. I curve them around her ass again, fingers toying with the seam of her leggings.

She hesitates when I dip lower.

"Tell me to stop."

"No. Keep touching me."

And so I do, running my fingertips against the seam of her leggings, and reaching around to stroke them over her pussy, only to find the fabric there is already damp with her arousal.

"Wet for me already?"

"Yes," she breathes.

I stroke my fingers over her core one more time then give her ass a squeeze as I rock her against me. I continue my path, giving into the insane need to touch every inch of her. Both hands wander over her stomach and up over her chest. My thumbs flick her nipples that are peeking out from behind her sports bra. Then I give those a squeeze too.

Reese moans this precious sound against my throat as she kisses over my stubble.

She's fucking perfect in my hands, but of course she is.

"That feels good," she whispers. "I like you like this. With your hands all over me. A little bit desperate."

"A little bit? Fucking please." I exhale a tortured laugh. "I'm fucking gone right now, but are you surprised?" Clamping a hand over her shoulder, I push her down onto me, making sure she can feel just how *desperate* I am. "You did this to me. You walk around my clubhouse in those goddamn high heels and with that goddamn attitude, making me want you."

She gasps as she lifts herself up, creating a bit of distance between our bodies to give herself a momentary break. I only give her a second before I press a palm against her lower back and push her back onto me.

"My clubhouse," she exhales.

"What was that?"

Bending to put her lips close to my ear, she repeats, "*My* clubhouse."

The rumble of my laugh quickly morphs into a moan when she wraps her teeth around the lobe and bites down.

I don't know if I've ever been so turned on in my life. The pressure of her body rolling on mine. Her hard-earned breaths panting in my ear. The fact that she has to be firm and in charge out there, but when she's with me, she's soft and pliable, mostly giving up control.

I let my lips wander over her jawline, kissing a reverent path and making sure each one counts. That each one brands her skin and will make her remember me.

She writhes into me, her chest flush to my own, and *fuck*, it's incredible. Having her skin on mine. Having my arms around her. I'm so blissed out that all I can do is drop my head back and let her take over the pace for a moment.

Fucking euphoria, I swear, watching her get herself off on me. I've never been so happy to be used like a toy in my life. I could throw my hands behind my head and just let her bounce on me until she comes. It'd be the view of a lifetime.

When my head falls to the side, I catch our reflection in the mirror.

The dim lighting paints her curves with shadows, and I follow the way they dance along her body as she moves over me. A spotlight illuminates her face, and *God*, I don't think she could get any more beautiful than she is right now.

It's unreal, watching this woman on top of me. We look good together. It's no wonder the boys have been giving me so much shit about my boss. Even I can see in the reflection just how gone I am for her.

"Look at us." I nod toward the mirror. "Look how good you look riding me."

Reese follows my line of sight, and I watch those blue eyes drag down the length of us, taking in the entire picture.

Her lips pop open but then close without saying anything.

"What are you thinking?"

Her eyes bounce over us again. "That it doesn't look wrong."

No. No, it doesn't.

She's mesmerized by the view, and I don't blame her, but she's so distracted by looking at the image of us, her hips have halted to a torturously slow pace grinding over me.

Coasting the backs of my fingers over her stomach, I dip them into the waistband of her leggings, and that earns her attention once again.

Wetness pools around my fingertips as I grip the stretchy fabric and yank her forward, restarting her movements.

"You're going to come," I tell her.

It's not a question, but more like an order.

Well, more like a statement, I suppose, because even if I wasn't here telling her what to do, she's close enough that it would happen anyway.

"*Yes.*"

Heat twines around my spine, simmering low in my hips, and I'm right there with her. And that feels like a war in itself. If this is my only chance to see it, I refuse to miss a second of watching Reese Remington fall apart on me simply because I'm too busy with my own orgasm.

With my fingers in her waistband, directing her movements, I let my thumb glide over the front of her leggings. One swipe and I find her clit with the pad of my thumb, rubbing tight little circles over the damp fabric.

"Fuck, Em." She falls forward with a shudder, her body unable to keep herself upright. Unable to control her movements.

Yet still she chases her orgasm, rocking against me.

She's not asking me to take over, because she's far too prideful to ask for that, but I do so anyway. Pushing off from the bench, I cup her ass and carry her to one of the mirrored walls.

She slides down my body as I set her on her feet, and when I flip her around, I press her flush against the mirror. Her tits smash against it in the most sinful of ways, her cheek is pressed to her own reflection, and the mirror is fogging with her warm breath panting out needy moans.

"Watch." I yank her hips away from the wall a few inches, giving me space to slip my hand down the front of her leggings. "Watch me get you off."

Pushing back, she rubs her ass against my crotch, and I move with her, rocking against her the same way as if I were fucking her from behind.

"Emmett," she cries, arching back into me.

"I know. I got you."

I find her clit with the pad of my finger, rubbing tight circles while using her own arousal to help it glide. She's so wet and warm and ready, and *fuck*, I just want her.

My knuckles are white with how firmly I'm gripping her hip, keeping her steady as I rock against her from behind. My cock slides against the seam on her ass as I drop my lips to her spine, placing worshipping kisses up a path along her back until, over her shoulder, I find her mouth.

I drop my forehead to hers. "You feel incredible."

"I'm going to come," she whines against my lips, fingertips leaving smudge marks against the glass as she looks for something to grasp onto.

Her attention is locked on the other mirrored wall to our left, staring at our reflection, and I follow her line of sight to watch us too. I can't get over how much it looks like I'm taking her from behind. How perfectly willing she is, pushing her ass back and rocking with me, while also chasing my fingers on her clit.

"I wish you were inside of me."

"Oh, fuck." I drop my head to the back of her neck, trying to compose myself. "Don't say shit like that or I might just do it."

She smiles that tempting smile before her mouth drops into an "O," her brows furrowing in concentration when my fingers circle again.

"Right there, Em."

"*God*," I groan. "I love when you call me Em."

"Yeah?"

"I love when you call me anything. I just like knowing I have your attention."

"Trust me." She reaches back, slipping her hand behind my head to pull my lips to hers. "You always have my attention. And that's the problem."

It's the worst reminder, on the brink of both our orgasms, that this can't happen again. That *we* can't happen ever.

I don't care how good she feels in this position, I just need to see her. So I flip her around to face me. Reese wraps her thick legs around my waist as I scoop her up and push her back against the mirror. And like finding their home, my hips effortlessly fall into the cradle of hers.

Then I kiss her, deep and long, letting my tongue take its time sliding against hers. I work for every moment. I memorize every sound. The little whimpers against my lips. The squeeze of her thighs around my hips as she gets closer. The way her arms wrap around my shoulders, fingers digging into my back as I rock into her.

I kiss her in a way that will make sure she remembers me.

And when her body tightens as we desperately move together, I hold her, letting her ride her orgasm out against me and making sure I get to feel it as it happens. Even through her leggings, I can feel her flutter and it draws my own orgasm that much closer to the surface.

She's fucking stunning. Spent and exhausted. Flushed skin and heaving chest. Coiled muscles and pretty sounds. Every reflection in the room gives me a different view of her coming undone.

I can't tear my eyes off her and don't know how I'm supposed to be okay with only seeing this once in my lifetime.

"Emmett," she cries, mid-orgasm, and my name has me falling over the edge with her.

One arm holding her up, the other is flat against the mirror as every muscle in my body begins to contract. I hide my face against her neck as heat zips down my spine. White light shoots behind my eyes as I muffle my desperate sounds against her. She's got her arms wrapped around me, lips attached to my neck, and I'm done for.

Right there in the gym, I come in my fucking shorts from dry humping my boss against the wall.

And holy hell, I'd like to do it again.

That was just enough to take the edge off, but my burning desire for this woman hasn't been stoked in the slightest. In fact, it might be worse now, getting a small taste of what it would be like to be with her.

We both take our time coming down, much of the previous tension settling between us.

Reese's beautiful body slumps in my hold and I ease back on the force with which I'm pinning her up.

"Thank you," she exhales through hard-earned breaths.

"A little less pissed off?"

"You could say that." Her eyes drop to the front of my shorts, and I can't quite tell if the wetness there is her release or my own. Couldn't care less either way.

You couldn't find a shy bone in my body right now if you tried.

"How about you?"

"I don't know if I'm more or less worked up now," I tell her honestly.

She bites on her lip as she keeps her eyes focused on where we're connected, and that hungry look in her eye seems like a good sign. If she's still wanting this, at least the postcoital regret isn't settling in.

I take the fingers that were down her leggings and slip the tips into my mouth to lick them clean.

It earns all her attention.

"For the record, you taste phenomenal."

Her jaw falls open. "You're not playing fair."

"I don't know about that. You just got an orgasm." I push her hair behind her ear, stroking my thumb over her cheekbone. "You're stunning when you come, by the way."

Her smile turns sheepish, a blush covering her cheeks. It's a bit of a mind-fuck to see this confident woman go shy, but under these circumstances, I revel in it.

"Honestly." She folds her arms behind my neck, keeping me close. "You shirtless in the gym is some really good spank bank material I'll be using later anyway. So, thanks for that."

"I was just thinking the same thing about you in this little outfit."

Her eyes find me, this soft yet sad smile on her lips. I'm almost certain my expression matches her own as we watch each other. She leans in and kisses me in a way that feels as if she were doing it for the very last time.

And if it's going to be, I'll make it last.

Soft kisses turn into desperate ones. Gentle touches morph into frantic, seeking hands. With her pinned to the mirror, we make out with each other like a couple of teenagers finally getting a bit of alone time.

A post-orgasm make-out is highly underrated in my books, and it goes on for minutes until, eventually, Reese pulls back, hooded eyes and kiss-swollen lips.

So beautiful it hurts.

And then I remember what happened the last time we were alone.

"What did Scott want when he interrupted our meeting earlier?"

She rolls her eyes, fingers still toying with the back of my hair. "He thinks he should be more involved with the baseball operations."

"He can get fucked. What did you tell him?"

"That *my* title is president and not his, and that I'm running the team how I see fit."

There's a proud grin on my lips as I look up at her. "That's my girl."

"I'm not your girl." She lifts a testing eyebrow. "I'm your boss."

"Ah, yes. How could I forget? Maybe it was the way you just came all over my cock that has me confused."

She playfully smacks me in the chest, but I grab her wrist and push into her, brushing my nose against her cheek, laying lazy kisses against her jaw. But not pressing my lips to hers just yet.

"You know this can't happen again, right?" she whispers against me.

"Yeah." I find her mouth and kiss her once more. "Definitely never happening again."

25

EMMETT

"This is the training room," I tell Milo. "And this is Dr Rhodes. She'll be overseeing any treatment you'll need."

Kennedy holds her hand out to shake his.

"Hi." He clears his throat, but his voice still comes out a pitch too high and it has me questioning just how long ago he went through puberty. "Nice to meet you."

"Welcome to the team. Let me know if you need anything on this end of things, and if you need anything out on the field, my husband Isaiah can help you out."

His eyes go impossibly wide. "Isaiah Rhodes? You're married to him?"

"I am."

"I'm a huge fan." He catches himself. "I don't know if I can say that anymore though, since I'm his teammate now."

Milo Jones is young enough that he's fanboying over his own teammates. Got it.

"That's okay. I'm kind of a fan myself sometimes. And heck, I'm married to the guy." She offers him a wave before she gets back to work. "Congrats on the call-up."

I cup Milo's shoulder, moving him along. The poor kid is practically shaking like a leaf under my palm. He's been a ball of nerves since he walked into the building earlier today and it hasn't subsided since we started this tour.

I don't particularly blame him. The day you get called up from the minors is one of the biggest days of your life. It's equal parts exciting and terrifying, but that fear is definitely compounded on this particular day.

Unsurprisingly, the city and the league have been in a state of pandemonium over Reese's decision to trade Harrison Kaiser to Houston. It cleared some room in the budget as well as a spot on the roster, but the fans have been in an uproar all day and I have a feeling it's not going to let up anytime soon.

It's far worse than I was expecting, and while yes, it could be perceived as a controversial trade to offer up a well-known veteran before we know our playoff potential, the headlines have been less focused on the move itself and more so on the fact that it was made by a woman.

Even if I didn't know Reese, I'd be disgusted by some of the things being said online. But I do know her. I know her intentions. I know her heart and love for this team.

Don't get me wrong, scrutiny from fans and media outlets over trades and pickups is all part of the game. But this is on a different level, and everyone in this building knows it.

I haven't gotten a chance to speak to Reese today. It's been a bit of a whirlwind with the media, Milo's arrival, and the usual changes that happen when a new player joins the team. All I can do is hope that she's stayed offline. The things people have been saying, the names they've been calling her . . . it doesn't matter how tough you are or how solid you stand in your business decisions, it's enough to make anyone break.

"What's in there?" Milo asks, pointing at a set of closed doors as we pass them.

Images of last night run through my mind as I stand outside the gym where I got Reese off. The way she moaned my name. The way she tasted on my fingers.

Thankfully, I did a deep clean of the mirrors before I left last night.

"That's uh . . ." I clear my throat. "That's just the gym, but let's keep the tour moving, yeah?"

He gives an unconfident nod of his head, and I feel for the kid. He's young, and the scrutiny of today isn't just landing on Reese—he's getting his fair share too. The pressure on his shoulders is far greater than it should be for someone's first day in the major league.

"You nervous?" I ask quietly.

He shrugs. "Wouldn't you be?"

"Oh, I was fucking terrified on my first day in the league." Out of the corner of his eye, I watch as he looks up at me. "Everyone has a first day. Then you'll have a second. Then soon enough you'll lose track of the days, and you'll forget why you were ever nervous in the first place."

"Pretty sure I'll never forget why I was nervous today. I just got called up for Harrison Kaiser. What the hell?"

"Yeah," I state confidently. "You did."

"No one thinks I'm ready for this."

"Okay. Do *you* think you're ready?"

He hesitates with his answer. "I don't know. The fans are pissed."

"Let us handle the fans. You just focus on doing your job."

He nods, but the fear is still evident, so I place a hand on his shoulder, stopping our walk down the hall to make sure he's looking me in the eye.

"This was not an unplanned decision. A lot of thought went into this. You're not here by chance. You're here because Reese thinks you're ready. I do too. So instead of worrying about the fans, how about you focus on proving them wrong and proving her right?"

He swallows hard. "Yes, sir."

"Jesus." I exhale a laugh. "Call me Monty. You make me feel old as fuck when you call me sir."

Milo chuckles and it's nice to hear the kid finally laugh on one of the biggest days of his life.

"And this is the clubhouse," I tell him as I open one of the double doors.

If I could get inside his head, I'd imagine it sounds a whole lot like the gates of heaven opening right now. His eyes are wide in awe, and it just makes him appear even younger.

I know I'm harping on his age, but it has me nervous. This is a lot of pressure for a grown man to handle, let alone a kid who's still coming into himself.

But then I remind myself that he looks around the age that I was when I came into the league for the first time. And that makes me think about Miller and how I became her dad shortly after that. Looking at Milo has me realizing just how young I was when I took on that role, and if I could handle becoming a single father of a five-year-old, then he can handle this.

"Guys," I call out, and every one of my players who is fucking around in the locker room turns in my direction. "This is Milo Jones. Milo, these are the guys."

There's a beat of silence, and I'm sure Milo is entirely in his head right now, thinking this team is pissed about Reese trading Harrison and pulling him up in his place.

But they're not. I think they're all relieved, even if they can't admit that out loud.

"Hey, man." Cody is the first to step forward, putting his hand in his and swinging his arm around to tap him on the back. "I'm Cody. First base. Congrats."

Milo breathes a sigh of relief. "Yeah. Thanks."

I can see him fighting the urge to tack on "I know exactly who you are," but it's probably for the best if he doesn't come on too strong in the fan department.

The rest of the guys introduce themselves and though I already knew they'd be welcoming to the new guy, I'm also proud that it's something I didn't have to worry about. We have a really decent group of guys, and though the team is currently under a ton of scrutiny after the trade news that broke this morning, they make it a little easier knowing their team dynamic isn't on my list of concerns.

"Isaiah," I say, calling over my shortstop. "Do me a favor and take care of him for me. Show him his locker stall. Make sure no one from the media is getting him to answer any questions. I'll be back. I just need to go check on . . . something."

"How's Reese doing?" he asks quietly, his voice laced with sincerity. For being a complete goofball most of the time, he's quick to pick up on exactly where my head is.

The guys have seen the headlines today too. They've all seen the names she's been called. They've seen their team owner undermined publicly more than any other owner has been before.

And I hate that for her for multiple reasons, but I can't imagine how hard it's going to be for her to continue to run this organization with confidence, holding her head high as she walks these halls, knowing her entire staff has witnessed her name being dragged through the mud.

She'll do it because she's a fucking boss and has bigger balls than any other owner in the league, but I hate that she has to.

"I'm going to go find out," I tell Isaiah.

With Milo settled with the guys, I slip out of the clubhouse and head straight upstairs for her office.

The top floor is brimming with stress. The offices are packed on this Monday afternoon.

People move from room to room. Conversations are hushed but frantic. It has my feet picking up pace to get to Reese's office while also hoping she's not in there. Hoping she's not surrounded with this kind of energy today.

I turn into her receptionist area, where, shockingly, there's still no receptionist sitting outside her office. And with how feral people are regarding this trade, the last thing I want is for anyone to be able to get to her.

Well, besides me. I still want to be able to get to her.

I push through her door, and when the field comes into view from the massive windows lining her office, I find Reese's desk chair empty.

She's not in her office at all, and it fills me with both relief and worry. Relief that she's not surrounded by the current chaos. Worried that she's getting even more shit about this trade somewhere out there than she would be if she were hiding in her office right now.

It doesn't take me long to piece together where she might be.

I tend to find her in the dugout when the players are gone and there's no baseball to be played. And while the guys are still here, today's practice is already over, so it's worth a shot.

I take the elevator down to the clubhouse level once again, keeping a casual stride down the tunnel to not draw anyone's attention or cause someone to join me outside. The boys are still chattering away in the locker room when I pass, but the tunnel is empty.

And so is the field when it comes into view.

I can't see anyone in the dugout either.

Until I turn the corner around the partition that separates the field manager's seat and find Reese sitting on the ledge above the bench.

She looks good in my seat but it's all a sharp juxtaposition. Her trouser pants are perfectly tailored to fit her body but are currently sitting in dirt that's kicked up on the ledge. Her legs are crossed, one red-bottomed high heel firmly planted against the old wooden bench that should really be replaced soon.

Blonde hair covers her face, because her head is tipped forward, staring at the phone screen in her hands. Her thumbs scroll endlessly, but I catch some of the words on the screen.

She's too focused to realize I'm standing right in front of her.

Every protective instinct in me flares, watching her sit there and read nasty things about herself, but along with that comes the helpless realization that I'm not going to be able to do much to fix this for her.

"Hey," I say gently, reaching out to cover her phone with my hand. "You don't need to be reading those."

Finally, Reese notices me, letting me take her phone from her. Blue eyes are rimmed in red, not from crying but from exhaustion. Her brows seem to have a permanent line between them from the constant furrow. Her skin is a touch dull, and don't get me wrong, she still looks fucking gorgeous, but she's also clearly wrecked.

"Shit," I exhale, slipping her phone into my back pocket. "Did you not sleep?"

She shakes her head to tell me no, and the selfish part of me wants to make sure it's not because she was up all night regretting what we did. But I know in my gut this isn't about us.

"Reese," I say, taking a step forward before stopping myself when I remember where we are.

I can't hold her. I can't comfort her. I can't do anything and it's eating me alive to witness her this way. That confidence I'm so used to seeing this woman exude is nowhere to be found.

"They hate me," she finally says, and it's the saddest admission that could ever slip from her lips.

"Fuck them."

"Em—"

"No, Reese. Fuck them. They don't know what we know, do they?"

Finally, she gives me the smallest shake of her head.

"I'm sure they're looking up that kid right now." I point toward the clubhouse. "And even though his stats are ridiculous, they're still going to convince themselves that you made the wrong decision. But you didn't, did you?"

"I hope I didn't."

"You know you didn't. And it's going to feel real fucking good when we prove them all wrong."

She looks up at me, eyes bouncing between mine as if she were searching for something. Maybe a bit of reassurance.

"You and me, right?" I ask gently.

We know what we're doing. We know how we want to run this team. Together.

She finally nods and gives me the smallest tilt of her lips. It's not much, but it's more of a smile than she's probably worn all day, so I take it.

"He has to do well." Reese circles the pads of her fingertips against her temples. "I know that's asking a lot of him so quickly, but he really needs to do well on this upcoming road series."

"I know. I'll take care of him."

She nods, fingers still massaging her skin, attempting to release a bit of the tension.

My eyes snag on the fresh pink polish. "You got your nails done."

I doubt anyone else would notice. The color is just a slight shade off from the light pink she had on yesterday. But I have images of her manicured hands stroking over my cock ingrained in my memory, so the color change is easily identifiable for me.

"I did." She holds her hands out to examine her fresh manicure. "I promised myself they'd look good today."

I'm not sure exactly what that means, but knowing Reese, there's probably something petty behind that promise that I'd fucking love to know about.

Taking a step forward, my shins hit the edge of the bench as I reach forward and tuck her hair behind her ear, letting my thumb coast along her cheek as I do.

She closes her eyes, leaning into my touch, but adds a warning tone onto my name. "Em."

"I know."

I run my thumb over her lineup of earrings before I drop my hand back to my side.

Blue eyes are pinched as she looks up at me. "Last night was reckless." The statement hangs between us. "A hell of a lot of fun . . . but reckless."

I huff a small laugh. "I know."

"There are more eyes on me than ever now. We can't . . ."

"Reese, you don't have to explain it to me. I know. And I agree."

She offers me a thankful grin.

"I don't like it," I tell her. "But I agree."

"I don't like it either."

The partition is covering me, so though I know nothing can happen between us, I don't move from my spot at the edge of the bench. I'm allowed to stand close to the woman. I'm just not allowed to kiss her. Or fuck her. Or call her mine.

"So, how'd I know I'd find you here?" I ask. "I believe this is the third time now that I've caught you sitting in my seat."

My seat that I never use because I like to watch the games from the spot right by the dugout stairs, leaning against the railing.

"I used to hide out here when I was a little girl," she admits, and for a moment, I'm startled by her honesty. Part of me assumed she'd make up some excuse or call it a coincidence, but maybe she's too tired to lie to me. Or maybe she just wants to tell me the truth.

"When I was growing up, I used to hang out here during practices or hide from my parents when I wasn't ready to go home just yet. I always loved that it had these partitions around it." She puts her hands flush to the walls on either side of her.

"Six-year-old me thought it was her own personal fort. If I couldn't see anyone else, they couldn't see me."

Fuck, that's sweet. My chest cavity seems to split at the mere thought. Especially knowing how much this woman loves this team and realizing it all started when she was just a little girl, sitting in this same spot.

"Then, last year, I found myself out here again when I came back to work for the team. I remembered what a great hiding spot it can be. It's a nice reprieve from the office, from all the eyes on me. A place where no one will know to come look for me. Well..." She nods in my direction. "*Usually*."

She's all human right now. All soft and vulnerable. It's a good reminder that while she holds her head high around everyone else, she still needs a place to rest. Even if it's done in secret.

I might not be able to protect her the way I want to, or shield her from the ugly headlines and names, but I could shelter her in a different way. Be a soft place for her to land.

Maybe it doesn't just need to be this secret spot that's a reprieve for her. Maybe I could be a resting place too.

"Well, this is *my* seat, you know." A smile cracks on her lips at my teasing tone. "But I don't mind sharing it with you."

26
REESE

I don't know if I've ever walked as slow as I am now, going from the parking lot to the team plane out on the tarmac at O'Hare. Trying to delay the inevitable of seeing everyone on board.

I've already addressed the team of course. I've spoken to the staff. But we've been under constant question since I made that trade, and it doesn't just extend to me. Every person in this organization is being scrutinized for my decision. And now, I have to get on an airplane with each and every employee I've unintentionally added stress to.

Are the remaining players good enough to bring this team to the playoffs?

Are the coaches supportive of losing a power hitter like Kaiser?

Is Reese Remington setting the tone of being the most impulsive owner in MLB history?

Actually, I think the wording was "emotional and impulsive," if I remember that headline correctly. Because of course I had to be labeled emotional by a bunch of fucking men. I'm a woman, after all.

I'm not an emotional person when it comes to business, but it feels as if I'm real close to becoming one. I pride myself on having a thick skin, but these past few days have shaken me. The headlines have been far worse than I was mentally prepared for. They've made me question my confidence, and I hate that

I'm allowing other people's thoughts and feelings to cause me to second-guess my ability to do my job.

People were loud when I took over the team, but the hate was never to this extent. And the overwhelming thought that's been playing on a loop in my mind since the trade announcement became public is that maybe my ex-husband was right. Maybe he should've been the face of this team.

Maybe if a man made this same trade, the chatter would've died down by now. Maybe my entire staff wouldn't currently be operating in crisis mode because the first big decision that the first female team owner ever made was to trade away a majorly sought-after vet.

I'm not ready for this plane ride, but we need to get Milo's first game under his belt and hopefully everyone will just move on.

I pass my suitcase off to one of the linemen just outside the aircraft and make my way up the stairs. As soon as I turn the corner and stand at the front of the aisle, every pair of eyes lands on me in a way I've been dreading all day.

Standing here splayed out for my entire staff to see, looking like shit because I've hardly been able to sleep or eat, all while knowing they've seen the headlines. They've seen the forums and the name-calling. They've seen me be undermined by every single reporter who has covered the story. They've seen the horrible things Harrison had to say about our club.

It's humiliating. No one wants to look weak in front of those they're leading, but it's a whole added layer of complication when it comes to my particular role. Me being my age. Me being a woman.

If a different owner makes a mistake, it'll be forgotten soon enough. However, if this trade is my first business mistake, it'll follow me forever.

I, more than anyone else, have to be perfect, and right now, I feel anything but.

My skin prickles with embarrassed heat as I stand in the aisle for everyone to see, and I wish I could just run away. I want to hide. To let this blow over. To apologize profusely for adding stress to anyone else's plate. But I'm in charge here. I made this decision. So, I do my best to hold my head up high and own it as I get to my seat in the third row.

Except today, my seat is currently taken. My entire row is taken, in fact, by a man and woman I don't recognize.

"These are the Walkers," one of my staff members tells me. "They were the winners of the charity fundraiser's silent auction we held toward the beginning of the season. They'll be joining us for this road trip."

Fuck. I completely forgot we were going to have guests with us on this trip and I'm in no shape to be seen by fans.

"Of course." I find my most convincing smile. "Welcome. I hope you have a great time with us."

They beam up at me, thanking me for allowing them to join, and expressing their excitement to see the behind the scenes of team travel.

I don't have it in me to tell them I completely forgot they were coming, but they also donated a ton of money to Chicago's public school system in exchange for this trip, so the least I can do is give up my seat on the plane for the week.

Emmett stands from his seat, the one that's directly in front of my usual place on the plane, and for the first time today I make eye contact with him.

It's shocking to me how centered I feel when he's around now. A bit more confident too, like I have a partner in this mess. Yes, it's just a work-related partnership, but it's nice being part of a "we."

I don't know if I've ever been part of a "we." It's becoming more and more evident that my previous marriage wasn't a partnership at all, and with Emmett . . . at least I know that even if every other person in Chicago hates me, he doesn't.

"Saved you a seat," he says, brown eyes equal parts soft as they are concerned. "Window okay?"

I nod, thankful that I have a place to hide away from everyone's attention. "Thank you."

He steps out into the aisle, giving me room to slip into the window seat next to his. I tuck my purse under the row in front of me then practically exhale a sigh of relief when I sink into the chair.

Emmett doesn't say anything when he sits back down, and I find myself thankful for the silence. It doesn't draw added attention, but just having him next to me feels like I can breathe a little easier.

He's really great at taking care of people, even if he doesn't mean to be.

It's taken everything in me not to call him the past couple of nights like he told me I could. Especially when he's the *only* person I've wanted to talk to about any of this. I've found myself wanting to hear only his opinion, in hopes it might drown out the others. To maybe let his steady confidence in me reignite my own sense of assurance.

But I need to take care of myself. I've been doing it for years at this point and he's got too much going on because of my decision to worry about the burden of my shaken confidence. And at the end of the day, I need to remember that he's still my employee, and though we've fucked around with some professional boundaries, I need to stay strong even around him.

I don't know if any field manager has been called for more interviews than he has in the past two days. And in each and every one he's taken accountability and blame, recounting the game he grabbed Harrison by the jersey. When asked what prompted the trade, Emmett has been constant with saying Harrison and the coaching staff couldn't get on the same page.

He and I both know that's not the case, but I appreciate what he's trying to do.

It's strange. After being married to someone who wanted to take this role from me, I haven't been able to quite wrap my head around Emmett. A man who not only wants me to have this job but wants me to succeed in it. Wants to protect me as much as he can, and has done so willingly, without even knowing whether he's going to be coaching here next season.

Emmett leans into the space between our seats, keeping his voice hushed. "When was the last time you ate?"

I shrug in reply because I don't actually know. Maybe last night. Or maybe I was so busy reading online forums about how much our fans hate me that I forgot to.

"Reese."

"I . . . I don't remember."

I tentatively allow my eyes to drift over to him only to find that he is pissed.

Emmett's jaw goes hard before he quickly stands from his seat and slips into the galley where the flight attendants are waiting to close the boarding door.

Food is the last thing I care about right now. Sleep too. It's kind of hard to focus on either of those things when all I want is to succeed in this role. I've been training for what seems like my entire life for this moment but am currently being told by everyone that I'm failing.

The only saving grace over the past couple of days, besides Emmett's interviews with the press, are the players' interviews. They've supported the trade, and maybe that's just a public appearance thing or maybe their field manager threatened them if they said something negative about my decision-making. But whatever the reason, them publicly having my back makes me feel as if I'm part of this team.

"Eat this," Emmett says, holding out a granola bar as he retakes his seat next to me. "Lunch will be served in the air."

"I'll be fine."

"Reese." His tone holds no room for argument. "You need to eat. Then you need to close your eyes and try to get some rest. I'll wake you up when food comes around, but you need sleep."

I've come to learn that though Emmett will bend on certain things, there are other beliefs he holds strong conviction in. And judging by the way he's forcing this bar in my direction, apparently something as minor as me not eating breakfast is a hard line for the man. Pretty sure he might feed it to me if I refuse to do it myself.

I'm sure that wouldn't raise any suspicions.

I take the bar from him. "Thank you."

"You're welcome."

I turn my body toward the window to eat this granola bar, but I catch him out of the corner of my eye every so often watching me with concern.

"How's Milo?" I ask quietly, attempting to get the attention off me.

"Don't worry about him, Reese. The boys are taking care of him."

I nod to myself.

"We should sit him the first couple of games, though. Give him some time to adjust."

I know it's the right thing to do. Let him learn our system and get a feel for the pace of the game at this level, especially with how much pressure he's got on his shoulders. But I also know what delaying his first game will do.

"But," Emmett continues, "I'm worried things are going to get worse for you if we don't just get him out there and let him shut everyone up."

My thoughts exactly.

"No." I shake my head. "We can't do that to him. I can handle it for a few more days."

He exhales a deep sigh. "I'm worried about you."

"I can handle it."

"Yeah, I know, but that's not the point. You don't have to be tough all the time, Reese. What's happening right now sucks. People suck. What they're saying online . . ."

I force out a smile. "I promise, I'm fine."

"Reese—"

"You're right, Emmett. I should try to get some sleep."

It's a three-hour flight to Miami and though I'd rather spend my time getting some work done or doomscrolling through nasty comments online, I don't think Emmett is going to allow me to do either.

Shifting, I angle my body toward the window and rest my head against the fuselage.

An arm lands on my leg and when I look down, I find Emmett's arm reaching across the center console to offer me his team-issued hoodie.

"Here," he says softly, and thankfully the engines have started and are loud enough that we can speak at a more normal volume without anyone else hearing us. "Use it as a pillow."

"Thank you." I take it from him, folding it up tightly. "How'd you know I was a pillow princess?"

A smile finally cracks on Emmett's lips and it's nice to see him a bit less concerned, even if I had to force out a mildly dirty joke to make it happen.

"Match made in heaven," he says quietly. "I would happily do all the work."

The skin around my eyes crinkles and it feels good to be a little lighter around him, even for a second.

Shifting, I situate his sweatshirt against the window and try to concentrate on getting a few hours of sleep. But as soon as I rest my head on it, his scent is the only thing I can focus on. It's practically melted into the fibers of this fabric and the smell instantly takes me back to the other night.

Images of us in the mirror. The way he could hardly control his breathing as he looked at me. The way his body felt between my legs, deliciously hard.

Everything was hard. His . . . yeah, that was hard too. And big.

Not too much of a surprise, I suppose. The amount of big dick energy Emmett exudes, I half expected it to be dragging on the floor. It doesn't, thank God, but he's definitely . . . *blessed* in that department.

I close my eyes and attempt to concentrate on anything other than how utterly fucked I am when it comes to the man sitting next to me.

Using one hand to prop his sweatshirt up, I place my other on the center console between us, fingers hooked over the edge of the mutual armrest. My arm is draped there for no more than a few seconds when I feel Emmett's arm join me.

Firm pressure from elbow to wrist, his skin on mine.

Then he reminds me that I'm completely done for when his pinky finger reaches out and grazes my own.

It's the smallest of touches, completely discreet if anyone were to look over here right now, but the back-and-forth slide of his finger against mine, reminding me that he's here, is all the comfort I need to finally fall asleep.

We sat Milo for the last couple of games, letting him get acquainted with his new team and how we run our system. I also had a delusional hope that allowing two games to pass would give us some time for the noise to settle down. That it might take some of the pressure off this poor kid's shoulders.

Unfortunately, it hasn't.

All this extended time has done is make people even more curious about the new guy on the team.

Will he be able to fill the role that was left by Harrison? I sure hope so.

Is he even ready for this? Again, let's hope.

Did Reese Remington make her first colossal misstep and take her team out of the playoff run before we've even hit the mid-year all-star break? Maybe.

Some of those questions could finally be answered tonight. Some of the chatter could be quieted if Milo comes out and has a strong first game. If he could just shut them up for me, that'd be great.

I think about that kid I found a couple of years back playing baseball for his local community college in New Mexico and could not feel worse that this is his introduction to the league. No one should have this kind of pressure to have such a solid showing in their first game in the majors, but unfortunately that's just the situation we're in right now.

The press interviews have taken it out of me this week. I'm usually on top of my game, ready with quick remarks to shut any bullshit questions down, but now I'm off, stuttering through my responses and finding the need to explain myself and my decision to move on from Harrison Kaiser.

It's what has me hiding in a visitors' office and watching the third game of this series from the television on the wall instead of finding a seat with a view.

Nervous energy rattles through me as Milo makes his way to the plate for the first time in the top of the second inning. I can see his tension through the screen too. He's hesitant in the way he digs his cleats into the dirt, and there's no fluidity in the way he lifts his bat into position.

He's stiff and locked up.

It only takes three pitches for him to strike out. He doesn't even get a single swing in.

In the bottom of the fourth, a pop ball heads in his direction in the outfield. It's an easy catch. A given out. The sun is in his eyes when he looks up for the ball and when it drops, it's not in his glove. It's two feet away on the grass by his cleats.

He strikes out again during his next two at-bats, and when he comes up to his fourth and most likely final in the top of the ninth, I'm staring at the screen with rapt attention. Praying for a miracle at this point because currently, with the way he's playing, we're going to get eaten alive in the press after this game.

He can do this. He *has* to do this. We're down one run, top of the ninth. We've got a player on third and one on first with two outs. All he has to do is get on base. Bring home the player at third. Get us a tied game and push us into the bottom of the ninth.

He's no more confident as he steps up to the plate than he was the first time he did it tonight. In fact, I would say the added pressure of this moment has his shoulders slumping even more. It's given him less power in his stance.

The first pitch is a slider, but Milo swings, giving me a bit of hope when he gets a piece of it. It's a foul ball and his first strike, but at least he had the timing to slice part of it. And at least he had the guts to swing.

His second foul ball earns him his second strike, but again, at least he's getting a piece of it.

The energy in the building grows, eagerly watching the new kid fight off Miami's seasoned pitcher. If he could just get on base. Give our fans a smidge of hope.

He slices another foul ball, keeping the count to 0-2.

On the fourth pitch, he fully connects, and his swing is solid and strong, sending the ball deep into right field. I'm out of my seat and nearing the television screen praying for it to stay left, to stay in fair play.

It doesn't. It curves right for his fourth foul ball during this at-bat.

Even from the office I can hear the sigh of relief from the Miami fans outside. If he had kept that in play, it would've been a three-run homer, putting us up by two in the top of the ninth.

Okay. He can do this.

The power behind that last hit gives me a little hope. Standing at the screen, I rest my palms on my knees and watch him take his position for the fifth pitch.

"C'mon, Milo," I mutter to the screen. "Just bring him home. Get on base."

The pitcher winds up and releases a hell of a fastball right down the center of the plate.

It zooms right past him. He doesn't even get a swing on it.

Milo strikes out looking, ending the game.

Head dropping between my shoulders, I instantly begin rehearsing all the things I need to say in the postgame press conference.

But the one statement that keeps swirling around in my mind is, *everyone else was right. I think I made the wrong decision.*

27

EMMETT

I should be asleep. Our current game schedule is way too brutal for me to be missing out on sleep, yet here I am, tossing and turning in my hotel bed.

I should put my phone down. That'd probably help. Cut down on the blue light or whatever. But I can't seem to find it in me to stop scrolling.

Tonight's game was brutal, and I feel for Milo. Sure, it was a pretty shit first showing, but it's all magnified because of the caliber of player he's replacing.

But even more so, I feel for Reese. I'm *worried* about Reese.

She won't admit that she's hurt by the things being said about her. She's doing her best to act as if she's okay. I understand why she hasn't come to talk to me about it in public yet, but I was hoping by now, she'd confide in me in private.

But she's headstrong as ever and determined not to appear weak. Even around me, I guess.

This is how I've spent every night this week. Lying in bed, unable to sleep, and thinking about how she's handling everything.

I've also spent my nights reading posts online and listening to commentators speak on things they have no fucking clue about regarding my boss. I'm not sure why I can't stop, all their takes are utter bullshit anyway, but there's something in me that feels as if I just need to be aware.

Not that I could do anything about it anyway.

I click on a suggested video from a guy I recognize as the host of a popular sports podcast, and from the clickbait headline alone, I can already tell I'm not going to like it.

"Let's get into the mess that's happening in Chicago," he says as soon as I press play. "All anyone can talk about is the Kaiser trade to Houston. Anyone with an ounce of baseball knowledge knows that was one of the worst moves we've seen in years. And to do it so early in the season? The Warriors don't even know if they're headed to the playoffs or not, and they're trading off huge-name players like Harrison Kaiser. They just traded away any hope they could have of a playoff run, and we aren't even halfway through the regular season yet. The Warriors already lost Kai Rhodes to retirement last year. What's next? What other disaster decision could they make over there? And by 'they,' I think we all know by now I'm referring to 'her.'"

Oh, get so fucked.

He continues to speak into that stupid little microphone in his hand. "In case anyone is living under a rock and doesn't know by now, Reese Remington is the granddaughter of former Warriors owner and acting president, Arthur Remington. He handed over the team during the offseason, and instead of hiring a president who actually knows a thing about the game, she decided she was capable of taking on the role herself." He laughs to himself, and I wish I could reach through the screen and wrap my hand around his throat. "I have no idea who let her believe so highly of herself. I'd be curious to know what Arthur thinks about his precious granddaughter running his team into the ground. If I were a Warriors fan, I'd be fuming that my team is the hands of someone like her. Hardly any experience. Clearly doesn't know the game."

He shakes his head, exhaling a long sigh. "It makes you wonder if there's anyone over there in Chicago with enough balls to stand up to this chick and tell her she has no idea what she's doing."

Fucking idiot.

"Now, let's talk about this new kid, Milo Jones. I'll give it to him. His minor league stats are impressive. I hadn't heard of him before this week, but it's clear by his numbers that Arthur found himself a possible future gem out of New Mexico. But the key part of that is 'future.' Today's game was evidence that this guy is *not* ready for the majors, and bringing a player up too soon can and will ruin his growth. I'm sure when Arthur filtered him in his minor league system, he had no intention of him being pulled up so soon. So, someone might want to inform Reese that you can't replace a player like Harrison Kaiser for a nobody. Maybe if she gave her team as much time and attention as she gives herself to get ready every morning, they wouldn't be in the situation they are in now." He holds his hands up in surrender.

"I hate to say it, but we're all thinking it." I can already tell whatever he's about to say, he's fucking thrilled to say it out loud. "You're out of your league, honey. Oh, and there's no crying in baseball, which we all know you're doing right now. So, clean up that mascara and pass the team off to someone who knows what the hell they're doing."

The clip ends there, and I'm tempted to throw my phone across the room in hopes it'll smash against the wall so I never have to hear his voice again.

The video previews another that will automatically start next, but I don't have it in me to watch any more. I don't have it in me to listen to another asinine take regarding someone they don't know shit about.

And by "they," I mean the podcasters who think that because they went and bought a microphone and started recording themselves they're now experts on the sport. But even the reliable reports in the industry can get fucked with how they've spoken about Reese this week.

They have no idea that Reese was the one who found Milo.

That she's so smart when it comes to both business and baseball.

That she probably hasn't cried once over the hate she's getting because she's afraid to show any emotion for fear of being called emotional by idiots with a platform.

I toss my phone onto the nightstand with a little more force than necessary, and as soon as I lay my head back on the pillow, a knock sounds at my door.

Startling, because it's the middle of the night, I lie there and listen carefully. These hotel walls are so thin, I'm not entirely convinced that knock was even coming from my door.

Maybe ten seconds later, it sounds again. It's a light tap, and it's then I realize the sound is not coming from my main door that leads out into the hallway. The knock is happening on the pass-through door that connects this room to the one next to mine.

Reese is staying in that room. It's not the first time we've shared a hotel wall. In fact, it's not even the first time we've shared a connecting door. And it's not the first time I've kept it unlocked on my side in hopes she might open it.

But this is the first time she's ever tried.

"It's open," I call out.

The handle turns, but there's a long pause before the door opens, as if she's making sure she actually wants to do this. The last time she was in my hotel room was almost a huge fucking disaster, but the situation is a whole lot safer when she doesn't have to go out into the hall to get in here.

Finally, the door cracks open just enough for Reese to peek her head through.

Fresh face without any makeup. Tired eyes. Apologetic smile.

"Hi," I say gently. "Can't sleep?"

She shakes her head to tell me no. "How about you?"

"Same."

She opens the door a bit wider, revealing the matching pajama set she's wearing. Because of course, even when she's not feeling her best, she's still put together.

"Could I . . ." She stumbles over her words, waiting for me to finish her sentence.

It'd be easy for me to. I know exactly what she wants to say, but I also need her to start being okay with asking for help, especially from me.

So, I don't say anything.

"Would it . . . would you mind if I stayed in here tonight?"

My chest feels like it's being split in two with how sad she looks. With how vulnerable her request is. She takes care of herself far too often, so this feels much more meaningful than her simply wanting to sleep in my bed.

I'm eager to give her a quick and resounding "yes," but I think she might be more comfortable if I at least gave her a little shit for it first.

I fold an arm behind my head as I watch her in the doorway. "Is your room too cold again or something?"

She catches on immediately, throwing a thumb over her shoulder. "I can go back in and turn down the temperature if I need an excuse."

A smile curves at my lips. "No need for an excuse. Come here."

I lift her side of the covers for her as Reese closes the connecting door and pads over to the bed. I fully expect her to climb in, situate herself along the furthest edge of the mattress from me, and face the wall.

But she doesn't.

As soon as Reese slips into the bed with me, she scoots her way across the mattress right to me, putting us chest to chest.

Tucking her head under my chin, she wraps her arm around my waist. Her way of silently asking me to hold her.

It's unguarded and sweet and it's the first time she confirms just how much she's hurting, even if it's done so silently.

"Hey," I soothe, slipping my palm into her hair and cradling her head against me.

I don't tell her it's okay because it's not. I don't tell her she's fine because, again, she's not.

Her fingers desperately press into the skin of my back as if she could just get a bit closer, things might start feeling better for her.

It does a stupid, irresponsible, possessive thing to my chest.

I scoot closer to her, curving my body around hers, covering her legs with one of my own and intertwining us as much as possible.

It'd probably be unprofessional to tell her how much I've missed her this week while she's been hiding out. It'd probably be just as unprofessional to tell her how good it feels to hold her.

At this point, I think we both know we've crossed any professional lines that may have stood between us anyway.

I fold both my arms around her back and drop my face to the area where her neck meets her shoulder, breathing her in. We lay like that for a long while, not saying anything. I draw soothing circles against her back. She holds on to me with this firm need that gives me a purpose. Like I can actually do something to help her after a week of feeling utterly helpless.

"I'm sorry," she whispers against me.

I pull back to look at her. "For what?"

"For making your life harder this week. For needing you to make me feel better."

"Reese." My tone is almost scolding because it's unfathomable to me that she could feel that way. "Tell me the truth. Do you really think that any part of you is a burden to me?"

She's quiet for a long while and I can tell she's really mulling over that question in her head. Finally, she answers with a soft and sincere, "No."

"No," I confirm. "I know that we're . . . well, I don't know what's happening between us, but it feels really good to be needed. Especially by you."

She burrows her head against me. "I'm not usually like this."

"I know." I move her hair out of the way, pressing my lips to her temple. "So thanks for letting me see it."

"Emmett, I think I made the wrong decision."

Shit. I was worried the noise would eventually seep in.

"Do you?"

It's almost as if having to repeat it for a second time is giving her pause to think. "I . . . I don't know."

"Do you actually believe you made the wrong decision, or do you think maybe Milo had one bad game when we really needed him to do well? Do you think if everyone would just shut up for a second and let you think clearly, you'd still regret making that trade?"

She pulls away from my chest and searches my face but doesn't give me an answer.

"Em, I need you to tell me the truth." Her eyes are pleading with me, even in the dark hotel room. "Even if I'm not going to like it. You're the only person I trust when it comes to the team. Do you think I made the right call?"

There's absolutely no hesitation for me to answer. And it has nothing to do with my feelings for her. Even if I wasn't completely gone for the woman, my answer would remain the same.

"I do."

Her brows slightly lift, and I watch as a wave of relief washes over her. "You do."

"Reese, I wholeheartedly trust your gut. I need you to try to block out the noise and remember what it feels like to trust yourself too."

She absorbs my words, the pinch between her brows softening a touch, and even more so when I run the pad of my thumb over the creased line.

She smiles gently. "I hope Milo is doing okay."

There she is.

"He's okay," I tell her, drifting my fingertips up and down the column of her spine. "Isaiah, Cody, and Trav took him out for a beer after the game."

That pinch between her brows returns. "Is he even old enough to drink?"

"Let's not ask questions we might not want the answer to."

Chuckling, she drops her head back against my chest, and fuck . . . I couldn't tell you the last time I felt like this. In fact, I don't know if *I've* ever felt like this.

Sure, I've been needed by others, but rarely do I let that be reciprocated. I pride myself on taking care of my people, but regardless that I'm the one holding Reese, comforting Reese, I think *I* might be the one who needs *her*.

But it's nice to think that maybe she needs me too.

She exhales a long breath as if she were shaking off the heaviness of the past few days. "So, how's Miller doing? Is she feeling okay?"

The shift is somewhat startling but only because I realize just how normal this feels with her. Laying with her in bed. Talking through the hard parts of the day. Her asking about my daughter.

I tighten my hold on her. "She's doing all right. She's more tired than usual, and is having some nausea, but she's handling it."

"Is that where Kai is? Did he stay home to take care of her?"

"Yeah, he did."

I feel her smile against my chest. "He's good to her."

"He is. I couldn't have asked for a better son-in-law."

She pulls back to look up at me. "What was it like for you finding out that one of your players was dating your daughter?"

I huff a laugh. "Well, he's the *only* one of my players that I would've been cool with dating Miller. And that's mostly because he's the only guy I know that could handle her."

Reese chuckles. "But he's also your friend, right?"

"Yeah, he's a good friend of mine. And sometimes I take on more of a fatherly role when he or Isaiah need it. Their dad isn't in the picture, so . . . yeah. And then I'm also their coach, so there's that. Our dynamic might seem weird, but it works."

"I don't think it's weird at all. I think it's sweet. I'm kind of jealous of your family." She breathes a nervous laugh as soon as that last sentence is out of her mouth. "So how did that all work? Him and Miller. Did he run it past you first, or did they keep it a secret? And how did you feel when you found out?"

It's wild to think that Reese wasn't here for that part of this team's history. That she wasn't there for that part of my life. I've never had someone ask for my point of view on the whole thing.

I find myself wishing she was around then. It would've been nice to have someone to talk to.

But I get to talk to her now.

I shift onto my back, one arm folded under my head, the other wrapped around her waist. Pulling her into my side, Reese rests her head on my chest and waits for my response.

And I can't help the stupid smile on my face when I say, "Okay, let me start from the beginning and tell you everything."

28

REESE

"We're the laughingstock of the league right now!" Scott yells, standing from his seat at the conference table.

"Do you understand what you've done, young lady?" That's Phil joining in.

Two more of the advisory board members tack on something about being disappointed in me and blah blah blah . . .

At this point, I'm kind of over it. I didn't call this advisory meeting, and anything they have to say, I've already heard it this week.

I also don't really care.

Of course, I want Milo to do well. I want our team to succeed. But I've given up on trying to make everyone happy. I made the trade I saw best for our future and I'm sticking by it.

My eyes drift to Ed. *Sweet* Ed who has had nothing but encouragement for me this week. He offers a smile full of apology for his fellow board members.

"Well." I stand from my seat. "If you're all done treating me like a child, I'm going to go now." Grabbing my bag, I head for the door of the conference room. "I'll see you tonight at my grandfather's retirement party, where I'm sure you'll all pretend you didn't just spend the entire morning disrespecting me in *my* building regarding the team that *I* own."

I push the door open, but Scott stops me in the doorway.

"How do you sleep at night knowing the entire league thinks you're running *your* team into the ground, Reese?"

Man, the fucking gall of this guy.

I contemplate his question. "Usually with a fan on. Thermostat set to sixty-seven, and like a fucking baby. Thanks for asking."

Ed laughs but tries to cover it with a cough, and with that final word, I leave.

Now that some time has passed and we've made it back home, there's definitely more confidence in the way I walk down the hall. I'm caring less about what everyone else has to say and more about what I think regarding the situation.

I've adopted this "me against the world" attitude that's been working well for me, but there's even more conviction behind the sentiment knowing it's not just me. It's Emmett too. And, even more so, it's the players having my back as well.

Every single one of them who's been interviewed this week has stood up for me publicly. And what I once thought might be rehearsed lines their field manager told them what to say, I now realize are their own words. Their own convictions. It's obvious in the way they've been ripping reporters to shreds if asked a disrespectful question regarding me.

So, I suppose it's the Warriors against the world. And that feels like a pretty good position to be in.

Tonight is my grandfather's retirement party, and after making it through a rough week, Emmett canceled today's practice to give the boys a break, while I gave the front-office staff the day off to get ready for tonight. Everyone will be in attendance later, so I'm hoping a day away from the field and a late-night party will act as a reset for everyone.

Though no one else is working today, I always planned to. What I didn't expect when I showed up to work was that I'd end up in an advisory board meeting that Scott called as if he had the authority to do so.

I don't have it in me for any of them to corner me in my office, so with the building to myself until the party planners start showing up in a few hours, I decide to hide out in the dugout for a bit. At least until the board members can get in their cars and leave.

It's peacefully quiet on the clubhouse level, a stark contrast to most days during the season. And I revel in the rare silence.

That is, until I'm startled with an overly cheery, "Hi, Reese!"

Isaiah jogs to meet me on my way outside.

Stopping in my tracks, I look back in the direction he came from, trying to piece together where the hell he just popped out of.

"Hey." My tone is laced with confusion. "What are you doing here?"

"Just using the restroom."

That earns a brow lift. "Which one?"

"C'mon, Reese. Not that one." His smile turns cheeky. "My wife isn't here."

I don't give myself time to think about what those two may or may not have done in there over the years. "I mean what are you doing *here*? At the field. Don't you have the day off?"

"Oh." We start walking together down the tunnel to head outside. "Monty asked a few of us to help him out for a couple of hours."

"Help him out with what?" But as soon as I step out into the dugout, my question is answered for me.

Out on the field, the portable batting cage is set up behind home plate. Milo has his batting helmet on, taking swings off Kai Rhodes' full-speed pitches. Travis is padded up and catching for his previous pitcher. Meanwhile, Cody and Emmett are leaning behind the cage, giving the new kid pointers on his swing.

"Well, I guess technically we're helping out Milo," Isaiah explains. "Monty called this morning to see if we could get together. He's trying to get his confidence up before the next game."

Well, shit.

And to think, there was a time I convinced myself I didn't like the team's field manager.

"Did he now?"

"Kid's got potential." Isaiah bumps his arm against my shoulder. "I think you made the right call."

"Yeah?"

"Yeah. We'll make sure everyone else realizes it too. Don't worry."

With that carefree statement, he jogs out to the field to join the rest of the guys, going to the far side of the cage and leaning against it next to Cody.

It'd probably be smart of me to head back upstairs to my office instead of walking out there to join them, because I'm fairly certain if I get too close I might just grab Emmett by the shirt and press my mouth against his to say thank you.

On their day off, he got his guys together to give Milo a confidence boost. He even got his star pitcher out of retirement for it.

Screw it. I'm not going back to my office.

I take the steps up the dugout stairs, walking on the balls of my feet when I hit the field so my stilettos don't sink into the grass. Emmett is on the near side of the batting cage, so that's where I go. Like a moth to a flame these days.

As I cross the field, I watch as Kai throws a nasty slider. Milo simply stares as it flies past him and into Travis's glove.

"At least get a swing on it, Jones!" Cody calls out from behind the netting.

"It's Kai Rhodes." Milo points his bat toward the pitching mound. "You try getting a swing off him."

Kai laughs. "Thanks, kid."

"Yeah," Cody says dryly. "I used to do just that. Literally last season."

"He's old and retired now," Isaiah taunts. "The guy ain't shit! Take a swing!"

Isaiah's brother gives him his middle finger as Travis tosses his pitcher the ball back.

"Milo," Emmett says just as I join him at his side. "If you can get a hit off Kai, you can hit off any pitcher in this league. You got it?"

"And if I can't?"

"Well, that's not exactly an option you have."

I fold my forearms over the metal framing behind the net, mirroring Emmett's stance.

He looks down at me with a soft smile. "Hey, you."

"How's this going?"

Milo squares up for the next pitch as Travis signals to Kai. Milo swings, and it's a beautiful swing, but his timing is completely off as he misses entirely.

"Shit," he grumbles right after it lands in the center of Travis's glove again.

"It's going," Emmett mutters.

Emmett doesn't give any advice, and I think that's done purposefully to see how Milo will handle his own mistake.

Milo immediately gets back into the batters' box and squares up for the next pitch.

When Kai releases the next one, anyone could see that it's going to be a ball that's curving wide to the left. But Milo reaches out of his pocket to swing for it and misses.

"You're chasing bad balls," Emmett calls out.

Milo immediately gets back into position for the next one.

"Step out. Take a breath. Fix your gloves. Anything that will separate you from that last pitch. You chased it because you were frustrated about the previous one. Reset yourself before it snowballs."

Milo's frustration is evident as he takes his coach's advice, stepping out of the box and exhaling a deep breath. He gives himself plenty of time and I can see him mentally trying to re-center himself.

"I'm not just saying this to boost your ego," Emmett continues. "But your mechanics are perfect."

Isaiah scoffs from the other side of the cage. "You've never said that to me, Monty."

"Yeah, that's because they're not."

A smile cracks on Milo's lips.

"It's all mental," Emmett goes on. "You're in your head. Everyone here can see that you're intimidated right now. It's the same way you looked during the game the other night, but there's nothing to be intimidated about here. This is just practice. No one is watching. Who cares if you mess up. You're getting to swing off a guy you idolize, but he's not on the other team. So, show him what you got and let it rip."

Milo nods, stepping back into the batters' box, and it's clear from his relaxed stance that he's already calmer.

Travis gives his pitcher a signal and Kai winds up, delivering a fastball right down the pipe, almost identical to the one that finished our last game with Milo at bat.

The crack of the bat is almost deafening as it echoes throughout the otherwise silent stadium.

"Holy shit," Travis mutters from behind the plate, throwing off his face mask to watch as the ball sails through the air, scaling over the ivy in center field.

There's an unmistakable thud when the ball hits metal, landing somewhere in the upper bleachers.

Every one of us is silent as we stare out into the distance in disbelief.

"I just hit a homer off Kai Rhodes." Milo's voice is laced with awe as he looks around for our approval, but we're all still staring out over four hundred yards away.

Emmett looks to his former ace pitcher. "You take anything off that?"

Kai shakes his head, brows raised and thoroughly impressed.

"I just hit a homer off Kai Rhodes," Milo repeats.

"Hell yeah you did," Emmett says. I can almost see the relief wash over him. "Now do it again."

Milo's energy is instantly lighter as he resets himself for another pitch.

"That's how he looked the day we went and watched him play in Vegas," I say quietly to the man next to me.

"He'll get back there. He's just having a crisis of confidence."

"I know a thing or two about those, don't I?"

Emmett chuckles, head resting on his crossed arms when he looks over at me. "You look good."

"I'm feeling better."

"Good."

I knock my shoulder into his and it does absolutely nothing to move the brick wall that is Emmett Montgomery. "This is sweet of you, by the way. To do this for him."

"Yeah, well, I'd be lying if I said he was my motivation here."

He did this for me.

His soft smile as he looks at me is enough to flip my stomach in the most irresponsible of ways.

He told me the other night to trust my gut, and right now, my gut is telling me to give in already. And he's making it awfully hard to remember the consequences of that decision.

"If you could try to make me like you a bit less, that'd be really helpful, Em."

His grin is lazy on his lips as he looks at me. "Can't help it, I guess. I think we both know I'd do anything for you."

There's not an ounce of me that wonders if that's true or questions his motives as to why.

And it's a liberating, yet terrifying, realization. Because I'm pretty sure Emmett Montgomery is everything I wasn't ever planning to go looking for.

29

EMMETT

I collapse into the couch in my office.

The heaviness from the week pushes my body down, and I quickly realize what a terrible idea it was for me to sit.

I didn't notice how exhausted I was. How wrecked I've been from worrying about Reese this week. How concerned I've been about Milo not playing up to his potential. But now that I'm paying attention to the stress, it's evident in the way it's locked in my shoulders and twined around my spine.

She looked better today. Brighter. More herself.

I can physically feel some of the worry beginning to melt away, sliding right off me as I sink into the couch cushions.

I really should get up though. I need to go home and get ready for Arthur's retirement party tonight, the same way Reese and the guys have already left to do the same.

At least, that's what I thought she did until, in the distance, I hear the unmistakable click of heels against concrete.

Reese struts right into my office like she owns the place because, yeah . . . she does own the place. But even if she didn't, it's nice to see that confidence back in her stride.

Across from me, she sits on the edge of my desk, legs stretched out and crossed at the ankles.

I've very seldom afforded the opportunity to look at this woman the way I want, so I take the rare moment to do so.

Regardless that no one else is in the office today, Reese is still dressed to the nines. A tailored pencil skirt paints her hips and stops around her knees. The silk shirt she's wearing is unbuttoned at the top, opening slightly in the most teasing of ways. And her heels . . . they're dark brown with a thin strap circling her ankle, and all I can think about is how I wouldn't mind getting on my knees to unbuckle them with my teeth.

I'd fucking love to be on my knees for this woman.

"I thought you left by now," I ask, not pulling my attention away from her body.

I take my time working my way back up. Following the long line of her legs over the curve of her tits, only to find a smirking grin waiting for me on her lips.

"I do need to get going. I just wanted to come by and say . . ." She hesitates. "Well, I guess I just wanted to ask. You know we need to stay away from each other tonight, right?"

"Yeah, Reese. I kind of figured with every person who has ever worked for this team coming here, I couldn't exactly get away with dry humping you in the gym again."

"Which is such a shame. That was by far my favorite workout I've ever had."

Fuck, I like this woman.

I like this woman on a foolish level.

She's honest with me. Funny with me. *Herself* with me.

"What are you planning to wear tonight?" I ask.

"A dress."

"And what color is this dress?"

Amusement dances in her eyes. "Why are you asking?"

"I don't know. Trying to mentally prepare myself, I suppose. Trying to give myself the best shot at controlling my future reaction when we're surrounded by our coworkers later tonight. But I have a feeling that no matter which dress you choose, it's going to make it awfully hard for me to stay away like you're expecting me to."

A blush warms her cheeks. "Don't say stuff like that."

"Why not?"

"Because I like it too much."

I like *you* too much.

"I . . ." She hesitates again. "I also wanted to come by and say thank you."

My brows pinch. "For what?"

Reese exhales a sigh as if she's got a whole list for me. "For that." She nods toward the field. "For letting me stay with you the other night. For taking care of me all week. With the press too. It made everything feel a whole lot less isolating knowing I had you in my corner. So, thank you."

I truly don't think I'll ever get over this sharp woman being soft with me.

"Of course. We're on the same team, Reese."

But we both know it's more than that.

She pushes off the desk, crossing the few feet to the door before closing it.

"You take care of everyone." The way she says it is done slowly and seductively, and the statement is punctuated by the click of the lock bolting into place. "But who takes care of you?"

Blood instantly rushes to my cock, imagining her being the one to. Because that look in her eye is telling me that's exactly what she's offering.

She slowly makes her way to me, standing between my spread legs.

Reese bends forward, hands on either side of me, anchored on the back of the couch. I look up as she looms over me, her mouth teasingly close to mine, but not quite close enough.

"Are you offering, Reese?"

Her lower lip slips between her teeth as she nods to tell me yes.

Fuck. Me.

She reaches up and behind me, the silk from her top brushing over my beard, her soft feminine scent invading my nose, and I swear I'm about to lose it.

Behind me, Reese drops the blinds to my office window, hiding us completely.

"Let me take care of you, Em."

We're very clearly about to cross a line and I can't seem to find a fuck to give about that anymore.

She slinks down my body, lips dragging over my jaw and down my neck before dropping to my chest.

"How are you going to do that for me?"

"By making you feel good." Lips run down my abdomen, the beat in my chest picking up speed the closer she gets to my cock. "You're stressed. I can tell."

"Yeah," I exhale, head dropping to the back of the couch. "I am."

"Because of me."

"No."

"Yes," she argues. "So let me be the one to fix it for you."

Reese drops to her knees between my spread legs, and it steals all my breath away.

She's fucking perfect and stunning and willing. But I also know what a big deal it is for her to put herself in a vulnerable position, here of all places. Where she's usually in charge. Where she doesn't want to appear weak.

But she's still got all the power, even from her knees.

"You are"—my breathing is already labored—"so beautiful down there."

She preens under the praise, a smile ghosting her lips when she runs them over the front of my jeans. Right over my cock.

"Fuck, Reese."

Her hands smooth up my thighs and I don't think I've ever been more ready for something in my life. I want her. I fucking *need* her.

Unable to tear my eyes off her, I unclasp my watch, tossing it onto the couch next to me so it doesn't get tangled in her hair when I wrap it in a fist.

Then I sink into the couch, drape my arms across the back of it, and spread my legs wider.

I'm mesmerized by her fingers toying with my zipper. Those pretty pink nails that are going to be wrapped around me soon enough. Mesmerized by the way she can't tear her eyes off the bulge in my pants.

"You're going to be good for me, aren't you?"

"Yes." She nods eagerly, a cheeky smile on her lips. "Just don't fall in love with me after this."

I rumble a contemplative sound. "Don't tell me what to do."

Reese runs her palm over my covered cock before reaching into my boxers and stroking it behind the fabric.

I drop my head back, eyes closed, concentrating on not coming from having her soft skin wrapped around my shaft.

"You feel good," I sigh.

"Do you think it'll fit?"

Oh, she's fucking with me right now. She has to be. She's going to make me come before I've had her lips around me because the last thing I'm thinking about fitting into is her *mouth*.

I crack my eyes open, looking down at her over the bridge of my nose.

Reese is wearing this too-satisfied smirk as she leans her cheek to rest against my thigh, her fist still tugging in long strokes behind my boxers.

It's innocent and seductive all at the same time. That push and pull, the constant teasing between us, is still evident here.

I sit forward, scooping my palm under her cheek to help her sit up before I use one hand to bracket her entire jaw.

"Let's check."

Holding her firm, I use my other hand to run two fingers over her lips. Breaking past the barrier, I push them through the seam and stroke them over her tongue.

Reese moans around my fingers as I work them into her mouth, all the way to the back of her throat, and when they meet resistance, she doesn't fight it. She doesn't flinch or gag.

"You like having something back there, don't you?"

She nods around me, ocean eyes blown out with need. Then she sucks my fingers as a preview, and I just know I'm going to lose it when I get to see them replaced by my cock.

I push my fingers in and out, letting her stroke them with her tongue, all the while she's still tugging and twisting me in her fist.

"Oh, you're going to suck me so well, aren't you?"

She nods again, her mouth too occupied to speak. But then she pulls my hand out, spits on my two fingers, and slowly wraps her lips around them again.

My jaw is hanging all the way open.

So much for not falling in love with her.

I groan. "You're not going to just be good for me, are you? You're going to go ahead and be perfect, huh?"

Using my other hand, I push my boxers and jeans down, lifting my hips to get them past my ass. My cock stands proudly out in the open in my office with Reese's hand wrapped around it.

It's dirty. A bit depraved. And I would happily lose my job for this moment right now.

"You're so perfect." I run my hand through her hair before gripping those silky straight strands in my fist. "But I want to see you dirty."

Leaning forward, she places a soft kiss on the head of my cock.

I let go of her hair and let her do her thing.

Arms draped wide on the back of the couch again, I look down and watch her through hooded eyes.

"Do you know how much I appreciate you?" she asks before placing another kiss. "You're so good to me." Using the tip of her tongue, she runs it over the slit. "I'm not sure you realize just how much I adore you."

"Fuck."

The words. Sweet and heartfelt.

Her mouth. Hot and sinful. And so fucking talented.

She looks up at me through her lashes. "I think about you all the time, Em. Do you know that?"

With that, she slips her lips over my shaft and takes me all the way in.

I can't tell what's going to make me come first. Her honest confessions or the way her warm, wet mouth is sucking me so perfectly.

"Oh God," I groan, eyes screwed shut for only a second. But once I've regained a bit of composure, I open them again so I can watch her work. "I think about you all the time, Reese. When I'm with you. When I'm not with you. All the fucking time."

She hums around my length, bobbing her head before taking me deeper.

She is pure heaven.

Not only does she feel unreal, but it's hard to believe this is happening after all the times she told me it wouldn't. Harder still to believe some of the words that are coming out of her mouth after the way we started off.

She's so eager as she takes me, but also so calm. Like she has nowhere else she'd rather be and all the time in the world to make this last.

Reese moans and I almost lose it right there.

Bucking my hips, she takes me to the back of her throat and swallows around my tip.

"I'm going to come," I hardly push out past gritted teeth, wrapping a fist around her hair to keep it out of my view.

That declaration ignites a fire in her eyes. Bright blue, just like the hottest part of a flame. She wraps her lips around me tighter then runs her tongue around the head, fully determined to make me live up to my promise.

"You like that, Reese? You like knowing that you're going to make me come while we're at work?"

She rumbles this satisfied sound that shoots a vibration straight through my cock.

"You're so good," I encourage. "So perfect for me." With my palm on the back of her head, I gently push her down as I lift my hips. "You can take it." I move in and out of her mouth, keeping her exactly where I need her. "There you go."

Releasing my hold, I let her breathe and the self-satisfied smile she wears as she pops off my dick for a moment is enough to end me.

She strokes me in her hand, still regaining her breath. "Please give it to me."

"Yeah. You want it?"

She nods impatiently, kissing the tip of my dick again. My throbbing, eager, going-to-come-all-over-her-lips-if-she-does-that-again dick.

"Are you going to let me come in your mouth? Swallow it for me?"

"Is that where you want to finish?"

Fucking hell, this woman. Asking me where I want to finish.

"This time, yes." I lean forward, tugging her chin to me until I can place a kiss on that talented mouth. "But just know that if we weren't at work and if your makeup didn't look so pretty today, I'd be painting your face with my cum instead of the back of your throat."

Her lips drop open, and I take that as an opportunity to guide her mouth back down around me.

Her fervent sucking in combination of her hand twisting around the base sends me right over the edge of my orgasm.

I don't have time to give her a warning, but it's clear she already knows it's coming by the way she grips my thigh and steadies herself in place. Pleasure zips down my spine, curling around my hips until I'm coming down her throat.

Blinding bliss with Reese's blonde hair twined around my fingers and her mouth wrapped around my cock. My hips chase the high until I'm fully spent, falling back on the couch behind me.

Heavy hooded eyes look down to watch as she slips off, mouth full of my release.

Reese stares up at me, swallows it all, then hums like it's the best thing she's ever had in her mouth.

"Good God," I exhale through hard-earned breaths. "How?"

How are you real?

How are you interested in me?

How can I make you mine?

She simply smiles at my rhetorical question.

"Come here." I tuck myself back into my pants as I pull her onto my lap. Holding her to me, I kiss her, tasting myself on her lips. "You expect me to stay away from you tonight after that?"

"I believe in you."

"I'm a much weaker man than you give me credit for."

She drops her smiling mouth to mine again, this time in a slow, sweeping kiss. It's patient in the way she takes her time. There's longing in the way her tongue slides against my own. There's care in the way she strokes her fingers through my beard.

There's no wondering whether she likes me. I know Reese likes me. But the question is, does she want me the way I want her? Because I'm pretty sure I'm willing to put everything on the line for a real shot with this woman.

When she pulls back, I slip her hair behind her ear, running my thumb over her earrings. "Is this the part when you tell me that can't happen again?"

Reese huffs a small laugh. "Exactly."

I hum. "Maybe one day I'll start believing you."

30

REESE

"All right, you two." The photographer holds his camera up. "We need a photo. This will be frame-worthy. The previous team owner and the current one."

I slip an arm around my grandfather as we pose together, getting our picture taken. Maybe it'll be one that I'll add to the walls during my own retirement party one day.

The photographer smiles at the screen on his camera. "Perfect." Then he moves on to take more photos of more party guests, snapping his way through the venue.

I glance around the room again, taking it all in. "Denise did a hell of a job."

My grandfather looks around with me.

We have an event space at the stadium, and it was only right that his retirement party took place here. So many of his previous players, coaches, and staff have shown up to help him bid farewell to this part of his life, and the whole night just feels really special.

One man's entire life's work in one room.

There's a dance floor in the center and a live band on a small makeshift stage. Multiple open bars are set up along the perimeter of the space, and the remaining walls are covered in photo collages, showcasing all the previous teams and memories my grandfather has made in this exact building.

"This is really something, isn't it, Reese's Pieces?" His voice goes thick. "I can't believe so many people showed up."

His emotion is evident, but how could it not be? I gained my love of this game and this career choice from him. He was the embodiment of "choose a job you love, and you'll never have to work a day in your life."

I run a hand across his back. "You deserve for people to show up."

I scan the room once again, recognizing so many faces from the past. And of course, plenty of ones from the present.

Our entire current roster is here, all suited up, because, like me, my grandfather enjoys the fancier parts of life.

The lighting is dim and moody. Cocktail tables are peppered throughout the space, as are plush couches for mingling. The food was divine, and it's clear that no expense was spared.

It's been special to spend tonight with my grandfather, but I'd be lying if I said that was the only reason I've been glued to his side. My self-control is utterly lacking as of late, so much so that I don't know what I'd do if I didn't attach myself by a metaphorical leash.

My attention drifts to the dance floor, snagging on the source of my lack of restraint.

Emmett is wearing this sweet, almost wistful expression as he looks down at his daughter. It's a tender moment, the two of them dancing together, and I'm unable to tear my eyes away from him. It's been my issue all night. We've successfully avoided each other for hours, but that doesn't mean I haven't looked.

Miller says something to him that causes Emmett's head to fall back in laughter and I can't help but smile at his contagious joy. He looks good when he's happy. He looks good, period.

"Arthur!" Scott calls out, drawing my attention away from the dance floor as he and the rest of the advisory board circle around my grandfather. "It is so good to see you. You're looking great."

My grandfather beams at the five men. "Thank you all so much for coming. It means so much to me."

"We wouldn't miss it for the world," Phil says.

"How have you all been? How's it going with my Reese? Giving her some good advice, I hope."

"Great advice." Scott puts his hand on my grandfather's shoulder in a chummy but slimy way. "Just waiting for her to take it."

My attention drifts to Ed, and he meets my eye, telling me he's thinking the same damn thing as me.

My grandfather looks around the group of men suspiciously. "What do you mean?"

"He's kidding." Phil laughs. "We're glad to be working with her. She's really . . . doing her own thing. Making this team *hers*."

Again, Ed and I share a look, silently calling out that bullshit.

"As she should." My grandfather beams with pride because he doesn't pick up on the nuance of their statements. He has no idea that four of the five members of his previous advisory board are furious with the direction I'm taking my team and think I should step down as Acting President of Baseball Operations.

I'm also not going to go run to him and tattle. I can handle myself just fine.

Ed gives me a squeeze on the arm as I excuse myself.

For the first time tonight, I'm alone without the safety net of company. I instantly feel the heat of Emmett's attention, the same way I have most of the night. Glancing back in the direction of the dance floor, I find him and Miller walking off as the song ends.

But as I assumed, he's watching me.

He looks stunning tonight. Fitted black suit, white shirt unbuttoned near his throat, and a perfectly trimmed beard leading to a bit of salt around his temples. It's not often I get to see him without his baseball hat, but it's a lovely change to witness his face without the shadow of a brim covering it.

Then you add those black lines webbing over his hands, falling out past the cuffs of his suit and starkly contrasting the rest of his look tonight, and I'm just kind of done for.

His lips are a bit too full but perfect all the same, especially when they fight the smile he shouldn't be sending me from across the room.

Emmett joins a group of his players, and I turn my attention back to the bar.

Grab a drink. Reattach myself to my grandfather. Those are the only two things I'm allowed to do.

"A glass of red, please," I request from the bartender, and as he's pouring it, my phone dings in my clutch.

Emmett's name is on my screen with a message below it, but when I look for him over my shoulder, he's mid-conversation with the guys on the team, standing around a cocktail table. No phone in sight.

Emmett: If I had it my way, you plus that dress would be the second-best thing I'd see today.

Honestly, screw the giddy, ridiculous smile on my lips. Something is truly wrong with me lately.

Me: What would be the first?

I press send and watch over my shoulder as he pulls his phone from his pocket and holds it under the table to read and reply while keeping it hidden from everyone else.

Emmett: You minus that dress.

This forty-something-year-old man has more game than anyone I've dated in the past. Confident and unapologetic all at the same time. And it just really does something to me. The way he's both hard and soft. Grumpy yet a huge fucking flirt.

Again, I look over my shoulder at him, and this time, find his eyes already on me. They take their time slowly tracking down my length, outlining my dress while his bottom lip absent-mindedly slips between his teeth.

"Aww," Miller coos, sliding into the space next to me at the bar.

I quickly pull my attention away from her father and focus on the glass of freshly poured wine in my hand.

"Mutual eye-fucking across the room. So cute." She thinks about what she just said before she audibly gags next to me. "I cannot believe I just said *eye-fucking* in regard to my dad."

Chuckling, I take a sip from my glass. "Sorry to break it to you, Miller, but your dad is very eye-fuckable."

"Oh God. Not you too." The look on her face is utter disgust before she rethinks that statement as well. "Actually, I take that back. You're just about the only person I'm okay with saying that."

I gesture to the bar. "Can I get you something to drink?"

"A beer would be life-changing at the moment."

"Yeah, I bet it would be. I'll happily buy you a beer once you push that baby out."

"Fine. I'll take a water. How boring."

We're shoulder to shoulder, saddled up to the crowded bar top, with our backs to the party. I've just asked for an ice water when Miller says, "My dad likes you," quietly enough that only I can hear.

I swallow hard. "Yeah. I like him too. We work well together."

"No. He *likes* you. In a way I've never seen before."

I'm beyond tempted to get all schoolgirl on her with a, "you really think so?" but I restrain myself.

Emmett's daughter was not the first person on my list I expected to discuss this with, and it would be so much safer for me if I could get back to my grandfather and spend the rest of the night trying to pretend that my field manager didn't exist.

"We just . . ." I speak in a hushed tone, discreetly checking my surroundings. "It can't be like that."

"Why not?"

How do I even answer?

Sure, as the owner of this franchise, there's nothing that would explicitly keep me from having a relationship with someone in my organization. But it's not about some metaphorical rulebook. It's about the way it would look. I'm his direct superior.

What would that do to my reputation? I'm still dealing with the mess that happened online this past week. I can already see the headlines now about me being a woman and sleeping with someone on my staff. Let alone just months after I took over the team. The situation would be entirely twisted to fit a narrative, and I have a responsibility to other women who are trying to break into this industry to not give us a bad name.

I'm his boss. He's up for a new contract. Who knows how messy that could get?

"Because . . ." Again, I hesitate. "I want to protect him. And myself too. He loves his job, I love my job, and he really loves you. He wants to stay in this city. He and I would just be . . . messy."

"I think messy is worth it sometimes." She mulls something over for a moment, taking a drink of her water. "I wouldn't normally be this bold—"

I lift a brow in her direction.

"Okay." She laughs. "I meant I wouldn't be this bold about someone else's relationship, but he's always been my favorite person, so I'm just going to say my piece on the whole thing."

She turns to face me, so I give her my full attention too. "I know he's been lonely. He may never admit it because he keeps himself busy, but I see it. I don't remember what he was like with my mom, but he's a completely different person than he was back then anyway. Raising a kid on your own that you didn't plan for and putting everyone else ahead of yourself will do that to you. But he doesn't look lonely when you're around. As an only child, that kind of means everything to me, you know?"

The backs of my eyes burn in a way I'm wholly unaccustomed to. I don't often cry, especially now. I've learned to overcompensate being a woman in a man's field by trying to take the emotions out of most things.

But this little speech might just get me.

"And I hear you on the whole job thing," she continues. "I don't know what that would look like for his career and your reputation. But I used to base a lot of my decisions off what I thought was best for him too. I used to travel for work all the time, constantly be on the go, because I thought staying away was the best thing for him. I thought it gave him the space he needed to do his own thing and live his own life after giving it all up for me. Then I realized that he just wanted me around."

She offers me a small smile. "I'm pretty sure he just wants you around, Reese. And if there's anyone who deserves to get everything they want, it's him."

Well . . . shit.

I can't imagine those words hitting harder than they just did, being delivered by the person Emmett loves most in the world.

I can't tell her how scared I am to like her dad. Or how much I already do. If that's something I were to ever admit, it'll be to Emmett himself. But I also don't think I can express to her just how much hearing her say that means to me.

But what I can say is, "He does deserve to get everything he wants."

"Who deserves to get everything they want?"

It's a deep, gravelly voice asking the question. One I'd recognize anywhere. One I haven't heard all night.

My plan of grabbing a drink and returning to my grandfather is failing miserably.

Miller and I make eye contact, silently asking the other how we're going to play this off.

"*I* do," she says, covering for me. "Carrying this baby for nine months. Do you know how many restrictions there are during pregnancy? And of course you get to drink a beer." She gestures to the glass in Emmett's hand. "I'm going to go give Kai some shit for this. This is all his fault anyway."

Miller takes off in a faux huff and her dad steals her spot next to me at the bar, eyes locked on her back in confusion.

"What was that all about?"

"Oh, you know Miller."

Miller, who loves her dad enough to practically beg me to open my eyes and see him.

But seeing him is not the problem. Quite the opposite, in fact. Part of me wishes I could go back to the days when I was unaware of just how big his heart is. It made it a whole lot easier to keep from falling for him.

"You look . . ." His eyes trail down my body. "Fitting for you to wear black tonight. My heart practically stopped when you walked in, and here you are, already dressed for my funeral."

There's that unapologetic confidence again.

"You're far too old to be joking about heart issues, Emmett."

He brings his beer to his smiling lips. "I truly wish I were kidding."

"Reese?" someone calls out. "No way. Is that really you?"

It takes me a moment to process who is standing in front of me, speaking as if they know me. Graying hair and wrinkled skin from too much time in the sun. I couldn't have been more than ten years old the last time I saw him.

"Mick?" I study him for a second to make sure I'm correct before I go ahead and hug a complete stranger. When he doesn't correct me, I set my wine down on the bar and open my arms. "Oh my God! It's been so long."

He gives me a tight squeeze. "Look at you, girl! You were just a kid the last time I saw you. I remember you used to always hang out in the dugout during practices. Didn't we have one of your birthday parties in this exact room? Me and all the guys went. And what was it that we all called you? Reese's Pieces! That's right."

I exhale a small laugh. "It's just Reese now." Shifting, I involve Emmett into the conversation. "Emmett, this is Mick. He played second base for the Warriors for over a decade. He was a part of the team when I first started coming around with my grandfather and fell in love with the game. Mick, this is Emmett. Our field manager."

The two men shake hands.

"So great to meet you," Emmett says kindly.

"Wow." Mick stands with his hands on his hips, shaking his head at me in disbelief. "So, you're running the team now, huh?"

Oh.

A flush of embarrassment rushes my cheeks. He knew me as just a little girl obsessed with being a part of this team. He remembers me always hanging around and wanting to be included. If I were him, I'd also assume my grandfather passed the franchise on as a way to appease me.

"She is," Emmett answers for me when I don't respond quick enough. "And she's doing a hell of a job."

"Of course she is." Mick smiles down at me. "You were always sharp. I remember that. Knew the game better than some of the grown men who were playing it. And you loved this place more than anyone. You were just a part of the family. It wouldn't make sense for anyone other than you to be running the team."

I can sense Emmett's proud gaze boring into the side of my face, but I don't have it in me to turn and indulge in it. I feel a bit splayed out being described by someone who was around when I had the luxury of being naïve about this business. But I won't lie, after a week of getting hell from the press, the words from an old player I adored back in the day mean more than he probably realizes.

"I need to go say hi to Arthur," Mick says. "Congratulate him on his retirement. Emmett, it was great to meet you. And, Reese, it's nice to see this team in the hands of someone who loves it so much."

We say our goodbyes and Mick heads off, leaving Emmett and me alone.

"So," he begins in a teasing tone. "Remember that time you told me that baseball is just a business?"

"Shut up."

I smack him in the arm with the back of my hand, but he grabs my wrist before I can pull away. He's close. Too close. Chest to chest with his long fingers wrapped around me, holding me softly.

"Dance with me."

It's a gentle plea and does something foreign and unpermitted to my chest.

"Emmett—"

"Dance with me."

"You can't just repeat what you said and expect me to change my response."

He does his best to bite back his smile.

I look around the room again.

It's packed with too many people who know exactly who we both are. Sure, everyone is occupied with doing their own thing, but still, someone would be bound to grow suspicious of a slow dance between the two of us.

"There are too many eyes," I tell him.

"At this point, I've danced with my daughter, your grandmother, and Denise. I think people would find it more strange if I *didn't* dance with you. We don't want anyone thinking the owner and field manager aren't getting along again, do we?"

"I think that might be a safer option."

"Dance with me, Reese."

His brown eyes are soft, his dark brows pinched together as he looks down at me. And when the song shifts and the live band begins to play the next one, I don't have it in me to turn him down again.

"Okay," I whisper.

"See." A proud smile hitches on his lips. "Different response."

"You're awfully annoying when you get what you want."

He pushes my wineglass off to the side along with his half-finished beer, then finds the small of my back to usher me out onto the dance floor.

We pass too many familiar faces. The dance floor is too crowded. Though, I suppose that might work to our advantage, hiding among the sea of bodies.

We catch the attention of many of our current players, but still Emmett doesn't hesitate, leading me right to the center of the floor. Like he has no problem if those close to us realize there's something going on here.

His recklessness has my nerves frayed. I should've never left my grandfather's side.

Kai and Isaiah are huddled together on the perimeter of the dance floor, watching us with ridiculously giddy grins on their faces. But when they realize I've caught them looking, they quickly turn away and pretend as if they've been occupied with something else this entire time.

"The Rhodes boys have no chill."

Emmett chuckles. "Tell me about it."

Turning to face me, he slides one of my arms over his neck, holding the other out to the side. Then he places his palm at a respectable height at my mid-back, and for that split second, I let myself believe others will find this perfectly professional.

This could be okay.

I smooth my hand over his shoulder, keeping my voice low. "You look handsome tonight."

He grins lazily. "Thank you."

"And you and Miller looked sweet together on the dance floor."

"Crazy to think that the next time I'll be dancing with her will be at her wedding."

The mental image has me smiling, but it drops the same time Emmett's hand sinks an inch lower on my back.

"So, what were you two speaking about earlier?"

It'd be a lot easier to lie to him. To make something up so we don't get into that kind of conversation here—while on the dance floor. In front of the entire Warriors organization, both past and present.

But he's always honest with me, so I don't how I couldn't be the same.

"She thinks you want me around."

I'm hesitant to look up and meet his eye, but when I do, I find that he has no issue watching me in the same way.

"I do want you around, Reese."

"No, I mean—"

"I know exactly what you mean. And my answer is still the same. I want you around. All the time, really. I just want *you*, but I think you already know that."

Oxygen has a tough time finding my lungs. There's no shyness to his statement. No hesitation. He's a man who knows what he wants and apparently, he wants me.

I discreetly check our surroundings. "Em, not here."

"Fine, but where I say it won't change my answer. I want you, Reese."

My eyes bounce between his. "Why?"

The question is out before I think better of it. Before I have time to remind myself to hide that insecurity. Before I can remember where we are.

Emmett's brows pinch together. "Is that a real question?"

Unfortunately, yes. It is. I didn't know there could be a why. I once thought you just loved someone for who they are until I learned that some people do have another reason why. An ulterior motive.

His palm on my back sinks another inch lower, and at the same time, he pulls me closer to him. Hard stomach to my soft. His hold on me is firm and unrelenting. Comforting in a way it shouldn't be with so many eyes nearby. All while continuing to sway us to the soft melody.

"You should never have to ask that question, but I understand why you are."

A small wave of relief washes over me that I don't have to explain myself. It's not talked about enough. How settling it is to be understood without needing to make someone understand.

The realization that Emmett has *always* understood me has me pliable when he takes my hand that's held out to the side and hooks it to meet my other around his neck.

His palm strokes against the bare skin of my arm until it also drops to my lower back.

"I don't know if my why is a tangible thing I can pinpoint, Reese. I don't know that I have a good answer for you to overanalyze. But I know some of the reasons why I *don't* want you."

Craning my neck, I look up at him, desperate to hear the next words out of his mouth. His mouth that's too close to be considered professional, but all I can seem to care about is the next thing that's going to come out of it.

"I don't want you for what you can offer me," he says. "I don't want you for job security. In fact, I think we both know that me wanting you will provide me the opposite of that. I don't want you because you suddenly brought me back to life or anything like that. I've had purpose. I love my life. I love my job. And I love my family. I don't want you for anything that you can give me, other than the hope I've been unable to ignore since you walked into this building."

My heart races in an unhealthy way, and I try to calm it by focusing on the small circles he's drawing with his thumb against my back.

"For someone who has gone twenty years assuming that I would spend the rest of my life only being a dad and only being a coach, there's a nagging hope I feel when you're around that I could also be . . ."

Someone's partner. Someone's equal.

He doesn't finish that sentence, because he doesn't need to. I already know.

There was so much of me that longed to hear exactly that, but then there's also another part of me that prayed he'd never say it out loud. That we'd never have to confront what's happening between us.

And here of all places. Locked in the center of people who can never know.

It's scary. Everything about him is scary. The way his mere presence has me questioning everything I once stood firm in is terrifying.

His confession brings us to a boiling point and we both know it. And I just wish that this song would end so I could get off this dance floor to keep from confronting what's right in front of us.

Emmett drops his head, lips ghosting the shell of my ear. "I know I promised you that I'd protect you and your reputation and the legacy you want to leave. And I'm fully aware that I'm breaking that promise by wanting you. And I don't know what the fuck to do about it, Reese. For someone who usually has all the answers, I have no idea how to *stop* wanting you."

"Emmett." There's a desperate plea in the way I say his name. "Please not here."

When I turn my head to look at him, I find this almost untamed need in his eye and it terrifies me for the next thing he's going to say.

"I don't think you understand me. It doesn't matter where I say it. I wasn't lying that day in the elevator when I told you to fire me. That's where I'm at. I'm not willing to risk your reputation, but I am willing to risk my own job to figure out what this might be. So fucking fire me already."

"No." I pull away from him in a somewhat dramatic fashion, but thankfully the song ends and plenty of people are separating on the dance floor that no one seems to notice. "Absolutely not."

"Reese—"

He reaches out for me, but I take a step back to create distance, then look around to remind him where we are right now.

He's lost his fucking mind if he thinks I'm going to let him lose his job over me. After everything he's done to get back to this place in his life. After everything he sacrificed.

"Absolutely not." I keep my voice sharp but hushed. "We aren't . . . that's not an option."

Can he hear how scared I am? Can he see it on my face?

"Don't bring that up ever again. I'm . . ."

Not worth it.

And that's not a lack of self-esteem speaking for me. I know my worth. That's the fear of him losing everything he's ever wanted to gamble on me. In that respect, I refuse to let him believe I'm worth that risk.

"I'm . . ." I try again. "I'm not going to have this conversation again."

Then I turn on my heel and leave the dance floor as I fast as I can without drawing suspicion. But as soon as I'm out of the main event space, I run.

31

EMMETT

"You good?" Kai asks as I bring the bourbon to my lips.

I relish in the burn as it slides down my throat. It's both delicious and needed.

I know exactly where Reese ran off to. We're at the stadium after all. But I'm not going to disturb her in her one safe space here. In the one place she can think clearly.

Instead, I'm going to down this drink and reminisce on what a fucking idiot I am for professing my unwavering desire to be with her while in the middle of all our coworkers.

I don't answer Kai because I don't have it in me to lie and I can't exactly talk this out with him right here and now. Instead, I lean my forearms on the cocktail table and take another long swig from the glass.

"I'll take that as a no, you're not good, and you don't want to talk about it."

I lift an impressed brow in his direction. "You know me so well, honey."

He chuckles. "I'm taking Mills home. She's not feeling great."

"What?" I stand up straighter. "Is she okay?"

"Sorry. Yeah, she's fine. Just more exhausted than she thought she'd be. We came with Isaiah and Ken, but they're not ready to call it a night just yet, so I'm going to get a rideshare for us."

"No. No need for that." I reach into my pocket, pulling out my keys. "Take my truck."

"You sure? Do you want me to drop you off on our way?"

Glancing back at the door where Reese exited, I will her to walk back in.

Still, she doesn't.

So, I finish the rest of the bourbon in my hand. I've only had this and half a beer, and as tempted as I am to get a little buzz going so I can think about something *other* than what just happened on the dance floor, I know I need to stay sober so I can apologize for making a scene when she comes back in.

"I'm going to hang here for a bit," I tell my future son-in-law. "I'll grab a rideshare later, but thanks."

He smacks me on the shoulder. "See you tomorrow."

Over the next hour, I mingle with my coworkers. I catch up with some of my former players. I stare at the door, waiting for Reese to come back inside.

I know she went and hid in the dugout, but it's been over an hour. She should've been back by now.

It's then the sobering realization sinks in that she isn't coming back to the party because she already left.

What is wrong with me? Why did I feel the need to tell her that here of all places? She preemptively asked me to stay away tonight. She essentially glued herself to her grandfather to ensure that I would.

And the second I had her to myself, I practically begged her to be with me. Threw my job on the line and everything. For someone who can usually read a situation through a clear lens, my feelings for Reese have me spinning out of control and ridding my brain of all rational thought.

I might not know what the hell I'm doing when it comes to Reese, but I do know if she's not here anymore, then I don't want to be either.

Making my rounds, I say a few goodbyes, congratulate Arthur one more time, then head out the side door to go home for the night.

A tinge of humidity still suffocates the air as I step outside, and the suit I'm wearing doesn't help the situation. But it's not nearly as bad as it'll feel later this summer. I pull up the rideshare app on my phone, request a car, and stand on the curb as I wait for it to arrive.

A few minutes pass and a car pulls up along the curb in front of me, but it's not the one the app told me to look out for. It's a little red Porsche that's far too pristine to be used as a taxi.

The tinted passenger window begins to descend and when I dip my head to look inside, I find Reese behind the wheel.

I know she has a couple of cars and apparently one of them is a Porsche. And unsurprisingly, she looks fucking unreal in it.

"Need a ride?" she asks.

I hold up my phone to show her the screen. "Just called for one."

The unmistakable click of the passenger door unlocking fills the silence between us.

"Cancel it. I'll take you home."

That desperation to talk to her comes back with a thundering amount of hope that this could be my opportunity to do just that. It's what causes me to cancel my ride and slide into the car with her.

It's not meant for someone of my size, that's for damn sure. But I can put up with a bit of physical discomfort if that means I might be able to fix what just happened between us.

Reese pulls onto the street and starts driving.

"I thought you left," I say into the otherwise silent car.

She hesitates for a long moment. "I just needed some time to think."

I watch her, and get the sense she's thankful she has to keep her eyes on the road.

"Are you okay?"

"I don't know, Em."

This is the part where I should apologize for springing that not-so-little confession on her. But something about the way she's slumped as she drives, and the exhaustion she's experiencing from overthinking for the past hour, has me keeping my mouth shut and saving it for another time.

The ride is silent. Every red light we sit at makes the tension grow. This car is far too small for this much pressure to build.

She takes a turn in the opposite direction of my apartment, and that's when I realize she has no clue where I live. I blanked on giving her directions, too preoccupied with her simply being here.

"I actually . . ." I throw my thumb over my shoulder. "I'm that way."

"Okay."

Reese continues to drive without looking for a place to turn around. Without even trying to.

I'm a smart enough man not to question her. Not tonight. She's equal parts confident and uneasy as she continues on, and I can't quite put my finger on what's going on. She takes a few more turns, the route an ingrained path for her, until finally, she pulls up in front of a building.

Her building.

The valet pops out to park her car for her, but before he gets to the door, I turn to her.

"Not that I'm complaining, but I thought you said you were taking me home?"

"I am. I just didn't say when."

She passes off her keys to the valet, and heads to the main entrance of the building, expecting me to follow.

And like a fucking dog, I do.

I quickly catch up to her, and together, we cross the lobby to the same elevator where I kissed her for the first time. Standing next to each other inside, we don't speak. The only sound is the instrumental music playing over the speakers.

It's soft and calming, vastly contradictory to the war raging inside of me. The confusion. The want. The hope that if I'm not going home just yet, that'll give us time to talk. Time for me to apologize.

The music doesn't match up with the woman next to me either. She's practically rattling with nerves, and they only seem to grow the higher we climb. More than anything else, that's what has my attention.

"Reese, if you don't want me to come up, I don't have to."

"It's not that. It's just . . ." She steels her spine as the elevator stops moving. "I'll explain inside."

She exhales a long breath as the doors open, then steps off into her condo, heading farther into the entryway. I take one single step into her place, but pause there, just on the other side of elevator doors, because I'm not actually convinced she wants me to be here.

The elevator closes behind me, leaving us alone. And finally, Reese turns to look at me.

"So, this is my condo." She sweeps her arms out, and her voice is laced with faux confidence.

I quickly glance around. It looks exactly as I would expect her place to be. Expensive. Luxurious. And it practically screams her name with the neutral color palette.

"It's beautiful."

The statement is hardly out of my mouth before she starts trying to explain herself. "I know it's indulgent and a bit over the top, but—"

"I like that you like nice things, Reese." Her blue eyes meet mine, this fear of being judged so clear in her expression. "And I like that you like me."

She sighs, her shoulders dropping. "I do like you, Emmett."

"I know you do."

Reese's expression is full of apology, as if she's the one who needs to apologize for leaving earlier when I was the one who ran her off.

She shifts on her heels as a pink hue flushes her cheeks. "No one else has ever been in this condo before. It's another one of my safe spaces, I suppose. Another place I can hide."

Oh.

Her nervous energy suddenly makes complete sense, and the gravity of what she's telling me settles onto my shoulders. Her allowing me to see her home feels a lot like she's allowing me to see *her*.

That realization changes this entire interaction. She's not tense because I was too honest with her earlier. She's nervous because she's trying to do the same.

Suddenly, the five feet of entryway between us feels like too much distance.

"I'm sorry for running off earlier."

"No." I take a single step in her direction. "No, Reese. I shouldn't have thrown all that on you, especially there."

"It's just that, I don't have the luxury of letting my walls down in public, Em."

"I know. I knew better than to do that, and I'm sorry."

"So, I guess that's why I wanted to bring you here. This place makes me feel safe to be myself." Her eyes meet mine. "*You* make me feel safe to be myself."

I want to cover the space between us, to take away the distance. But I can tell by the way she's hesitating that she's trying to conjure the words she needs to say to me.

And I want to hear every single one of them.

"You're a safe man, Emmett. I know that might not seem like the most glowing of compliments, but I promise you, you being safe is everything to someone like me."

Safe. Maybe if I were young, I wouldn't love the description. But as a grown man who knows better, safe is the only word I want her to use to describe me. It's the only way I want her to feel around me.

Her honesty has me frozen in the entryway of her condo, unable to tear my eyes off her and praying that she keeps going.

"I think that might be your superpower. Being safe."

Her ocean eyes are soft but look like they might well up at any moment, and I have a feeling whatever she's about to say could make mine do the same.

"You make your players on the team feel safe enough to come to you with whatever they need. You made the Rhodes boys feel safe enough to think of you as both a father and a friend. You made Miller feel safe enough to know that she was going to be loved by you when she lost her mom. And Claire . . ." Reese smiles sadly. "You made her feel safe enough that when it was her time to go, she knew she could leave her daughter with you. I can't imagine the relief she must have felt, knowing her daughter would be safe with you."

It's hard to breathe. I'm unable to swallow past the lump in my throat. It's more overwhelming than I assumed it'd be, being seen in this way by someone you desperately want to know every part of you.

"And me," Reese continues. "You make me feel safe enough that when I'm around you, I can take off my armor. Even when I have to continue wearing it around everyone else. When I'm with you, you allow me to shut off my brain because it feels safe enough to know that everything will be taken care of, and I don't have to be the one to handle it."

She swallows, seeming like she's on the verge of crying, and it's then I realize I've never seen her cry. Even over the past week, while she was being torn to shreds, she didn't cry.

Reese straightens her shoulders, and boldly says, "My heart

has waited a long time to be wanted by someone like you, and that terrifies me."

And now I'm positive all the oxygen has left the room. I certainly can't seem to find any.

"Why does that scare you, Reese?"

"Where do I start?" She breathes a sad laugh.

"Anywhere. Start anywhere. Just tell me everything."

"Well." She gestures in my direction with frustration. "I'm scared because I tried and failed to stay away from you. I'm scared of what the headlines would say if anyone found out. I already feel traumatized from this last week as it is. I'm scared for your job, regardless that you say you're willing to lose it. But *I'm* not willing for you to lose it. And I'm scared that the one thing I've *ever* wanted, which was this career, feels overshadowed by how much I want you."

Those final three words play on a loop as I take a step toward her.

"I'm scared of this career slipping through my fingers before it's really even begun, which is also exactly how I feel about you. And most days, those two things don't feel like they can coexist, so that's scary too."

She takes a breath, recomposing herself. "But the thing that scares me the most is knowing that there was safety and security in not looking for someone to add to my life. I truly was fine being alone because turning off the desire to find a partner meant that I turned off any chance that someone could let me down again. I wouldn't have to question someone's motives for wanting to be in my life. So, the thought of switching that back on is . . ."

"Scary," I finish for her, taking another step in her direction.

"Terrifying."

"Don't think you're alone in that. You terrify me just the same, Reese. I've only ever wanted one other person in my entire life, and I lost her. Wanting someone again, opening myself to possibly losing you is fucking petrifying."

Her head tilts, brows pinched. "Emmett."

"But my fear doesn't stop me from wanting you."

She swallows hard. "Neither does mine."

I take another step in her direction, risking it all when I ask, "So what are we doing, Reese?"

"I don't know." She throws her hands up in defeat. "I have this internal war raging inside me at all times. I feel calm when you're around, but also like every inch of me is on fire. You're both safe and simultaneously the most terrifying person in my life. I have never been so unsure about what to do while also being so steadfast and certain about you. I have no idea what I'm doing, while at the same time knowing exactly what I want. And, Emmett." Her shoulders drop, every inch of her giving up the fight. "I want you."

It's overwhelmingly surreal to hear that you're wanted by a woman who doesn't need anyone.

"Say that again."

Her eyes narrow with confusion. "Which part?"

"The last part."

"I want you."

"That's the one. That's all that matters."

I close the distance between us, standing right in front of her.

Hopeful and vulnerable and terrified blue eyes look up to meet mine. "What if we risk everything and we don't work out?"

"But what if we do?"

The words sit in the small amount of empty space left between us.

"Emmett," she whispers, so clearly exhausted from overthinking all night. "I'm tired of fighting this."

"Yeah, baby. Me too." I drop my forehead to hers. "So, let's stop fighting."

32

REESE

My calves hit the chaise that lives at the end of my bed.

I'm not paying attention to where I'm going, though I know I'm at the edge of something big, seconds away from tipping over. Metaphorically, that is.

I want to fall.

Without restraint. Without worry.

I want to fall, knowing he's coming with me.

My eyes stay glued to the stunning man in a suit standing just inside my bedroom doorway. Watching as he unclasps his watch from his wrist. Watching the methodical way he lays it on my dresser by the door so he can remember to grab it tomorrow.

Emmett takes slow steps in my direction as his fingers work at the cuff buttons of his shirt.

I get to work as well, reaching down to unfasten the buckle on my heels.

"Leave them on," he says coolly. "I'll be the one to do that."

He shrugs his suit jacket off and cuffs the sleeves to his white button-down shirt, showing off those tattooed forearms.

"You know exactly what you're doing, showing me those."

A knowing smile lifts on his lips, but he keeps his attention on his shirt, folding the cuffs precisely how he wants. I'm not sure why he's so adamant about fixing his sleeves when the whole thing should just be coming off already.

But he looks hot, so I don't say anything.

He drops his suit jacket onto my chaise and when his long legs bring him to me, he takes my face in both of his hands and drops his mouth to mine.

Confidently. Possessively. And when his tongue sweeps past my lips, it tells me exactly who I belong to.

Which is fine by me.

He stands behind me in public. Allows me to lead the way I need to. I'll happily bend to him behind closed doors.

The kiss turns a bit frantic. Desperate hands. Eager mouths.

After so many confessions tonight, it's nice to busy my lips with kissing him instead of talking.

He lifts me in his arms, rounding the bed to lay me flat on the mattress, and with both of us still fully clothed, he climbs right over me.

We move together immediately. Needy, searching hips looking for each other.

Mouths melded together, he reaches between me and the mattress and pulls my zipper down my spine, opening my dress in one easy motion. He pushes it down to pool around my waist.

"Please, baby," he breathes against my mouth, rocking his body over mine. "Fucking please."

"Em, are you begging?"

He breathes a laugh. "Yes. God, I need you, Reese."

The confession is soft, a sharp juxtaposition from his hard body and the firm grip he has on my hip.

It's one of my favorite things about him. The hard and soft.

"Show me."

My request has his pupils blown out. This sheer determination etched on his face. "I'll show you all night."

But then he looks down at me, partway undressed with my dress wrapped around my hips.

And shakes his head. "But the first one might be kind of quick because holy shit, Reese. Look at you."

Maybe that statement shouldn't be such a turn-on. But the idea that this stunning man, who is still fully dressed, already knows he's not going to last long just from looking at my almost naked body . . .

Yeah, my confidence is through the roof.

His hands gently roam my bare skin, reverent touches followed by warm lips laying worshipping kisses. Emmett works a path over my jaw, down my neck, and across my collarbone. His mouth drags over my strapless bra, lips brushing right along the cups until he reaches behind me and flicks the clasp open at my back.

He pulls it away, discarding it somewhere on the floor.

"Fucking perfect."

It's a whispered prayer chanted right against my nipple, and the warmth of his breath is a maddening tease. It only worsens when Emmett tenderly drags his lips right over the peak. That minor graze causes my entire body to shudder with need.

"Emmett. Mouth." They're the only words I can push out, incoherent and under his spell already.

He gets the message regardless, and though I half expected him to fire back a "don't tell me what to do," instead he wraps his mouth around me, bites me gently, then sucks.

I arch into his mouth. "*Yes*, baby."

He growls against me, but the way his tongue lashes at me, I'd say he's perfectly okay with the accidental pet name.

"Been dreaming of these, Reese."

"Hmm." I hum, so ridiculously turned on already. "So, you're a tits guy."

"If we're referring to yours, then yes." He flicks his tongue over my nipple. "In which case, I'm an ass guy too."

His mouth works on one breast while he grabs the other in his rough hand and squeezes. Then he gives it a light smack to watch it bounce, and the sudden sharp sensation has me squirming as wetness pools between my legs.

It's not a lot, but from him, it seems like it might be enough to make me come. That's how badly I want him. How desperately I've been fighting myself to stay away.

I've touched myself to the thought of him far too many times over the last few months, that having the real thing, having his hands on me, having his mouth taste me . . .

We're on the same page about not lasting long.

His shoes drop to the floor, and at the same time, he pulls my dress down my hips and legs, adding that to the pile as well.

Kneeling between my legs, he lays wet, messy kisses over my stomach, his hands touching every part of me he can get to. And for that brief moment, I let myself remember a time I would've been insecure in this position, sprawled on my back on full display with someone's hands and mouth all over a part of me that's not my smallest.

Seeing Emmett's fingers knead into my flesh with this desperate need, listening to the hungry sounds coming from his throat as he attempts to kiss every inch of my skin as if he needs to brand me as his, has me questioning how I could ever be self-conscious when the view is this good.

I run my fingers through his hair. "You look good like this, Em. Between my legs. Exactly where you should be."

He smiles against my skin. "You think I look good? You should see yourself from my view."

His eyes flash up to meet mine just as he places a gentle kiss right over the front of my panties.

"*Fuck*." I shudder, sucking in a harsh breath.

"You're so wet already, Reese. When did this start?"

I try to find a coherent string of words. "When you walked into the party wearing that suit tonight."

He groans. "So you've been a mess for hours."

He presses his mouth more firmly, sucking me through the fabric.

"*Em*," I cry out, fingers gripping his hair, needing something to hold on to.

"Let's add 'pussy' to that list of things I'm a fan of. Because I'm already a huge fan of yours."

He takes the elastic waistband between his fucking teeth and yanks them over my hips. Lifting my legs in the air, he uses only his mouth to pull the fabric completely off my body.

He spits them out to add them to the floor with the rest of my discarded clothes.

Primal and dirty and so fucking hot.

It's then I realize that other than my high heels, I'm completely naked while he's still fully dressed. And when he pushes my legs apart, splaying my open, I realize exactly why he cuffed his sleeves earlier.

Because right now, this man is on a mission to get to work.

His dark eyes are locked right on the glistening wetness between my legs.

"Heels?" I ask.

He doesn't look up at me, too fixated on my pussy.

"With how many times I've wanted to bend you over your desk while you're wearing those at work, they're staying on for now."

He lifts one of my legs to his lips, placing a reverent kiss to my ankle bone. His eyes take a leisurely path over my entire body until he finds my face.

"You're beautiful, baby."

I feel myself glow under the praise. "Thank you."

There's an edge of disbelief as he rakes over me again, this slight shake to his head as he does. There's not an ounce of me that questions if Emmett finds me beautiful. Not only does he tell me with his words, but his touch says the same thing. His mouth does as well when he runs it over my skin, peppering thankful kisses.

He kisses me *everywhere*.

Absolutely everywhere that he can reach.

And it's a torturous tease when he does so on my inner thigh. Closer and closer, but not quite where I need him.

Until he is.

"*Oh*." I lift my hips into his face when I get his mouth where I crave it most. But his big hand instantly presses on my stomach, keeping me pinned to the mattress.

I can hardly move with the force in which he's holding me down and it's a delicious realization that I don't have control right now. I couldn't move if I tried.

I melt into the bed at the thought. Turn my brain off. Feel his tongue flick against my clit. Revel in the sensation of his lips kissing my pussy.

He kisses me there the same way he kissed me everywhere else. Like he can't possibly get enough. Like he's so thankful I exist.

"Your mouth—" That's all I can get out because that mouth sucks my clit between his lips in a way that has me about to come undone already.

He comes up for a quick breath, only long enough to say, "You taste so goddamn good, Reese. I've thought about it since I tasted you on my fingers."

Then he goes right back to owning me.

I should maybe feel a bit self-conscious about being naked and splayed while these insane needy noises escape from my throat, but I don't care. I've never wanted someone as much as I want him. I've never wanted anything as badly as I want to come right now.

His coarse facial hair scratches against my sensitive skin and it has me out of my mind. I can only imagine what a mess I'm making on his face. But the way he's devouring me, it's almost as if that's exactly what he wants.

Then he lifts my hips and runs his tongue in a rough line down my seam until he reaches my ass. He licks a circle around that before retracing the same path back to my clit.

"*Holy shit*," I cry out. "Do that again."

I feel him smile against my sex, but he gives me what I want and repeats the motion.

"Please make me come. Please, Em."

"Are you begging for it?"

"Yes. Yes, yes. I learned from the best." I truly don't think I've begged for anything in my life. If I want something, I just do it myself. But there's no way I could make myself feel as good as he's making me.

"Sounds lovely coming from you, but you don't have to beg, Reese. You ask for anything from me, and you'll get it. Understand?"

"Will you make me come?"

His answer is silent and comes in the form of two fingers rimming my entrance. He flicks a rhythmic pattern with his tongue that makes me boneless, but when he adds those fingers, slipping them into my pussy, he has me shaking.

"*Oh, fuck*," I cry, trying to writhe against the bed but unable to move with the hold he has on me.

He strokes. He licks. He moans against me, and I fall right over the edge, coming on his tongue.

It's an unnerving high. A peak I've never been to. It steals my breath. It momentarily takes my vision. There's no restraint in my sounds or the way my body fights to move.

It's utter bliss.

Tight muscles untwine themselves as I settle back into the bed. The fog begins to clear, and when I look down between my legs, I find Emmett staring at me. Awe and wonder etched on his handsome face.

"I thought I was only going to get to see that once in my life. Thank God that wasn't true." Then he licks his lips to clean up the shine, but I still see myself glistening in his beard.

Emmett sits up on knees and the bulge in his suit pants is impossible to ignore. It's as if hearing me, watching me, and tasting me are the sole reasons he's about to bust behind that zipper.

I sit up, my naked body to his clothed, and stroke my hand right over the front of his pants.

"You are awfully good at that," I tell him, laying hot kisses against his stomach, placing them right over the buttons on his shirt. "Thank you."

He sinks his fingers into my hair, groaning when I dip to kiss below his belt.

"Don't thank me. I think that was as much for me as it was for you."

I squeeze his length.

"Fuck, Reese." He tosses his head back. "I almost came when you did."

"Glad you didn't." I fall back onto the bed, putting myself on full display for him again. "I'm going to need you to come inside of me this time, and I don't mean my mouth."

The pure agony on this man's face could almost be qualified as entertaining when he screws his eyes shut. "I need to get inside of you before you keep saying shit like that."

Hands around my waist, he shifts his hips forward in one languid thrust, his erection hitting my swollen, sensitive core. As if he were testing what it's going to feel like when he finally fucks me.

"*Fuck*, we're going to be perfect." Then he gently smacks my pussy before climbing off the bed.

Confident is the only word I can think of to describe him.

Confident in the way he knows he can please me.

Confident in the way he knows exactly what he wants.

Confident in the way he holds such intense eye contact with me as he unfastens his belt.

I've seen him before. I've had him in my mouth. But this proud display he's putting on steals all my attention. As if he's proud to show me himself. Proud that he's the one I'm with.

There's no arrogance in his movements. Just a solid assurance of knowing he's right where he should be.

With me.

"I know I probably sound like a broken record." His eyes wander over my splayed body as he drops his shirt to the floor. "But I have been dreaming of this."

"Me too, Em."

"Yeah?" That comes with the release of the button and zipper on his pants. "Show me."

My eyes flash with heat and they only blow out even more when he drops his pants, leaving him in only his boxer briefs.

"Show me, Reese. Show me what you do when you're dreaming of me."

Eyes locked on him, I bring my hand between my legs.

His smile turns wicked at the sight. "What do you dream about?"

"You. On top of me. Inside of me."

He hums, joining me at the edge of the bed, standing over me as I touch myself. He gently strokes my hair and cheek as he watches my fingers rub circles over my clit.

"What do *you* think about?" I ask.

My eyes land on his erection, so close to my face as he stands over me.

He rubs his other palm over my belly, smoothing down to join my hand between my legs. "Drowning myself in this. You sitting on my cock. You sitting on my face. Really just you sitting anywhere on me kind of does it for me."

Chuckling, I stroke a hand over his bulge. "I want to sit on this."

"Yeah?"

I nod innocently before reaching into his briefs and pulling out his dick.

"You can do anything you want with that."

It's thick, angry, and swollen around the head. And as I'm lying on the bed with him over me, I slip my lips over the crown and take him into my mouth.

"Yes, Reese." He strokes my hair tenderly. "You're so good to me."

I keep my mouth open, keep my throat unlocked for him to use me. But he doesn't use me like that. He rocks his hips slowly. Gently. Languidly. Pushing himself against the inside of my cheek. Teasing himself just enough. In and out. In and out.

He rubs his fingers over my clit in pace with his easy thrusts and *holy hell*. Just seeing him keep this kind of control is so much hotter than I assumed it could be.

The restraint. The testing himself. Why is this doing it for me?

Then again, everything about Emmett does it for me.

My hips chase his circling fingers, ready to come again, and as if he can read my mind, he stops. He pulls himself out of my mouth, wraps his hand around my throat, and bends down to kiss me roughly.

"Not yet," he says against my lips. "Your next orgasm will be around my cock. Understood?"

I nod.

"That's my good girl." He punctuates that with one more deep kiss. "You're going to be good for me all night."

Emmett sheds his boxer briefs, adding them to the pile on the floor before climbing onto the bed with me. He sits on his heels between my spread legs, stunning naked body proudly showing off. Thick cock jutting out and pointing right at me.

He lifts my foot to his mouth, placing a kiss there before he unbuckles my heel, tossing it to the floor, joined a second later by the other one. He crawls up my body, once again getting his lips anywhere they can reach. Like there's no place on my body that's better to kiss than the next. It all needs equal attention.

And it's tender and possessive and bossy all at once. Like he's lovingly marking me as his.

Hard and soft.

But the only thing I can feel is *hard*. Solid, throbbing, and thick pressed against my hip as he lies next to me.

"I'm on birth control."

He drops his head to my shoulder with a groan. "Are you asking me to fuck you bare, Reese?"

"No," I say breathlessly. "I'm telling you to. I want to feel you when you come inside of me."

His cock pulses against my hipbone.

"Please, Emmett. I need you."

His eyes bounce between mine, nodding quickly to agree. Then he kisses me in the most tender of ways. Exploring my mouth. Taking his time.

His hands move at the same pace. As if we have all the time in the world.

But I'm burning up with need.

I open my legs. He fits himself between my thighs. He keeps most of his weight off me, leaning on his forearms on either side of my head, but still, it's this delicious comfort having his heavy body covering mine.

He grabs a pillow, ushering me to lift my head, smiling down at me as he tucks it underneath. "For my pillow princess."

I exhale a laugh, but it dies as soon the head of his cock grazes my entrance.

"There's no going back after this," he reminds me, watching for my reaction to the news.

"Good." I lean up and press my mouth to his. "I only want to go forward with you."

His eyes blaze this warm brown, as if that's the only thing he needed to hear.

Between us, I reach down and line him up to my entrance.

There are no other words that need to be said, so with his eyes on me, Emmett tilts his hips and pushes in.

Slowly at first. Just the tip. Then the blunt head. He pulls out and pushes in again, feeding me another inch. He continues that torturous but needed cycle.

His strong body is shaking above me. Muscles tight. Sweat beaded along his forehead. Taking all his restraint to not just slide home.

But he's big. Overwhelmingly big. And I'm thankful for the slow stretch.

"I can take it, Em." He steals my breath with his next thrust. "Give it to me."

With my nails scratching along the skin of his back, he groans this desperate sound as he gives me that final push.

I tremble below him. "*Oh my God.*"

His forehead drops to my shoulder, holding me firmly. "Don't move, baby," he grits out. "Just. *Fuck*, you feel incredible. Just give me a second."

I'm thankful for the pause. Even though he was the one who asked for it, I need it too.

I'm profoundly full. And it feels profoundly right.

Emmett eases his hips back before pushing forward, testing himself. Testing *me*. And when I lift to rub against him and meet him in pace, I feel his feral smile spread against the skin of my neck where his face is hiding.

Then he moves, his tempo picking up slowly. We find a rhythm together. I grasp at him frantically. He rocks his hips into me. We share breaths and kisses and curses.

A quick, needy ache builds low in my belly as we join together. As we move together.

The sound in the room is a mix of panting breaths and pounding skin, so I decide to add, "I've never been fucked like this," out loud for him to hear.

It was supposed to be just a realization I was going to internalize, but I'm glad I didn't.

Because Emmett whimpers at my confession, head dropping to my sternum to place a few humble kisses there. "I'll fuck you however you want, Reese. Whenever you want. Please just let me."

I run my fingers through his hair. "Just like this. This is perfect."

He continues to thrust into me, snapping his hips, until suddenly he pulls out and leaves me empty. "You're going to make me come."

"*Yes.*"

"No." He slides down between my legs. "I need you with me."

Then he devours me with his mouth again. Licking and sucking. Pulling me right to the brink with him.

"Okay. Okay." Toes curling, I tighten my thighs around his face. "I'm right there. Come back."

He gives my ass a playful bite before leaving me.

I'm both eager for more and unsure how I could possibly take it. He's all-consuming in the best way, but holy hell, this guy can fuck.

Emmett swoops me up with an arm, his tattoos flexing in the most distracting of ways when he sits up against the headboard and brings me flush to his chest.

"Sit on it, Reese."

And apparently *that's* how I'm going to take it. That commanding tone in his voice could make me do anything right now.

"Do you want to see it from the front or the back?" I ask.

Emmett drops his back with a groan. "Jesus, woman." He grips the base of his dick in a desperately firm hold. "You're tempting me to make a fool out of myself here."

I chuckle, lifting to line myself up with him again, deciding I'd rather see his face when he comes. "You couldn't make a fool out of yourself if you tried. I think I'm in love with your dick."

That earns a laugh.

Emmett's rough hands roam my body, gently caressing every inch of my skin.

Hard and soft.

"I want to feel you take me." A wide hand presses against my pelvis and that is so stupidly hot to imagine, so I center myself and slowly sink down. "Goddamn," he breathes. "You're going to be so full."

I know he can feel me trembling on his lap. He's so much deeper in this position.

But still, I fit myself over him, watching as he disappears inside me completely.

"*Good God*, Emmett. You seriously have the biggest . . ." My eyes meet his to find an arrogant lift of his brow. "*Heart*."

His throat protrudes when his head falls back in a hearty laugh, and it might be the most beautiful sound I've ever heard.

He's beautiful. Breathtakingly stunning. And not just the way he looks.

He is good and kind and maybe even mine.

I'm a big fan of his big heart. Both of them.

The shift in the air is evident. Face-to-face like this, it feels even more intimate. There's more touching. More kissing. More thankful words whispered in my ear about how glad he is to be here. How incredible I feel. How he wants to do this again and again and hoping that I do too.

It's tender and desperate and still so fucking hot as he pumps into me from below. My hips roll and his hands settle on them to help me find a rhythm.

"Em," I whisper through shaky breaths.

His eyes flutter shut. "I feel it. You're going to come, aren't you?"

I don't have the oxygen to speak as my body winds itself tight, so I just nod frantically.

"Me too." His thumb circles my clit with shocking accuracy. "Just keep going. You're doing so good for me, Reese."

I do as he says, continuing my cadence, even as my body tightens again in jerky movements. Still, for him, I try not to change anything.

But he's everywhere.

His hands. His dick. His *attention*.

It covers me like a blanket, wanting to catch every moment of my release so he can steal the memory for himself.

His chest rattles right in front of me with uneven breaths. His fingertips dig into my hips with so much force I'm sure I'll get to see myself branded with marks tomorrow.

He gives me one more thrust and I'm a trembling, panting mess. I think I cry out his name. I believe I fall into his chest. My entire body pulses as I come on his cock, exactly the way he told me I was going to.

But what I'm more focused on is the way his eyes can't leave mine, even when they want to screw shut. He forces them to stay open and on me. He's so close so I lean forward, kiss the spot under his ear and beg—no—I *ask* for what I want, knowing he'll give it to me.

"I really want you to come inside of me."

"Oh God, Reese. Take it. Fuck, just take it."

Then he does exactly as I ask of him.

He forcibly holds me down on him. Chants my name. Worships me. Praises me. Then he spills inside of me.

He's stunning to watch as he works through it. But it's even more lovely to feel his orgasm for myself.

It's shockingly intimate, holding him while he finishes.

Emmett is gentle with me as he comes down, this blissed-out expression on his handsome face.

His firm grip loosens on my hips before he tenderly caresses my body. Softly squeezes my breasts. Lays languid kisses across my collarbone.

"Thank you," he whispers.

"Not sure why you're thanking me when you just fucked me so thoroughly."

He chuckles against my skin. "Well, thank you for letting me."

We kiss and come down for a while, and when it feels like the right time, I rise up on my knees.

"No." Emmett grasps my hips. "Keep it in."

There's that commanding voice again that makes me do anything he wants. I sink back onto him, and he sighs when the back of my thighs press to the top of his.

I run my fingers through the hair on his chest. "In case no one has ever told you, you can really fuck."

He exhales a laugh, our hips moving in slow circles together. "You make it easy. Everything you do turns me on."

He's so open with his words. So forthcoming with how he feels about me.

"Speaking of turn-ons." I run a hand up his neck, cupping his jaw. "I think maybe you should stop wearing your hat at work. And the baseball pants. And running without a shirt. That should stop too."

He smiles lazily at me. "Is this your way of saying you want to set some ground rules?"

Again, I'm understood without having to ask him to understand.

"Yeah, we should do that. But you're still inside of me, so I don't know if it's the best time for that conversation."

"Me inside of you is the only way I want to talk about work. In fact, this is the only way I want to conduct any conversations with you going forward."

I can't help but lean forward and press my smiling lips to his.

His hips move in an unhurried way, but there's a clear rhythm that I subtly chase with my own.

"You're not quitting your job," I say adamantly. "And I'm not firing you."

"Yeah. I gathered that."

"I just don't know what to do yet."

He moves my hair behind my ear, the way he does so often. "But you know you want this?"

There's a pleading glint in his eye as he asks for confirmation.

"I know I want this."

"Okay. That's all I need."

"Okay."

We're absent-mindedly rubbing together, but when I shift my hips and ground my sensitive clit against his pelvis, a gasp escapes me.

Emmett's expression turns a bit wonderstruck as he looks down to the space where we're connected. His hands are gentle on my hips, slowly guiding me to move with him.

I know he can see the shock on my face too. I thought we were done, but judging how my body is warming, I think I could come again. And with the way I can feel him thickening inside of me, I think he can too.

He picks up an even tempo, but it's still unhurried. Like an early Sunday morning kind of fuck.

Arm around me, hand cupping my ass, Emmett flips us, putting me on my back. And when his big body drapes over mine again, he moves inside of me until he takes me over the edge again.

This orgasm is a slow, soft ripple through my body. Thank God for that, because I don't think I could handle one as intense as the first two. I writhe my way through it, riding out the slow wave. It's a gentle pass and leaves me perfectly satisfied and sated on its way out.

"Yes," Emmett pants into my ear when he feels my body tighten around his. "I could fucking live between your legs."

He's got his arm between me and the mattress, holding me in place as he slowly rolls into me.

"I'm going to come again." Disbelief is laced in his tone. "I'm gonna co—"

And then he does, small shocks passing through him as he trembles on top of me.

It might be my favorite way I've seen him. Unexpected and a bit surprised. Shocked and a bit humbled. An unplanned moment of blinding pleasure all because of how much we want each other.

He falls into me with an exhale, face hiding against my neck. "Thank you," he repeats.

"You don't have to keep thanking me."

"I went a lot of years without knowing you, Reese. I can thank you for finally being here if I want."

Oh, I am so done for. So utterly gone for him.

He nuzzles against me, so much wonder in his voice when he asks, "What the hell are you doing to me?"

I don't hesitate. "Hopefully making you mine."

He lifts to look at me, eyes bouncing between my own. "Is that what you want?"

"Yes. I'd really like to call you mine, Emmett."

"That's good." He kisses me softly. "That's really good, Reese, because I've been yours for quite some time already. I'm glad you finally realized."

33

REESE

For the first time since moving into this condo, I don't wake up alone.

Warm sun spills into my bedroom, and when I take that first deep breath of the day, it smells like summer and sunshine and Emmett combined. Though I'm not sure there's much of a difference between those things. Warm and dreamy. It's the best time of the year. He's the best part of my day.

A firm, protective arm is wrapped around me, keeping me close, and as consciousness begins to creep in, I'm reminded of where I am and who I'm with. With my face pressed to Emmett's chest, I brace for the incoming dread to seep in. For the worry and the anxiety about the line we not only crossed last night, but obliterated.

But it doesn't come.

The only thing I feel is peace, lying here next to him.

Even in his sleep, he keeps me close. He covers me, protects me. The same way he does with all his people. I've watched him for months now, even last season when we hardly knew one another. I've witnessed him take care of everyone. How could I not want to be included in that?

This was inevitable in a way. In my bones, I knew eventually we'd be waking up tangled together. We've been tangled up for months now, haven't we? Blurred lines. Boundaries crossed. Enemies. Friends. Coworkers. Lovers.

A tangled web, indeed. And I've never enjoyed a mess as much as I do this one.

The sun shines over his face too, and I steal the opportunity to look at him. Really look at him. We've woken up a couple of times together, but not like this. I've never had the chance to take him in like this.

Emmett is handsome when he sleeps. Lashes a bit too long. Jaw that's a bit too sharp. A big hand, that only a few hours ago was all over my body, rests against his chest.

Perfectly content with himself after ruining me last night.

"Enjoying the view?" he asks, eyes closed, voice laced with sleep.

I attempt to hide my face against him, but I'm sure he can feel my smile form on his skin.

"I was just checking on something." I run my fingers through a bit of the salt that lives around his temples. "Is that new? Did you age in your sleep? I remember you looking younger last night."

His chest moves in a laugh. "I didn't hear you complaining about my age while I was fucking you through multiple orgasms."

No, no he didn't. I had never been with an older man until last night, and I learned that they know exactly what they're doing in bed. At least, this older man does. The soreness between my legs is evidence of that.

Finally, he cracks his eyes open, turning to look down at me. "Morning, Reese."

His sleepy rasp does something sinful to my body. It has me shifting my legs, rubbing my naked skin against his. "Morning, Em."

The hand that's keeping me close reaches up to run softly through my hair. "You're beautiful in the morning."

"I just called you old, and you call me beautiful?"

"Yeah. And I hope you feel terrible about it for the rest of the day."

I crack a smile. "You've woken up with me before, you know."

"I know. But not like this."

Definitely not like this.

Scooting up, I press my lips to his, then cross my arms over his chest, leaning my chin on my hands.

Emmett's attention bounces over my face, soft smile on his lips, and fingers toying with my tangled hair.

He's so comfortable. So at ease in my bed, like he's got nowhere better to be today, even though both of us are aware we need to head to the field soon for a game.

"How's that brain of yours?" he asks. "Running in circles?"

"Nope."

There's an edge of surprise on his face.

"Just happy."

"Yeah?"

"Very happy. You look awfully good in my bed."

His smile turns boyish, a stark contradiction to the gruff man I'm accustomed to.

"And you look awfully good naked and on top of me." Lifting, he kisses me once more. "But we should probably discuss what's going on here. I know we mentioned it last night, but maybe you were right. Maybe it's best if we have this conversation while I'm not inside of you."

"Your dick didn't hypnotize me into saying something I didn't want to, if that's what you're worried about."

"I guess I'm worried you might walk it back. The way we've tried to so many times before."

"I'm not," I tell him easily. "I'm in it. With you. I just need to figure out how this is going to work *at* work. But I want this. I want you."

"Okay." He softly smiles. "We'll keep it between us for now. Until we decide what we're going to do."

I nod in agreement. "Thank you."

"Coffee?"

"Yeah. That sounds nice. I'll make us some."

When I move to peel myself off him, he tightens an arm around me, keeping me in place.

"What?" I ask, confused.

"I was asking if you wanted some, not if you'd get up and make me a cup."

"I know, but I can do it."

"Good for you. So can I." He slips out from under me, flipping me onto my back and cradling my head until he rests it against a pillow. "Lie down. I've got it."

Emmett stands from the bed, proud naked body on full display. Big, thick, and all man, walking around my bedroom without a shy bone in his body.

"How do you take yours?"

How do I take my coffee? I don't know if I've ever had to tell someone else that. I don't remember a time anyone has ever made me a cup in the morning, though it's something I do for myself daily. I'm about to tell him I'll take my coffee any way he wants to prepare it for me, even though I have a very specific order, simply because I'd be thankful for anything.

"Um," I hesitate. "Splash of cream. A bit of brown sugar."

I don't tear my eyes off him as he bends to pull his boxer briefs back on. But that's all he puts on his body.

"You got it." He comes back to me, crouching down on the side of my bed. "And to make this clear, I don't do things for you because I don't think you can do them for yourself. I do them because I want to. And because you should know what it feels like to be taken care of."

He kisses me one more time before he heads into my kitchen, which I have a perfect sightline to from my bed.

Emmett opens a couple of cupboards until he finds the mugs. He locates the brown sugar and the utensils. He opens my fridge like he's done it a thousand times. And before he leaves the kitchen, he washes the spoon he used to stir my cup.

It's a bit mesmerizing to watch him. He moves around my place with so much confidence, as if he innately belongs here. As if he fits seamlessly between these four walls.

Laying in sheets that smell of him, watching him treat my condo as his own, I realize that maybe he does. Maybe he belonged here all along. With me.

Those were my suspicions last night. As soon as he stepped off the elevator, he looked like he belonged. And that's what this morning confirms.

It's so simple, this coffee he hands me in bed. But when you go so long with no one else taking care of you, something as simple as a cup of coffee takes on a whole new meaning. I'm more grateful. More appreciative of the man he is. All because I went so long without him.

Emmett slips under the covers again and we drink our coffee together. We laze around for the morning, talking and touching until we run out of time.

He needs to change before heading to the field, so eventually, I take him home, the way I promised him I would last night. But when I return to my condo, the emptiness is glaring.

It's lonely.

In a place that, up until yesterday, I loved to be alone in, even craved its solitude, today I don't. Today I want him to be here too.

That's the only dread that finds me today. The realization that my own company no longer compares to his.

I may have no idea what I'm doing or how I'm going to go about keeping Emmett on my staff, but one thing I'm certain of is that he's the biggest risk I've ever taken and simultaneously the surest decision I've ever made.

I just need to figure out the rest.

My pregame visit to the dugout was short-lived. There were too many players milling about that I knew it wasn't safe for me to stay long. I couldn't keep a straight face around Emmett today if I tried. Not when images of his tattooed hands gripping my hips to help me move on top of him are replaying on a loop in my mind. I can't look at the man without thinking of last night. Without hearing his sounds. Without seeing that grateful expression he wore as we laid together afterward.

And anyone with eyes would see the shift between us today. It's too fresh. Too obvious.

So, I hid in my suite and have stayed here for the entirety of the game.

We're heading into the bottom of the ninth with a tied game and possible extra innings ahead of us. But the way we've played today has me shockingly hopeful and energized.

You'd think I would be tired. I *should* be tired. Sleep was sparse last night, but the hours I did get were deep and restful. The kind of sleep you get after working your body to the bone all day.

Or alternatively, the kind of sleep you get after being fucked so well you're not sure how your legs still work.

I cross said legs, watching the game from my suite above the third baseline.

It's the start of a home series against Boston, and we need a win. After a rough couple of weeks, we all just need a win.

We've played well. Our starting pitcher went deep into the game, and our defense has been on point. But it's the hits that have been lacking on both sides, keeping a score of 1-1 in the bottom of the ninth.

The sun has long set. The fans are still filling the seats, but they're growing restless with the lack of scoring today. And even with a glass wall of windows separating us, I can still feel their frustration when Boston's closer strikes out our first two batters of the inning.

Then that frustration quickly shifts to a collective dread when the crowd realizes that Milo is next in the lineup.

I notice a lot of them looking around, as if they're contemplating calling it a night, since it's already late, or staying for the extra innings. As if those extra innings are inevitable because of their lack of faith in the new guy on the team.

I find myself briefly allowing those same thoughts before I catch myself. I know what he's capable of. It's why he's here.

The first pitch is a slider and a strike.

The crowd groans.

Milo steps out of the box and even from here, I can see the change in his demeanor from the last game he played. He's calmer. He's able to collect himself.

The second pitch is a fastball, and Milo gets a solid swing on the ball. It sails deep. The fans gasp. It's deep enough to be a run, but at the last second, the ball curves wide outside the foul pole in right field.

Two strikes.

Milo steps out of the box again, and this time turns to Emmett in the dugout. I can't hear what Emmett says to him, but whatever it is Milo takes it in, nods to himself, then repositions himself at the plate.

I don't need to know what he said. I know Emmett. The guy is steady. Steady enough for everyone around him.

The typical anticipation for a tied game in the bottom of the ninth is lacking tonight. It feels as if everyone in this crowd has counted Milo out already.

But then he decides to prove everyone wrong on the third pitch he's given.

The crack of the bat is sharp. It practically screams at the crowd to pay attention to him.

It sails deep, deep, deep into left field.

Boston's pitcher stands with his hands on his hips as we all watch the ball sail over the fence and into the bleachers.

The stadium erupts. The added shock to their elation causing an insane buzz throughout the building. It's deafeningly loud in here as Milo tosses his bat to the side and starts his jog to round the bases.

Because he not only got his first hit in the majors, but he just got us a walk-off win.

I'm on my feet, screaming and cheering for him, slapping the glass as if I were anywhere close enough for him to hear me.

The boys rush out of the dugout to meet him at home plate, and I don't miss the relieved smile he wears as he rounds second.

I could not be happier for him. Immeasurable pride sits on my chest as he touches the third base.

My attention ticks to the dugout, the way I've tried not to all night.

I wish I could be down there to celebrate with the field manager.

This is a victory not only for the team or for Milo, but also for us. After going through hell in the press, this feels like a big fucking win.

There's a stunning smile on Emmett's face as he cheers for his new player, clapping his hands together. I half expect Emmett to be out there with his team, waiting to greet Milo when he touches home, but apparently, he's going to leave that moment to the players.

Instead, when Milo runs into the pile of his teammates, Emmett turns his back to the field to look in the opposite direction.

Up. Right at me.

He claps his hands together along with the rest of the crowd, but unlike them, Emmett isn't celebrating this moment with the team and the fans. I think he's still in the dugout so he can celebrate this moment with me.

His proud smile and discreet wink confirms my theory.

The elevator opens on the top floor with only Emmett inside.

He's got this knowing look on his face, as if he knew I'd be the one waiting on the other side when the doors open. As if he rode this elevator to the top floor for no other reason than to see if I'd get on it with him.

I step inside, slightly in front of him, both of us facing the doors and trying our best to keep things professional while other people are still here from the game.

"You seem excited," he says low in my ear.

I smile at my reflection. "Of course I am. We just won. Milo just hit a homer off one of the best closers in the league. And I got laid last night. Life is good."

Emmett chuckles from behind me. "Are you sure you're not just excited for this postgame press conference you're about to walk into?"

He knows me far too well.

"I might be a little eager to put some of these reporters in their place after last week."

"Any idea of what you're going to say?"

"Might not say anything. Might just hold up two middle fingers and call the press conference done."

Emmett slides a hand over my ass to my hip, squeezing me there. "You're spicy today."

"Thank you."

As we slowly descend to the clubhouse level, a heavy forearm wraps around the front of my chest, pulling me until my back is flush to him.

"I'm proud of you," Emmett says quietly, punctuated by a tender kiss on my hair.

I swallow. "For what?"

"For getting through the worst of it. You have every right to go in there and tell them they can all go fuck themselves for how they spoke about you."

I grasp his arm with both my hands, eager for that small amount of physical touch. "I'll kill them with kindness. Answer their questions politely. Act professionally and all that. But they'll have to ask them while knowing I read the things they said about me."

"And that's also why I'm proud of you." His lips move to my neck for another kiss, and I can't help the upturn of my smile, feeling him nuzzle against me.

"Good game today, Coach."

"Thank you, baby." Another kiss. "Good game to you."

When the elevator stops on the clubhouse floor we break apart without hesitation, creating a bit of distance. Through the reflection I see that both of us have regained our straight faces in time. When the doors open, there's a swarm of players and staff celebrating, but no one is really paying us any attention.

Still, we're careful to ensure that when we walk off the elevator, there's nothing warm or flirty about our departure from one another.

"Emmett," I say, retreating to the media room.

"Reese," he responds, headed in the opposite direction.

34

EMMETT

"Well, this was a nice surprise." I push my empty plate away, unable to take another bite if I tried.

"We just wanted to pop in," Miller says. "Say hi. See how you're doing."

"Oh, is that so?"

I know exactly why my entire family showed up to my apartment on the morning of a game day to have breakfast with me. And it's not to simply say hi. I see these five almost every day, and they're way too obvious this morning.

Kai, Miller, and Max showed up with a bag full of groceries to make breakfast. Then, minutes later, Isaiah and Kennedy just *happened* to be on my side of town and wanted to stop by.

"Yep," my daughter continues. "You know, give us some time together in case there's been anything on your mind that you wanted to tell us. In case there was anything new or interesting in your life that you wanted to share."

"Geez, Mills." Kai laughs. "Give the man a break."

On the opposite side of the dining room table, Isaiah sits forward. "Absolutely do not give him a break. I want to know what's going on too. I mean, I think we all know what's going on, but I'd like to hear that I'm right."

"I have no idea what you all are talking about." I look down at Max in my lap. "Do you have any idea of what they're talking about, Bug?"

He just smiles up at me, causing me to smile back at him.

"That's exactly what we're talking about!" Isaiah points in my direction. "That freaking smile that's been plastered on your face for weeks. That's not normal, Monty."

"Maybe I'm just happy to see my family."

"You see us every day!"

"Exactly. Which is why I'm wondering why you're all here."

"We want to hear some news about you and the team owner, okay? That's why we're here. So, freaking spill already."

Kennedy's brows furrow, looking at her husband. "You're awfully invested."

"The entire team is invested in these two! That's all anybody talks about these days."

That earns my attention. "Wait. What?"

My eyes bounce between Kai and Isaiah.

"Yeah." Kai rubs the back of his neck. "The whole team kind of already knows."

"They know what, exactly?"

"That you two have been fu—" Kennedy smacks her husband's arm to stop him, nodding toward Max in my lap. "Fff-riendly," Isaiah corrects. "That you two have been *friendly* with each other."

That's one way to put it. Reese and I have been awfully *friendly* with each other. We've been friendly every night since Arthur's retirement party. I've stayed over at her place, woken up with her there, showered with her there, all except the past two days because she had to attend an owners' meeting in New York.

And I miss her.

I miss her so badly I can feel the ache down to my bones. I've gone so many years without her, and suddenly, two days apart feels more like a lifetime. I didn't know that, at my age, you could miss someone like this. I thought this was a phase you grew out of. But apparently, with the right person, you don't.

I don't know how to define it. It feels juvenile to call Reese my girlfriend. We haven't put a label on us, but that particular one also doesn't seem to fully encompass the way I feel about having her in my life.

She seems bigger than that. *We* seem bigger than that.

My days are better, simply because she's included in them. My nights are better too, that's for damn sure. But having someone for *me*, I don't know how to explain it. After so many years of being alone in that regard, I just feel . . . really grateful to have met her.

She'll be home today, and I'll get to see her at the field before our game. Which has me eager to get there already.

"You're not denying it, I see," my daughter says, bringing me back to the conversation.

"I'm not here to confirm or deny anything." I pop a kiss on Max's dark hair before getting him to his feet. I stand as well, gathering the dirty dishes from the table. "I need to get ready to head to the field and so do all of you."

Isaiah groans. "You're killing me, Monty."

As I load the dishwasher, Miller joins me in the kitchen.

"So, now that everyone who works for her is in the dining room, let's hear it. Are you two together or what?"

"You were way too obvious with this family breakfast, by the way."

"Dad. Please just tell me. You seem happy."

I pause on the dishes, setting them in the sink and leaning back on the counter to face her. "I am happy."

"Good. You deserve to be happy. But as your favorite daughter, you've got to tell me. Is this happiness thanks to a certain curvy blonde that used to drive you insane?"

I chuckle, because again, I'm just so damn happy apparently. "I've always been happy, Miller." I toss my head from side to side. "But yeah. You could assume that, lately, that's been a contributing factor."

A smile slowly creeps up on her.

We're on the edge of a conversation that is completely foreign to the two of us. We've never broached the topic of me seeing someone who isn't Miller's mom. I haven't dated anyone since Claire passed, so it hasn't been needed until now.

I can assume how Miller will feel about Reese and me, but I don't know for certain.

I decide to test the waters and find out. "This isn't something we've ever talked about before."

"I don't think we've ever needed to, right? As far as I'm aware, you haven't dated anyone in an awfully long time."

"I haven't."

There's a beat of silence between us.

"So, she's got to be pretty special then."

"She is."

Miller watches me observantly. "You deserve all the good, Dad. If you're hesitant to talk about it because of my mom, don't be. I know you loved her. Look what you did for her. Look what you did for *me*. But you're allowed to move on."

I didn't expect to have this kind of conversation this early in the day. And I sure as hell didn't prepare myself for it.

I wrap my arm around her shoulders, pulling her into me for a quick hug. "Thanks for saying that, Millie. It's not that I'm hesitant for you to know. I just wasn't sure how you'd feel about it. Me meeting someone new. Me and Reese."

She pulls back to look at me. "You and Reese, huh?"

"Yeah." I try to bite back my grin and fail miserably. "Me and Reese."

She chuckles, leaning back on the counter to face me. "Look, Dad. It was always just the two of us, and I loved growing up that way. But our family is growing now." She gestures to the dining room. "You sacrificed your entire life for me, but I'm not a kid anymore. You're done raising me. Regardless of my opinion, and I'm freaking stoked about this by the way, you deserve to have someone care for you the way you've always cared for all of us."

I can't seem to find the right words for her, but I find myself grateful for her permission. Of course, it wasn't going to stop me from living my life, but at the same time, it feels like a breath of fresh air to hear her say she's happy about Reese. It's a comfort, knowing that my most important person wants me to add another important person into my life.

"And I think you should invite her to the wedding."

I rear back. "Miller. No. I couldn't do that. That's your big day. It's not about me."

"It's about you too. I would literally not be here if it wasn't for you. It's your day too, Dad. And you deserve, for once, to have someone there to celebrate with you. I'm going to have my person there. You should have your person there too."

My person.

Maybe that's exactly what Reese is. Maybe that's the word I've been searching for.

I try it on for size, and the weight feels right.

"You'd really be okay with that?" I ask.

"I'd be more than okay with that. You've watched us all find our person over the years and have supported us along the way. It's time we do that for you. And I like how happy she makes you."

"I like how happy she makes me too."

A knock sounds at my door, interrupting our conversation.

Groaning, I push off the counter. "Who else did you invite to this ambush?"

I open the door, expecting to find Cody or Travis. Maybe even the entire team.

But instead, Reese is the one standing in the hall. Two coffees in hand. A nervous smile on her lips.

"Hi," she says uneasily as she looks up at me.

I'm stunned. I'm thrilled.

"What are you doing here?"

She swallows, so clearly anxious about putting herself out there in this way. "I missed you. I hope that's okay?"

Oh, fuck me. I'm so done for.

I'm a bit speechless, seeing her here, so I'm hoping my excitement is overtaking the shock on my face.

"He missed you too, Reese!" Isaiah calls out from behind me.

Isaiah. Goofy little fucker that I, for some reason, call family.

Reese's blues go wide at the realization that not only are we not alone, but members from the team are here. "Oh my God."

I close my eyes for a moment, collecting myself. Then I quietly whisper, "I'm so sorry for this," before I fully open the door.

Moving out of the way, I let her see who's behind me at the table.

Cheshire-level grins on all of them, I swear.

"Oh." Her eyes bounce over my family members. Three of whom she signs paychecks for. "I'm just here . . . I'm here to discuss work. This is a work-related visit."

"Yeah?" Isaiah asks. "I heard you two have been discussing work *a lot* lately. Heard you've also been fu—"

Kennedy slams a hand over his mouth to stop him. "Reese, if I give one massive apology for my husband, will that cover a lifetime, or is this something I'll need to do daily?"

I lean a shoulder on the door, propping it open. "So, everyone knows apparently."

The panic is evident in the way Reese is holding herself stiffly on alert. "I should go."

"No. You should stay." Slipping a hand to her lower back, I usher her into my apartment then return my attention to my family. "But you all need to go. Now."

Kai is the first to stand from the table and Kennedy follows him, but Isaiah and Miller are more hesitant to leave.

"Millie."

Miller scoffs. "I'm your only child."

"Exactly. I'm trying not to traumatize you. Please leave."

My attention moves to my favorite little guy as he makes his way toward me. "Sorry, Maxie." I bend down on my haunches to give him a hug. "I wish you could stay but your aunt, uncle, and parents are being weirdos."

He giggles, hugging me in return. "Weirdos."

"Right? I know."

Eventually, the five of them make their way out of my apartment, Kai bringing up the rear to usher the group ahead of him.

He halts in the doorway, turning back to Reese. "If it makes you feel any better, the entire team is absolutely stoked for you two. And so am I."

I catch the small crack of a smile on Reese's lips as Kai closes the door behind himself.

But that smile drops as soon as they're gone, and the realization sinks in. "Emmett. The team knows?"

"Don't freak out. They won't say a word."

"Are you sure?"

"I'm positive. You might not believe me, but they want to protect you as much as I do."

I watch as that statement settles onto her shoulders. They've proven just how loyal they are to her in the media lately. They'll continue to prove it by keeping this secret for us.

I don't hesitate any longer, taking the coffees from her hand and placing them on my table so they're out of my way. Both hands sliding into her hair, I bring my lips to hers in a desperate kiss.

She sighs into me. I sigh into her.

"Hi," I whisper.

"I'm so sorry. I should've called first."

"No. I'm glad you didn't. This is the best surprise."

She wraps her arms around my neck, leaning up to kiss me again. "I need to get to the field, but I wanted to see you."

I check my watch. I need to get out of here too if I'm going to make it to work on time. But I also don't want to miss out on time alone with her when we won't get it again all night.

"Wait for me?" I ask. "I need five minutes to shave quickly then we can walk down together." I drop a kiss on her mouth before grabbing my coffee from the table and taking a sip. "Thank you for this, by the way."

"You're welcome."

Slipping into the bathroom, I project my voice so she can hear me still. "So how was your meeting?"

I pull my shirt off, toss it in the hamper, and turn on the faucet.

"It was good." Instead of staying out in the main room, she follows me to the bathroom, leaning on the doorway with her coffee in hand. "I think some of the other team owners actually felt bad for me about the heat I took in the press."

"So, they didn't treat you like an outsider this time?"

"Well, I wouldn't go that far."

I lather up my shaving cream, spreading it under my jaw so I can clean up my beard. I feel Reese's attention the entire time. In the mirror, I watch as she moves fully into the bathroom and sits on the counter at my side, facing me.

I love how comfortable she is here. How she moves around my apartment the same way I move around hers. Like she belongs wherever I am.

"Can I do it?" she asks, setting her coffee on the counter next to mine.

I hold up my razor in surprise. "You want to do this?"

She nods in confirmation.

It's a shockingly intimate request that I give into immediately, handing the blade to her. "I just need the line cleaned up."

I grab her hips, shifting her closer to me, then stand between her spread legs. I keep my palms on her thighs as I tilt my head back, giving her better access.

Her eyes are locked on my jaw in concentration, figuring out exactly what I need taken care of.

Running the razor under the faucet, Reese returns her focus to my neck.

She bites her lip as she runs it in a slow, cautious line up my throat to my beard. It's gentle and methodical. Careful not to hurt me.

She smiles a bit, proud of herself when the first swipe comes up clean. "Easy."

Reese runs the razor under the faucet again before going in for the next swipe.

"So," I begin, speaking cautiously so as to not move my throat too much, "who all was at this meeting?"

Her blue eyes are lasered in on her task at hand, her other palm cradling the back of my neck to keep me steady.

"The commissioner. The owners."

I knew that. I knew that's why it was hosted in New York, where the commissioner's main office is.

"Anyone else?"

She breaks her concentration for only a moment when a knowing smirk lifts on one side of her mouth. "Are you asking if my ex-husband was there?"

Yes. Yes, that's exactly what I'm asking.

There's no part of me that thinks Reese would ever go back to him. I just don't like the guy and don't want him around her. Sure, I don't know him, but I do know what he tried to pull when he was married to her, and that's enough information for me.

I don't like that he's in our line of work. I don't like that he works for the commissioner's office. And I don't like that she will most likely have to see him multiple times a year.

Part of me hates that he got to know her before I did. But part of me is glad because it taught her what she deserves in a relationship.

And all of me is fucking thrilled that I'm the one she's allowing to give that to her.

"He wasn't there," she answers her own question, resuming her careful strokes.

Over the bridge of my nose, I keep my eyes locked on her while all her focus is lasered in on her task. She takes her time. She's gentle with me. Tender with me.

It seems so simple. But she's attentive in the way she takes care of me.

It's foreign. It's unexpected. And it's really *nice*.

I don't know if I've ever been taken care of. Not like this. That's usually my role.

"I missed you too, Reese," I say into the quiet bathroom. "I didn't get to say it earlier, but I missed you too."

Smiling to herself, she takes her careful last swipe, running the razor under the water to clean it off. Then she looks over her handywork, checking the line of my beard.

I would check for myself in the mirror, but I already know it looks perfect. She gave way too much effort, cares about me too much, for it not to be.

I stroke my thumbs over her inner thighs, keeping my hold on her. "Thank you for taking care of me."

"You're welcome, Em." She punctuates her statement with a soft kiss to my freshly shaven jawline. "So handsome."

Slipping my hand into her hair, I hold her against me for a

moment before we'll have to break away for the rest of the day. She wraps her arms around my waist. I breathe her in. She does the same.

My person.

My daughter's words play on a loop again, but this time there's no asking myself if that's the correct label or not.

Because there's not a doubt in my mind that Reese is my person.

35

REESE

"I don't know if there was one specific thing that contributed to our win tonight," Emmett says into the microphone during the postgame press conference. "Our pitching was phenomenal throughout all nine innings. Our defense was sharp. Our base running was aggressive at the right times. Overall, it was a team win."

I watch from my spot in the back of the media room. Behind all the reporters, I lean on the doorway that leads out into the hallway.

"You guys are on a five-game win streak," a reporter says. "Can we contribute any of that to Jones joining the lineup?"

"I think having Milo join the team has been great. He has an eagerness to learn. The vets are enjoying having him around. Overall, I would say the entire organization has a new ... *energy* lately."

Emmett's eyes flick to mine for the briefest of moments, a smirk tilting one side of his mouth.

He and I definitely have a new energy lately.

"And by the way." He sits forward to speak into the microphone. "Our current President of Baseball Ops, Reese Remington, is the one who discovered Milo a few years back. Thought I should clear that up for all of you. And if you ask me, he was a hell of a find."

A few heads turn my way.

He didn't need to give me that credit, but of course he did so anyway.

Standing in the shadows, I offer a polite lift of my hand to get the attention off me again. I shouldn't even be in this room, but I have a hard time staying away from the field manager these days.

Once they turn their attention back to the front stage where Emmett sits under the bright lights, I risk another glance his way.

Smug and satisfied, resting back in his chair with his arms crossed over his chest. So proud of himself for dropping that little anecdote.

The postgame interview continues, winding down the long day, but I should get going. I've been on the road for the last two nights and instead of going home this morning when I landed back in Chicago, I headed straight for Emmett's place.

I decide to stay for one last question, simply because I enjoy Emmett's point of view on his team, when someone slides into the space next to me.

"Reese."

Unfortunately, I'd recognize that voice anywhere.

Every muscle in my body goes rigid at the realization of who is next to me. In this building I love so much. This place that holds so many of my favorite memories. I had mentally prepared myself to run into him while I was in New York, but not here.

"Jeremy. What are you doing here?" I ask my ex-husband.

He leans onto the wall next to me. "One of our umpires has been missing some calls. I needed to watch him live. He happened to be calling your game today, so I figured it was the perfect one to come see."

I hate that he's here. I hate that we're in the same industry and it's his literal job to come to my stadium. I also hate that he tried to take it from me.

And I hate that I wasn't angrier about it then. I was hurt, yes. But I should've been angrier.

Because how dare he?

Now that I'm here and this is all mine, I can't begin to fathom the idea of losing it. I can't imagine having it taken away, but even more so, I can't conceive how someone who I thought loved me would ever try.

A slow fire begins to stir in my bones. I might be a few years late but I'm angry now.

"So, you and Monty, huh?"

I whip in his direction. "What?"

His laugh is dry. "Really, Reese? It's clear as day. I saw the way you were looking at him up there. I just find it hard to believe that you left me over this job and now you're risking it by sleeping with your employee."

Shit.

Fear and anxiety twine around my stomach. Realization steals the color from my face. How did he pick up on that? How did he notice something that he's never witnessed for himself before?

One thing is for certain, I never looked at Jeremy the way I look at Emmett.

He can't be the first person I tell. It doesn't feel right. What's going on with Emmett is far too special for Jeremy to be involved in it in any way.

My attention shifts to the front of the room to find that Emmett's previous smile is long gone. The muscle in his jaw tics as he answers reporters. His eyes continue to flash to me and my ex-husband after every couple of words.

"Don't worry," Jeremy whispers. "I'm not going to say anything."

"I don't know what you're talking about."

"Yes, you do, Reese. Don't forget that we were married once. I know you."

Wow. He can go fuck himself with that.

"What's so wild about that statement, Jeremy, is that, married or not, you've never known me. That's become very clear."

Not in the way I feel known now.

I risk one more glance in Emmett's direction, and he looks downright lethal sitting at the front of the room. Tension is clear in his posture, clearly frustrated that he can't get to me right now. The way he's angrily focused on Jeremy seems similar to the level of the fury I have brewing inside.

Pushing off the doorway, I turn to leave.

"Oh," I add before I go. "And I didn't leave you because of a job. I left you because you tried to take something from me that wasn't yours to have. Maybe if you had helped me protect it instead of attempting to steal it, I would've been inclined to share. But I'm glad you didn't." I point down the hall. "So, I'm going to go. To my office. Which is on the top floor of the stadium I own. Have a good trip home, Jeremy."

Once I'm out of that room, the fire doesn't tamp down in the slightest. Every step I take away from him seems to stoke it. It's as if the hurt and anger I should've already worked through is all coming to head at this very moment.

And it hits me like a brick wall as to why it's happening now.

The reason it's sinking in all these years later is because I've met someone who would never dream of doing what my ex-husband did. In contrast, Emmett wants this so much for me that he'd do anything to protect it. He'd risk his own career for the sake of mine.

And that makes me angry.

Because for years, Jeremy let me believe that the only way I'd be loved was for what I could offer. I'm angry at myself for believing that.

I'm angry that he fucked me up so badly I thought being alone was my only option. I'm angry that he broke something inside of me.

Emmett came around and healed something that wasn't his to fix, and I'm angry that he had to.

I hesitate when I reach the elevator, tempted to go hide in the dugout and clear my head the way I so often do. But I don't want any part of that safe place to be tainted by my anger toward someone who tried to steal this from me.

Instead, I go to my office, exactly as I said I would.

Passing the empty receptionist desk, I slam my office door closed.

Fuck him for coming here without giving me a heads-up. I could've prepared myself. He knew what he was doing, catching me off guard.

Rounding my desk, I push my chair out of the way and stand over it. Palms flat on the top, head hung low.

I was in survival mode when I took over this role. Desperate to prove myself. Equally desperate to prove my ex-husband wrong. I don't want to go back to that place mentally, but I can feel the anxiousness stirring inside. I'm worked up. I need an outlet.

I need . . . I don't know what I need. I just need to forget I was ever his.

My door flies open.

"What the hell is he doing here?" Emmett booms, charging in like he owns the place.

It's no wonder everyone thinks there's something going on between us. Throwing open my door like he has every right to.

"You can't just barge into my office!"

"Then hire a fucking receptionist to keep me out!"

Something stirs in me from hearing the anger in his voice.

Maybe this is what I need. Maybe I need a fight. I never used to fight with Jeremy because there was nothing to fight for. But with Emmett, it feels safe to fight with him because I know we're fighting for the same thing.

Emmett's tone drops to a menacing level. "What the hell is he doing here, Reese?"

"He's working. What do you want me to do about that?"

"Kick him out. I don't want him in your stadium."

Your stadium.

We so often banter about who has the right to what. The dugout. The clubhouse. The team. But with the conversation involving my ex-husband, the way Emmett gives me full ownership doesn't go unnoticed.

Emmett is still worked up the way I am as he takes slow steps toward my desk.

"In case there's any miscommunication here, let me clear a few things up for you." He dips his head, eyes piercing mine under his heavy brow. "You are *mine*. That night we finally got together, when you said you wanted to make me yours, that goes both ways. You are mine, Reese, and if I need to go make sure he fucking realizes that, I will. Or is it you who needs reminding?"

This. This is what I need.

I need to feel like his.

I need him to remind me that I am.

I need him to erase any memories of a time that I wasn't.

Lifting my chin defiantly, I look him square in the eye. "Prove it."

He stops in his tracks, brows lifting. "What did you just say to me?"

"Prove it. Prove that I'm yours."

He exhales an ominous laugh, turning to pace his same path. "Don't say something like that to me unless you want me to follow through. You don't want to play this game with me, Reese. I'm too fired up to be smart right now."

I don't care that we're in my office. I don't care that this is a terrible idea. At this point, I'm too worked up to even pretend to care.

"Prove. It."

Those two words settle into the space between us.

He slowly nods, tongue running over his teeth. "Just remember that you asked for this." Tension lines the room as he flips the lock on my office door. "You know that I respect you, right?"

I roll my eyes. "Yes. Of course I do."

"Good. Remember that. Because it's about to seem like I don't."

"What does that me—"

"Hands on the desk." Emmett comes up behind me, running a palm over my spine before pressing down on my neck. "Face too. I'm not taking it slow with you."

I do as he says, folding in half and squeezing my thighs together at his commanding tone.

"Oh, no, no, no." He nudges my feet apart with his own. "Don't be shy now, baby. You started this."

Standing on the balls of my feet, thanks to my heels, I press my cheek to the desk and look over my shoulder.

Emmett is towering over me, big body covering mine from the wall of glass behind us, even though it's a one-way window. With his baseball hat still on, he flips the brim to the back and *fuck me* with that little move.

His fingertips skim the back of my thighs, teasing the hem of my pencil skirt. "You want me to prove you're mine, Reese?"

"Please."

"You want me to make you forget about anyone else?"

Exactly. I'll never get over the way he knows me.

"*Yes.*" I squirm, pushing my ass back into him.

He tugs my skirt up, yanking it over my wide hips and leaving it to circle my waist.

The cold air is sharp against my ass and so is the slap he delivers to one cheek. "Love this view. Love the way this bounces on me."

"*Em.*"

"Shh. You're going to stay quiet for me. Remember where we are."

How could I ever forget? My face is currently pressed to the desk I sit at to sign his paychecks.

His fingers run over the seam of my panties and I'm so needy, so desperate already that I moan, trying to muffle the sound against the desktop.

"What did I just say, Reese?"

"I'm sorry."

"Keep yourself quiet or I'll have to do it for you." He sticks two fingers in my mouth to show me what he'll do if he has to.

Can't say I'd mind that one bit.

Then he takes those wet fingers and strokes them over my pussy again. I focus on not making a sound all while pushing my hips to chase his touch.

"You're soaking wet, Reese. You like fighting with me, don't you?"

I nod against the desk, eyes locked on him over my shoulder. "I like that I can."

Understanding washes over him, his face going soft. "Yeah, baby. You can fight with me about anything you want to, okay?"

He presses up against me, hands roaming over my hips and ass. But then his softness disappears again. He keeps his eyes on me while using one hand to undo his belt and drop his zipper.

My focus falls from his face to between his legs as I watch him pull his dick out, wrapping a fist around it in one long stroke. He keeps his pants up. He still has his shirt on. And everything about this image is filthy.

It only gets more depraved when he uses two fingers to pull my panties to the side, and in my next breath, he fills me completely with his cock.

"*Oh, fuck,*" I cry as quietly as I can.

He sighs with relief. "God, I missed you."

He gives us both only a second before he begins to move, his thighs slapping against the back of mine. It's dirty and fast, both of us are still clothed. It's also exactly what I need.

My mind goes blank, only focused on the way he feels inside me.

He feels like mine.

"You need me to fuck the anger out of you, baby?"

I nod desperately, chasing his thrusts.

"Are you going to be done with the attitude after this?"

"Are you?"

His chuckle is dark. "I don't like seeing him with you."

"Why's that?"

"Because I hate that he got you first. I hate that he messed with your head, but I also love that he fucked it all up. Because you're mine now, huh?"

I whimper into the desk, clawing at anything I can get my fingers around. Reaching back, I find his thigh, cupping my fingertips around the back of it to keep him close.

"Oh, fuck me," he breathes out. Then he covers my hand with his own, offering this sweet moment while he takes me in an obscene way.

He cups his other palm over my shoulder, using me as leverage as he pounds into me from behind.

"The way you fit around me, Reese. You take it like you're mine."

"Yes, Em."

"The way you cry my name sounds like you're mine too."

Oh God. I'm going to come.

"The way you clench around me feels like you're mine." He snaps his hips. "You feel incredible. You always feel so fucking good, Reese."

It's practically a growl the way the confession rips from his chest.

His hand slides between me and the desk, fingertips circling my clit.

"Oh my God, right there. Please. Please keep going." I practically beg the words.

His other arm slips under my body, his palm circling my throat as he folds over me. Emmett lays adoring kisses along the back of my neck, a stark difference to the way he's defiling me so perfectly.

"Do you want to be mine, Reese?"

I whimper. "I already am."

His beard scrapes over my jaw as his mouth finds my ear. "You know what else you are? You're a fucking boss, Reese. You don't let other people come in here and make you question that. All of this is yours. I'm yours too. So remember who the fuck you are."

"What's that?" I ask through strangled breaths. "Yours?"

He exhales a laugh. "That too."

"Emmett."

"I know. You're going to prove it by coming on my cock, aren't you?"

I can't speak, too overwhelmed by him moving inside me, the way his frame is folded over mine and pinning me down. So, I simply nod to tell him yes.

"You should see yourself, Reese. Ass up, blonde hair sprawled on your desk. Being fucked by your field manager. Naughty little thing."

I moan, rocking against him.

Slipping a hand around the back of his neck, I hold him to me. "How long can I be yours?"

He melts into me with a sigh, his hips continuing their punishing rhythm. "For however long you want to be."

"And how long are you going to be mine?"

"Always," he admits easily. "Even if there comes a time you don't want me to be. There's no getting over you for me, Reese. You've ruined me."

I want to tell him he's done the same, but my words are stolen when he pushes into me one more time. My entire body tightens with a force that takes not only my words but also my breath.

Emmett follows, holding himself deep inside as we both come together yet fall apart right there in my office. Shared breaths, warm skin, equally spent.

I slump onto the wooden desktop, letting him relax on top of me as we slow our breathing. A bit of sweat clings to his temples, but it looks so sinfully good in combination with that backward hat.

"Well, fuck me," he says playfully, dropping his head to mine.

I laugh with him. "You're insane."

"That would be your doing." He presses a kiss to my bare neck.

I practically purr in response, so fully satisfied, trying to remember what the hell I was so upset about in the first place. I can't recall anyone other than this man laying on top of me, running his hands over my arms, down my sides, and over my ass.

His whole *you know I respect you* thing was never really a question, but just to be sure I remember, he trails his warm lips down my neck and over my spine leaving soft, worshipping kisses in their wake. He takes his time touching every inch of me as I stay bent over my desk.

Emmett pulls out of me, holding my panties to the side. Over my shoulder, I watch as he stares at what I know is his release dripping out of me. I can tell by the satisfied glint in his eye and the way his focus is locked between my spread legs.

Instead of cleaning me up, he simply puts my panties back in place. "You better clench for the rest of the night, Reese. You're keeping that in to act as a reminder of who you belong to in case you run into him again."

I can't contain my shocked laughter. "You are out of your mind, you know that?"

"Yes, I'm aware." He bends to playfully bite my ass cheek before pulling my skirt back down to cover it.

Turning to face him, I lean back on my desk. My legs are a bit too wobbly to walk just yet.

Emmett tucks himself back in before he takes his time straightening me out. Fixing my hair. Adjusting my top. Cleaning up my makeup from under my eyes with the pads of his thumbs.

"How do I look?" I ask.

"Like you just got bent over your desk."

"Great."

He smiles, so proud of himself.

I wrap my arms around his neck. He slips his hand into my hair, pulling my lips to his. So much softer with each other than we were a few minutes earlier.

"We should get out there," I eventually say.

He nods, helping me to my feet. Emmett opens the door for us, allowing me to exit first. As I pass him, he leans down to my ear and whispers, "Thanks for a great meeting, boss."

36
EMMETT

When we're playing a home series, Reese and I know we'll end up together at the end of the night, usually at her place, sometimes at mine. But it's much harder to draw a line when we're traveling and don't have the luxury of spending our nights together.

When we're on the road, we'll go to dinner together because that's easily played off as a work meeting. We'll extend our pregame lineup chats to steal more time. But we don't risk either of us sneaking into the other's hotel room unless we have a connecting door.

Seems a bit extreme after how many times we've fucked around at the stadium back home, but when we're not blinded by need for one another, we both have smarter decision-making skills.

I won't lie, though. I like being stupid with that girl.

That's what sucks about this road trip. Reese's hotel room is on the opposite end of the hall from mine, so our time together has been limited over the past few days.

But on the flip side of that, the thing that's so great about this road trip is that we're in Colorado. Back in the city I once played for. Back in the place I raised Miller until she was eighteen.

I knock on Reese's room, leaning a shoulder against the wall as I wait for her to answer.

Blonde hair half clipped up. Under-eye patches on and a

coffee in hand. Wearing both a matching silk sleep set and a bright smile as she opens the door.

"Well, good morning to me."

I chuckle, keeping my hands in my pockets so I don't tempt myself to touch her until we're alone. "Missed you last night. Any chance you're free this morning?"

"I can be. What's up?"

"I want to take you somewhere."

Her eyes sparkle at the idea. "Just you and me?"

"Just you and me."

"Yes. Yeah, I'm down for that. I need to change quickly. Meet you downstairs in five?"

"Perfect." I lean in to kiss her before stopping myself, arched halfway over in her doorway.

Things have progressed so naturally between us the past few weeks. Easy kisses and simple touches are second nature at this point, that it takes a conscious effort to remind myself of our positions while we're at work.

Which is what I have to do now.

I stand straighter, backing away from her door and pointing in the direction of the elevator. "I'm just gonna . . ."

She laughs at me. "See you soon."

I rented a truck for this specific outing, so I drive it up to the front entrance of the hotel and wait for her there.

A few minutes later, Reese walks out wearing a sweet floral sundress in a light pink shade. Similar to the color of her nails. It's feminine and easygoing, so different from how she dresses at work. She's beautiful both ways, but I don't miss that she dresses softer when we're outside of work. More colorful too.

It's nice to see her allow herself time away from being the boss.

"You rented a car for this?" she asks as I open the passenger door for her. "We couldn't have taken a rideshare?"

"Nope. We have a bit of a drive ahead of us." As soon as she's sitting, I pull her seat belt across her body, clicking it into place. I don't know what possesses me to do it. I suppose partly because I just need her safe. And partly because I rarely get to dote on her unless we're hidden in one of our apartments.

Arm still reached across her body and hand still covering the buckle, I glance up at her. "Sorry."

She lifts her hand, running it against my beard. "Don't be. It's nice."

Don't kiss her. Not here.

Clearing my throat, I push off, closing her door before rounding to the driver's side.

As soon as I'm in my seat, she finds the only thing in this car, which is a half-eaten bag of candy that I left sitting in the center console.

"What's this?" There's a playful edge to her question as she holds the bag up.

"Candy."

"Since when are you into Reese's Pieces?"

A shy smile pulls on my lips. "What can I say? They're a new favorite."

She chuckles to herself, pouring out a small handful and popping them into her mouth before she returns them to where she found them.

As soon as we pull out of the parking lot, I shift to drive with my left hand on top of the wheel, sliding my right across the center console and over her thigh. Without missing a beat, Reese slips her palm into mine, lacing our fingers together.

Easy. Natural. Connected as we always are when we're alone.

And we stay that way for the hour-long drive.

Once the streets turn into single-lane roads and trees begin to canopy the path, Reese finally asks, "Are you going to tell me where you're taking me?"

I squeeze her hand in mine. "Soon. We're almost there."

She doesn't push for more answers. She just relaxes back into the seat as I continue to drive the ingrained route, trusting I'll explain when the timing is right.

Soon enough, I slow my speed and turn onto a long gravel path that takes me to a cabin-style home. It blends subtly among the surrounding foliage. It's quiet and understated. The lake behind it acts as a serene backdrop, and it's exactly what I needed at the time I bought it.

After Miller and I talked that morning in my kitchen, I knew I wanted to bring Reese here. That conversation acted as all the permission I needed to involve Reese in every part of my life. Even the parts that came before her.

Regardless, I did call my daughter this morning to double-check she'd be okay with me bringing Reese here. She probably rolled her eyes at me on the other end of the line, but then answered my question with a swift, "Absolutely."

Killing the engine, I hop out of the truck and open Reese's door for her.

She slowly takes in her surroundings as she steps onto the gravel path that acts as the driveway.

"So, this is my house," I tell her. "It's used as a vacation rental these days, but I still own it."

"Really?" Her eyes trail over the roofline. "Your house from when you played here?"

"Not exactly. When I was playing, I shared an apartment in Denver with some of my teammates. But I bought this place after I left the league." I gesture to the house. "This is where I raised Miller."

Realization dawns on her. "Emmett."

She runs her palm down my arm before slipping her hand into mine. Reese focuses back on the house, her eyes trailing the cabin more carefully as she studies the details. She takes her time understanding the meaning and importance of this little place.

From behind, I wrap my arms around the front of her shoulders as we look at it together. "I wanted you to see it. I didn't have someone to share that part of my life with, so I was hoping I could share it with you now."

"I'd love to see it, Em. But is Miller okay with that?"

My chest tightens at her question.

I love how often she thinks of my daughter. Grown or not, Miller is still my kid. Every time Reese considers her, it reaffirms what I already know. That she's what I was missing from my life. That she's my person.

I drop my lips to her hair. "She is. Miller and I had a nice talk. She's more than okay with . . . *everything*."

I watch the smile spread on Reese's mouth. "That's good to hear."

"Come on. Let me give you a tour."

I don't manage the property myself, but I have access to the rental schedule, so I knew the place would be empty today.

Using my key, I unlock the door, and let Reese enter first.

The furniture has all changed. The wall colors too. But the bones are still the same.

"When I adopted Miller," I begin, closing the front door behind us, "I didn't know much about what I was doing, but I knew Miller needed some stability. So, I bought this little house for us."

I take her to the living room first.

"Here, I'd watch game film for the college team I was coaching. The first few years we lived here, I was not only trying to figure out how to be a dad, but also how to be a coach. At that point, I had only ever been a player, and I wasn't much older than some of the guys playing for me. We had a coffee table right here that Miller would sit at and color while I worked."

Reese smiles softly, listening to me speak, putting her hand in mine to follow me on this tour.

I bring her into the tiny kitchen and explain that though it's not much, Miller learned to bake here. That she found her passion right here in this little cabin on the lake.

I show Reese where the dining table used to be. The same one I'd sit at and help my daughter with her homework. Same one where we'd eat dinner together that Miller most likely prepared because she was a far better cook than me.

Down the hall, I take her to the first of two bedrooms. I explain that Miller painted this room a dark green when she was a preteen, and that I built shelves for her and screwed them into the walls so she could display her softball trophies.

Then I take her to my old bedroom. The one where, when we first moved in, I'd lie awake at night, trying to figure out what the hell I was doing. Though later, once I gained some confidence in the parental department, I'd lie awake trying to figure out how to be a better one.

I explain how the years spent in this house were the hardest of my life, but also some of my best. And that even though they weren't easy, I wouldn't change the thirteen years we spent here, just Miller and me, for anything.

"And right on the lake," Reese says, pointing out the windows on the back door of my old bedroom. "It's beautiful here, Emmett. You did a good job. For Miller, but for yourself too."

I push her hair behind her ears, running my thumb over her earrings. "Thank you for saying that."

"I mean it." She steps into me, head against my chest, and I wrap my arms around her to keep her close. "Miller is lucky to have you. And I am too. Thank you for bringing me here. This is really special to see."

Much in the same way that she had never let anyone into her condo, I had never let anyone into this part of my life.

It does feel special. *We* feel special.

"It's special to me too, Reese."

"Will you show me around outside?"

"Yeah. Of course."

Opening the back door, I follow Reese out onto the porch then lead her to the dock that'll take us to the water.

It's a perfect summer day. The sun is reflecting off the water, but we're surrounded by enough trees that provide plenty of shade from the heat. The air is crisper out here than back home in Chicago. But that's not saying Chicago doesn't have its own charms. That city has been a needed contrast to the years of solitude I spent out here.

We walk down the dock together, and when we reach the far end, Reese kicks off a sandal and dips her toe to test the water.

"It feels nice."

She looks beautiful, standing on the edge of the water, trees surrounding her. If we didn't have a game tonight, I'd happily spend all day with her out here.

But we still have a couple of hours at our disposal, so I toe off my shoes and toss my socks off to the side before taking a seat on the edge of the wooden dock. "Sit with me."

Letting my feet sink into the water, I usher Reese to do the same. She kicks her other sandal off and I settle her between my legs with her back to my front.

We're quiet for a long while, the sounds of nature playing their own soundtrack for us. She closes her eyes, dropping her head back on my shoulder as the sun illuminates her face.

Utterly content and at peace. With me. Just me.

From an outside point of view, it doesn't seem like I can offer her much. I can't provide for her financially. Though I make more money than I'll ever need, she will always make more. Materialistically, I can't give her anything that she can't give herself.

But I can provide for her in every other sense of the word. I can take care of her in every other way. I can make her a part of my unconventional family that I love so much. I can listen when she's had a hard day. I can fight with her when she needs a safe battle. Be her sounding board when she needs to talk something through.

I want to spend so many more days making her laugh, flirting with her, encouraging her, and challenging her the way she challenges me.

I want to be her closest friend because she's mine.

I wonder if she knows that.

"Reese," I whisper.

Eyes closed with the sun on her face, she hums in response.

"I know I told you that there was no part of me that wanted to be your friend, but I think you might be my very best one."

A smile curves her lips. "That's good, Em. Because it's been occurring to me that I'd like to hang out with you for a lot of years to come, and that might be kind of hard to do if we aren't friends."

My chest splits with the easy confession. "A lot of years, huh?"

"A whole lot of years."

I tighten my arms around her middle.

There's something different about falling in love this time than when I did in my twenties. When I was young, finding love seemed like a rite of passage. A guarantee. A part of life everyone gets to experience and that it was simply my turn.

But now, getting this chance with Reese, it's filled with more gratitude that I somehow found it again. There's more of a fight to hold on to it. More desperation to keep it. Love feels more sacred this time around because I didn't think I'd get the chance to experience it again.

It's on the tip of my tongue to tell her, but I keep that information locked up for another day.

"Can I ask you something?" she says quietly.

"Of course. Anything."

Reese is silent for a moment. She swallows hard as a pinch forms between her brows. Whatever this question might be seems to have been weighing on her for a long while. "Do you think you have it in you to move on?"

Move on from her? Absolutely not.

"I don't understand."

She shifts between my legs, pulling her feet out of the water to turn and face me. "There's no wrong answer, Em. I'm just trying to manage my expectations here. That first night I slept in your room. The night you told me about Miller and her mom. You said you didn't have it in you to move on. I'm just wondering if that's changed for you."

She studies me for my answer before the eye contact becomes too much and she forces herself to look away.

But I'm sitting here trying to rack my brain for what the hell she's talking about. I retrace that conversation in my mind until I get to the part she's referring to. The part when she asked me if I ever moved on after Claire.

I was drifting to sleep and didn't have it in me to fully explain. I thought she understood, but it's clear she's been holding on to my words since that night.

"Reese." I cup her face, bringing her eyes back to mine. "You misunderstood, baby."

"How?"

"When I said I didn't have it in me to move on, I didn't mean emotionally. Or that my heart was still taken. I meant that I *physically* didn't have it in me to move on. I was a single dad. I was exhausted all the time. I didn't have the time to focus on someone who wasn't my daughter. I was too busy trying to figure out how to do right by her. And by the time Miller was old enough to be on her own, I was older too and thought I'd missed the train on the whole 'finding a life partner' thing."

Her brows lift in surprise. "Oh."

I chuckle. "Yeah. Oh."

"Well, that makes a lot of sense."

She offers me a sheepish smile before turning back to the water, resting her head on my shoulder again.

But there's something else she should know. Something that I haven't said to anyone else because it hasn't mattered until now. Until her. And she, more than anyone, needs to understand.

"I loved Claire."

Reese nods against my shoulder. "I know."

"But we had one year together, and it's been over twenty years since. After spending some of those early ones grieving—for myself, but mostly for Miller—I've been able to shift that grief to gratitude. The thing I love most about Claire now is her daughter. I thank God every day that I met her when I did because Miller needed me. She is the best part of my life and I'll forever be grateful to her mom for trusting me to raise her. But I'm not still in love with someone else."

I'm in love with you.

But still, I hold those words in. Wanting to use them at a time that can't be misconstrued with needing to prove a point.

Everything I said sinks in for Reese and as she melts into my chest, I feel the weight of them release a bit of the pressure. And when I crane to look at her, her nose is a shade of pink I'm not accustomed to seeing.

"That's a really lovely outlook, Emmett." Her voice sounds thick. "I just needed to understand where your head was at, for my own expectations."

"My head is here, Reese. My heart too. You've got the whole thing."

Turning to look at me, she runs a palm over my jaw, cupping my face. "Just know that you can talk about her with me whenever you want. It doesn't make me uncomfortable. I'm glad you had someone to love you before. That would have been a long time to go without it."

I drop my forehead to hers. "Are you calling me old?"

She exhales a laugh, and it helps her to swallow down some of the emotions. "Miller should know about her. Max too. So don't ever feel like you can't speak about her when I'm around."

"Thank you for that."

Reese pops a quick kiss on my lips before she drops her head back to my shoulder, letting the sun shine on her face again.

I don't know if I'll ever be able to wrap my head around her. Having her in my life. Being able to share parts of me with her. This house. These conversations. My important moments.

It reminds me of another important moment I want to share with her.

"Kai and Miller's wedding is coming up."

"Yeah? She's going to make a beautiful bride."

"She is." I grin at the image. "Will you go with me?"

Reese slowly sits up, turning back to face me. "To your daughter's wedding?"

I nod.

"I . . ." Her mouth closes, trying to find the words. "That's big, Em."

"It is big. So will you go with me?"

"But Miller—"

"It was her idea." I cut Reese off before she tries to tell me that Miller might not want her there. "She brought it up."

"She did?"

"I believe her words were along the lines of 'our family is growing, and you deserve to have your person there.'"

Reese's smile slowly blooms. "Your person, huh?"

"Yeah. Whether you like it or not, you're my person, Reese. And I'd really like to celebrate that day with you. The guest list is small. Just the team and a few friends. It's out in the middle of nowhere. The only people who will see us together will be those who support us. It'll be safe."

She thinks it over for only a moment before she gives me her answer.

"Okay." She leans in and presses her smiling lips to mine. "I'll go with you."

"Yeah?"

"Yes. I'd love to."

I kiss her once more before the energy flowing through me becomes too much. I'm too amped up. Too excited. Too fucking giddy around this woman.

Slipping out from behind her, I stand and strip off my shirt, tossing it onto the dock.

"What are you doing?" There's so much joy in her tone, matching the way I feel.

"Going for a dip. And you're coming with me."

She bursts a shocked laugh. "No, I'm not. I don't have a bathing suit."

I drop my pants, kicking them off to the side.

"You don't need one. There's no one else for miles."

"I'm not skinny-dipping with you, Emmett."

"And why not?"

"Because we're not kids."

"Then why do I feel like one?"

That admission halts any retort she may have.

Yeah, I feel like a kid with her. Excited for what life has to offer. Excited to spend it with her.

Reese stands from the dock, joining me with an eager smile on her lips.

"Come on, baby. Slip that dress off and have some fun with me."

And she does, letting it pool on the wooden planks before she takes my hand so we can jump in the water together.

37

REESE

I hesitate with my fist held up to the front door, ready to knock.

But I can't. I've been out here for a few minutes already, baking in the summer heat, and still, I can't find it in me to let them know I'm here.

As soon as we landed back at the Chicago airport, I got in my car and came here.

My grandparents live about forty minutes outside of the city limits, and I came all this way. So why can't I find it in me to knock on the door?

Because everything is about to change, that's why.

Closing my eyes, as if that's going to help anything, I drop my fist against the wood. Then I do it a little harder two more times.

The wait afterward is the worst part of the anticipation. I can no longer run back to my car and leave, pretending I was never here. I'll have to go inside. I'll have to have this conversation.

One that I'm terrified of.

"Reese?" My grandmother beams as she opens her front door. "What are you doing here, honey?"

Her arms are wide to hug me before I've even told her the reason for my visit.

I love my grandparents. They're kind and sweet, exactly how you'd hope your grandparents to be. Sure, my grandfather became my business mentor when I got older, but when we're not at the field, he's just my grandfather.

Which is why I wanted to have this conversation here, I suppose. At his home—where I've celebrated almost every Christmas and more than a handful of birthdays over my life. As if the familiar territory will soften the blow of what I have to tell him.

I give my grandmother a hug before she pulls back, hands on both my shoulders to look me over. "Is everything okay with you?"

Lying, I nod. "I was hoping to talk to Grandad."

"Is that my Reese's Pieces?" I hear my grandfather call out. His wife moves out of the way so he can see me. "It is! Come in! What a lovely surprise."

I step into their family home, closing the door behind me.

"She wants to talk to you, Arthur." My grandmother's tone clearly hopes to convey something to him. Not that she knows what.

"Oh." His previous cheery tone settles. "Okay. This seems like it may be serious. Should we talk in my study?"

My attention bounces to the French doors that lead to his study, but there's a reason I came here instead of having this conversation in my office. There's a part of me that's hoping he'll be my grandfather more so than my business mentor today.

"Would you mind if we talked in the living room?"

"Great idea." My grandmother pats me on the back. "You two talk in there and I'll make you both some tea."

My grandfather eyes me cautiously, a bit resigned in the way he's holding his shoulders. As if he knows he's not going to like what I have to tell him.

We wordlessly make our way into the living room. This one is less formal than their sitting room with all the stiff antique furniture. It helps add to the comfortability. I'm desperate for a bit of comfort today.

My grandfather takes his usual seat in his worn-in leather recliner. But I can't even attempt to relax, so instead of taking the matching one where my grandmother usually sits, I opt for the sofa across the room.

It'll give me a bit of space to breathe from his inevitable disappointment.

Awkward silence stifles the air. I don't have it in me to start this conversation and he clearly doesn't want it to happen at all. As if not having to hear whatever I'm going to say would give me the chance to fix it. To change it on my own.

But there's no changing this. Even if I wanted to.

Our family photos line the walls of the room. There are a few photos of my dad's mom too, but any of the ones where I'm older than a baby, the woman who I now call my grandmother is in them. In every photo, there's only five Remingtons. My grandparents, my parents, and me. As an only child, who didn't see myself having my own children one day, I assumed I'd probably never have a family bigger than this. As if that was the only way it could expand.

But here I am at thirty-five, feeling like I'm on the edge of it growing bigger than I ever imagined.

"Reese." My grandfather uses his professional voice. "What's going on?"

I look him over, soaking in the mental image of this moment. Because there's an awfully good chance this is going to be the last time he views me as a respectable businesswoman. Or as the girl who was so eager to follow in his footsteps. The girl he was so proud to lead the way for.

"Are you stepping down?" he finally asks, unable to bear the silence any longer. "Is that what this is about?"

"What? No. No, that's the last thing I want."

Relief washes over him. "Then what's going on? You're scaring me."

"It's Emmett."

"Monty?" He sits up in his chair. "Is he okay? What happened?"

"He's okay."

"Is it his contract? I don't understand why you haven't had him sign an extension yet. Time is ticking, Reese."

None of this is going to be easy, is it?

"I don't know if I can extend his contract," I admit.

My grandfather rears back. "Why not? He's the best man for the job."

"I know. I fully agree. It's just that he and I . . ."

I pray for that to be enough. That he won't force me to finish the sentence.

"He and you, what?"

I guess not then.

"What?" he asks again. "You two aren't getting along still? Reese, you have to move past that. For the good of your team. You need to think about the future of the club—"

"Grandad," I interrupt. "We are getting along. That's what I'm trying to tell you. We're getting along *too* well."

His gray bushy brows narrow in confusion.

I love the man, but I hate that he's not piecing this together.

"Arthur," my grandmother says from the entryway off the kitchen. She's behind his recliner, two glasses of iced tea in hand. Adoring eyes locked on me across the room. "She's trying to tell you that she and Monty are together. Romantically."

There they are. The words are out there in the open now.

I offer my grandmother a grateful smile. She nods toward the kitchen, silently telling me she's going to let us have this conversation privately.

I look anywhere else I can. The wall. The carpet. My lap. Finally, my eyes hesitantly track back to my grandfather.

"Reese." He says my name coolly. "Please tell me that's not true."

The dissatisfaction in his voice. The hurt on his face. It's already burning the backs of my eyes. This is the last thing I wanted, for him to be disappointed in me. But after our trip to Colorado, with the way I feel about Emmett, I had to tell him. It was time.

"I can't lie to you anymore."

"Oh, Reese." He sighs heavily. "I told you not to give them anything to talk about. The press is going to eat you alive for this." He stays silent for a long while until he eventually asks, "How long?"

"Long enough."

He closes his eyes and drops his head back as he takes in that statement.

"I'm sorry. I'm so sorry. I didn't mean to."

"You didn't mean to what?"

"I didn't mean to fall in love with him."

His expression earns a bit of understanding. "Oh, Reese."

"I'm sorry," I choke out. "I tried not to."

He takes a long moment to collect himself and once he does, he settles me a bit by saying, "You can't apologize for loving someone, honey."

"But I'm still sorry. I know you trusted me with this franchise. And after everything that happened with Jeremy, I'm sure you think my decision-making skills are absolute shit. And now here I am with the field manager of the team."

He sits forward in his recliner. "Let's get one thing straight. I do not think your decision-making skills are shit, so get that out of your head. I would have never held on to this team for you if I didn't trust your gut. If I didn't trust you. And Jeremy tricked all of us, Reese. That wasn't your fault. Monty, on the other hand . . ." He leans back in his chair, shaking his head. "They're not the same, okay?"

No. No, they're not.

"I thought you two hated each other?"

"Well, apparently not anymore."

He chuckles, but the way he's looking at me, his expression is full of sympathy, as if he knows whatever happens next is going to be a terrible decision for me to make.

"You couldn't have picked a better man, Reese. More than anything, know that."

That is something I undoubtedly already know.

I nod, trying to swallow back the thickness in my throat. I can't fight the emotions today. My heart feels heavy. This conversation has been weighing on me. Being in love with someone you're not supposed to is really fucking scary.

"I need to take my grandad hat off now," he says. "We need to talk business."

I brace myself, already knowing what he's going to say. He and I are both aware there's no way things can continue the way they are now. We're both aware that's why I finally came to him.

"Grandad, I promise I'm not trying to ruin the franchise you just left behind."

"Then don't." His eyes are fiercely glued on mine. "You don't have the luxury of doing whatever you want, Reese. That's something you gave up when you took on this position. You have a responsibility bigger than yourself. You don't get to be selfish, and you don't get to have a choice. Do you understand?"

I nod. "Yes."

"This is a business, Reese."

"I know."

"Good. Then you also know exactly what you have to do, whether you like it or not."

38

EMMETT

Reese was right. Miller does make a beautiful bride.

Did I cry a little when I saw her in her dress for the first time this afternoon? Yes.

Did I tear up while I walked her down the aisle then again during her vows? Also, yes.

Today has been special for a lot of reasons. Kai and Miller asked me to officiate the ceremony, so I got to stand up there with them and lead them through it. Isaiah and Kennedy acted as the only members of their bridal party, standing on either side of them.

And of course, Max was with us too, wearing a button-down shirt that refused to stay tucked in. He's had a ring of something around his mouth all day, chocolate milk if I had to guess, and could hardly stand still as he listened to his parents make vows to each other.

It was perfect.

And every once in a while, when the timing was right, I'd look into the crowd and catch Reese's eye. Sitting in the second-to-last row, wearing a pretty lilac dress and a sweet smile on her face as she watched.

It's nice to see her enjoying herself. Since we got home from Colorado, she's been a bit off, burying herself with work. When I asked if I could help with anything, she assured me she had everything handled—whatever that means.

But today, it's clear she put all of that on the back burner and has been fully present and in the moment with me. It's been more special having her here than I could've imagined.

When Kai and Miller had their first dance, I got to sit with her as we watched them together. She had her hand in my lap, stroking soft lines on my thigh the whole time. When Isaiah gave his best man speech, I had my arm around her chair and whenever she laughed, she'd fall into my shoulder. After Miller and my father–daughter dance, Reese is who I came back to.

It means more than she'll ever know, getting to share today with her. Getting to talk to her. Getting to sit next to her. Getting to take photos and dance with her. Getting to experience this all with her.

I know she was hesitant about being out in public with me for the first time. Although the team has assumed correctly about the two of us, they've never seen us together in this way or had our relationship confirmed. That changed today.

She was nervous at first, looking around anytime I reached for her hand. But soon enough, she settled.

Yeah, every one of the guys gave us shit at one point or another, but it was all good-natured. And it was nice. Being *us* in public for once.

But thankfully, other than the wedding guests, no one else is privy to seeing that.

It's an intimate gathering of Kai and Miller's closest people. There's got to be fewer than fifty of us in attendance. The team is here, as are a couple of other athletes who play for Chicago—two hockey players and a basketball player. And a couple of other friends as well.

The wedding location is secluded and private. We're a couple of hours outside of the city, but it feels as if we're in the middle of nowhere in the best possible way. It's all greenery and nature here. Oak trees envelop us, adding to the privacy factor. Two long tables and a makeshift dance floor are set up under string lights for the reception.

And just on the other side of the tables, yurt-style tents are scattered around the property for all the guests to stay the night after the party. The camping vibe works for the two of them. After all, Miller used to travel the country living out of her van before she landed in Chicago.

"It's kind of annoying how happy we are, huh?" my daughter asks from the seat next to me.

I wrap an arm around the back of her chair. "Yeah, the smile on my face is a bit painful. I could go for less of it."

She drops her head to my shoulder as we keep our eyes on the dance floor.

Isaiah stole Reese for a dance and Kai took Kennedy. Max is passed out asleep in his mom's lap, exhausted from the party, so I stayed behind too.

"She's a good addition," Miller states, nodding toward the dance floor.

My attention finds Reese, laughing at whatever it is Isaiah is saying to her.

I smile that same smile I've worn all day. "Yeah. She is."

"What are you two going to do about work? You can't keep your relationship a secret forever."

"I don't know, Millie. It's either her name gets dragged through the mud for dating her employee, and we both know that's going to stain her reputation forever, or I quit my job. I'm only okay with one of those options."

"But you love your job."

"Yeah, but I lo—" I stop myself.

"Oh shit." She smacks me in the chest with the back of her hand. "You're in love with her! Of course you are."

There's no use denying it, but I don't confirm either. I should probably tell Reese before I tell anyone else.

"Have you told her?"

"Not yet."

"Wow." Miller drops her head back onto my arm. "She really is going to be my new mommy, isn't she?"

"Let's not scare her off with that weird shit, please. It's her first time around the whole family like this, us being together, and I've already got Isaiah saying God knows what to her out there."

But I can't stop the smile from stretching my lips as I watch those four on the dance floor. Reese is holding her own just fine with Isaiah, saying something that causes his head to tip back in laughter. And Kai is joking about something with his sister-in-law as they finish their dance together.

The music fades out as the song comes to a close.

The reception has almost come to a close as well. A handful of the guests have already made it back to their tents for the night. But then you have the guys from the team who I have a feeling will be up partying until the sun rises.

That's the benefit of Kai and Miller getting married on a random summer Monday, I suppose. We don't start our next series until Wednesday, so everyone can recover tomorrow.

The four of them make their way back to our end of the table. Isaiah takes a seat, and Kennedy slips onto his lap. Kai presses a kiss to the top of Miller's hair before lifting their sleeping son into his arms to give her a break. And Reese stands behind my chair, sliding her hands over my shoulders and crossing them at my chest.

I had convinced myself I didn't care that I was the only one in my family without someone. But now that Reese is here, I know I was fooling myself before. This feels right. The seven, soon-to-be eight of us, feels right. Unconventional little family that we may be.

I reach up and hook a hand around Reese's wrist, holding her to me.

On the way to the bar, Cody and Travis stop by our end of the table.

Cody looks up at Reese then down to me, repeating that pattern a couple more times. "I don't know if any of the other guys on the team are going to tell you, so I'll be the one to say it. You two are hot together."

"Jesus, Cody." Travis shakes his head.

"What? It's giving 'power couple.'"

"It's giving 'he can bench your ass, and she can trade you.'"

"Exactly. Power couple. And they wouldn't." Cody looks at us. "Would you? You love me too much. But out of curiosity, with three happy couples here and all, just how many hookups have happened at the stadium?"

"I'm so sorry for him." Travis pushes Cody to keep moving and doesn't let up until he's far enough away from our table.

"I'm not here to judge! You can tell me!" Cody yells over his shoulder at us.

I feel Reese silently shake in laughter behind me.

"What?" Kai laughs. "Mills and I have never hooked up at work. Well, if we don't count any of the road trips from that summer she was nannying for Max."

"Yeah, for sure," Kennedy adds. "Same here. No hookups at work. *Definitely* not."

Isaiah scratches the back of his neck. "But also, maybe don't use the women's restroom by the clubhouse."

"I knew it!" Reese bursts. "You two looked guilty as hell when I found you in there last year."

"Really, guys?" I ask. "The bathroom?"

"You two probably have no room to talk." Isaiah lifts an accusatory brow. "Why don't you go ahead and tell us what rooms *we* should avoid at work, huh?"

Reese stays silent.

"How about we don't," I answer for us.

"*Please* don't." Miller visibly grimaces. "I'll never be able to go to another game there if this conversation continues. For the love of God, can we talk about something other than my dad's sex life?"

She holds her left hand over her eyes to shield herself.

"Oh, Miller," Reese sighs from behind me. "I hadn't seen your wedding band yet."

The conversation shifts as my daughter excitedly holds out her left hand to show her.

Reese takes it in her own, examining the diamond band nestled against Miller's engagement ring. "It's beautiful," she says. "It pairs perfectly with your mom's ring. I love them together."

Miller beams, checking out her own hand. "I love them too."

Taking Reese's hand that I still have in my own, I bring it to my lips and press a kiss to the back of it. She didn't miss a beat when I told her the significance of Miller's engagement ring, which is just another reason I love her.

"We should get this kid to bed soon," Kai says with Max's cheek pressed to his shoulder.

Miller cranes her neck back to look up at him. "One more dance, the three of us, and we'll call it a night?"

He wears this soft smile as he looks down at her. "Sounds perfect, Mills."

"What do you say, wifey?" Isaiah asks Kennedy. "We've got a second wedding coming up ourselves. Maybe we should go practice."

"This music is a little different than what I'm accustomed to getting married to."

Isaiah laughs, standing to carry her out to the dance floor, following his brother's lead.

Hand in mine, Reese backs away from the table, urging me to stand and follow her. "Come on, Em. I can't let my final dance be with Isaiah."

"Hey!" Isaiah interjects. "I'm an excellent dancer, Reese. Isn't that right, Kenny?"

Kennedy hesitates. "Let's just say I think it's good we have time to practice before it's our turn again."

Reese leads me out to join everyone else, walking backward and facing me, a single hand of mine in two of hers.

It's so different from the last time we danced together. I had to practically drag her onto the dance floor at her grandfather's retirement party. Now, here she is, on display in front of our entire team, pulling me to follow her.

She doesn't have to force me, by any means. I'd literally follow her anywhere.

Taking her arms, I drape them around my neck, then settle my hands onto her lower back. Chest to chest. Cheek to cheek. The song is slow, and we move to that same tempo.

"Thank you for being here today," I tell her quietly. "It means the world to get to share it with you."

"I wouldn't miss it for anything."

"Has everything been okay with you? You've seemed stressed at work since we got back from our last road trip."

Reese goes silent for a moment before she says, "Everything is okay."

"Can I do anything?"

She smiles up at me, hands on either side of my face. "Let's not worry about work right now. Not tonight. Everything else can wait until tomorrow."

I study her, trying to understand what's weighing on her. But she's right. It can't matter tonight. I press a kiss to the top of her hair before she rests on my shoulder again, the two of us dancing as the party winds down around us.

Her fingers toy with the line of my hair. "You did such a good job officiating today."

"You think so?"

"It was perfect. It was so special to hear you talk about them. The stories were personal, and the advice you gave them was delivered with so much faith in their future."

"I do have a lot of faith in their future." *I have a lot of faith in ours too.* "I was a bit nervous, though. It was my first time doing something like that."

"Yeah, I didn't know you did weddings." She pulls away, tilting her head as she looks up at me. "Ever consider doing one as the groom?"

I huff a laugh. "Don't tempt me, Remington."

I've had the question on my mind for some time now, and standing up front during the ceremony today has only brought it to the forefront. I can't think of a better time to ask.

"Reese, no wrong answer here. But could you ever see yourself getting married again?"

Her brows lift in surprise at my blatant question. But she doesn't give me a yes-or-no answer. Instead, she asks, "Is that something *you'd* want?"

"I've never gotten the chance to be married before. I think I'd like to be."

Her smile goes soft. "If I could have it my way, I'd marry you, Emmett. If that's what you're asking."

I slip her curled hair behind her ear, running my thumb over her line of earrings. "Well, maybe one day, that's exactly what I'll be asking."

39

REESE

Cloud nine.

I'm not sure I've been on it before, but it sure feels like it today.

I probably shouldn't allow myself to feel so carefree this morning, but I can't help it. Thoughts of last night have me floating right down the hall to my office.

Being out in public with Emmett, spending time with his family, I wish every day could be like that. If we met under different circumstances, if he wasn't my employee, it could be.

But it never could have been someone else, could it?

It was always going to be Emmett. We were two people who were lonelier than we realized and only found each other because we had the same hiding place.

It only makes sense that the person I fell for is the manager who spends as much time at the field as I do. Who loves the team the same way I do, even if I didn't want to admit it initially.

The players are off today, no doubt still recovering from last night's wedding. But I have too many meetings ahead of me to do the same. The top floor is full. All of the front-office staff is working today. I offer a few smiles and waves as I pass by their office windows, headed for mine.

I'd find the skip in my step to be a bit annoying if I were watching me strut down the hall. But I can't help it. Life is good.

Stopping by the coffee station, I pour myself a cup before adding a splash of cream. Then I take a brown sugar cube from the small glass jar and plop it in my mug. Brown sugar cubes were an addition I found here one morning a few days after my grandfather's retirement party. No doubt Emmett's doing.

With my mug in hand, I turn in for my office, coming face-to-face with the empty receptionist desk just outside my door.

The interviews I conducted for a new receptionist were promising. There were some good candidates. Some great ones, even. But I didn't have it in me to hire someone. I know I should. I know I technically need one, but there's something about having an open door this season that I've enjoyed.

I enjoy that players can come to me if they need something.

I enjoy that the staff can come directly to me with any concerns they may have.

And I enjoy that Emmett can get to me anytime he wants.

I don't know. Maybe I won't hire anyone. Maybe the door will remain open for the rest of my time here.

But that notion flies right out of the window when I step into my office and find Scott sitting in a chair opposite my desk, his back to me, looking out my view.

Sure, I have a lineup of meetings today, but none of them are with him.

"Scott?" I ask, rounding my desk and placing my mug on the coaster I leave next to my computer.

"Reese."

"I don't have you on my schedule, and I don't have extra time today."

"If I were you, I'd make time for this conversation."

My senses go on high alert, prickling my skin uncomfortably.

"What can I help you with?" I ask.

And why were you in my office without me?

I don't look at him, firing up my computer and focusing on a few emails I need to reply to. Trying my best to not let his presence throw me off.

Out of my periphery, I watch the smug bastard lean back in the chair, stretching his legs out and crossing his hands over his stomach. "You can help me by involving me in the team as I've been requesting all year."

I roll my eyes, but they're locked on the computer screen. "We've discussed this, Scott. You're involved with the advisory board, but I've taken over the baseball operations for the club. I'm glad you were able to help my grandfather when he needed it, but I do not need that same help."

The truth is, he didn't help my grandfather. He made slimy moves that pushed us into debt, knowing my grandfather was too tired to notice. But I don't have the energy to explain all that today. I don't owe him an explanation anyway.

Scott, as well as the rest of the advisory board, are compensated well for their advice. Even the ill-intentioned advice that's delivered in a disrespectful manner. I've kept them on as a courtesy to my grandfather and because it felt like the right thing to do when I took over this role. I was new. I wanted to learn. But they haven't wanted to teach me anything. They've wanted me to fail.

Or in this case, they've wanted my job.

"You see, about that." Scott sits forward. "I don't just want to help. I want the title I deserve after all the years of work I put in with Arthur. I want you to name me President of Baseball Operations."

I don't even look in his direction. "No."

"You're unqualified, Reese."

"Just because you want to assume I'm unqualified doesn't make that true. I have trained for this position for my entire life. This is not up for discussion, Scott."

"You've trained for this your entire life, yet you're willing to risk it?"

That finally earns my attention, and my eyes tick up to look at him. "What does that mean?"

His smile slowly stretches his mouth. It has a superiority to it, as if he were seconds away from calling checkmate. "Did you have fun last night, Reese?"

What the hell?

My stomach dips at the mere insinuation.

I keep my eyes glued to him, willing him to explain the rest.

"Not so confident playing the big scary boss now, are you?" He pulls an envelope from behind his back, tossing it on the desk between us. "It looked like you had a great time to me."

I don't touch it. I don't want to play this game.

"Go ahead, Reese. I think you'll agree. You looked fucking thrilled in those pictures."

Keeping my eyes locked on him, I hesitantly grab the envelope, opening the flap and finally glancing inside.

The first thing that catches my eye is the bright lilac of the dress I wore last night.

Then Emmett's dark green suit.

The flashes of bright string lights dotted along the top edges of the photographs matching the same ones that illuminated the dance floor last night.

Anxiety wraps me up, stealing the color from my face as I piece together what exactly I'm looking at.

The first photo is of Emmett and me sitting closely together, my head on his shoulder during the reception.

The next is an image of us dancing together, his hand holding mine to his chest, his smiling lips dangerously close to mine.

In the third you can clearly see his tattooed hand palm the back of my head as he bends to kiss me.

And the last one I'm able to stomach looking at is a photo of me talking to Miller, but that's not the focus of this image. The reason Scott included this particular photo is because of Emmett. As I talk to his daughter, his eyes are locked on me. Physically, nothing in this photo is incriminating. But it's the way he's looking at me. Adoration lines his features. He's watching me as if he were in love with me.

My heart hammers in my chest. My skin chills with panic. Dread twists my gut.

There's plenty more photos, but I don't flip through them. I don't need to see any more.

There's no use in denying anything. It's clearly us in these photographs, and I hate that images from a night as special as Emmett's daughter's wedding are going to be used against us.

I close the envelope, tossing it onto the desk.

Somehow, I manage to push the words past the lump in my throat to ask, "You had us followed?"

"Found a kid on the catering staff who didn't sign an NDA. Threw him a few hundred bucks to confirm my suspicions." He admits it so carelessly, as if this isn't the most intrusive thing he could've done. And of all nights, of all places, he had to do it there?

"And you printed them out? First of all, what year is it? And second, there's nothing that says that Emmett and I can't have a relationship."

"Oh, bullshit, Reese! Legally, maybe not. Apparently, you get to do whatever the hell you want being the sole owner of this club. But morally?" His laugh carries an evil edge. "You're his direct supervisor. He's up for a new contract. You know how easy this is going to be to spin in the media? Either you'll be the owner who coerced her employee into a relationship, or he'll be the field manager who slept his way into a new contract. You're fucked either way, and so is he. He'll be lucky if he lands himself another coaching job after this one."

I push up from my seat, hands on the desk. "Do *not* threaten him."

He stands as well. "Then don't make me."

We stand off with one another.

I couldn't care less about my reputation right now, but I am worried about his. If I could do anything in this moment, it'd be to protect Emmett.

"What do you want?" I finally ask.

"You know exactly what I want. Name me president and I won't say a word."

"You're blackmailing me? Seriously?"

"That's a strong word, Reese. All I'm suggesting is you name me president so those pictures won't go anywhere. Monty keeps his job, but you'll step back. You'll still be the owner, of course. No one can take that from you." Scott uses his hands to imitate that he was reading off a marquee sign. "The first female team owner in the league. Geez. What a bad look, Reese. Way to represent women in sports, or whatever the hell you thought you were doing."

He pushes the envelope toward me. "Go ahead and keep those. I have more."

I think I'm going to be sick.

"Don't look so sad about this," he continues. "We'll have an advisory board meeting tomorrow. We'll call for a vote. Make it look like an in-house decision for you to step down and for me to take over. Or . . ." He tilts his head from side to side, as if he were contemplating another option. "Those photos get leaked to the right people. We both know by now there's plenty of media sources who aren't your biggest fan. They'll get the word out. Then it's good luck to you in hopes of ever being taken seriously again."

Scott takes a deep breath, a satisfied grin on his mouth as he says, "Do the right thing for the team, Reese. You're a liability at this point."

Then he exits my office, leaving me alone with an impossible decision to make.

40

EMMETT

I have to tell her. I should've done it last night.

Shit, I should've done it weeks ago.

Reese should know that I'm in love with her.

Sure, there's a good chance she already knows, but she should hear it from me. I've learned that life is too short not to tell people that you love them.

Reese had to leave the wedding venue early this morning to get to work, but I needed to stay back and make sure everything was cleaned up and paid for. As she sat at the end of the mattress we slept on last night, buckling the strap on her high heel, I almost told her then.

I swallowed the words down, though. It didn't feel big enough. It didn't feel special enough to tell her while she was getting ready for work, and I was lying naked in the bed we shared the night before.

I almost said fuck it and told her when I walked her to her car, but then a couple of my players passed by and ruined the moment.

But as soon as she drove away, I regretted not telling her. At this point, she just needs to know. And truthfully, I can't think of a better place to tell her than at the field. So that's where I am. On the team's day off. I'm just going to pop in and let her know that I'm in love with her.

I take the elevator to the top floor where her office is. It's a Tuesday, so even though the team is off today, everyone else from the front office is here to work.

A normal day for all of them.

I couldn't tell you the last time one of my days felt normal or mundane. Life is exponentially brighter lately and today feels like another one of those vibrant days. Even more so after last night.

I turn into Reese's office, passing the vacant reception desk, only to find her office empty too. Her bag is here, hanging on the hook on the wall. There's a full mug of coffee sitting on her desk, but it looks cold at this point.

I give it a few minutes, waiting for her to come back from wherever she ran off to, but soon the silence becomes more than I can handle, and I decide to go in search of her instead.

There's only one other place she could be, especially on a day the players aren't here.

Taking the elevator to the clubhouse level, I walk down the tunnel that leads to the dugout. Glancing to the right, two red-bottom heels stick out past the partition, legs stretched over the bench, ankles crossed. Turning the corner, I find Reese sitting on the ledge where I've found her so many times before.

Her attention shoots to me immediately. "Emmett." There's an edge of panic in her voice. "What are you doing here?"

I step forward, shins to the bench, getting as close to her as I can, but she pulls her legs back as I do.

"I need to tell you something, Reese."

She tracks the space around us, unable to focus on me. Too worried about someone else walking up on us, I guess. "Yeah," she exhales. "I need to tell you something too."

Her words don't come out eager the way mine do. Instead, her statement is laced with dread.

"Is everything okay?"

"No." Her throat bobs in a thick swallow. "It's not."

Panic pricks my skin. This heavy impending doom settles between the two walls on either side of us, suffocating this small corner. When I examine Reese more closely, there's an almost vacant look on her usually expressive face.

I slide my hand over her thigh. "Reese, tell me what's wrong."

So I can fix it, I silently add.

Looking around again, she takes my hand off her leg and drops it at my side. "You can't do that, Emmett. Not here. Not anymore."

Okay. We've literally fucked in her office here, so I'm not sure why she's tripping out over me hardly touching her while no one is around.

But then that last part replays in my head. *Not anymore.*

Alarms sound off as my stomach sinks to a nauseating level.

"You're freaking me out, Reese. What's going on?"

Her deep blues trail over my face, as if she were memorizing it. Tracing the shape of my lips. The line of my jaw. It's almost unnerving in a way, but only because I plan to be right next to her for a long time to come. She doesn't need to memorize anything.

At least, that's what my dwindling hope is trying to reassure me. *We're still okay. We still have plenty of time.*

On the ledge beside her, Reese grabs an envelope and holds it in her lap before finally extending it toward me. She doesn't explain the contents, but as soon as I open it, she doesn't need to.

My heart hammers when I see the first picture, but in the best way. Because these pictures so clearly show how much I love this woman. How right we fit together. How happy we are.

Were, my brain screams.

These pictures showcase how proud she is to have me next to her. How adoringly I watch her even when she's not looking. Honestly, some of these should probably be framed so I can have a couple in my apartment. I think they may be our very first pictures we've taken together, other than the professional ones that were snapped last night. And for only a second, I truly enjoy flipping through them.

Until I realize what they are.

Someone took these last night and it wasn't the wedding photographer.

"Where did these come from?"

My eyes flit up to Reese to find her watching me thumb through the photos. She's overwhelmed, checked out, but there's an underlying apology in her features.

"Scott."

"What do you mean, 'Scott'?"

"Scott paid someone to take them last night. I walked into my office to find him waiting for me this morning with that envelope."

I could fucking kill him.

I slip the envelope into the back pocket of my jeans. "Where is he?"

"Emmett. No."

"Where the fuck is he, Reese? I'm not playing around here. Whatever this is, if he wants to threaten us, he can threaten *me*."

I turn to leave, anger pulsing through my veins. I don't even know what he wants or what he thought he'd get out of *stalking* us like a fucking psychopath, but I will very quickly teach him that I'm the last person he wants to play this game with.

Reese grabs my arm to stop me, standing from her seat on the ledge as she does. "Emmett, you cannot go after him. It's bad. What he's threatening is *bad*. Do not give him any reason to follow through."

A bit more of her natural fire shines through, and I realize now, she's been trying to disassociate herself from whatever the hell happened in her office this morning.

I reach up to cup her face, wanting to touch her. Wanting to comfort her. But I drop my hand again before I can, knowing the last thing she'd want right now is to give someone else the opportunity to see us together. "What does he want?"

She exhales a sharp breath, bracing herself. "He wants me to make him President of Baseball Operations."

"Abso-fucking-lutely not."

"It's not that simple, Em."

"It is that simple! That is *your* position. Something you've worked your entire life for. Someone else has already tried to take it from you. I'm not letting fucking Scott steal it from you over some pictures."

"*You're* not letting him do anything! This is *my* decision."

That stops me in my tracks, tamping down a bit of my fight. We're supposed to be in this together, but it sure doesn't sound like we are.

"You can't be seriously considering this, Reese."

She looks up at me, holding her ground, but doesn't say anything.

She *is* considering this.

I shake my head vehemently. "No."

"I don't have to explain to you what those pictures will do in the wrong hands."

I want to argue with her about that, but I know she's right. Our relationship could so easily get spun to appear to be something it's not by anyone who wanted to sell that story. By someone who doesn't like that Reese is in the position she's in.

"Is that what he's threatening? To give these to the press?"

"Yes."

"And the only way to stop him is by giving up your position?"

"Yes."

"Reese." There's resignation in the way I say her name because that's exactly how I feel right now. Utterly defeated.

This is the last thing I want for her. I'm supposed to protect her, but instead, I was careless. I was too comfortable with the fact we hadn't gotten caught by the wrong person yet. I promised her she'd be safe in public with me and look what happened. This is my fault and she's going to lose everything she's ever worked for, everything she's ever wanted, because of me.

"I'll be fine," she forces out. "There's going to be an advisory board meeting tomorrow. He wants me to step down then."

"Tomorrow?"

That gives her no time to prepare. No time to think this through. No time to find a different option.

"Reese." I have no clue what else to say to her other than, "I'm so sorry. This is my fault."

She shrugs, trying to act casual, but she's so clearly heartbroken. "It's not your fault, Em. And there's nothing to be sorry about. I'm still glad I was there with you last night. I'm still glad I met you. I don't regret anything that's happened."

I hate everything about the way those words settle into me. They feel . . . *final*.

Here I was, coming to tell her how much I love her, and now I can't. Now I might never be able to. Not when me telling her might cause her to make a decision she thinks is best for me and not for herself.

"Do you want me to come by tonight?" I ask. "We can talk it out. Look at all our options."

She steels her spine and puts her best professional face forward. The one I haven't seen in a while. The one she always used to wear when she first got here.

"I think it'd be best if we were more careful right now. We don't need to give anyone else a reason to make this worse for us."

I think I'm going to be sick.

"I'm going to . . ." She points up, telling me she needs to get back to work. "Let me handle this, okay? I'll take care of it."

That's the last thing I want her to do. I want to figure this out together. I want to protect her from all the bullshit that's running circles in her head right now.

But there she goes, being adamant about taking care of herself again.

I'm desperate to ask her if we're okay. If we'll be okay. But I'm also terrified of the answer.

So, I don't ask.

I just let go back to her office alone.

After I give myself some time outside, wrapping my head around what the fuck just happened, I swing by her office to let her know I'm heading out.

But when I go to turn the handle, I find that, for the first time ever, her door is locked.

41

EMMETT

I can't sleep.

It's the only time since Arthur's retirement party that Reese and I have actively chosen not to stay together. Of course, there are the nights on the road we can't get to each other, or the two days she was away for an owners' meeting. But we've never *chosen* to be apart.

Until tonight.

I didn't choose shit, actually. And after being alone for more than twenty years, I've very quickly become terrible at sleeping without her next to me.

But even if she were lying in bed with me, I'm not entirely sure sleep would find me anyway. Guilt is too busy gnawing away as I toss and turn. Stress is too demanding of my attention for me to find any sense of calm.

It's taken everything in me not to call her. To apologize for putting her in this position and for not protecting her the way I should've. It was selfish, asking her to come to Miller's wedding with me. I was greedy, and now look where that got us.

But I haven't called her tonight because I'm afraid if I say anything right now, it'll push her to make a decision she'll feel obligated to make.

Reese didn't have to spell it out for me. I already know that if she steps down as president, I'll be able to keep my job. Scott *wants* me to keep my job.

If and when news got out about Reese and me, it would be a whole lot less damning if she were simply the distant team owner and not my direct supervisor on the baseball side of the business. If she didn't directly control my contract extension, if she wasn't involved in the daily decision-making, there wouldn't be a whole lot to say.

And that's exactly why she's going to give up her position.

She's going to step down to keep my job safe.

There's also the option that maybe she'll end things with me and try to protect me that way.

I'm not good with either of those outcomes.

Another question swirling in my mind is if Reese does hand over the presidency to Scott, allowing us to stay together, how long until the resentment builds? Another man has already tried to take this from her, and though I'm not going about it in the same way, if she lost her job, the result would be the same. How could she not resent me for losing the only thing she's ever wanted?

Even if she did decide to fight it and Scott gives those photos to certain journalists who simply want to sell a story without knowing the facts, *I* can't handle watching her go through the hate again. She doesn't deserve that.

If we had more time, if Scott hadn't insisted this happen tomorrow, we could come up with a plan to get our story out in the right way. We *should've* already done that, but Reese wasn't ready, and I don't blame her. She just got through hell with the press. She's not ready for another round.

Lying here, alone in my dark apartment, I'm done.

I'm done feeling helpless. I'm done *being* helpless.

I have always prided myself on taking care of what's mine, and that's exactly what I'm going to do.

There's still a way for Reese to keep her position. She didn't mention it earlier today because in her mind, it's not an option.

But if I quit my job, what's the press going to say then? My contract extension is the most damning part of this all. It could easily be spun to look as if I was only with her to renew my job. But if I took that off the table, not just the extension but my entire position, what would the press have to say then? Nothing. They'd have no fucking story.

Two people fell for each other, so one of them left their job so they could be together. Pretty boring story if you ask me.

I promised Reese I'd take care of her because she deserves to be taken care of, and tomorrow, I'm going to do exactly that.

"Hey, what's up?" Isaiah asks, closing my office door behind him. "You wanted to see me?"

His eyes trail to find his brother in my office as well. Kai has a shoulder leant against the wall, arms crossed over his chest, just as confused as to what's going on. He thought we were having a pregame pitching lineup meeting until I told him we needed to wait for Isaiah.

Standing from my desk, I round it to the other side, sitting back on the edge. "I wanted to talk to both of you before the game."

Kai and Isaiah look at each other, silently asking the other what's going on.

"I just needed you boys to hear it from me that after the game tonight, I'm going to be stepping down from coaching this team."

Kai pushes off the wall, standing up straight. "What?"

"Nothing is going to change between the three of us. We're—"

"Hold up." Kai screws his eyes shut, holding his hands up to stop me. "What the fuck are you talking about, Monty?"

I don't know why I thought this was going to be easy. I suppose because my conversation with Miller this morning was.

As soon as I told her I was stepping down, she completely understood where I was coming from.

But it's different with Miller. She's been questioning what Reese and I were going to do about work for a while now. This was on her radar.

It clearly wasn't on Kai or Isaiah's.

I exhale a long breath. "Miller already knows. I talked to her this morning, but I asked her to let me be the one to tell you guys. I'm going to be stepping down after today's game. Things are complicated right now. There's some stuff happening behind the scenes."

"What kind of stuff?" Isaiah asks, frustration lining his tone. "What does that even mean?"

"Threats to Reese's position. Threats to make our relationship look bad in the media, and I need to protect her from that. This is how I can do that. This is the *only* way I know how to do that."

Silence fills my office.

Kai's brows are furrowed. His face is etched in anger and confusion.

Isaiah's expression is a bit blank. His mouth is parted without words to say.

"Nothing will change between the three of us. You guys are my family. Have been since I met you. And hell . . ." I gesture to Kai. "You're legally stuck with me now anyway."

The humor doesn't diffuse anything. Both of them are still silent, staring at me in disbelief.

I'm doing my best to make this easy, but the truth is, telling them is breaking my heart. The three of us met here. We've become family because of our time together here. I've loved being involved with this team, both on and off the field.

I'd like to believe that nothing is going to change, but certain things will. I'll still be their friend. I'll still be Kai's father-in-law. But I don't know that I'll still be the guy they come to for advice or when they need to talk something out. Baseball has bonded us in that way. Me being their coach has made our dynamic what it is, and I can only hope that it stays the same when I'm no longer involved with the team.

"Someone say something."

"But you love your job," Isaiah finally chimes in.

"Of course I do, but . . ." I scrub a palm over my face, swallowing down the lump in my throat. "Look, I've lost someone once before and I can't go through that again. As much as I love my job, it's not worth losing Reese over. Not even close."

"Whatever is going on, you're not going to lose Reese over it," Kai argues. "There's no way."

"I don't know that for certain, and it's more complicated than that anyway. It's not just a matter of us staying together. Which, yeah, that is a question on my mind. It's also about doing what's best for her, even if that means I need to sacrifice some things. That's worth it to me. I can't just sit back and watch her lose everything she's worked for. I wouldn't want her to want that version of me. Someone who doesn't fight for their people."

They both lose their arguments, understanding beginning to settle in.

"You two know better than anyone that you take care of your family first, and this is me taking care of mine."

"I get it," Isaiah finally agrees. "I would do the same thing for Kennedy. Hell, I *tried* to do the same thing for Kennedy. I tried to leave my job so she could have hers. And you supported me in that decision. I don't like this, but I understand your reasoning."

I look to Kai, but he's got his arms crossed at his chest, not budging on his anger. "There's got to be another option."

"Yeah, if we had more time, we'd probably have a different solution here. But Reese is being told to step down from baseball operations tonight. Right after the game. So, we're out of time."

His jaw tics in frustration. "This is bullshit."

"Couldn't agree more."

"I'm not coaching under someone else."

"Shut the fuck up. Yes, you are." I exhale a laugh, and it feels nice. "Look, I've made peace with this decision. I made peace with this decision months ago, in fact. It's just a job. I'll get another one. So, let's not be so dramatic about this, okay? I'll probably be at your house for dinner in like two days."

"Fine. This is stupid though. Anyone who knows you two or has seen you together would know it's genuine. The fact that anyone could spin this differently is bullshit. But Reese is under more scrutiny than anyone else in the league, so I guess I get it."

I smack him on the shoulder. "It'll be all right."

"Fuck this." He uncrosses his arms to give me a hug. "Love you, Monty."

Isaiah does the same. "So do I."

"Love you both too, but let's go. We have a game to win. No way am I going out with an L."

I may have told the Rhodes boys not to be dramatic about this decision, but *I'm* being dramatic as hell about it.

I try to hold on to every moment of my pregame ritual, knowing it's my last time doing it.

Filling out the lineup card for the final time.

Meeting with our bench coach, base coaches, and pitching coach to go over tonight's strategy.

Doing pregame media interviews.

I soak it all in, trying to hold on to it for a day I know I'll be missing it a little extra.

I try not to dwell on the fact that this place has become my second home or that this team and staff are my second family.

As I said, I'm being dramatic.

But nothing is as dramatic as the way a rock lodges in the back of my throat when it's time for my pregame speech to my players.

In the clubhouse, they all sit in their respective locker stalls as I go over the strategies we have in place for tonight. They all listen intently as I discuss the opposing team's batting lineup and our own.

We go over a couple more housekeeping items, and that's usually where I end these meetings, but before I call it done, I add one more thing.

"And um . . ." I clear my throat, tapping my game notepad against my palm as I attempt to get my shit together. "I don't say this often enough, but I truly love each and every one of you guys. Getting to coach you has been one of the best things I've done with my life."

My attention ticks to Isaiah but he can't look at me, eyes locked on the carpet, head tilted low.

Cody and Travis keep glancing over at each other, silently asking what the hell I'm on about.

Poor Milo sits in his locker stall, eyes wide and so fucking confused.

"This job and the years I've spent here brought my passion for the game back. I found a lot of myself again here. And I can't thank you enough for allowing me to coach you all."

Silence suffocates the typical rowdy clubhouse. Tension lines the wall. Confusion sits heavy on everyone's expressions.

So much for me not being dramatic about this.

"So, uh . . . yeah." I nod along. "Let's go win a game!"

That does absolutely nothing to get the energy back in the room, but I wasn't sure if I'd get a chance to talk to them all as a group again after tonight and I couldn't risk not having the opportunity.

Thankfully a bit more fire ignites under the guys when they take the field for warmups, and that pregame focus really zeros in for everyone as the time ticks down closer to the first pitch.

Like a fool, I allow myself to hope for a dugout visit from Reese.

I wait for it. I long for it.

It never comes. *She* never comes.

And when I look up into her owner's suite, needing just a glimpse of her, I find it empty. And it stays that way for the entire game.

42

EMMETT

Well, I'm going out with a win, so that's something, I guess.

I wasted as much time as I could. Held off as long as I could as I sat in my office. But now the players are gone, and the advisory board meeting is going to be starting any minute if it hasn't already.

It's not that I'm dreading this part. I'm not at all, actually. I know in my bones this is the right thing to do. That my motives are true. But these are my last few moments being the field manager for the Windy City Warriors and I want to soak in every second I can.

So yeah, I'm taking my time.

That time dwindles down as I ride the elevator to the top floor, and I take it all in on the long walk down to the conference room. I give Reese's office door a long stare as I pass by it.

It's not as if I'm never going to be back here. Reese will still own this team. Isaiah will still play here. Kai and Kennedy will still be on the staff. But this is the last time I will be.

As I near the floor-to-ceiling windows that make up the conference room walls, I spot Scott already running his mouth about something.

Pompous in the way he leans back in his chair.

Smug in the way he smiles at Reese.

Reese.

Sitting at the head of the table, she's dressed to the nines per usual, and not showing any signs of weakness as she listens to him. Blonde hair is styled sharp to hit just below the line of her jaw, and she's wearing heels that look severe enough that she could puncture Scott's tiny little dick if she wanted.

Her expression, as she listens to him ramble on, is screaming that she wants to.

It's the first time I've seen her since she showed me the pictures in the dugout yesterday morning. Just seeing her again, even through a glass partition, reenforces my resolve to do what I need to do.

I push open the door to the conference room, just as Scott says, "We'll take a vote. All in favor of Reese stepping down as President of Baseball Operations, raise your hand."

Scott's hand flies up immediately.

"There's no need for a vote," I cut in, letting the door close behind me. "It won't matter. I quit."

Silence stalls the rest of the group from voting before chaos ensues in the conference room.

"What?"

"No, you're not!"

"Absolutely not, Monty!" are all blurted out by the advisory board members as they talk over one another.

"You're not quitting," Scott states, a bit of panic etched on his face.

"Yes, I am. No way in hell will I work for you."

"That's not part of the—"

"Part of the what?" I test. "Were you going to say it's not part of the deal? Is that what you're calling it now?"

"What is he talking about?" Phil asks, eyes shooting to Scott.

The room is uneasy. There's an obvious confusion happening, from both me storming in here to quit my job as well as Scott randomly coming up with a vote to take Reese's position out from under her.

"Emmett," Reese says coolly, standing from her seat at the head of the table. "You're not quitting your job. Take a seat. I've got this."

"Yep. Great." I do as she says, taking the chair next to Ed.

Ed smiles at me, as if he were welcoming me to a dinner table and not the battleground I just stepped into.

Reese looks absolutely lethal with the way she stands at the head of the table, hands flat on the top of it, blue eyes scorching Scott in his seat.

So fucking hot, I swear.

"We're not *voting* on anything here."

He lifts a testing eyebrow. "You really want to play this game?"

"We don't vote. That's not how it works, and you especially don't get to vote me out of my job. There's only one opinion that matters, and it's mine. This is *my* club. This is *my* team. Whatever I say goes.

"I've let the four of you intimidate me for long enough. You seem to have forgotten who signs your paychecks. You work for *me*, not the other way around. In this working relationship there's only one of us that's irreplaceable. And that's me. Understand?"

"Reese," Scott seethes. "What the hell are you doing?"

"Firing you."

Fuck me, she is so hot.

"I'll release them." Scott stands from his seat as well. "Do not test me."

"Release what?" Phil asks.

"Photos of Emmett and me," she says simply. "Oh yeah, we're together. Surprise! And Scott had us followed and photographed so he could blackmail me into giving him my position."

Phil and the rest of the board, besides Ed, seem utterly shocked. Maybe over the news about her and me. Maybe over the realization of what Scott did.

"Go ahead, Scott. Release them."

His jaw tics. "They'll eat you alive, Reese."

She shrugs so casually. "I can handle it."

Reese has said that phrase to me so many times before. *I can handle it*, or *I'll take care of it*. I've always insisted that she shouldn't have to. And it's true again this time. She shouldn't have to deal with the shit the press is going to say about her, but that's not the point here. The point is, Reese can handle it.

Of course she can.

Here I was, thinking I was going to come in and save her, but she's too busy saving herself.

Scott retakes his seat, but she stays standing, looming over the table.

There's an eerie calm about her. She's got so much fire in her, but it's controlled and wielded perfectly to get her exactly what she wants.

I fucking love it.

She makes her next words perfectly clear, careful to enunciate each one slowly.

"Do not dare threaten me or what's mine, ever again." She points my way without looking in my direction. "And that includes him."

I smack Ed in the arm before pointing to Reese. "That's my girl."

A grin twitches on Reese's lips, but she doesn't break her ruinous stare from the other four men.

"Reese . . ." Phil cuts in with a nervous chuckle. "We had no idea that he was—"

"I do not care if you didn't know about this or if you weren't involved with what Scott was attempting to do. You four"—she gestures to everyone but Ed—"have disrespected me all season long. You have undermined me, attempted to set me up for failure. But this is my building. This is my team. I gave you months to remember that, but time is up." She retakes her seat, leaning back in her chair. "You four are fired effective immediately."

"You can't do that!" one of them argues.

"Actually, the crazy thing about me being the sole owner of this club is that I can! And the beautiful piece of all of this—honestly, it worked out so lovely for me—is that your salaries will help relieve some of the pressure on the budget and give room for Emmett's well-deserved raise next season. Isn't that just great? Remember, Scott, when you wanted me to focus on the budget? Look at me. I found a solution!"

Scott stands from his seat, frantically trying to find a shred of hope for his plan. "You cannot be his boss! No one would think that was appropriate."

I wave him off. "Oh, sit down and shut the fuck up, Scott."

"It's okay, Em," Reese cuts in. "He's right. I can't be."

My attention shoots to her. What the hell does that mean?

"But what you didn't know, Scott, is that for the past week and a half, I've been meeting with our legal team as well as human resources, working on a solution so that I wouldn't be Emmett's direct supervisor. So I could still keep him on my staff."

The last week and a half? We only found out about Scott's threats yesterday.

"I know you thought I wouldn't have had time to find a solution, seeing as you only gave me one day's notice of this meeting, so lucky me, things were already in motion."

She turns toward Ed. "Ed here will now serve as Vice President of Baseball Ops. He'll be handling the coaching staff of not only our major league team, but also our minor league system. All coaching hires, promotions, and salary negotiations will go directly through him, while I'll continue to do the same for the players. The new title comes with a nice raise too. So, congrats, Ed! Good on ya."

He smiles knowingly at her. "Thank you, Reese. I'm looking forward to working with you."

"Well . . ." She exhales a long breath, a self-satisfied smile on her lips as she looks around. Four speechless and stunned men stare back at her. "That should about do it. Oh, one more thing." She reaches into her bag, pulling out three packets and sliding them across the table to three of the four freshly fired board members. "Your severance. Not that you deserve it, but I've got to keep things above board around here. Clearly, you broke your contract, Scott, with that little threat of yours, so nothing for you."

She stands, hands on her hips, and nods as she looks around the room, really playing up the whole thing.

"Okay, yeah. That's all I had. Great meeting. Thanks for calling everyone together, Scott." She grabs her bag, slinging it over her shoulder. "Security will escort you four to your cars."

On her way to the exit, she runs her hand over my shoulder, giving me a squeeze before she goes. And as she walks out the door, her head is held high, as it should be.

This woman is truly in her own league in every sense of the phrase.

I'm sat here utterly speechless, and so fucking in love with her.

What the hell just happened?

I spent the past twenty-four hours mentally detaching myself from this job and coming to terms with losing it. But here I am, still employed, sitting in the field manager's seat in the dugout, and trying to wrap my head around that.

Trying to wrap my head around *everything*.

It seems too good to be true. I'm still here. Reese is still here. We're good. There's a part of me that doesn't want to quite trust it yet. That doesn't want to get my hopes up that things will be okay.

But it's hard not to feel hopeful after watching Reese handle business the way she just did. Anyone who ever doubted she has what it takes to run this place should be eating their words right about now.

"I thought I might find you here."

Reese turns the corner, finding me sitting on the ledge above the bench behind the small partition, the same way I've found her here so many times before.

"I stole your spot."

She tilts her head. "I thought we were sharing it?"

"Yeah. We are. Come here."

Reaching out, I slip my hand around the side of her neck, pulling her mouth to meet mine. I kiss her. Firmly and with a mixture of desperation and relief to quiet that small part of me that thought I might never get the chance to kiss her again.

She sighs into me, kissing me back with the same eagerness.

"Are you okay?" I whisper against her mouth.

She nods, kissing me one more time before she pulls back so she can look at me, one perfectly shaped brow arched high. "You were going to quit your job?"

"Of course I was. I wasn't willing to lose you."

"Lose me?" Her head rears back, hands dropping to my thighs. "You could never lose me."

"I don't know. It felt like I was losing you yesterday. Things seemed oddly final when we left here." I chuckle half-heartedly. "I thought you might break up with me."

She's so utterly confused in the way she's looking at me.

"Why would I break up with you? Emmett, I'm in love with you."

Oh. Wow. It's surreal to hear those words come out of her

mouth. They hit differently after not hearing them for so long. After believing I might never hear them again.

It also hits differently hearing it from the one woman you've been desperate to tell the same to.

"I was going to tell you first."

A smile curves her lips. "Well, be quicker next time."

"Don't tell me what to do."

Her head falls back in a laugh and it's such a lovely sound to hear after a stressful day. I think I could live off that sound.

Pulling on her hips, I bring her in. "Come up here with me."

Holding her steady, she steps onto the rickety wooden bench, before I settle her on one of my thighs while I sit on the ledge.

She wraps her arm around my neck, her other hand stroking gently along my jaw. "I'm sorry if I made myself seem distant yesterday. I was overwhelmed with how much I had to do. I was up all night, finalizing things with legal, making sure everything could be ready to go quicker than I had planned. I didn't mean to make you doubt anything. I was just trying to protect you the way you do so often for me."

I shake my head in disbelief. "When did you start all of this?"

"Right after we got back from Colorado." Her smile is a bit sheepish. "I drove straight to my grandfather's house from the airport to get his advice. I don't know, Em. I've loved you for longer than that, but something about spending that day together made me realize it was time to stop hiding it."

Ten days. She's been working on this for ten days. She told her grandfather ten days ago, after our trip to Colorado. After spending the day with me in a place that holds so many special memories that I wanted to share with her.

It may not seem like a big deal to publicly declare our relationship, but for Reese, she's risked everything to do just that.

And more importantly, she made that decision for herself. Her hand wasn't forced by some bullshit threat.

So yeah, it's a big fucking deal to me.

I drop a kiss on her shoulder. "Why didn't you tell me? I could've helped you."

"It was the week of Miller's wedding. I didn't want you to be distracted by anything else. I didn't want you worrying about me. I was planning to tell you this week. I was going to set up a meeting with you and HR, then everything happened so quickly. After yesterday, I just needed to handle it. You've taken care of a lot of people for a lot of years, Em. For once, I wanted to take care of you."

It feels vulnerable, in a way, allowing someone else to take care of you. But having someone like Reese, powerful in her actions yet thoughtful in the way she goes about them, to be the one who has my back, how could I not feel secure in that?

She takes care of me in the same way I take care of her. With the other's best interest in mind.

We're a team, and I couldn't have picked a better teammate.

Arm wrapped around her hip to keep her steady on my lap, I stroke my thumb over the softness there. "There's something we still need to be prepared for. Scott is going to release those pictures. After you bruised his little ego in there, he's probably already sending them off to someone."

"Do you think I made him cry? I've always wanted to make a grown man cry."

My chest rumbles in a silent laugh. "I have faith you'll be able to accomplish whatever you put your mind to. You were terrifying in there and it was so fucking hot."

Her smile goes wide. "Yeah?"

"Poor Ed had to sit next to me while I was just drooling over you. Don't know if I've ever been so turned on."

Chuckling, she drops her mouth to mine again. When she pulls back, she reaches into her back pocket and pulls out her phone.

"This is the other thing I've been working on." With her thumb, she scrolls through her email. "I did an interview last week with a big-name sports magazine. There's a woman on staff who had reached out to me a few times wanting to do a piece on me being the first female owner in the league. But the timing never felt right. And I didn't feel like I had enough to say yet." She clicks on something, allowing a news article to take over her screen. "But this felt like the right time and for the right reason. I wanted to control the narrative about our relationship as best I could. I wanted a woman journalist to be the one to write the story. I know so many people are going to have so much to say, but maybe it'll help if we get ahead of it. Get our side out first. That's the other thing that kept me occupied today. She was finalizing the article so it could go live once I showed you and got your approval."

Reese hands me her phone. "I'm hoping for it to go live first thing in the morning, if you're okay with that."

I don't even need to read it to know that I'm okay with it. That I'm great with it.

I will never get over how bright this woman is. How strategic she is when she needs to be. How thoughtful she is always. Even now, holding on to an article that will paint her in a better light than anything Scott could come up with, but sitting on it to make sure I'm good with what she had to say. That I'm good with our relationship going public.

"So just to be clear here, you're not breaking up with me?"

"I think we can confidently agree that option is off the table." Her laugh is soft. "You're my person, Em. It took me thirty-five years to find you. I'm not letting you go now."

Oh, fuck. That confession hit right where it needed to land. Reese has said I'm her safe place, but she might not know she's mine. Giving me that kind of reassurance, I'm not sure she realizes how safe she makes me feel too.

"Hey, Reese." I push her hair behind her ear, running my thumb over her gold earrings, the way I so often do. "I'm in love with you too."

"I know." There's a sweet smile on her lips. "Even if you never told me, I already knew. It's clear in the way you look at me. In the way you speak to me and speak to others about me. My hope is to make you feel as loved as you make me."

"You do, baby. I . . ." I shake my head. "I didn't know if I'd ever feel like this again, and I'm not letting you go."

She gestures to the phone in my hands.

I begin to read the article. It's mostly about Reese, as it should be. Her experience, her education, her background and history with this baseball club. She speaks about the pressure she's under, being a woman in this industry. I've witnessed that pressure, and know her feelings surrounding that. But it's kind of beautiful to see her tell the world how vulnerable she feels.

She's worn a metaphorical suit of armor since she got here, letting the hits bounce off her, and not allowing anyone to know when one landed. It takes an enormous amount of strength for someone to admit how badly you want something and how scared you are to not do well. And that's exactly what Reese is doing in this article.

Eventually, I get to the piece about me.

There's not a lot, and there doesn't need to be. This is about her. But there are some lines that stick out.

"He's my most trusted sounding board."

"I feel fortunate to know that he has the team's best interest at heart, the same way I do."

"When I came back to the Warriors, I walked in with the idea that I was going to treat everything as a business. The staff, the players. They were all pieces of the business. Emmett doesn't do that. This is his family, and being around him this season reminded me of that. Of what it was like for me to grow up around the team. Baseball has always been about family."

But I think the last line is the one that might stay with me forever.

"How lucky am I to have found the person I love most in the place I love most."

"Reese," I exhale, clicking the side of her phone to lock the screen. "This is everything. This is perfect. Thank you. I'm so proud of you."

"I'm proud of me too. But there are a few other things that didn't make the article. Things I need to say that are for only you to hear."

I give her my full attention.

"Before you, I had never felt seen."

Oh, my heart.

"I didn't have someone to witness my every day. The mundane moments, but also my biggest accomplishments. No one was there to see them for themselves. Even if they were technically there, no one ever saw me. It's easy to get lost when you're no one's number one. Easy to be forgotten. It was strange and lonely, even if I didn't admit it, to go through life without being seen. But I think you see me, Emmett."

I swallow back the emotions sitting in my throat. She has no idea just how blessed I feel to be the one granted the opportunity to see her.

"Yeah, baby. I do see you. And it's been one of my greatest privileges, to witness you live your life. To see you for who you are."

Her eyes are a touch glassy as she nods, soaking in my words.

"And I hope you trust me when I tell you that I love you, Emmett. I'm an overthinker. I've already thought of every reason why I shouldn't and yet I still do."

My chest rumbles with a silent laugh. "I know you do, Reese. I love you too. Any plausible reason not to flew out of the window a while ago. Maybe the day you walked back in here. I didn't know that love would find me like this, but you've had my attention for a long time, and I can't look away."

She bites back her smile before pressing her lips to mine once again.

"And lastly," she says when she pulls back. "You need to know that I would've given my job up for you, the same way you tried to give yours up for me. There's not a question in my mind. This career is no longer the thing I want most out of life. You are. But I'm glad I didn't have to give this up because when I picture our future together, I see us here. Together."

Here. On this field. Running this team together for a lot of years to come.

In the place I love most with the person I love most.

"You and me." I slip my hand into her hair, gliding my thumb over her cheekbone. "And when we're done here, who will be next? Who's going to take over for you?"

She shrugs so casually, as if she doesn't already have a plan. "Who knows, maybe Max will take an interest in baseball. Baseball is family, after all. We should keep it in ours, don't you think?"

Epilogue
REESE

A Few Months Later

I turn the hot water on, letting it fill my bathtub.

It may only be the middle of the day, but life has been nonstop for months, and our season just ended two days ago, so I'm stealing every extra minute I have to relax.

The media was not very kind to me after Emmett's and my relationship became public knowledge, but it was nowhere near as bad as it would've been if I hadn't had the opportunity to get our side out first.

The headlines were predictable, and I felt bad for all the noise it caused around the team. The boys though, they were great. They didn't care at all about the circus it created. They truly are so supportive of their field manager and me, that every time one of them was asked about us in the press, instead of getting defensive, they liked to gush over our relationship. Sometimes to a comical level.

Eventually, it seemed that reporters got bored of only receiving positivity in response to their intrusive questioning, so they stopped asking.

It wasn't easy, seeing certain things said about me, but it was expected. Something I learned this year is how important it is to pick a partner that you don't feel like a burden to. Emmett never shied away from listening when I needed to vent, or defending me at every opportunity.

And it was different this time than it was the last time when I made an unexpected trade that had the entire league up in arms.

When Milo first joined the team, I was questioning my own decision.

But with Emmett, there was no doubt in my mind. I didn't question a thing. It made it a whole lot easier to block out the nonsense knowing there was no other choice. There's not a world in which I wouldn't choose him.

And eventually, the noise quieted as it always does. It especially helped when we made a strong playoff run. We eventually lost in game six of the Division Series, but for my first season, I'd call it a win overall.

On the bathroom counter, as the bathtub fills, I grab a hair clip that's sitting next to Emmett's toothbrush.

His spare toothbrush has been here for months, but as of yesterday, everything else he owns made its way over to my condo too.

The day after our season ended, he moved in with me, and it only took us that long because of how busy our game schedule has been. We were practically living together anyway, either at his place or mine, but now it's official.

It feels good. It feels right to share this space where I'm able to find peace and calm with the person who brings that same peace.

I turn the water off once the tub is full.

Clipping some of my hair up, whatever is long enough to actually stay up, I step into the warm bath. I let the water envelop my body as I sink in, feeling the weight of the day drift away.

The heaviness has been slipping off my shoulders, slowly, day by day, for a while now. I no longer feel the need to prove anything to anyone. I no longer have the desire to do twice as much, simply to get recognized as the right person for my job.

Going forward, the only person I'm going to prove anything to is myself.

I already have been.

Emmett often likes to reiterate how proud he is of me, so even though I don't need to prove anything to him, his recognition means the most of anyone's.

Closing my eyes, I drop my head to the edge of the porcelain tub. But when I hear the elevator open in the main living space, I can't stop the grin that stretches my lips.

Emmett was added to my elevator's access months ago, and I'm not sure I'll ever get over the idea of him coming home to me.

I hear him move around a bit, hear the undeniable pop of a cork, before his footsteps grow closer, coming my way.

Emmett comes into frame, leaning on the bathroom doorway, glass of red wine in his hand and eyes freely roaming down my body that he can see perfectly clearly through the water.

"Hi, baby." He pushes off the door before bending over the tub to kiss me. Then he hands me the glass of wine.

"You're too good to me." I take a sip from the glass.

"I'm dating a younger woman. I got to keep her happy. Can't have you going anywhere."

I chuckle. "You do a good job at that."

Eyes locked on me, he begins to unbutton his shirt.

"Did everything go okay at the field?" I ask.

"Yeah, just tying up some loose ends for the season. A few of the guys were there, cleaning out their locker stalls, so that was nice to see them."

His shirt gives way to his bare torso and inked arms before he slips it off his shoulders and tosses it to the floor. Unclasping his belt, Emmett moves to unzip his jeans, pushing them down his wide thighs to join the rest on the ground.

The boxer briefs are next, leaving him standing proudly naked in our bathroom.

Drinking my wine, I let my eyes trail over him, the same way he's looking at me.

He's so hot. But also so kind. So protective. So *mine*.

"Let me slide in with you."

I arch a brow. "You can slide in somewhere else, looking like that."

His dick twitches at my insinuation, and a grin hitches on one side of his mouth. "I will be soon enough. We both know that."

As I move forward in the tub, Emmett wedges his big body behind mine. A bit of the water sloshes over the side because neither one of us are small people, but I couldn't care less.

Legs open wide on either side of me, bent at the knees so he can fit, Emmett pulls me back to lie against him.

"I like coming home to you," he says, dropping a kiss to my damp shoulder.

"I like hearing you call this place home."

He smiles against my skin before he dots another kiss on my neck.

Emmett reaches for my wine, taking a sip before putting it back in my hand.

"So," he begins, hands smoothing over my hips under the water. "You've officially finished your first season. How are you feeling?"

I drop my head back to rest on him. "Good. Sad that it's over, but proud of how this first year turned out."

"You should be proud."

"So should you."

His hands move up my stomach. "I am. It was a good year. Shit, it was a great year."

"I want to go all the way next season. Now that we have the staff and the players we want. I don't know. It feels like we're all in it together. We have such a good group, and I want to win a championship with them."

"Then let's do it."

I huff a silent laugh. So much easier said than done, but I'll take his vote of confidence that we can.

His inked hands roam, moving over my breasts, squeezing them in his palms on his path over my body.

"Are you going to hire a receptionist next season?"

A soft moan escapes me when his thumb circles my nipple.

"I don't know. I should."

His lips trail over my ear. "Just don't keep me out."

I shake my head against him. "Never."

Emmett's hands run over my thighs, but I squeeze them together, needing a bit of friction.

"Don't keep me out of here either. Spread your legs, baby."

He can't always get me to do what he wants. We tend to challenge each other before giving in. But when we're naked together, sometimes it shocks even me how compliant I am. How easy it is for me to give up control.

And that's exactly what I do, opening my legs wider, pushing them flush against his. One of his arms wraps around my middle, his other hand running teasing circles just above where I need him most.

"Em," I whine.

"I know."

Finally, he puts me out of my misery when he glides his hands between my legs, middle finger running over my clit.

I drop my head back on his shoulder with a moan. "*Yes*."

"Hold on to your wine, Reese."

Tightening my grip on the stem, I can't help but smile up at the ceiling, eyes closed, his fingers slowly playing with me exactly how he knows I need it.

"I could get used to this."

His mouth finds my ear, his other hand toying with my nipple as I writhe against him. "So could I. Coming home to you. Feeding you wine. Playing with your pussy until you come. We can do this every night, Reese."

I grip onto his thigh with my free hand as he continues toying with me. His dick is pressed against my ass. It's hard, but I'm not surprised. Getting me off usually gets him off. And it's sinfully hot that my enjoyment is what does it for him.

"Fuck, Reese. You're soaked right now. I could slide right in."

Then he does, with a finger, his palm keeping pressure on my clit.

He adds a second and I'm about crawling onto his lap with how close I am already.

With the hand that's not inside of me, Emmett takes my wine from me and places it on the floor next to the tub. I wasn't paying attention to it, but with how uncontrollably I'm rocking against him, I'd imagine I've probably already spilled a good amount.

"Watch the way I touch you, baby. Look down."

And so I do. Looking down, through the water, I watch as his fingers move in and out of me. It's mesmerizing, seeing the way his inked hand flexes as he brings me closer. Over the months we've been together, he's learned my body, and I've learned his. It doesn't take long when he knows exactly what to do and when to do it.

His arm around my middle is holding me firm as I writhe against him, squirming as my orgasm builds.

"You're going to come." He exhales the statement, groaning as he continues to play with me. "I can feel you tightening around my fingers. Please. Fuck, you're so good. Please come for me."

Pushing back against him, I shift onto his lap, the bath water sloshing all around us. His dick glides against my pussy as we move together, and soon enough, I can't take it anymore. I want more.

Reaching between my legs, I circle his width and line myself up. Emmett removes his fingers, bringing them back to my clit as I drop myself onto his cock.

It's quick and the stretch would be uncomfortable if I wasn't already so turned on.

"Goddamn." He rests his head on the back of mine. "You feel incredible. Fuck, I love you so much."

I lift and drop.

"Oh my God," Emmett moans, holding me steady as his head falls back against the porcelain tub. "Do that again."

So I do, riding him in the bathtub and making an absolute mess.

Heat stirs low and I'm close. He is too. I can tell by his sounds. By his frantic hips chasing my rhythm.

With one arm around me, Emmett pushes out of the tub, taking me with him as he sits on the ledge.

He gains more leverage, being out of the water, and takes full advantage of the new position. He moves me how he needs me, bouncing my hips on him. Wet, slapping skin fills the bathroom, mixing with the echoing of our moans off the tile walls.

It's a desperate chase to the finish and when we get there, we get there together.

He hugs me tightly to him, his face buried in the crook of my neck as he comes inside of me. My body winds tightly around his, doing the same.

It's all hot, panting breaths and sticky, soaked skin. Soft caresses and lazy kisses. Emmett toys with my sensitive clit as we ride it out together.

We touch and writhe. He runs his hands all over my body, the way he does so often. He whispers praise in my ear, always telling me how well I did for him.

Eventually, we come down, slumped together and satisfied.

Chuckling, I drop my head back onto him again. "I love you, Em."

He smiles against my hair. "I love you."

Slowly, I find a bit of strength to stand in the tub. He helps me, and as I lift up, he slides out of me.

So much bath water covers the tile floor. My wine is all over the place. The clothes he took off earlier are soaked.

"We made a mess."

Emmett doesn't look at the ground, only stares between my legs where his cum is dripping out of me. Reaching between them, he gathers it on his fingers and pushes it back inside. "Yeah, we did. My favorite kind of mess."

I shake my head at him in disbelief, but he's smiling proudly. "You have no shame, Montgomery."

"Not an ounce."

"Your family is coming over for dinner for the first time tonight. We should probably clean this up before they get here. And you should probably not have your dick out either."

He gives my ass a slap before he stands. "Fine." Dropping another kiss to the top of my head, he climbs out of the tub. He grabs a towel, wraps it around my body, and picks me up, not putting me on my feet until he's carried me away from the wet floor.

He tucks another towel around his waist before he gets to cleaning up the mess we made.

"How are you feeling about that?" he asks. "Everyone coming over here?"

He pours the rest of the wine down the sink since half of the glass was filled with water from the tub. I grab his wet clothes and add them to our hamper.

Things are easy between us. We move together like a well-practiced partnership, regardless that we've only been doing this for a handful of months.

"Good. This is your home now too. They should feel welcome here."

"I know, but it's kind of been your hiding place until you let me in."

I remember only a short time ago, how scared I was to let someone in again. Not only into my condo but also my life. But plot twist: letting Emmett in has not only gone well, it's the best thing I've ever done, and life has only continued to get better from there.

And at this point, with how much time we all spend together, Emmett's family has started to feel like my own. Of course they should be here.

"I don't feel the need to hide anymore," I tell him honestly. "I want them to be here."

Emmett stops what he's doing and looks at me with an edge of disbelief. "I love that you want them here."

I slowly make my way to him, wrapping my arms around his waist. "Well, I love you."

He holds me against him. "You keep surprising me every day, Reese. How lucky for me that I'll never finish falling in love with you."

Epilogue

EMMETT

One Year Later

I lean my elbows against the railing in my usual spot in the dugout.

It's the same place I've stood during every game this year. The same spot I've watched every game in my coaching career.

But this game is different.

World Series. Game 5. Playing at home.

Something in the air is telling me this is the game. We're up 3-1 in the series, heading into the bottom of the ninth. I probably shouldn't be so confident. The game is tied after all. But I've been confident in this group all year.

And it just seems like fate that this record-breaking year, one of the best of my life, would be topped off with a World Series Championship.

The energy is humming around me. From both the guys in the dugout, as well as the packed stadium of fans. Then, of course, there's all our families sitting in the section directly behind us.

Home or away, for this whole playoff run, Reese has bought out that entire section for the players to have their families close by. Sure, some of these guys make ridiculous money. They don't need the help in purchasing expensive game tickets. But there are others, like Milo, who are still on a rookie contract and shelling out that much for tickets to his World Series games wouldn't be feasible.

So, Reese bought them for everyone. Without being asked to. Because of course she did.

She'll tell you herself, baseball isn't just a business anymore.

It's been fucking adorable how stoked Milo gets before every postseason game when he finds his parents in the crowd. He's really grown into his own this year as a player and is now someone that every other team dreads to see at the plate. His confidence has skyrocketed. Partly thanks to him playing well, and partly due to the help from the vets taking him under their wing.

Milo was Reese's very first business move, and it's going to be hard to beat.

But this offseason, she made some other strategic shifts, bringing on a couple more guys. They've been the missing puzzle pieces to our equation, and we've been the most winning club in the league this season because of it.

I'll never forget the commissioner's conference last year when I told Reese I wanted to finish the season with a better record than every other owner who treated her as if she didn't belong.

This year, we did exactly that. Together.

We spent the offseason traveling together anytime she needed to do some scouting. We went on a couple of vacations. One with the whole family. One with just her and me.

Reese was a missing puzzle piece in her own way.

She fits seamlessly into our little family. She gets along so well with both Kennedy and Miller, and of course, the Rhodes brothers think she's great. Five of the six of us spend every day together at the field, and Miller and the kids are here whenever they can be, so it's not surprising how close Reese has grown to them. She loves my family like they're her own, and because biology doesn't mean shit around here, that's exactly what they've become.

That was evident shortly after our last season ended when Miller gave birth to her and Kai's daughter, Emmy. Reese came with me to the hospital to meet the newest addition to the family and when *my* daughter told me that *her* daughter was named after me . . . yeah, I was a fucking mess in the best way possible. I vividly remember looking over at Reese, who rarely gets emotional, to find her crying along with me.

That day solidified it for me. That she was a part of this. Our little family of eight.

When Kennedy and Isaiah got remarried before the start of this season, renewing their vows back in Vegas, Reese was there too. In the pews, watching me proudly, the same way she did at Kai and Miller's wedding.

One of the best parts of this year together has been watching Reese's confidence grow in her work. She was always confident on the outside, held her own when needed, but last season when the media had something to say about her, I'd see it invisibly weigh on her shoulders. But only when we were home and never at the stadium.

But she's taken her team to the World Series in her second year. It's hard to argue with those facts or find something to complain about. And more than just being the first female team owner in the league, Reese wants to be known for winning.

So that's exactly what we're going to do.

I've won a World Series as a field manager before. I have the ring. But nothing else will compare to this one if we can pull it off. Winning it for Reese. Winning it *with* Reese.

The crowd erupts when Travis gets his fourth ball, giving us a man on base. No outs. Bottom of the ninth. Still a tied game.

A calm confidence settles me as I watch, because I know it's going to happen. We're going to win it all. At home. In Reese's stadium.

Isaiah bumps his shoulder against mine. "Hey, Monty. Remember that time you gave a speech last year about loving us because you were going to quit your job but then you were back the very next day?"

I burst into a laugh, and I'm sure any camera operator that's focused on me right now is confused as to why I'm smiling when I should be stressing.

But I can't help it. This is fun. All of this is fun.

"You're a little shit, you know that?"

Isaiah flips the brim of his hat to the back, leaning on the railing right next to me. "I'm aware."

Milo Jones makes his way to the plate, and the whole scene is just poetic. Not only that he's become one of our biggest offensive threats, but because we're playing against Houston tonight. Against the player that Reese got so much shit for trading.

Except Harrison Kaiser has hardly contributed to Houston's success this year. He's been suspended twice. He was sent down to their triple-A team for a couple of weeks mid-season. Their field manager told me earlier in the series that they're itching to get him off their roster after his contract expires at the end of their season.

Which hopefully is tonight.

Not that I had any doubt in my mind, but Reese clearly made the right decision last year.

As Milo approaches the plate, I look up. To the owner's box. Reese's eyes are already on me, a proud and meaningful smile on her lips. She knows it too. It's about to happen. I can see my own confidence mirrored in her.

Her parents and grandparents are up there with her, and I just know that Arthur is beaming with pride for his granddaughter as he watches this game.

Reese gives me a wink before I return my focus to the field.

Milo's first pitch is a ball.

The second, he gets a piece of it, but it goes wide. It's a foul ball, earning him a strike.

Isaiah swings his arm over my shoulders when the pitcher winds up for the third pitch of the sequence. Their closer is nervous, that's evident. His team's entire season is resting on his shoulders and he's up against one of the best young hitters in the league.

And when he releases the pitch, he sends it straight down the center of the plate. Milo's swing is flawless, and when his bat connects, he sends the ball deep. Deep into center field, over the ivy, much in the way he did that first day he hit a homer off Kai.

I couldn't even tell you where the ball lands because it doesn't matter. All that matters is that it's gone, and we just won.

We just won the whole damn thing.

The stadium erupts in madness. The team rushes out of the dugout, meeting Travis at home plate before they charge Milo after he rounded second, dogpiling him there in the infield.

The bullpen flies out, joining the celebration, and Kai heads straight for his brother.

The next few moments are a whirlwind. My coaching staff comes over to celebrate with me. There's a shit ton of cheering and shouting and hugging.

Finally, I run up the dugout stairs, joining our group on the field. Kai is the first person I find there. He throws his arms around me, and I do the same. Then Isaiah jumps in, and all three of us are celebrating. Champagne soaks my shirt, but then I'm handed a new one that says, *Windy City Warriors. World Champions.*

"Holy shit, we did it!" Isaiah yells next to my ear.

"I love you guys!" Kai shouts.

Isaiah slips his new championship hat on, and Kai grabs a bottle of bubbles, chugging some before passing them to his brother.

But I look around the crowd because there's only one person I want to celebrate with.

"Where's Kenny?" Isaiah calls out. "Where's my wife?"

Kennedy and the rest of the medical staff eventually make their way onto the field, and he sprints in her direction.

"Where's Mills sitting?" Kai asks me, searching the family section for his wife and kids. I point up at those three, and when he finds them in the stands, he runs over to help them down onto the field.

Reese still isn't out here. There's got to be about a hundred people on the field already and she's not one of them. I frantically scan the space, looking up to the owner's box to find Reese's parents and grandparents, but not her.

"Monty!" A reporter and camera operator run up with a microphone extended. "You just won the World Series, tell us what you're thinking."

"I'm thinking I need to celebrate with my girl, but I can't find her."

There's literally only one person I want to talk to right now. One person I want to celebrate with.

The reporter points me in the right direction.

Finally, sharp blonde hair peeks out from the dugout tunnel. I can practically hear the click of her heels against the cement, the way the sound is so ingrained in my memory, as she makes her way to me.

The smile on my lips is instant.

Pushing through bodies, ignoring anyone who tries to stop me, I race across the field to her just as she takes the stairs up. She practically throws herself at me. I throw myself at her. As I lift her up, her legs wrap around me.

Now, I can celebrate.

"We did it!" Reese exclaims. It's a mixture of disbelief, shock, and pure joy.

"Yeah, we did!" I press my face to her neck, holding her tight. "I love you so much."

"I love you! I can't believe this!"

"Believe it, Reese. We just did that. *You* just did that."

"Marry me."

That halts me in place. It's loud on the field, so chaotic, that there's no way I could have heard her correctly.

Pulling away, I make sure to look her in the eye this time. "What?"

"Marry me."

Yeah. I did hear her right. Holy shit.

"Is that a question?" I ask.

"No." She shakes her head, biting back her smile. "Marry me, Emmett."

"Don't tell me what to do."

She laughs with me before I lean in and kiss her.

"Reese, baby, I'm really going to need you to stop beating me to things." I set her on her feet before reaching into the back pocket of my baseball pants and pulling out the ring I've kept in there for the past two games, just in case.

But I'm glad this is happening here. On her field.

I get down on one knee, holding it out to her. "I don't know that this ring will be able to beat the one we just won."

She nods frantically, so much surprise written on her face. "It absolutely does."

"Good." I smile up at her. "Marry me, Reese. And no, I'm not asking either."

Her laugh is watery. "This is the only time you get to tell me what to do. But just know that if you were to ask, my answer would be yes."

Then I slip it on her finger, eager to fill the rest of her hand with many more rings to come.

THE END

ACKNOWLEDGMENTS

This book was such a joy to write! It reminded me of why I love writing and creating so much. This story had been brewing in my head for a couple of years before I had the chance to get to it. Emmett has been my favorite character since he was first introduced in *Caught Up*—Windy City Series Book 3—and to me, he was the most deserving of a happily ever after. I had so much fun giving one to him. And Reese became a comfort character to me. I saw a lot of myself in her (we're both in love with Emmett Montgomery, for one!) I enjoyed learning about them equally and looked forward to writing, regardless of the POV I was writing from. I hope you loved them as much as I do (but I'm not sure if that's possible!).

My first thank you is to you, the reader. Because of your support on the Windy City series, I've been able to continue to write stories I love. Thank you to everyone who has shared their love of my books. It means the world to me!

Allyson—I'm always better at writing about how grateful I am for you rather than trying to awkwardly spit it out in person. Which I suppose this is why I'm an author. But written or spoken, I'm not sure I'll ever be able to fully express how thankful I am to have you in my corner. I am so lucky to have one of my best friends working with me. You make this process so much more fun while also taking so much off my plate and protecting my peace. Thank you for taking over and keeping the business running when I needed to step away at different times this year. Love you so much.

Chas & Sierra—Thank you for being the first eyes on the first draft. And all the hype comments that keep me going. I appreciate you both so much!

Sam & Kristie—Always my first readers of the finished product. It's a vulnerable feeling to share that first look, but I always look forward to our group texts. Love you both.

SJ— For being the best friend and hype woman. I'll never forget you reading chapter 29 with a straight face while you sat next to me in a London emergency room. Memories.

Erica—Six books together! So grateful for your talent and your friendship!

Entangled & Hodder—Thank you so much for your belief in me and my storytelling. This book is the one I've been most excited about, and you eagerly jumped on board.

Jess W & SDLA—Thank you for all your hard work you do for me to make my stories accessible to more readers. I am so appreciative of the whole team.

Andrew & Peter—This past year was a rough one for us, but I'm very thankful to have both of you.

To all my author friends, you know who you are—I am so grateful for you. This industry can be isolating at times but having friends who cheer you on every step of the way and simply understand is *everything*. Thank you for your friendship!

Marc—Six for six, my guy! The playlists have quickly become one of my favorite parts of creating these stories and it's partly because of the music, but mostly because I get to collab with one of my best friends. Unfortunately for you, I have a lot more books to write…

Lastly, but most importantly, to my mom—I love you. I miss you. Thank you for being the most incredible mother and friend. I am who I am today because of you.